rome for the holidays

Lit Lovers
Book Two

ciara blume

Rome for the Holidays by Ciara Blume

Published by Dolce Villa Press

www.ciarablume.com

COPYRIGHT PAGE

For Ruth and Sol, who fed my insatiable appetite for the world of make-believe, buying me old books at the book barn, by the brown paper bagful. I'm grateful for a childhood full of found object (including tampons) puppetry, dollhouse dramas and dress up clothes.

Thanks for believing in me and for all those years of insisting I needed to write a book. Or two.

Pretending is a very valuable life skill.
— Meryl Streep

prologue: emily

. . .

KENT, my ex, tries to sweet-talk me into it at first. He does that thing where he convinces you he's doing YOU a favor. It's a Jedi mind trick. If you blink, he might even make you think it was all your idea to begin with.

"This is the background for a feature in a nationally syndicated magazine, Em. Millions of people will read it. One week of travel, first class, with all the perks. And needless to say, unprecedented access to a celebrity relationship guru."

I snort. "A little ironic, isn't that? Too little, too late?"

"Come on, Emily. It's Italy. You've been dying to go back. Take a little extra time. It's the least I can do for you."

No. You've already done the least. This isn't a gift. It's a favor. I have to stand my ground. No more mind games.

"What about the byline?" I ask.

"Well." Kent hedges. "The thing is, I haven't really cleared sending someone else with the editor."

"So, what do you imagine is going to happen? Blaze Smith is going to send a driver to the airport for you and get me instead? Won't that be a little awkward?"

"No, that part is all worked out. Blaze's manager is fine with me sending a proxy to do the interview. I'll prep you with a list of questions. And I told them that I trust you, implicitly, more than anyone in the whole wide world, Em."

Too bad that's not a two-way street.

This thought is followed by a moment of pity for Kent's wife. His very *pregnant* wife. The whole reason he can't go on this assignment. My pity fades fast.

"Think of the food, Emily. All that pasta and gelato …"

Is that asshat actually trying to woo me with the idea of binging on Italian delicacies?

Begrudgingly, I have to admit to myself that this is actually a solid plan. Without Kent there to carb shame me, I might actually enjoy myself. The one time we flew through Milan, he threw away the beautiful, crusty bread that came with our airport salami and cheese plate. Without even asking me if I wanted it first.

What he had asked me was, "Are you really sure you want to drink that prosecco? You know how much sugar is in that stuff?"

Just as well we hadn't had time for a stopover. Keto Kent is the last person you'd want to tour Italy with. Instead of *Eat, Pray, Love,* you'd just be praying. Mostly for him to shut up about how many steps it will take to burn off your spaghetti.

"I'm sorry, Kent. I'm still not seeing why I should do you this favor. You're the one who cheated on me with your coworker. You're the one who insisted that you never even wanted kids. And now you are asking me to do your job for you, and I won't even get a lousy byline?"

"I'll split the money with you."

"Sixty/forty," I say. "And that's generous if I'm doing all the legwork. It's a whole week of my life."

"Are you shitting me? I'm about to have two more mouths to feed. Plus, we're getting a doula. And a night nanny. Do you have any idea how much that costs?"

"So, find another gig. Forget about this one."

"Fine," he capitulates at last. "Sixty/forty, and you tell no one. I've already sworn Blaze's team to secrecy. His manager owes me a favor. You're in, you follow him to a few events, you do the interviews, you're out."

"Plus, three days in Tuscany," I negotiate. "You pay for my car rental and a B&B, or I'm out."

"Jesus. You want my kids to starve?"

"You can get them on keto early," I say. And then, because I know not having an answer today is going to make him suffer significantly more, I tell him I'll think about it. "Give me a day or two."

I don't call him back for three.

emily

. . .

I SHOULD BE LOOKING FORWARD to this trip. Who wouldn't look forward to an all-expense-paid, ten-day trip to Italy two weeks before Christmas?

But first, I have to finish recording this podcast.

"Today on the *Lit Lovers'* podcast, we're headed to a very special city." Jackson sets up the intro. "Consider the number of romantic comedies set in bella Roma."

I hadn't wanted the trip to be the subject of this episode, but I'd been outvoted, three to one. We'd already done a holiday episode, and Jackson, the main host, was desperate for filler.

"Roman Holiday!"

"All Roads Lead to Rome!"

"When in Rome!"

"To Rome with Love!"

"Don't forget about the *Lizzie McGuire* movie."

Alexis and Chelsea, my two other podcast cohosts, pepper me with rom-com titles, and I try not to twitch. I'm already stressed about the gig. It isn't helping that my friends and podcast cohosts are gleefully "shipping" me off, suggesting I treat myself to a holiday tryst with a stranger. They seem to be forgetting it's a work trip. But that's showbiz. It's better content for the show. So, I play along.

We're recording at my house because I have the best acoustics. Plus, I offered to buy dinner if everyone came to me.

The only evidence of the XL house special pizza we devoured before recording is the ghostly grease stains on the empty cardboard box on my coffee table. The shapes form continents. I superimpose my imminent journey halfway around the world on this tan map, picturing a tiny toy plane crossing quietly across the cardboard sea, past marinara mountains and olive juice islands.

Jackson and Alexis are stretched out opposite each other on my living room's two jumbo, leather sofas. Chelsea and I have claimed the matching, oversize club chairs at either end. It's a chilly fall night, but I haven't put the heat on yet, so all four of us are wrapped up in colorful afghans. I've knit at least one afghan a month since my breakup eight months ago. The clashing stripes and checks and cables make us look like members of a colorful cult. We're all staring off in different directions, speaking into our individual microphones.

As a rule, we try not to make eye contact while we record. We can't risk getting the giggles. I glance at my phone. There's a countdown clock counting down the hours left until I leave for the airport. It just hit single digits.

"So, Emily, what's the first thing you want to do when you get to Rome?" Chelsea asks.

Jackson tosses a throw pillow to get her attention, then taps his watch and pantomimes yawning at her. The two of them are siblings. Usually, he's sticking his hands over his ears to avoid hearing anything too spicy about his little sister. But that's not the problem here. Chelsea's question isn't salacious enough for the midpoint of the podcast.

"Here's a suggestion for you, Emily. How about a memorable, one-night stand with a mysterious Roman stranger?" Alexis jumps in. Here we go. She asks this provocative question in her sexy, husky, "podcast host" voice. The voice doesn't quite match the girl in the long-distance running shoes, baggy sweats, and oversize college hoodie.

Alexis and I have known each other since the fourth grade. Neither of us is the type who'd hook up with a complete stranger. But Alexis, who is all about female empowerment and putting an end to slut shaming, likes to pretend she's fearlessly promiscuous when we're riffing on *Lit Lovers*.

Now it's my turn to roll my eyes. I'm the resident square on this podcast. No acting required.

"How about a memorable STD?" I reply.

"Oh, come on, Emily, it's Rome. Let your hair down a little. Taste the local flavor."

"Fine. Find me a sweet stranger who's an ice-cold rockstar, smooth as silk, and goes by the name of Nocciola, and I'll take him to bed with me." I smile.

"Oh my God! The gelato in Rome is probably at least as good as sex." Chelsea moans, wrapping her afghan tighter around herself. "But so many calories."

"Who cares?" Alexis says. "You can just burn them off *during* the sex."

"Well, Emily," Jackson says, "we're going to miss you while you are off visiting the city that put the rom in romance. And we can't help but hope for a little vicarious fling. Throw us a bone? Or at least throw some coins in the fountain for us?"

"You want me to throw a coin in a fountain for YOU? Aren't you the one who thinks love is all ones and zeros?" I tease Jackson.

Jackson likes to pose as a nerdy logic lover, looking down his nose at the silly notion of true love and poking fun at rom-coms. But we're all onto him. He's dedicated his life to cracking the code to true love. Like the ancient alchemists, trying to turn lead into gold.

"It couldn't hurt," Jackson says noncommittally. "I mean, it probably won't help, but I'm open to experimenting. At any rate, you can tell us all about your trip when we get together for our next episode. That's right, everyone. Emily will be joining us live from Rome next week when we'll be discussing one of my, I mean … your … that is to say … romance fans' favorite tropes. Join us then!"

After we conclude the episode, I carefully wrap my head-phones and place them in my carry-on bag. Just a few hours to go before the uber driver gets here. I still have to pack.

"I got you something for the trip." Jackson pulls out a sleeve of condoms from his jacket pocket. They unfold and accordion out, hitting the floor.

I laugh. "That seems rather optimistic."

"You couldn't even tie a bow on your gift?" Chelsea scoffs at Jackson.

Alexis rolls her eyes but takes the condoms from Jackson, folds them back up, and shoves them into my bag.

"Time for you to go, bro." Chelsea pushes Jackson toward the door. "Alexis and I have to get our girl packed up now. We'll take it from here."

———

"It was nice of you guys to record here," I say. "I was stressed about getting everything done tonight."

"Have you finished the book yet?" Chelsea picks up the copy of Blaze Smith's *Go Your Own Way* that's sitting on my nightstand and turns it over, reading the cheesy slogan on the back.

"Ready to do some trailBLAZEing?"

"Ugh." I groan. "He's too much, isn't he?"

Normally, I prep thoroughly before an interview. For some reason, I can't seem to read this book. The tan man on the cover, with the smoldering, gray eyes, seems so smug and so … full of shit.

I keep falling asleep every time I open this book. Or losing it. I'd left the book at Celestial Pet Boutique when I went to interview Georgia Starr. Then I left it at the diner when I stopped in for coffee.

"I'll read it on the plane," I say.

Chelsea drops the book and joins Alexis, who is picking through my closet, pulling items out from the far back.

"You need to pack this dress, and this one, and these shoes, oh, and definitely this sweater." Alexis carries her haul to the bed. Predictably, she has pulled out the most bodycon items in my wardrobe. She wags her eyebrows.

"Are you still on about this one-night-stand fantasy?" I ask. "We both know that's not happening. The closest I'm coming to sex with a stranger is going to involve a turkey baster and a contribution from an anonymous donor."

That's my plan. If all goes well, I'll be pregnant by late spring. No more waiting around for Mr. Right. No more wallowing in "what ifs." I have decided that I'm just going to go for it. Even if "it" doesn't include a partner. Bring on the yoga pants.

"Ew," says Chelsea.

"You know what I think?" Alexis says. "That's all the more reason to have a fling. Maybe you'll get knocked up the old-fashioned way."

"With legal complications and an STD? No thanks."

"Too bad she can't pack this." Chelsea pulls out the regency-era dress that I wore to a masquerade last month. "You looked super hot in this."

I put the costume back in the closet and return to peruse the pile accumulating on the bed.

"Where do you think I'm wearing this, exactly?" I ask, holding up the cleavage-baring, red dress Alexis selected for me. "Or this?" The other dress is black and more formal, but just as tight. "Have you never heard of cobblestones? Do you want me to break my neck on the Spanish Steps?" I hold up the high heels.

"Oh, come on, Emily. You're going to be there with Blaze Smith. He'll have a driver. He'll probably have staff to carry you around, if needed. Or maybe he'll carry you himself, if you ask him nicely." Alexis winks. "He seems very gentlemanly."

"I don't want to give the poor man a hernia." I gesture toward my curvy self. I've put on at least fifteen pounds since Kent and I split up, but you know what? Fuck it. I actually enjoy feeling like a real woman. And I love eating pasta.

I pity Kent's poor, pregnant wife. He's probably rationing her protein bars right now. Last time I looked at her Instagram, you couldn't even tell she was pregnant with twins, aside from her perfectly round belly. She and Kent were still partici-pating in half marathons till her sixth month.

"Shut up, goddess. You know you are luscious. I would kill to have your booty. Not to mention that thick hair and your weird, hazel eyes." Alexis makes a show of pointing out my attributes like she is conducting a PowerPoint presentation, minus the laser pointer.

"Honestly, I don't see myself partying on this trip," I say.

I want to look professional, but it's a tricky trip to pack for. Not like my usual European assignments. I don't know how formal any of the events will be, or if I'm even expected to attend them. So, I have no clue what to bring. I don't usually follow celebrities around on their book tours. I bite my lip.

"Just pack the dresses. You won't regret it," Chelsea says.

"These boots are coming. NOT that sweater." Alexis returns a baggy favorite to the closet. "Yes to the pashmina. Now, what about pajamas?"

"I thought I'd sleep in a tee."

"No, Emily. You are an adult woman going on a solo trip to Europe, traveling first class," Alexis argues.

"Actually, I'm not sure about that," I say. "The reservation was for premium economy, but when I tried to check in online, I got a message that I need to check in at the counter for a seat assignment. God, I hope it's not a middle seat."

"I would gladly take a middle seat if it meant I got to go to Rome." Chelsea sighs wistfully. "You are so lucky!"

"I wish I could pack you in my luggage." I give her a quick hug. Chelsea has really grown on me in the six months since I've moved here. She's like a little sister. Suddenly, I feel guilty for my complaints and worries. I *am* lucky to be going on this trip. I hadn't accepted this assignment just for the money. It's a welcome distraction from the fact that this will be the first Christmas since my dad died.

The first holiday I'm spending alone.

"Then you'll need to pack a robe, too," she says. "Just a second."

Alexis gestures to Chelsea, who ducks out of the room and returns with a pink shopping bag stuffed with tissue paper.

"We hid this in your coat closet!" Chelsea grins triumphantly. "It's a going-away present."

"Own your hotness, Em. Kent was an asshole. He did not deserve you. You're so much better off without him."

"I already know that I'm better off without him," I say.

Anyone who would cheat on me while I was grieving for my father, and do a total one-eighty on his views about fatherhood when he knocked up a coworker, is not worth pining for.

"I know you're over *him*," Alexis says, "but I'm not sure you've fully recovered from what he did to you."

She has a point. I don't miss Kent one bit. But I do miss the old me. Sometimes I worry that Kent might have sucked all the fun out of my soul, along with the sugar in my diet.

I sink onto the bed and play with the lock on the suitcase that is sitting splayed open. I'd already tossed in an assortment of comfort items. Mostly ragged tees and pilly, old socks. I pluck the most worn ones out, extracting them like a surgeon.

"Thirty-two is not too old for anything. You've got your whole life ahead of you, and as someone who has known you for over twenty years, I think you've yet to peak. Your time is now. Try to enjoy it. Be a little frivolous. And wear some decent pajamas."

Inside the bag are three impossibly soft, jewel-toned, silk nightgowns, embellished with lace and whisper-thin ties. There's also a matching robe with a paisley print that contains shades from all three of the nightgowns. Chelsea grins. My mouth falls open, and I laugh.

"Are you two for real? What is this, my trousseau?"

"Why wait for our friends to get married to buy them lingerie? This stuff isn't for some guy. It's for you. You don't have to fall in love. Just try to have a good time in Italy. Appreciate yourself. Take some sexy selfies."

"I hope it's not too much. But uh … the gift receipt is in the bag if you hate it." Chelsea wrings her hands nervously.

"I love it," I say. Alexis is right. I'd much rather stand at my balcony window, eating my breakfast pastries and toasting my Kent-free future, while wearing a beautiful, silk nightgown.

"They're perfect."

blaze

. . .

"We all come to forks in the road in both life and relationships. These moments can lead to a lot of anxiety. Do I go left or right? Am I choosing the wrong way? Will I miss out on something wonderful if I opt for the wrong path? Will this choice have consequences for the rest of my life?"

— Blaze Smith, *Go Your Own Way*, on Facing Crossroads

"BLAZE, are you even listening to me?" Steff is exasperated. "The photos have been leaked everywhere. Even the tabloids here in Rome have them. It doesn't look good."

I'm already in my bed at the Seattle Airport Hilton. I floss my fingers on the starched, white sheets of my king-size bed as I field her late-night call. The room feels empty. It smells like canned air. Nothing but a faint whiff of chemicals designed to erase all scents of humanity. At least the bed is comfortable.

"What do you want me to say, Steff? Vivian and I aren't married. We've barely seen each other for the last six months."

Maybe longer. I do some mental math. When did Viv and I attend that gala? There was an awards dinner last March, and I'd popped by her studio in early April.

"That's beside the point. You haven't announced your breakup. I thought you both agreed to wait till the end of the book tour."

I'd thought so too.

I sit up, flip on the bedside lamp, and rub the bruise on the back of my shoulder. Baby goat yoga isn't for me, but I'd let my sister talk me into it. I'd spent the past month on her farm in eastern Washington State helping out with the goats, playing handyman, and running errands into town without a single person recognizing me. It had been glorious. If I'd had my way, I would have stopped doing events in September. But Steff wouldn't hear of it. We were just gaining traction on the Continent, Steff insisted. She'd worked overtime, pouring her heart and soul into this last leg of the tour. A media blitz just before Christmas. She'd dubbed it "Rome for the Holidays."

We'd be hitting bookstores, talk shows, and reality TV show tapings with "relationship advice and ideas for keeping the fire lit (pun intended) during one of the most stressful times of the year for most couples." That was the pitch anyway. The response had been fantastic. Everyone's looking for easy filler in the week leading up to Christmas. Phoning it in. Counting the days till their holiday breaks begin. My content is a no-brainer.

I'm not sure what that says about me, exactly.

"Did you know Vivian was seeing him?" Steff slows down for a moment, allowing a note of sympathy to creep into her normally tough-as-nails tone.

"No," I confess. "Did you?"

Steff has known Viv even longer than I have. They were sorority sisters. It was Viv who set me up with Steff's agency when my career started to take off.

"Oh my God, Blaze! Of course not!" Steff gasps, laying it on way too thick. That's how I know she's lying. Vivian had probably sworn her to secrecy, and she was honoring that oath. Or perhaps she was trying to spare my feelings. But I don't care. I'm not hurt. Annoyed perhaps, but not hurt. The timing sucks. She couldn't have waited a month?

My supposed girlfriend is dating "Titanium Man," and I could give two flying fucks about that.

I lift my phone off the charger on the nightstand and reluctantly scroll through the photos that Steff has texted to me. I'm waiting for the feelings of betrayal and jealousy to set in. But they don't.

My first thought, actually, is good for Vivian. She's always been a fan of that franchise, and let's face it—everyone is obsessed with Rafe Barzilay. He's the hottie du jour. I'm kind of happy for her. She looks like a real person in the photos. Relaxed. Her face doesn't have that awful, frozen, talk show host mask.

But then I do a Google search, and I see the rest of the photos that the paparazzi shot in Cabo. Vivian is laughing and putting sunscreen on the actor's three-year-old daughter. Blowing bubbles. Doing her hair. The same Vivian who's always made it clear to me she isn't mommy material and doesn't want any "dirty little rugrats." Perhaps the progeny of superheroes gets a pass.

I laugh, a little bitterly.

"Blaze, this isn't a joke. The whole world knows she's dating him now. We're going to have to respond quickly."

"Does it really matter? Does anyone care?" I try to keep the truculence out of my tone. "Who actually gives a damn about who I'm dating or not dating?"

Steff sighs her long-suffering celebrity manager sigh, putting me in my place as the clueless client whose messes and foibles she is once again forced to fix. Off to the timeout chair with me.

"You are a celebrity relationship guru, Blaze. You just released a bestselling book. You simply can't appear to get dumped right now. Have you ever heard the phrase, 'You can't trust a skinny chef'?"

"That sounds rather sizeist," I mumble. Steff sighs again.

"Blaze, I hate to say it, but I think we are going to have to fabricate something. It's unorthodox, but given the timing and what's at stake here"—she speeds up, cutting to the chase with her plan—"I'm prepared to be your decoy for the remainder of the tour."

A beat of silence as I take this in.

"My decoy?" I laugh. "As in my sitting duck?" I'm picturing a wooden duck with Steff's face, floating across a placid pond. There are paparazzi with giant lenses, snapping away from the shore.

I suspect Steff hasn't had her coffee yet. She's not making sense. It's still early morning in Rome. She's gone out a few days ahead to make sure everything is settled.

"Come on, Blaze. Decoy as in fake girlfriend. It's just for a couple of weeks."

I've grown so used to her pushy presence on my tours that I can almost hear the clacking of her heels as she paces the lobby. Short, sharp, stabby steps. Steff's weird and colorful couture shoes and fake eyeglasses might look friendly, fun, and approachable. But this is a ruse. That costume masks a ferocious PR beast. I like to joke that she's my "PRanha." There is no one I know who is more qualified to handle a crisis.

But a fake relationship with her? Not happening. The very suggestion makes me queasy. It makes everything in my life feel like a sham.

"I can't ask that of you." I rake my hands through my unkempt hair, enjoying the length and mess of it. I'd decided to leave it this way as long as possible, despite the certain knowledge that Steff will have a cow when she sees me.

Now I'm doubly grateful for the natural disguise. Since those photos of Viv are out there, I'm bound to be stalked by paparazzi and groupies who've been waiting for this opportunity. But none of them are looking for this version of me. I run my hand over my beard and give it a satisfying, little tug.

Blaze Smith fans are all about the clean-shaven, spray-tanned, rich-looking dude on the cover of the book. He isn't me. That guy? He's a suit I wear to the office.

"I hate to say it, Steff, but maybe we need to call it. It was already a lot to cram this tour in so close to Christmas. If it's going to turn into a PR nightmare, I'd just as soon spend more time with my family."

Not that I have much family to spend it with. But I could help my sister get my mom to the all-inclusive resort I'd booked us all into for Christmas.

"Absolutely not. Canceling at this point would be a career-ending move!" Steff argues. "Oh, and Blaze? I hope you haven't forgotten we have a journalist joining us." Steff pauses, checking something. "It's not Kent Larson, though. He's sending a colleague. Kent's wife is pregnant with twins. He can't risk being out of the country right now. You're cool with that, right?"

"Whatever," I respond. This is the last thing on my mind.

I kick off the duvet. The air in my hotel room suddenly feels close. Suffocating. Outside the window, I hear the distant sound of jets taking off, and I wish I could board any of them instead of the one I'm ticketed for. I'd rather ride shotgun through an asteroid storm with Titanium Man than go along with Steff's plan.

"I hope I don't have to remind you that a lot of people are counting on you, Blaze. Your mom and your sister. The book-sellers. The bookers and event planners who have worked to get you press here. Me," Steff lectures. I bristle like a teenager who's just been reminded, for the thousandth time, that he needs to take out the trash. As if I wasn't already aware. There's no point being resentful, though. Steff works for me. She's just doing her job. And I'm sure she's doing her best.

"I appreciate you, Steff," I say.

"Great. So, can you stop making this so difficult? It's barely a week. We'll get through it. I'm here for you."

"Fine." It's my turn to sigh. Fuck my fabulous celebrity life. "Walk me through your plan."

"I booked a penthouse suite for the two of us. The story is that we go way back. We've been working together for a few years, and one thing led to another and it's blossomed into something more. We're finally ready to tell the world. Viv will say she's known for a while and she's happy for us."

"You already spoke to Viv?"

"She feels terrible, Blaze. She was sure the resort was secure and there was no way they'd be seen."

I hate the plan already.

It was one thing to keep up the appearance that Viv and I were still dating long after the relationship ended. It was mutual. It had worked out well for both of us. But pretending to be in a relationship with my manager now? Even if she wasn't my employee, there's never been anything of that nature there. It feels wrong. Toothpaste and orange juice wrong.

I examine my surroundings for clues like it's an escape room and not the Airport Hilton. The generic, snow-capped-mountain painting hanging on the wall offers me no comfort. It makes me think about the Donner Pass. If worse comes to worse, fake a relationship with your client? At least she isn't planning on eating me.

"There are two rooms in the suite?"

"There's a couch in the sitting room," Steff assures me. "But we should probably take care to make it look convincing. The staff are bound to talk. I can purchase some lingerie to leave around your bedroom. Do you prefer neutrals or color?"

I reach over my shoulder to find the goat-yoga injury with my right hand. I survey the edges of the bruise with my fingers, then press the tender spot hard, like I'm doing some kind of penance for even considering this deceitful ruse.

"I don't know. Let me think about it," I finally say. "It's late here, and I'm tired. Maybe I'll come up with something else."

"Honestly, this plan is not a problem for me, Blaze. So don't sweat it. If you think about it, it might even be fun." Her voice sounds falsely bright. Cringeworthy. Like wearing fluorescent colors in the sunshine with a hangover.

"You're a trooper, Steff," I say.

"I think that journalist is on your flight, by the way. Probably in coach, but you'll meet her at the airport. The driver will fetch both of you. Let's make sure our story is straight by then, okay? Just remember, you're Blaze Smith. International Love Doctor. You weren't dumped. You're going your own way. And you've got to look happy, healthy, and well rested when you get here, so shave, please!"

I flip off the light and set my phone on the nightstand. Just five hours before I have to head to the airport. Six if I don't shower and shave first. I reset the alarm. Screw Steff's orders.

emily

. . .

IN MY DREAM, there's a swarm of bees near my face. Buzzing. So much buzzing. I swipe to slap them away and end up waking myself up as I send my phone flying across the bedroom. It clatters to a halt under my dresser. Still buzzing. I hadn't turned the ringer back on after we finished recording last night.

I dive for the phone, answering it at the last possible moment before it goes to voice mail.

"Emily Romano? Your 4:45 shuttle is outside. Please be advised that the driver has two more pickups and can't wait for more than five minutes for you to come out and load your luggage."

"I'm coming!" I dash down to the front door and throw it open, waving at the man in the blue van parked out front. Thank goodness I slept in my travel outfit and put the suitcase by the door. I kick the heavy carry-on out onto the porch with my bare feet.

The driver heaves a sigh, puts his phone down, and gets out of the van to help with my suitcase.

"Be right back!" I call out. "I'm just going to pee!"

I run back into the house, use the toilet, and sprint upstairs to retrieve my carry-on. What else? The knitting project I was working on when I fell asleep is laying on the floor. I drifted off without even setting my alarm. I shove the soft merino wool and needles into my bag, next to my laptop. I pull on a packable down jacket and slip my feet into the comfy pair of sheepskin boots that I left beside the bed last night. Finally, I reach for my favorite pashmina before glancing out the window. The driver is standing on the lawn, looking up impatiently. I knock on the window and give him the thumbs-up sign. There's no time to make my bed. I have the awful sensation that I'm forgetting something. Something important.

I can't believe I overslept.

I dash down the stairs and lock the front door behind me. At this point, anything I've forgotten will have to be purchased on the road. I lay my hand on the door, touching the wrought iron plaque with its hand-painted, Italianate ceramic numbers.

"Such a lucky number ... 333!"

I can still hear her voice in my head. My grandma was very scaramantico (superstitious). She almost never left the house without touching the iron scrollwork, "tocca ferro," to ward off evil spirits.

It still doesn't feel entirely like *my* house, yet I'm feeling the tug of homesickness at the thought of leaving.

"Wish me luck, Grandma," I whisper. And then, "I promise I'll be back in time to get the Christmas tree and lights up." Then I quickly kiss the plaque.

"You coming or what?" the driver asks impatiently, tapping his watch. I duck into a seat in the back of the shuttle.

Thanks to the driver's lead foot and the other passengers' ability to set their alarms, we beat rush hour, arriving at the airport a full forty-five minutes earlier than expected. There's only one agent checking bags for my flight, and I'm the first one in line. I hand over my suitcase and cross my fingers for a window seat.

"I'm sorry. Looks like there's an issue with your ticket. They'll assign your seat at the gate," the attendant manning the check-in station tells me.

"Is that normal?" I ask, willing away my pre-flight jitters. Knowing my seat number and looking it up on an app is one of the ways I help calm my fear of flying. Xanax, of course, is the other. "I thought flying premium economy guaranteed a seat choice?"

"Normally, but it looks like that cabin class is oversold. I wouldn't worry about it. They'll probably offer you an upgrade or a really sweet travel voucher." He shrugs and hands me a boarding pass. "Just check in with the crew at the gate for your seat assignment."

"Okay."

"That way." He points toward security. "Buon viaggio!"

I'm expecting a long line, but it takes me less than twenty minutes to get through security. Naturally, I head directly to the gate. Even if there wasn't an issue with my seat, I'd be making a beeline. This is a rule of mine. I always go directly to the assigned gate. Even if I have to use the restroom or want to grab a cup of coffee, I go to the gate first. It's like touching home plate. You're not safe till you go to the gate.

But this morning, I'm particularly anxious to get there before any lines can form. I'm not going to be able to relax until I get that seat assigned.

Of course, there's nobody else there. The destination isn't even listed on the sign above the desk yet. The flight isn't leaving for another four hours. FOUR HOURS. It's ridiculous. But for someone with flight anxiety like me, too early is a thousand times better than too late. If I'd waited another forty-five minutes for the shuttle, we would have hit rush-hour traffic. I would have arrived at the airport at the same time as hordes of other travelers. Then I would have had to wait in long lines to check in and get through security. I still would have made the flight. Probably. But with no time to spare. No thanks.

Better to be early and find a comfy place to grab some break-fast and read. Preferably not too far from the gate. I scan my surroundings and locate a coffee shop and bookstore/news-stand/convenience store a few gates away. I head in that direction.

It's only as I am walking past the rounder at the front of the store that I remember what I forgot in my bedroom.

Again.

The damned book.

An employee is just pulling up the wire mesh barrier to open the shop.

"Morning," she mumbles as I stand there, frowning at the pyramid of books displayed front and center in the entryway. Dozens of smiling Blaze Smiths are posed in front of a street sign with an arrow and the bold title, *Go Your Own Way.*

I pick one of the books up and turn it over. The copy on the back assures readers the "guidance tools" to "map out" a fulfilling relationship that promises to take you on the ride of your life. I stifle a gag.

What a crock.

I've never been a huge fan of self-help books. But I am self-actualized enough to admit that the end of my eight-year-long relationship, eight months ago, could be influencing my reaction to this one in particular. How many times have I tried to crack it open and read it? I'd started to read three different chapters, only to slam them shut, two paragraphs in.

I forget what the chapters were even called. I'd retitled them: Things That Should Have Been a Red Flag, Stuff You Ignored Like an Idiot, and This Is Why You'll Always Be Alone. And then I'd gone out and bought an armload of books on artificial insemination and single motherhood. I have one of those books in my bag right now. But what I don't have with me is Blaze Smith's book. That one is still sitting on my nightstand at 333 Poinsettia Lane.

This is the third time I've left it behind. I'm going to have to buy another copy.

I glance around the shop. May as well grab a couple of magazines too. And a Toblerone. Chocolate calories consumed at altitude don't count. I burn time browsing and deliberating over magazines before finally making my way to the register.

I get in line behind an exhausted-looking mother who is bent over a stroller, trying to soothe her toddler. It doesn't look easy. Traveling with a small child and no partner to help you looks debilitating, frankly. I wave at the toddler, who is now staring directly at me, fat tears rolling down her face. Actually, she's not looking at me. She's looking at the Blaze Smith book I'm holding. And crying.

"You and me both, kiddo," I mumble, turning the book over in my hands. Look how smug this guy is with his shiny, slicked-back hair, barbershop shave, and perfectly cut jacket. He's got just the slightest hint of crow's-feet at the corners of his ash-gray eyes and three dimples, if you count the one in his cleft chin. Usually, I'm quite partial to dimples, but in this case, I'm offended. What a waste of a perfectly sexy chin on this chump.

"So, I take it you're not a fan?" the man in line behind me comments, and I turn around.

"Pardon?"

"Blaze Smith." The man crouches down and makes a goofy face at the toddler, who bursts out giggling and proceeds to stick her tongue back out at him.

"Seems like this little one is NOT a fan, and judging by what you just said, neither are you. But then again, you're buying the book. So, I'm curious."

He shrugs and sticks his tongue out again at the little girl, who bursts into laughter again. Her mom drops a stack of magazines, several bottles of water, and a veritable mountain of snacks onto the counter. The checker gives her a look.

"Don't judge me," the mom warns, throwing two candy bars and some gum onto the pile. The checker quirks a smile.

I turn to check out the man behind me. He's taller than me. Maybe just over six feet? His dark, wavy hair is thick, shaggy, and desperately in need of a cut. And that beard … it's just prolific. He definitely looks like he's from rural Washington. Like he just stepped off a mountain pass. He's wearing faded jeans, a red, plaid flannel, a blue, fleece Patagonia jacket, and a blinding orange puffer vest. The kind hunters wear to avoid being shot. A pair of sunglasses with purplish-green lenses are dangling from a yellow bungee around his neck.

Who does he think he is? Dawn's emissary? Is he trying to make sure the search and rescue team can locate him in an avalanche? It's far too many colors for this early in the morning. I turn away, blinded, but still processing the details in my nearly photographic memory.

No ring. Not exactly shocking. I don't even know why I checked. It's a habit I've picked up since becoming single again. Like patting myself down for my phone, wallet, and keys when leaving the house. Another ritual.

"A bunch of people recommended I read it," I speak over my shoulder, "but honestly, I don't think it's my jam. I think this guy is probably full of shit, you know? I don't trust these self-help guru types. But what the hell, I've got a long flight ahead of me."

He grunts in a sage, mountain man way. "I heard he got dumped recently."

"Really? That's interesting." I make a mental note to investigate this further and glance back at the man. The colors are less overwhelming this time. "Where'd you hear that?"

"Tabloids," he says, pointing to a trashy news mag by the checkout. There's a photo of a blonde woman on the cover and the headline, "Titanium Man Douses the Blaze. Vivian's Burning New Beau."

"Wow," I say. "That's a little harsh."

He plucks a copy of the tabloid off the stand and adds it to his collection of goods. He's got the same kind of water as me and two Toblerones, plus a bag of potato chips.

"I dunno. I love reading these. And they're handy for lining birdcages." He smiles, and I'm momentarily dazzled. His smile is one of those whole-face smiles. Completely sincere. It's so bright, his clothes now seem almost normal. It's my turn to check out.

"Is that everything?" the clerk asks me. I glance at the potato chips the man in line behind me has.

"Where'd you get those?" I ask.

"Take mine," he says, holding them out. "I'll just grab another bag."

"Thanks!" I pay for my items and pass the man again on my way out.

"Safe travels." I smile.

"Good luck with the book." He tips his head.

And then I head for the restaurant with the bar because with the state of my nerves and four hours to kill, I'm probably better off with a Bloody Mary.

blaze

. . .

"It really isn't all that complicated. Think about where you're going. Think about how you're going to feel when you get there. Really think about it. Maybe you want to stand out. Maybe you want to blend in. You definitely don't want to get frostbite. If you don't feel qualified to pick appropriate clothes for this trip, get some help. But not from your mate. They're not your mom. It's not their job to dress you."

— Blaze Smith, *Go Your Own Way*, on Dressing for the Journey

I WATCH the woman go and smile to myself. I probably shouldn't be smiling, but I'm just so happy that my "disguise" is working. So well, in fact, that she just told me that she thinks my book is full of shit. It's kind of ironic that the more colorful my clothes are, the less people notice *me*. They're too busy trying to process my outfit to recognize me.

Then again, the clothes I'm wearing might make me look like a clown, but that woman had still opened up to me enough to tell me that she thought that the well-groomed, styled, and perfectly pictured man on the cover of that bestseller was a charlatan. Aside from the trolls on Amazon, that's the first honest opinion I've heard in ages. So, who's the real clown?

As usual, I'm overthinking.

I'm so tired of coming up with deep analogies. It's exhausting. With most of the couples I've counseled, it all comes down to the simplest of rules. Things like, "Don't be a dick," and "Tell the truth," and "Have some empathy." Yet so many people get it wrong. Myself included.

A popular news site once wrote an article that claimed all self-help books could be boiled down to about a dozen universal truths. The trick was turning each of those truths into a metaphor that people can understand and apply to their own lives.

In the case of my current book, *Go Your Own Way*, I use the metaphor of a journey, a road trip, in particular. You're on this trip whether you've got a partner or not. But if you're traveling with someone else, there's going to be some amount of negotiating. You aren't always going to want to go to the same places. You might want to take different routes. And then there's the issue of choosing who's going to drive, who's going to navigate, who's going to pick the songs on the radio.

Sure, it sounds simple. Remarkably simple. Maybe even too simple for the likes of that woman who was just buying the book. She had a real "No shit, Sherlock" attitude about her that I found completely refreshing. Most of the stuff I say in my books absolutely deserves a big, fat round of No-Shit-Sherlocking. But what can I say? Some people take a little longer to figure it out. And even when they do, they're still going to fuck it up.

It takes practice.

I'm my own perfect example. Here I am, a big, successful relationship guru, traveling in disguise because my sham relationship is over and I'd rather not face the music. It's like I'm on the lam. Why should anyone trust a damned thing I have to say about relationships?

I pay for my stuff and consider how I'll fill the next four hours till my flight boards. I could have slept in a little longer at the hotel, but I decided to get to the gate early to avoid crowds as much as possible. I thought I'd eat some breakfast here, have some coffee, and try to come up with a solution that doesn't involve a fake relationship with my manager. Odds are fifty/fifty still that I won't actually get on the flight.

I glance at the latest texts from Steff. She sent me three more links with the photos of Viv and Rafe Barzilay, the buff, Israeli actor who plays "Titanium Man." She's also sent over the complete schedule for the week. It's crammed full of appearances, meetings, book signings, and events starting the moment we land. That will have to be reworked. I'll need time to shave. I snap a selfie and send it to her, imagining her horrified reaction.

> You might want to give me a few hours to freshen up.

Her response is swift.

> No. No. NO, Blaze! Nobody can see you like this. What the hell are you thinking? Isn't there anywhere in the airport you can take care of that? Maybe in one of the private lounges?

> Think of it like a disguise. I just stood in line behind someone who was buying my book, and she had no clue who I was.

> If this look of yours gets out, I'm going to kill you. You've gone from sexy guru straight to creepy cult leader with this.

NO!

I pocket my phone and head toward the lounge, passing the one open restaurant on the way. The woman from the shop earlier is inside, arguing with a waiter.

"Why can't I order a Bloody Mary with my Eggs Benedict? Is that not a bar right there?" She points at the bar that is mostly covered in upside-down stools.

"Bar's not open yet, ma'am," he says.

She frowns. "Okay, but the vodka is right there. How hard would it be to make me a drink? I don't think you understand. I'm terrified of flying. And if I take my meds now, I might fall asleep before I get on the plane. Just one drink. It's an act of mercy."

The waiter looks like he's heard it all before.

"Bar's closed, ma'am. I think there's a Sports Bar in Terminal Three that starts serving at 8 a.m."

She lowers her forehead to the table, moans, and then sits back up straight. "Fine. Forget it. Give me a minute to think. I want to look back over the menu."

Impulsively, I slip into the seat across from her.

"Hey, I think I can help you out," I say.

"Excuse me?" She glances up, a little shocked to see me. And then she looks embarrassed, plus a little worried. She peers over her shoulder and slides her carry-on bag between her furry, boot-clad feet.

"I know where you can get a drink without leaving the terminal."

"I'm not a lush," she says. "I swear. I just have an irrational fear of flying."

"Admitting you have a problem is the first step toward the solution." I smile gently in an attempt at humor.

"I just said I'm not a lush," she insists defensively.

"I believe you." I backtrack. "You said you have an irrational fear of flying. The fact that you realize it's irrational is half the battle. But that probably doesn't make you feel any better, does it?"

"Not really. It makes me feel ridiculous. I don't know why I get like this." She fans her face, and I notice her beautiful, hazel eyes are getting a little watery.

She really is dealing with something here. Tread lightly, I warn myself.

Whatever it is, I'm suddenly overwhelmed with the simple urge to help her with it. To make a difference. To have a positive effect on just one person. I want to do something real for a change.

"You know," I say and smile in a way I can only hope reads conspiratorial despite all the bushy facial hair, "I'm not all that fond of flying either. In fact, I've got a few hours to kill before my flight, and I've got one of these." I pull a small, silver, metallic card from my pocket—the golden ticket that grants access to the Priority Club Lounge. "I hate hanging out there alone. So many stuffed shirts. I can bring a guest."

She eyes me warily.

"You can bring a guest?"

"I can."

"And there's no extra charge for that?" she asks.

"One of my company perks," I assure her.

"I've always wanted to check out the club lounge here," she says. "Is it true that there's all kinds of free food in there? I've heard they serve Japanese breakfast."

"I love miso soup in the morning." I grin. "And there's always an open bar. Even at 7:30 a.m. I won't judge you if you order a breakfast cocktail."

"It's noon somewhere." She smiles and stands up, holding out her hand. "Emily Romano," she says. "Nice to meet you, Mr. —"

"Smith," I say. "But you can just call me Smitty."

―――――

The tabletop is entirely covered with samples from the buffet. Half-eaten mini quiches, donuts, a few pieces of bacon, assorted nuts, fruit, and crackers, plus two tiny bowls of miso soup, vie for space. There are also assorted fruit juices, coffee beverages, glasses of water and, as promised, a Bloody Mary. We chat and nibble, sharing random tidbits about everything and nothing. Favorite TV shows from our childhoods. Best place travel pillows. Worst flavors for potato chips—neither one of us cares for BBQ.

After she finishes her drink, Emily cautiously mentions her ex. It's too bad she's not interested in reading my book because women like her are the reason I write the books I write. Or maybe it's the other way around. Maybe it's all the piece-of-shit ex-boyfriends who are keeping me in business.

"This trip is a sort of reward for making it through the past year," Emily says. "I've always wanted to find out a little more about my family's heritage. My grandmother came here in the 1940s after the war to marry my grandpa. She lost touch with her family, though. Never went back."

Emily passes on a second drink when the waiter offers, then continues the story.

"Pretty sure her family is all gone now, but her childhood best friend is still alive and kicking. I only located her and found out she's still alive a few months ago. I don't want to wait. She's in her nineties."

"This sounds amazing, like a book." I top off our waters. "Have you been to Italy before?"

"Only the Milan Airport, which hardly counts." Emily shrugs. "I've always wanted to go, but it never seemed to work out."

"Work?" I ask.

"I guess." She nods. "My ex and I are both freelance writers. We traveled constantly. Our schedules were crazy. But that was what we wanted. We wanted to be that writing power couple, always jetting off to another destination, covering another story. It's not as glam as it sounds. You go where the work takes you. You don't get to choose."

"Sounds exhausting." I wrinkle my nose and shake my head. "I'm more of a homebody. I'd rather hole up in a mountain cabin. Read books in front of the fireplace."

"In a rocking chair?" she asks. Even though we just met two hours ago, her gaze is familiar and personal.

"Bingo!" I say, grinning at her. "Preferably wrapped up in a cozy, handknit afghan or two."

"You don't say?" She looks at me teasingly. "Why am I not at all surprised to hear that? This is going to sound weird, but I feel like I've known you forever."

"I think that's the magic of making friends in airports. All the pretense of your 'real' lives falls away, and you get to know each other on accelerated schedules." I pop an olive in my mouth.

I haven't actually told her all that much about myself. I'm being careful. I don't want to reveal too much, and I also don't want to lie. But I have told her I'm a writer too.

"So, what do you write, Smitty?" she asks, using my nickname from high school.

"Believe it or not"—I improvise, praying she doesn't catch on —"I write self-help stuff."

"Shut up." She laughs. "Well, I certainly hope you offer better advice than this guy." She taps my book.

"What do you have against poor Blaze Smith?" I ask.

"Look at him. He's *too* handsome. And he looks so smug."

"You think he's handsome?" I raise an eyebrow.

"I mean, in a totally self-absorbed and slick kind of way. I bet his girlfriend dumped him because he's a narcissist." She flips the pages of the book, speaking confidently.

"That's a big assumption. Is it possible you're projecting because of your ex?" I ask.

"Hmm … maybe?" She hiccups and ponders this for a moment. "I guess that's possible. I shouldn't be so quick to judge. But I still don't trust slick-packaged self-help gurus like him, you know? Nobody can be that perfect. They can't be for real." She waves her hand dismissively, and my eyes return to her perfectly open face. No games. No subterfuge. No agenda.

I'm suddenly overwhelmed with an intense urge to kiss her. She's staring at my mouth too. Our eyes meet and she blushes, looking away quickly.

"I'll tell you one thing. If I ever meet this Blaze character and it turns out he's on a keto diet, I'm going to kick him in the nuts." Emily palms a handful of sugar-roasted almonds from the bowl on the table, pops one in her mouth, and crunches.

I cross my legs. What was I even thinking? I was supposed to be trying to be helpful.

"So, your ex-boyfriend, whom you dated for over eight years and who didn't want children, suddenly knocked up another woman?" I ask to clarify her story.

"Keto Kent," she confirms. "What a disappointment he turned out to be."

"Asshole." I nod in agreement and help myself to a slice of bread with jam. Emily looks on approvingly.

"I'm glad you're not afraid of a little strawberry jam, Smitty. You got a little here." She uses her hand to brush some crumbs off my beard, and as I turn, her fingers graze my lips, sending a white-hot current through my entire body. The force of it takes me by surprise.

I toss back the rest of my espresso and attempt to refocus.

"So now this bastard is having a baby with someone else," I recount, "and you're like, 'What the fuck, dude? You made me give up on this dream only to give me the finger and go for it without me?'"

"Yes!" She smacks a hand on the table. "That sums it up. You're a good listener."

I can't take my eyes off the curve of her lips. There's an incredible divot at the peak. Everything about this woman is deliciously curvy and swirly, I'm noticing. Her hair, her eyelashes, her hip-to-waist ratio. It's like she was drawn by an over-enthusiastic calligrapher.

I shake my head to try and clear it. "But I still don't understand why you're afraid of flying."

Her eyes suddenly fill with tears. Shit. Shit. Shit. Too much. I pushed it. I should have let her lead. I let my curiosity get the best of me.

"My dad," she says, struggling to regain her composure. "He was a pilot."

"Oh my God." I put a hand on her shoulder. "He didn't? He isn't?"

She shakes her head, allowing the tears to fall down her cheeks. A few cling to her lashes. Even her tears are curvy. She takes a few deep breaths before continuing.

"He is dead," she finally says, "but it wasn't a plane crash. It was cancer. I just … I don't feel safe in planes since he died. When he was alive, everything made more sense to me. Life. Planes. Flying." She takes a big sip of water before continuing. "But after he died, I started to question everything. I started having panic attacks every time I flew. Made it hard to travel for work. That's when Keto Kent found himself a new playmate."

"Fucker," I say under my breath. It's so nice to be able to express an opinion so freely. Obviously, with a patient, I couldn't just call their ex a fucker. Inevitably, they'd get back together if I did.

"Mega fucker," she agrees. We both sit in silence for a moment. "I'm sorry, Smitty. You don't even know me. And here I am unloading my entire life story on you. That's weird, right? It's not normal."

"We're in the airport," I say. "Normal rules don't apply when you're traveling."

"Ha! That's what my friends said. They tried to convince me I should have a one-night stand on this trip."

The minute it's out, she slaps a hand over her mouth, as if she could stuff the words back in. She blushes.

I bite my lip.

Emily stares directly at me for a very long moment without talking. Too long, really. But neither of us looks away. I'm aware that my heart rate is steadily accelerating, like someone's pressed the gas pedal down hard. We're getting on the highway, gathering speed in order to merge. Her pupils are very dilated. I imagine mine are as well.

Finally, I take a deep breath and clumsily attempt to break the tension.

"Can I give you a hug?" I ask, holding my arms open wide.

I'm not even sure what I'm going for here. I think it's platonic? No. The way I'm feeling is definitely not platonic. But it's not like I want to feel her up either. She seems like she could really use a hug right now, and if I'm being honest, so could I.

"I wasn't suggesting we ... I mean ... I'm not going to have sex with you, Smitty," she says.

"I'm pretty sure we'd get kicked out if you tried." I laugh. "Then again, they do have nap rooms." I shrug.

She looks horrified.

"I'm kidding!" I sigh and lower my arms. "You just seemed like you could use a hug, and the truth is, I could too. I'm headed into a really shit situation. I almost didn't come to the airport at all today. My entire career might be in the crapper if I don't go along with my colleague's plan, but if I do, I won't respect myself."

Emily scoots closer in the booth and places one arm on my shoulder. "I'm sorry, Smitty. I've been talking a lot about myself. I don't usually do that. Do you want to talk about it?"

I don't bother telling her that I have that effect on a lot of people. But in her case, I didn't mind. It's been a welcomed distraction.

"That's okay," I say. "I'm the one who invited you here. I'm grateful for the company."

"You've obviously got some shit on your mind too. Why don't you tell me about it? Airport stranger to airport stranger?" She raises her eyebrows and takes a sip of her coffee, quietly waiting. Her eyes urge me to go on.

So, this is what it feels like to be on the opposite side of the conversation. I should be better at talking about my feelings.

"My work/life balance is way out of whack. I miss working with people one-on-one. I miss making a difference in people's lives. I feel like all the writing I've been doing has been getting in the way of that," I explain. Speaking the truth gives me palpitations. Now that I've said it, I'm actually going to have to do something about it.

"I bet you're a great therapist, Smitty. You've been a wonderful listener. You know what? You've totally helped me. It was good to talk about my dad. I feel better about flying today. Thank you." She wraps her arms around me in a hug, and I bury my face in her hair. It smells like honey.

Reflexively, my arms go around her as well, pulling her closer. My heart is still hammering, but eventually, it slows. My breath and pulse adjust to match hers. We stay like this for a long time. A crazy long time. She tucks her head onto my shoulder and sighs.

"Excuse me. Can I take these?" An attendant asks if they can clear the table, and we reluctantly pull apart.

I feel strangely sated. Like I just took a really great nap.

"Well, that was weird," Emily says, searching my eyes. "I've never done anything like that before."

"Me either," I confess. "But there's a first time for everything."

"You won't mind if I tell my friends we had a one-night stand? Just to get them off my case?" Her eyes glint mischievously as she pours her ice water into her metal water bottle. The cubes click. Instantly, I'm feeling that other tension again. My heart is pumping its way back onto the freeway, zooming to catch up.

"I can still ask about the nap rooms if you like," I suggest. I'm only half-joking.

"Maybe the next time our paths cross, Smitty." She smiles wistfully. Then she slides out of the booth and places her empty cup back on the table. "I think we should leave well enough alone for now. Because this"—she gestures between us, across the wrecked dishes of assorted food we've tried—"this was really wonderful. I wish you safe travels and a simple solution to your work troubles. Be true to yourself."

She leans over to peck me on my hairy cheek, and I take one last hit of her honey scent.

"Don't give up on love because of one asshole, Emily. The right guy might still be out there. I think your ex-boyfriend was a fool."

Then I coil one of her enticing curls around my finger, cup her chin, and kiss her on the lips, slowly, properly, and deliciously.

"Thanks, Smitty," she says, swaying a little as she steps back. "Now I've got to go see someone about my seat assignment."

emily

· · ·

WHAT THE HELL WAS THAT? Did that actually happen? Or did I just dream the last three hours? I feel disoriented as I ride the elevator down from the Priority Plus Lounge. I consider texting Alexis. What exactly would I say?

> I just made out a little with a bearded stranger named Smitty, after the most amazing free breakfast buffet in the club lounge...

My fingers hover over the send button, and then I delete the message. She wouldn't believe it. She might send out a search party. Or worse. She might want to talk about it on the next podcast episode.

The TV screens displaying flight times and gates have changed over the last three hours. I scan for my flight and am dismayed to see that there's been a gate change. My flight is now on the opposite side of the terminal. I'm going to have to hustle to get there and get in line to get a decent seat, even with an hour till departure time. Dammit. Why hadn't I checked sooner? My app hadn't even pinged me.

Oh, wait. It had. I'd silenced notifications while I was talking to Smitty.

Thinking about him now makes me smile. And to think, I'd had such a negative reaction to him initially. There was just something about him. Something intense, for sure, but in a good way. Like he was a bonfire and I needed warming. I wanted to hold my hands up and absorb his heat. Inch my feet closer and curl my toes.

That kiss had definitely made my toes curl.

I didn't catch whether he wrote for print or digital. I imagine him dishing out practical solutions to modern problems via a down-to-earth advice column on some well-respected health site or magazine. He's like the anti-Blaze Smith. No slick suits or sly, disarming dimples needed. Why didn't I get his full name so I could at least follow him on social media?

Then again, if I knew his whole name, it might ruin everything. The whole charm of this airport encounter was that I didn't know all that much about him. It was a perfect moment. I'm going to carry this memory around with me in my pocket, like a lucky, polished rock, I decide.

I'm flooded with feelings of optimism that I haven't felt in a long time. This crazy trip is off to a much better start than I expected. Who knows? I might even actually get that upgrade.

Halfway down the length of the terminal, as I hustle past yet another shop displaying yet more Blaze Smith books, I realize that I've done it again. I left the freaking book on the bench at the lounge. I smack my forehead. Stupid, stupid, stupid!

There's no time to go back and no time to buy another copy. I'll just have to download it digitally once I get my seat assignment. I won't be able to take notes in the margins like I usually do. But at least if it's on my phone, I won't keep losing it and leaving it behind.

By the time I get to the gate, there's already a long line. At least it moves quickly. It's mostly people swapping seats to sit together. It looks to be a pretty full flight, but the gate agents are in a good mood. Several of the passengers are carrying wrapped gifts or wearing holiday-themed outfits. It infuses the atmosphere with a contagious sense of festive expectation. Most of these people are either headed home or headed to be with loved ones for Christmas.

I might be the only passenger who is doing neither of these things.

"Emily Romano." The gate agent over-enunciates my name as she reads my ticket. She's wearing a necklace that looks like a tiny string of Christmas lights. They are blinking merrily at me. "I see here you don't have a seat assigned. Let's see if we can get that sorted."

"I'd prefer a window, if possible," I mention, crossing my fingers behind my back.

She winces. "Oh dear. I don't think we can accommodate that. I am truly sorry. But hopefully, an upgrade will make up for that. I've got you on an aisle seat, in 3B."

"Upgrade?" I ask, hopefully.

"Yes. You were in premium economy, but I'm bumping you up to business class. Merry Christmas!" She smiles and prints out a new ticket for me, just as another agent announces that business class passengers are welcome to board at any time. "Anything else I can help you with?"

"No, ma'am," I say. "I'm just going to pinch myself. Seems almost too good to be true."

blaze

. . .

"There's no Google Maps or Waze for relationships. You can read up on the route, consider ongoing construction, and avoid road closures. You should factor in timing and make sure your tank is full. But at some point, you just gotta go. You won't know whether you'll have the whole road to yourself, or if you're destined to stall out in traffic, until after the merge. That's just how it is. You can prepare, but you can't always predict."

— Blaze Smith, *Go Your Own Way*, on Hitting the Road

AFTER EMILY LEAVES THE LOUNGE, I text a bit more with Steff.

> I can't get you out of the appearance tomorrow morning, Blaze. You need to go clean up before you get on that plane. I've confirmed there's a shower and razors you can use in the lounge.

As if by magic, a lounge attendant appears and asks me if I'd like an escort to the showers. I sigh. May as well get it over with and spare myself the stress of having to deal with it upon arrival to Rome.

As fun as it had been to have breakfast with Emily, it isn't real life. I'm tired. I still don't have a solution to my PR problem. I've got forty-five minutes, so I may as well shave now and get what sleep I can on the plane.

Ok, Steff. You win. I'm going to shave. If I miss the flight, it's your fault.

You have 45 minutes.

It's two months' worth of growth!

I argue with her, but I'm already planning my attack. I'll start with the electric razor.

Fifteen minutes later, I'm staring at my own pale, naked face in the mirror. I turn my head back and forth like I'm looking at a stranger. I hadn't realized how used to the beard I was. I liked how it softened all my features, sort of blending and blurring my face into anonymity. That beard made me feel free.

The cleft in my chin was the trickiest bit. I'd nicked myself and had to stick some toilet paper on it till it stopped bleeding.

Fortunately, the gate isn't too far from the lounge. Less chance of being recognized. I check my chin to see if the bleeding has stopped and discard the toilet paper. Then I return to the lounge and brace myself to run the gauntlet to the gate.

Before I shaved, I could just stroll through the airport, chatting with beautiful strangers. Now I have to plan my route like a tactical op.

My phone dings, and I scan the latest text from Steff.

That journalist is on your flight. Her name is Emily Romano. Keep an eye out for her, and don't say anything stupid.

"Sir! Sir! Excuse me, sir." The lounge attendant rushes over before I can finish processing the text. "I'm so glad you're still here. You left this book in your booth before."

He looks at the cover of the book, then at me, then back at the book, his mouth forming a perfect o.

"Thanks," I say, holding out my hand for the book. I've already left a generous tip on the table.

"Safe travels, Mr. Smith," the man says as he hands Emily's book to me. I have to admit, I'm a little bummed that she left it behind. I'd liked the idea of her taking a little piece of me with her. Even if we'd never have the chance to discuss it.

Something clicks, and I glance back at my phone, rereading that last message in disbelief.

Her name is Emily Romano.

"My ex and I are writers."

"Keto Kent."

Keto Kent couldn't be Kent Larson, the celebrity biographer who was doing the story on me, could he? And then I recall what Steff said last night—Kent is sending a colleague to do the interviews because his wife is pregnant with twins.

Everything lines up in my head with a sort of satisfying kachunk, like I've just unlocked my gym locker.

"Is everything okay, Mr. Smith?" the attendant asks.

"Sure, fine, great," I say. I shove the book in my backpack. "I just gotta run. My flight is boarding."

I don't bother waiting for the elevator. I've learned the hard way that elevators are the perfect place for fan ambushes. Instead, I race down the stairs and jog through the concourse to the gate number that is printed on my ticket. I can hear the boarding announcement urging all passengers on the flight to Rome that they should be boarding at this time.

But when I get to the gate, there's nobody there. No passengers, no flight crew, no signage. Nothing.

Motherfucker.

"Paging Blaze Smith, Mr. Blaze Smith, your flight is now departing from Gate 33."

A quick glance at the boards confirms that there's been a gate change, and I'm clear on the other side of the terminal from where I need to be. I fire off a quick text to Steff.

> Brace yourself. I may actually miss this damned flight now. I was so busy shaving that I didn't see the gate change

> No! Blaze, you can't miss it. Run!

Taking a deep breath, I slip my arm into the other backpack strap so it's evenly balanced on my back. It's a clear shot to the other end of the terminal. The length of it is broken up by a few stretches of people movers, which could work to my advantage given the fact that it's not particularly crowded today.

I realize that people are starting to look at me. One woman opens her mouth to say something, staring at me as the announcement comes on again.

"Blaze Smith, please report to Gate 33. Your plane is waiting."

"OMG. You're …"

But I'm already running, sprinting for it. As my feet hit the people mover, giving me that extra boost, the adrenaline kicks in. I might not be Titanium Man, but running through the airport like this, I do actually feel a little bit like a superhero. I'm sure that Steff would not approve, but I don't give a damn. I bite back the goofy grin, realizing I've always wanted an excuse to sprint through an airport terminal. And I can't help it. I keep picturing Emily Romano at the other end of this dramatic sprint, waiting for me to … what? Give her the book back?

Three hours ago, I was looking for almost any excuse to miss this flight. And now I'm running for it like it's the last sortie out of a war-torn nation.

I wonder how she'll react when she realizes who I am.

My phone dings again in my pocket, but I don't bother checking it. I've got one more bank of gates to clear, and then I'm there.

"Excuse me! Pardon me! Trying to catch my flight! Sorry!" I shout as I weave through slower moving groups of travelers.

Finally, I reach Gate 33, and thank the Lord, the doors are still open. I'm a little winded, but not as winded as I would have thought. Apparently, the last month working on my sister's farm has been good for my body as well as my soul. I reach into my pocket and pull out my paper ticket for scanning.

"That was close." I gasp.

The gate agent looks disdainfully at me. "Pilot's a big fan of yours. He was doing extra instrument checks to buy you time. But you'd still better hustle."

I nod my gratitude and jog down the jet bridge.

emily

. . .

I'M TOO enamored of my seat to waste any more time on pre-flight jitters. The seat is upholstered in cream-colored leather, and there are fresh blankets and pillows piled on the desk opposite. A large, flat-screen television is showing previews of all the movies available on the flight over. I see they have the Titanium Man release that's still in theaters. If only I didn't have to read that stupid book!

I settle into the oversize seat with my bag beside me and check out the Wi-Fi situation. Not much signal. Hopefully, there's still time to download the book. I start the purchase and set the phone on the desk in front of me, propped up so I can watch the download progress—3 percent … 5 percent … 7 percent. So slow.

Around me, other passengers are filtering onto the plane. I feel vaguely guilty as the coach passengers slip by, looking at our seats with envy. Then a man my age, carrying a Gucci murse, pauses beside me, arms akimbo, elbows in my face. He takes stock of my sheepskin boots and travel leggings and rolls his eyes, glaring at me. He clearly doesn't think I belong in business class. He's headed to the far back of the plane, judging by the number on his ticket. Hopefully, to a middle seat.

I check the download progress—12 percent … 17 percent … 21 percent. Come on Wi-Fi!

There's another seat cozied up next to mine, but I see there is a divider that can be pulled up between us, so I shouldn't have any problem maintaining my privacy. The last thing I want is for some stranger to be reading Blaze Smith's pearls of wisdom over my shoulder. Or even worse, commenting on them. I've been on too many flights with seatmates who have wanted to turn my reading assignments into an opportunity to host an impromptu airborne book club.

A flight attendant makes the announcement about stowing bags and preparing the cabin for takeoff, and I stash my carry-on in the compartment by my feet.

"We're just waiting for one more passenger," the flight attendant says as she hands me a glass of champagne. "Apparently, he didn't get the memo about the gate change."

"I almost went to the wrong gate too," I say.

She glances at the seat next to mine and whispers confidentially, "Normally, we wouldn't wait, but this one's a bit of a celebrity. I probably shouldn't say anything, but let's just say A LOT of women would love to be sitting where you're sitting right now."

My interest is piqued. "Oh really?" I reply. "What kind of celebrity?"

The flight attendant glances at the Titanium Man preview playing on my screen, then makes a show of zipping her lips and giving me a wink before moving on to the row behind me with another glass of champagne. I sip my drink and check back in on the download—27 percent … 31 percent … 34

percent. Whoever he is, he'll be doing me a favor if he just takes his sweet time.

Suddenly, I hear a loud thunking commotion as someone comes jogging down the jet bridge. Drama much? Could this be the late arrival?

Download progress—44 percent … 52 percent. Oh, come on. I just need five more freaking minutes.

"Right this way, sir," the flight attendant gushes. "Let me get you some fresh champagne, Mr. Smith."

I'm still staring down at the phone screen when I see the familiar-looking pair of jeans, flannel shirt, and Patagonia jacket coming toward me. Smitty! What are the odds that my bearded buddy would not only be on my same flight, but he's seated next to me?

It's funny how we hadn't shared anything about where either of us was headed. It was like we both just wanted to exist solely in that moment and not go anywhere else.

I can feel the smile blossoming across my face as I look up expectantly at Smitty.

Except, it's not him. The man standing in front of me is wearing Smitty's clothes, but he doesn't look like Smitty. Or smell like him. He smells like shaving cream and hotel soap. He is perfectly clean-shaven, and he has three dimples, if you count the one on his chin.

I freeze, my expression going from pure joy to shock and horror in a millisecond.

"I think you left your book in the club lounge, Emily," he says, dropping the book on the desk in front of me.

Then he slides past me into the seat next to me, brushing up against me in the process.

Download progress—79 percent.

The flight attendant spies my phone. "Sorry, ma'am. I'm going to have to ask you to put that in flight mode now. We're closing the cabin doors."

blaze

. . .

"Expect the unexpected. Embrace it. That way, when it happens (and it will), you will be able to appreciate the bonding power of off-roading together. Make your own maps. Chart new territories. Slay some dragons."

— Blaze Smith, *Go Your Own Way*, on Detours

EMILY DOESN'T SAY a word to me. She takes the book, shoves it in her bag, and pulls out a pair of oversize headphones.

"Emily, I …" I try to say something, but she holds up a finger and shakes her head at me, silencing me.

She won't make eye contact. As the plane taxis, she pulls on the headphones. Then she closes her eyes for takeoff. She's doing some kind of measured breathing. Deep breath in. Hold. Deep breath out. Hold. I watch her chest rise and fall as we climb. Her hands are gripping the arm rest. Her knuckles are actually white, I note. I study her smooth, olive-skinned hands. They are narrow and her fingers are long. Her nails are oval-shaped, painted a pale, natural peach color. A single gold chain encircles her wrist, and she's wearing one ring, on her right hand. It's vintage—a rose-gold flower with a ruby at the center. The petals emanate from the ruby in delicate arcs of filigree.

Mid-climb, while banking, the plane hits a pocket of turbulence. Emily gasps, her breathing pattern shattered. The hand I've been staring at flails and flutters, reaching for the seat in front of her and back to the armrest in search of solid ground.

I take her hand in mine.

Much to my surprise, she lets me. I count as her breath returns to its measured pattern. By the time we level off, she has relaxed and I release her hand. She remains still, eyes closed, breathing evenly. I don't dare disturb her. Instead, I flip through the selection of films.

The airline is featuring Titanium Man's latest. I turn off the screen and close my eyes as well. It's a long flight. There will be time to talk later. And in the meantime, I've got to make a decision about what I'm going to do. The way I see it, I have three options. I weigh the pros and cons.

First option: I can call the tour off. Pros include having more time to spend with family and not having to do the tour. This is a huge and compelling pro. Steff and Vivian had always insisted that public appearances would get easier for me, and they were right, as well as wrong. I no longer suffer from stage fright. Going through the motions has become second nature. But there's still that moment of cognitive dissonance that I experience every time I see myself in the mirror, freshly touched up by a makeup artist, or catch a glimpse of my on-camera self in a monitor. "Who the fuck is that guy?" It's no less shocking over time. If anything, it's worse.

The cons of calling the tour off are less clear. Steff seems to think I would be torpedoing my entire career. What would that mean, exactly? I've got plenty of money to live on for now, and thanks to my recent celebrity, my mom's and sister's lives are far more secure than they've been in decades. But is that something that I could sustain after a major blow?

Second option: I do the tour and pretend nothing's up. Freeze out the questions. Refuse to talk about my own love life. It would be uncomfortable, and my credibility would no doubt be questioned. I would be poked fun at. Perhaps there'd be a way to spin my own "heartbreak" about being dumped into a relatable moment?

Quickly, I reject that notion. It amounts to another layer of bullshit slapped on bullshit. At some point, the bullshit is going to be slathered on so thick, there'll be no way to strip my soul back down to bare wood. I like being able to recognize myself in the mirror.

And that brings me to option three, which is, frankly, ludicrous. There's no way I am pretending to be in a relationship with Steff. The two of us go back—way back—to grad school where I'd first met Viv. But there's never been anything even remotely romantic between us. She was my girlfriend's friend and sorority sister, and then she became my tour manager. End of story.

The flight attendant wheels up a trolley and offers us lunch. I choose salmon. Emily tucks her headphones back into the bag. She opts for the pasta.

Silently, we both stare at our food.

"I don't know about you, but I'm still full from breakfast," I say, pushing away the uneaten lunch plate on my tray table.

She closes her eyes for a moment and sighs, then turns toward me. I'm struck, once again, by her bright, hazel eyes. Shimmering speckles of green, gold, and brown outlined by a darker brown. They stand out like gems, framed by her long, thick lashes. Even though we've just met, I feel a shock of recognition when I look at her. It's like looking at a beautifully drawn map of a place I already know well. How can this be?

"Look," she says, and I hear the slight waver in her voice. "This is beyond awkward. I can't believe I was so unprofessional with you. I understand if you don't want me to do the background for the article now. If you could just let me know as soon as possible? I'm going to have to figure out how to split my travel expenses with Kent, and maybe he can make some other arrangements."

I have been sitting here for the last forty-five minutes thinking she was pissed off. Why hadn't I even considered that she might be embarrassed?

"Jesus, Emily, I don't want anyone else to do the interview. Least of all, Keto Kent. Are you kidding me?"

"Well, Kent's read your book, at least."

"Good," I say. "He probably needs it far more than you do."

She smirks at this, and I can see I've redeemed myself, if only a bit.

"I love that you didn't kiss my ass, Emily. I kind of even love that you haven't read my book."

"Yet." She holds it up. "We have twelve hours of flight time ahead of us."

"So we do." I smile. Twelve more hours till we get to Rome, and I have to make a tough decision.

"Quick question. Can I still call you Smitty?" She smiles sheepishly.

"Probably best if we stick to Blaze. I haven't been called Smitty since high school," I admit.

"Why didn't you tell me who you really were?"

"My father's." She looks sad. "He was an only child. After my grandparents passed away, they left their house in Ephron, Washington to him. Now it's mine. I moved in six months ago. Found these letters in a closet."

"What about your mom?" I ask. "Is she still in the picture?"

"My mom's still alive and well." Emily reaches for the letters and carefully stashes them back in her bag. "But she's in Africa working for Doctors without Borders. We're not close. She isn't the nurturing type. She and my dad divorced when I was pretty young, and she got right back to her career. She hasn't been that much of an influence, aside from her efforts to talk me out of ever having children."

"Which was fine with Keto Kent?" I guess.

Emily shrugs.

"Honestly, it was just an assumption. We never talked about it explicitly. Not until my dad was sick." She picks up her fork and pushes the pasta around on her plate without eating it.

"When my dad was dying, he told me how sad he was that he'd never get to meet his grandkids. He said this with such utter certainty, not like he was trying to talk me into it. Like he *knew* I was going to be a mother someday. Like he already knew. And in that moment, I knew too. And it also broke my heart. I don't know. I guess deep down, I always wanted kids."

"But not with Kent?"

Her eyes are shining now, glossy with unshed tears. She reaches back in the bag and pulls out the yarn and needles, continuing on with her knitting.

"I can't believe you're doing that thing again."

"What thing?"

"Getting me to talk about myself. First rule of interviewing: NEVER talk about yourself unless you are agreeing with what the interviewee is saying, thereby encouraging them to continue talking."

I prod. "Yes, yes, tell me more."

She sighs heavily and reaches in her bag, pulling out a bottle of pills. "You've given me no choice. I'm going to take a tactical Xanax now, and in another twenty minutes, I will fall asleep and sleep soundly and silently, all through the night, until we arrive in Rome."

"No!" I protest. "How will you read my book?"

"I'll read it when we get to Rome, and I'm … less distracted," she replies.

"Please don't go to sleep."

"Too late." She swallows the pill. "As soon as this plane lands, the tables are going to turn. I'm going to be the one asking the questions, and you're going to be the one giving the answers."

"You can ask me anything right now," I say. There's a list of no-fly topics Steff sends over whenever we accept an interview. I know I saw something in my inbox this morning, but I'm not even going to open the email. I'm going to do this my way.

"How long ago did you and Viv really break up?"

"Pardon?"

"Cut the act. 'Smitty' hardly seemed heartbroken at the newsstand. I figure you've had plenty of time to get over her."

"You're very perceptive." I tip my imaginary hat at her.

"So, you aren't shattered by Viv's hookup then?"

"Did it feel like I was shattered when I kissed you?" I turn to face her. Her hands stop flying in circles and clutch the needles tighter, blushing. I watch as she bites her beautiful lower lip. I'm dying to do it again. I desperately want to kiss her.

"That never happened," Emily asserts. She looks away from me, concentrating on her knitting. Her needles pick up speed.

"It happened," I say. She drops a stitch and frowns as she picks it back up before continuing her interrogation.

"So, you're saying you're cool with those photos of Viv?"

"Not all of them." I sigh. "But I would prefer you don't share this part in your notes for Kent."

I pull the tabloid out of my backpack and open to the story, careful to make sure nobody else is watching us. I open to the page where Viv is tenderly applying sunscreen on Rafe's tiny daughter. In another photo, the toddler is seated on her lap, arms wrapped around her torso.

"This one." I tap on the photo. "This is not cool."

Emily raises one eyebrow and looks quizzically at me. "Explain."

"Off the record." I speak in low tones, grateful for the hum of the plane that drowns out all conversations beyond a two-foot radius. "Viv and I were together for almost six years, and one thing that never changed was that she was vehement she didn't want children. More than that. She *hates* kids. Calls them career suicide bombers."

"Sounds like she has a lot in common with my mother." Emily bites her lip when I wait for her to go on. "I'm sorry," she says. "What I meant to say is, how did that make you feel?"

"Frustrated. It was a fundamental flaw in our relationship. I knew it was bound to break us up one day. It was like I'd already checked out online before leaving the premises," I admit. I haven't said this out loud before. It feels good to stick a pin in my feelings and label them.

"And is this that day?" she asks.

"No. We haven't been intimate for over a year. We agreed to keep up appearances till the end of the book tour. I'm not surprised. She's always had a crush on Rafe. And truly, I don't begrudge her a little happiness. But the playing at the 'happy family' part stings. Not gonna lie."

Emily nods sagely. "I get that."

"I thought you would," I say.

She yawns and stops knitting again, wrapping up her yarn around the needle.

"Oh no you don't. Stay with me till dessert," I say. "I think they've got gelato."

"Ooh, they do?" Her eyes light up instantly, like a child's. I love how small things seem to delight her.

"What are you making?" I ask.

"Some booties." She shrugs. "I stress-knit. I'm always making stuff. My poor friends have a million hats and scarves."

"Lucky friends," I comment. "Who are the booties for, then?"

She pauses for a moment.

"These? I don't know. Kent's kids, I guess?"

"What? Are you kidding me? You are knitting booties for your ex's babies that he is having with a woman he cheated on you with?"

"I'm a stress knitter. This is therapeutic."

"And I'm a therapist, and I think you're too nice." I shrug. "It's one thing to take this job—and I assume you're going to share a byline—but the booties?"

"We're not sharing the byline," she says.

"Give me that bootie." I reach for the needles.

"No!" she protests, laughingly shoving it into her bag. "What are you going to do with it? Throw it out the cabin door?"

"Maybe," I say.

"What are you going to do about the negative press?" She changes the subject deftly.

I sigh. "Touché. That is the question of the moment."

Reaching into my pocket, I pull out my phone. I still haven't read the last messages that I got, presumably from Steff, while I was running for the plane.

I flick the screen.

> Operation decoy is a go! I got a few items to
> sprinkle around our room.

There's a photo of lingerie spread out on a bed. Garish neon thongs, purple crotchless panties. In a second photo, Steff has posed suggestively with a large bottle of "erotic" massage oil, tongue peeking out, her bug-like, blue eyes rolling back.

> Lmk if you want any nudes. I should probably
> send some nudes to make it seem authentic,
> right?

Frantically, I try and delete the messages before anyone sees them. I only wish I could unsee them. Is that the sort of lingerie Steff actually wears?

I really don't want to know.

"What's that?" Emily looks at the phone, and at me, stifling another yawn. "You looked pale for a minute there. Like you saw a ghost."

I shake my head.

"What was it? More photos of Viv? Is she visiting an orphanage or something?"

"No," I say, weighing whether I can truly trust Emily or not. She already knows about Viv, and she's compromised herself as well. We're both vulnerable here, and we're stuck on this drive together. I may as well tell her the truth. Maybe she'll be able to help me think of another option that doesn't involve ending my career or living a complete lie with my over-eager manager.

"That was a text from my manager. She's worried about how the news of the breakup is going to affect the tour and, ultimately, my career. So, she's proposed that we fake a relationship for the duration of the book tour."

I feel dirty just saying it. I can't even look at her.

Emily snorts. "That's what you were talking about in the lounge! You're not actually considering it, are you?"

I plant my face in my hands and wait for the shame to pass.

"I don't know. It feels beyond wrong. I'm thinking I should call the whole tour off. I don't know what I'm going to do. I told you I needed a hug. I wasn't kidding."

Emily reaches out and pulls my hand away from my face.

"You can't call off the tour," she says. She looks genuinely concerned.

"Yeah, but what are my other options, really? I can't pretend I'm sleeping with my *manager*." I whisper the last part.

We stop talking when the flight attendant appears with two tiny cups of gelato. "I didn't realize you two already knew each other," she says, looking accusatorially at Emily. "How sweet that you arranged a secret rendezvous on such a long flight." She plunks down the gelato and purses her lips, blinking cannily at us like she knows something. "Don't worry, your secret's safe with me. What happens in my cabin, stays in my cabin." She winks before walking away.

Emily's eyes dart from the flight attendant to me and back and forth again a couple more times before her confusion morphs into laughter. She glances back as the attendant resumes her ice cream delivery service.

"OMG, is she for real?" she asks. "Does that sort of thing happen a lot to you?"

"You have no idea." I shake my head. "I'm not safe now. The speculation is just beginning. And I'm sorry you've been implicated. I'd hate for you to get in trouble with your editor."

Emily shrugs dismissively. "Actually, Kent didn't tell anyone that he was sending me to gather the background material. That's why I can't ask for the byline. As far as his editor knows, Kent's getting the story and writing the story. He said your manager owed him a favor, and she wouldn't spill about my being the one who actually spoke with you."

That sounds like Steff, though I hate to imagine the circumstances that led to the debt. What "favor" had Kent granted her in the past?

"Steff didn't mention any of this to me." I frown.

"You were just joking about canceling the tour, right?" Emily peels back the lid to her gelato.

"I mean, I probably shouldn't have even gotten on the plane. But I was really anxious to give you your book back."

She raises an eyebrow at me, eyeing me suspiciously.

"I'm calling you out now. That's bullshit, and you know it. There's got to be another solution. You'll figure something out." She dips her wooden spoon into the gelato and swoons. "Mmm."

"You think this crap is good? Wait till you get to Rome," I say. "What's your favorite flavor?"

"Well, my grandma used to make nocciola. But I don't know. I haven't really sampled many other flavors."

"When we get to Rome, I'm taking you out for gelato," I say. "You and me. We're going to try all the flavors."

"That actually sounds dreamy." Emily smiles. "But what about the press? What about the book tour? What's everyone going to say? I mean, you saw how that flight attendant jumped to conclusions."

"Fuck them all," I say, leaning over to wipe a bit of gelato off her chin. "Let them jump."

She turns her head, and my thumb brushes against her lips. So warm. So soft. This urge to kiss her is like a hunger pang. Sharp and physical. And that's when the obvious solution hits me, as plain as day.

We stare at each other for a second, and I can see the idea coming together for her as well. I feel certain she is thinking the same thing I'm thinking. Fuck them all. Let them jump to conclusions.

Emily could be my parachute.

It's like we're in a freefall, daring each other to reach the same conclusion, playing chicken to see who'll say it first. Just as I'm about to ask, she pulls the ripcord.

"I'll do it," she says.

"Pardon?" I reply, afraid to hope that she's suggesting what I think she's suggesting.

"I'll do it. It doesn't have to be your manager. I can be your fake girlfriend. Nobody knows why I'm really here, and I'm already traveling with you."

"How did you know that's what I was going to suggest?" I ask. "And are you aware of all that would entail?"

Emily rolls her eyes at me. "Give me a little credit, will you? I happen to host a romance genre podcast. I'm familiar with all the tropes. Fake relationships are a classic."

"Mind if I grab a cup of coffee for you to sip while we discuss this? And you should probably put your seat back up in the fully upright position. I can't have you conking out on me just yet," I say.

"Sure, sure." Emily rolls her eyes but presses the button to raise her seatback.

"I'll be right back," I promise. It only takes me a couple of minutes to fetch the coffees from the galley, but she's looking sleepier by the moment. We have to talk fast.

"Listen, Emily, I feel like it's a big ask. I know what's in it for me. I'm just not so sure what's in it for you."

"Besides the privilege of being publicly recognized as romance guru Blaze Smith's new squeeze?" She smirks.

"A great privilege indeed, but I'm guessing from our earlier conversations that one wasn't on your bucket list." I stir some sugar into her coffee.

"You know, the most common motivation for fake relationship tropes is revenge—making an ex jealous," Emily muses. "Though it usually revolves around a wedding."

"Or the holidays," I add, wondering if I'll need to make an appearance at any office parties to seal this deal. It would mean extending the fake relationship out past the tour, but I'm willing to commit to this if she asks. "Are we just talking about making Kent miserable, or are there any other skeletons in your closet whose bones I need to rattle?"

"It's just Kent. But that's not going to work." Emily dismisses this idea with a wave. "I don't have any desire to make him jealous, and even if I did, he's not the jealous type. All Kent really cares about is getting his byline. He'd probably put on a dress and try to date you himself if he thought there was any chance of the article not happening."

"I suspect Steff might be more my type than Kent." I grimace, suddenly coming up short and feeling foolish. "If I can't make your ex suffer, and there's nothing else in it for you, maybe I really should just go ahead and cancel the tour. It was just a silly idea. I shouldn't have mentioned it."

As if on cue, the plane lurches, and we lose altitude in a sudden drop. My stomach plummets, and my heart follows. The coffee sloshes on my tray. Emily's arm shoots out, and she grabs my hand and grips it tight while we both wait for the plane to level out again.

"It's fine," I say. "Just a little pocket of air."

"You CANNOT cancel this tour, OKAY?" Emily's brows are drawn, and she is squeezing the hand she is still holding.

"But you just said—"

"If you cancel the tour, there's a good chance the article will also be canceled. And if the article is canceled, Kent's going to be an ass about it. He's never going to cough up the cash to reimburse me for what I've already spent on this trip. I don't know what I'll do. I can't afford to spend ten days in Italy on my own dime right now, and if I have to turn around and go right home, I have no idea when I'll be able to come back."

I feel like an idiot that none of this has even occurred to me. I don't know if I should offer to reimburse her for her troubles or kiss her at this moment. I want to do both. But neither action feels quite right. Instead, I apologize.

"I'm really sorry to have put you in this predicament," I say.

"Don't be ridiculous. It isn't your fault," Emily says. "Although you probably should have told me who you were from the start."

"Maybe I could help with your expenses?" I offer.

"No. I don't want your pity money. I just want to do my job and get to spend a few days on my own special mission. I really don't mind being the decoy if that's what it takes. You clearly need some help with your whole situation, Doctor *Amore*." Her lips twitch with amusement.

I look away, staring straight ahead at my TV screen, which has somehow reset itself. The preview for the Titanium Man movie is playing again. I jab at the screen to turn it off.

"Okay, now you're making me seem pathetic," I say. "I don't need your pity." I can feel my face burning.

I am pathetic.

"Look at me?" Emily touches my arm lightly, and I turn back to face her. She stares deep into my eyes, and I feel the tug again, like I'm the skein of yarn waiting to be woven into her work. I almost wish for another pocket of turbulence that would give me the excuse to grab her, to pull her back.

She sighs and squeezes my arm before speaking. "It doesn't have to be such a big deal, does it? Think of it this way. We're just two friends doing each other a simple favor." She arranges her blanket around herself and reclines her seat all the way back.

"Wait. What are you doing?" I ask.

"I really need to get some sleep," she murmurs. Her eyelids are starting to get seriously heavy. "I think we're good here. We don't need to discuss this anymore right now."

"You're really sure you want to do this?" I ask, reaching across to tuck her in.

"It's fine, Smitty." Emily pats my cheek. "Ooh, that's smooth. You have baby-soft skin."

I brush a stray curl from her forehead and recline my seat as well, turning toward Emily as if to spoon her, which is a ridiculous thought, and not only because the seats make it impossible.

emily

. . .

I AWAKE twenty-five thousand feet above the Eternal City, about an hour before we land. It takes a few minutes for my brain cells to fire up and report for duty as I observe the man sleeping in the seat beside me. Right. I'm on a plane, on my way to Rome. And I'm with Blaze Smith. Who is also Smitty. Was I just dreaming about kissing a man with a beard?

There's a little drool on my pillow.

Blaze is still asleep, lying half on his side and facing me. His jawline is called out by a dark dusting of stubble. I want to reach out and run a finger across the cleft in his chin.

Instead, I get up, go to the bathroom, wash my face, and brush my teeth. When I get back to my seat, I crack open and read the first chapter of his book.

So far so good. No mentions of tantric sex, and no bro-code lists on how to "neg, if you want them to beg." Not that I was expecting anything like that. In fact, most of it seems almost painfully obvious. Stuff we learned in kindergarten, like "be nice" and "do unto others." Maybe that's what makes bad breakups so painful—knowing that our partners couldn't even keep up kindergarten standards.

I fold down the page and put the book back in my carry-on when Blaze gets up.

"Morning, Sunshine." He stretches lazily. "Sleep well?"

"I'm feeling oddly well rested and ready to report for duty." I smile.

"Good." His eyes probe mine. "So, no change of heart?"

"Nope." I shake my head. "I'm still in."

Blaze smiles and nods. "Me too. But we should discuss the details," he says, raising his seat up.

"I was just about to say the same thing," I agree.

Fake Relationship 101. There have to be clear boundaries. Rules can't be unspoken. They have to be spelled out.

But before we can hash anything out, the nosy flight attendant advises us that it's time to adjust our seats for landing.

"Talk more on the ground?" Blaze asks. I nod and try to ignore the turbulence, keeping myself calm by focusing on my task list.

As soon as we land, I'll check how much it would cost to change my ticket, just in case. And I'll check in with Maria, my grandmother's friend, later today to let her know I'm here. And, of course, I'll text Alexis.

The plane hits another air pocket.

Wordlessly, Blaze takes my hand. The instant he does, I feel better. And worse. Now I'm calm about the plane and freaking out about the man.

What the hell am I thinking?

Everyone knows that fake-dating scenarios are an accident waiting to happen. Cute and funny in rom-coms. Preposterous in real life. Except, celebrities get away with it all the time. Don't they? How hard can it be?

Blaze massages my palm with his thumb every time we hit a bump, sending swirling feelings throughout my entire body. It seems to short-circuit my panic reflex. His hand on mine is warm, steady, and reassuring. We stay this way until we touch down and the pilot eases up on the brakes.

As we taxi to the gate, I realize that I'm not even sure where I'll be staying anymore. Should I assume the original arrangements his manager made for me are getting scrapped?

"Do you want to share a cab into the city? You can drop me off at my hotel," I suggest.

He looks at me quizzically and shakes his head.

"No, Emily. Steff arranged a car for both of us. We'll go straight to our hotel and bring Steff up to speed on the new plan there, okay?"

"Okay."

As usual, the moment we deplane, I'm anxious to get to the carousel where I'll be reunited with my possessions. But much to my surprise, as soon as we enter the terminal, Blaze guides me away from the baggage area. He waves at a bald man in a suit who is holding a tablet with a simple flame logo.

"This way, please," the man says.

"Wait. Where are we going?" I ask.

"Private arrival lounge," Blaze says. He hands the attendant our baggage claim tickets.

"Do you always travel like this?" I ask.

"Not always. I met you at a newsstand in SeaTac, remember?"

"Was that an aberration? Or is this?" The journalist in me takes over as we are shown into a private waiting room. I'm curious what it's like to be him.

"Honestly, I prefer to fetch my own luggage and buy my own bottled water, but there are certain times and places where it's not feasible. Roman paparazzi are legendary, and my tour has been well publicized. And when you add the recent round of articles about Viv and Rafe, I'm a story. I can't risk my luggage being stolen, and I don't have the energy to deal with selfie-seekers after a long-haul flight." He sounds a bit defensive.

I hold up my hands. "No judgment from me. This spread looks awesome." I point at the table with fresh fruit, a coffee carafe, and pastries. "Is it all for us, or will Oprah be joining us today?"

"It's just us." Blaze laughs. "They'll bring our luggage to us shortly. Have you ever had a cornetto?" He hands me a horn-shaped pastry.

We both check our phones and sip our coffee while waiting for our luggage. Blaze answers a few messages. I send a photo of the pastries to Alexis.

"Check this out." Blaze holds up a photo of what appears to be a fuzzy muppet. "My sister has a goat farm, but she's just started raising alpaca as well. I helped deliver this one last month. Have you ever seen anything more adorable?"

"That's a real thing?" I laugh. "I mean, I love knitting with alpaca wool. I just never realized how adorably unreal their offspring look."

"Carina's working with a spinner. She can hook you up with some great stuff," Blaze says. He pockets the phone.

"You'd do that for me?"

"So long as you promise not to knit anything for Kent and his progeny."

The lounge guy is back with the luggage and has an agent in tow whom he's brought to review our passports. We both stand and gather our bags. Blaze puts his hand on the small of my back as I dig in my purse to retrieve my document case. I have to pull out his book, my earphones, and my laptop to get to the pouch with my passport and the letters.

"That bag is seriously like a clown car," he whispers in my ear. The touch of his breath against my neck gives me goose bumps. "And I'm sorry to spring this PDA on you, but we're being watched." He kisses the side of my neck, and my knees instantly go weak. I need to squeeze my thigh muscles to hold myself upright.

The passport agent and the lounge guy observe us and exchange a knowing look, similar to the one the flight attendant gave us. I wonder how many secret rendezvous between famous people airport staff have observed. And who they've shared those stories with.

Blaze pulls me closer and buries his face in my hair, kissing the top of my head. His hand is now wrapped around my waist. He seems relaxed when he smiles at the agent stamping our passports.

Of all the random strangers I could have kissed in an airport lounge on the one and only time I've let my guard down enough to do something so reckless, it had to be this guy. My assignment.

But it's fine, right? It's like I said last night. We're two friends just helping each other out. It doesn't have to be a big deal.

Maybe if I keep repeating it, I'll believe it.

It feels totally natural to lean into this man. He smells like vanilla and coffee with a hint of bourbon. Cinnamon bark too.

It's such a solid way to smell. Real and reassuring. Not at all what I would have imagined him smelling like based on the cover photo on his book.

"Grazie," I say as the agent hands back the passports.

"Arrividerci piccini (Goodbye, little ones)," he replies.

Finally, we're escorted out of the airport via a private exit that leads to a covered driveway. It's a brisk morning with fast-moving clouds that zip across blue skies as if they are in a hurry.

A big, black, shiny Mercedes van is waiting to ferry us to the hotel.

The driver, a stout man in a full chauffeur's costume, places a step stool to make it easier to climb in. He insists that I use it, placing his hand on my elbow to assist as if I am too fragile or elderly to step up on my own. Blaze jumps in behind me. There's enough room for at least ten people in the van's luxuriously upholstered interior.

Flashback to the beater van shuttle I'd raced to catch less than twenty-four hours ago. How can that have only been yesterday? The shuttle to SeaTac feels like it happened in another lifetime.

Our driver finishes loading our luggage and comes around to the side door.

"Andiamo (Here we go)!" he says and slams the sliding door shut.

He clambers up into the front seat and takes a moment to settle himself. I can see him programming our route into a tablet on the other side of the privacy panel. I can't tell if he's waiting for something. I glance out the window, curious to see if anyone else is coming.

"Before you ask, Oprah is not joining us in the van either," Blaze teases. "It's just us. The ride's forty minutes. I was hoping we could talk. Hammer out the details?"

"I might need a minute. That VIP treatment was crazy for me," I admit. "Are you used to it at this point?"

"For the most part. I don't think about it," Blaze says. "I have to apologize. I should have given you more warning before diving into the PDA back there. I don't trust those VIP guys not to talk to the tabloids."

"I assumed as much," I say.

"I hope it was okay," Blaze says.

"You did what you had to do."

The intimacy had indeed taken me by surprise, but not half as much as my own reaction to it. Foolishly, I'd assumed that after some sleep and a professional reframing of our relationship, this man would have less of an effect on me.

I thought I'd wake up and the memory of Smitty would be easy to wall off and file away.

The driver puts the van in gear and pulls out with a jerk, forcing me back in my seat. We circle the airport, following the signs indicating the way to Rome.

Blaze hands me a bottle of water.

In the light of day, without the bushy beard and after stashing his colorful, flannel shirt and puffer vest, Blaze Smith bears little resemblance to the wild mountain man who was Smitty. I note that his jeans, though faded, are expensive, and so are his shoes. The blue Patagonia fleece and black tee, worn on their own, are understated, classic. He's done something to tame his hair too. It's settled into an organized mess that looks completely intentional. It's annoying how good he looks.

My hair, meanwhile, looks like seaweed. It is twisted into a tangled and clumpy topknot and suffering from a bad case of airplane air.

My comfy flight clothes aren't doing me any favors either. My leggings are speckled with gray fuzz balls that resemble tiny bugs, and there are cornetto flakes clinging to the cuffs of my coat. I brush them off and cross my legs. My outfit looked more at home in the SeaTac budget shuttle than it does in the back of this luxury van.

For a moment, I miss Smitty and the crumbs in his beard.

Blaze Smith hasn't got a single crumb hitchhiking on his nearly perfect personage. He's staring at me, smiling slightly.

"What are you smiling about, Smitty?" I ask.

"I thought I told you not to call me that," he mock chastises me, shaking his head. "What were you just thinking about? You looked so serious."

"I was thinking that I miss your beard." I shrug. "And I was thinking about the article. This is virgin territory for me. I don't normally accidentally make out with people I've been assigned to profile."

"But I'm not technically your assignment, am I? No byline, nothing to link you back to the story?"

"It's a morally gray area," I say. "Other people might not know that I'm here to interview you, but I know."

And therein lies the problem.

"As do I." His pale eyes flicker with something. He licks his lips. Looking at his lips makes me need to squeeze my thighs together.

Is he toying with me?

There's no way I can maintain journalistic distance if I'm sleeping with this man. If that's even something that's on the table. Hooking up with a bearded stranger was farfetched enough. Hooking up with a celebrity? Someone I'm supposed to be profiling for an article? That kind of thing isn't even on my radar.

I recall the looks that I got from some of the other passengers on the plane who didn't seem to think I was VIP status worthy.

"Do you think people will buy that we're a couple?" I ask, covering my insecurity with a joke. "I mean, I clean up okay, but it's hard to hold a candle to the incandescence of Smitty."

He laughs. "Admit it, you're a beardie. You have a thing for dudes with beards."

"Admit you have a thing for airport damsels in distress."

"Only those with curly lashes and beautiful, sassy mouths that like to make a mockery of my life's work."

"I'm a relative nobody, Blaze. I haven't got star power, unless you count the handful of followers of the rom-com podcast I cohost."

"I definitely want to hear more about that." Blaze raises an eyebrow. "Is it just books that you talk about?"

"No. We discuss films and music as well. We did a whole episode on Taylor Swift," I say. "Why? Were you going to try and pitch yourself as a guest?" I'm just joking, of course. We get the occasional author and entrepreneur on our show, but we don't get A-listers like him.

"I think I'd love to be a guest on a podcast like that." Blaze shrugs noncommittally. "We should talk."

Jackson would die.

The thought of Blaze seated in my living room, stretched out on my sofa, is almost too much for me to imagine right now. My mind glitches as it tries to paint different versions of this man into the scene. Would Smitty stay behind after the episode ended? Would Blaze wait till everyone left to kindle a fire? And then what? This fantasy is not productive. Or helpful. I take a swig of my water and steer the conversation back to business.

"We don't have long till we get to the hotel. Let's go over the terms of this fake relationship thing. We don't want there to be any confusion, or hurt feelings, if we're really doing this," I say.

I feel pretty confident asserting myself here. You don't host over thirty episodes of a rom-com podcast without learning a thing or two about tropes. This is standard procedure with fake relationships.

"Isn't the whole point of making the rules in fake relationship tropes breaking them?" Blaze asks.

"Okay. Whatever. Here's the deal. WE are not going to break the rules." I fold my arms across my chest.

"What makes you so sure?" He raises his eyebrows at me, like he's issuing a dare. I'm not sure what the dare is, but I can imagine a lot of things it might be. And so can he, judging by the cold fire in his eyes.

"Because we are not characters in a rom-com movie. This is real life."

He sighs.

"Back to the ground rules." I pour a packet of vitamins into my water bottle and shake it hard, enjoying how it fizzes before settling back down.

"It's not too late to call the whole thing off, Emily. We could take a different path. I could cancel the tour, book us a cottage up north somewhere. I hear there's a great Christmas Market in Bolzano. We could hole up with some good books. Somewhere with a fireplace and a rocking chair. Maybe you could knit me an afghan?" Blaze attempts to give me puppy-dog eyes, but I'm not buying it. That puppy's a wolf.

"You wish I'd knit you an afghan!" I laugh. "You'll be lucky if you get a pair of mittens out of me."

"Your loss." He shrugs. "My beard grows pretty fast in the winter."

"We both know that can't happen," I say, speaking a little more sternly than I intend to. My heart is pounding and my hands are shaking. I have to will myself not to imagine that cabin now.

"It's only a week. We can do this, and we can both maintain our dignity. By the way, I have much nicer clothes packed in my bags. Or I can pick up some new stuff."

"I don't give a shit about your clothes," Blaze says. "Just like you didn't seem to give a shit about mine back in Seattle."

"You kissed me, remember?"

"You kissed me back. With tongue." He closes his eyes and rakes a hand through his hair.

I still want to kiss him.

I tap my water bottle impatiently against the padded armrest. "Are we doing this? Because if we really are, we need to sync up on the ground rules—and fast. We're almost there. Tell me exactly what you want me to do."

"Do you really have to put it that way?" he says, turning to stare out the window. "Because what I want and what I need might not be aligning perfectly at the moment."

"Tell me how we're going to sell this fake relationship," I rephrase.

"Fine." He takes a long drink from his own water bottle before continuing.

"You don't have to come to all the events, but we should make at least one public appearance together daily. We have to make it convincing, but not too graphic. Hand holding. A few kisses in public. Respectable stuff. I think you look just fine, but if you want to buy any other clothes, if it would make you more comfortable, I'll have Steff expense it."

Simultaneously, both of our phones ding. We ignore the incoming texts and continue to go over the terms.

"We'll eat all our meals together, unless they're part of an event," Blaze continues. "I hate to say it, but you probably can't tell your friends and family we're faking it for now. It's too risky. I'm sorry, it's just one week," Blaze says.

"I think that's a good call. I'll keep it vague," I promise.

It won't be easy keeping the truth from my friends back in Ephron, but I suspect we'll be busy. Plus, I'll have the time difference to blame if I don't get back to people right away.

"Which brings us to the sleeping arrangements," Blaze says. His voice gets lower, rougher. "We should talk about what happens in private too."

I take a deep breath. "I think you mean, what *doesn't* happen."

Our eyes meet.

"You sure about that, Emily? We're both consenting adults." I swear his gray eyes are flickering, like pale twin flames. Teasing me. Tempting me. Testing me. "Tell me you're not thinking about it right now?"

I can't tell him what I'm thinking because it's so utterly, entirely unprofessional. It involves a roaring fire, and a rocking chair, and his naked body wrapped up in one of my afghans. What is it with him? Is he some kind of charismatic cult leader? Am I a groupie now? My face feels hot. My lips feel dry.

I pat on some peppermint lip balm, hoping to cool myself off. He takes a deep breath as he watches this, and then it's my turn to close my eyes.

"I'm thinking that I would never forgive myself if I slept with someone I was supposed to be interviewing. Even if I was doing the work on the DL, as a favor to a colleague."

My eyes are still closed when I hear him let out the breath that I didn't even realize he was holding.

"I respect that, Emily," he says quietly. "Shit. I'm being such an asshole. I'm sorry."

I open my eyes, surprised to see him looking so genuinely abashed.

"I already feel like I'm implicating you in a falsehood. It's complicated, and confusing, and probably not fair to either one of us," he says.

"Then no sex, you agree?" I ask.

"Yes, I agree, as much as it pains me, and I assure you, it does." He groans. "And do you think you can put up with me for the week, despite how slick and smug and full of shit and beardless I am?"

"I mean … I can try?" I smile nervously. "As long as we stick to the rules."

"I solemnly swear not to try to seduce you as long as you are on assignment profiling me," Blaze says, holding out his hand to shake.

I take it tentatively. "Why does this feel like I am making a deal with the devil?" I joke.

"I've been called worse." Blaze shrugs. He fiddles with the zipper pull on his jacket. "There's just one more detail we need to discuss. We should talk about what happens *after* you're done with the article and the tour is over."

Our phones ding again. And again. And again. It's obvious that whatever is going on, someone is desperate to get ahold of both of us.

"You better check that," I say.

"Yeah. You too."

We each fumble with our phones as they continue to blow up with fresh messages.

I have six texts in my queue. They are from Jackson, Chelsea, and Alexis and include photos that are taking forever to load. Captions include: *WTAF, are you shitting me?* and *I knew it!*

I hear Blaze suck in a deep breath after opening his messages, and then his phone rings. He picks up immediately.

"Yeah, Steff. I see it. Yeah, I know. Uh-huh. She's here. Here here. As in here in the car with me. No. She hasn't seen it yet. I guess it was someone on the plane? Yes, I will put you on speaker."

The pictures on my phone finally load, and I gasp when I see them. Grainy and a bit out of focus, but unmistakably, Blaze Smith and me appear to be making out on the plane. It's not a flattering angle. My eyes are droopy and I look stoned. His hair is sticking out at crazy angles. It's been shared from a "Celebs on Planes" Instagram account.

When was this shot taken? Judging from the number of comments, it had to have gone up several hours ago. Possibly mid-flight? I look again. The caption says, "Fire in the Sky. Will Blaze and Emily Join the Mile-High Club?"

It must have been shot after we had lunch, after I took the Xanax. I vaguely recall him tucking the blanket around me right before I fell asleep.

Blaze puts Steff on speaker.

"What the fuck, Blaze?" she says. "We had a plan. I invested in props. Everything was all set up."

Blaze flinches. "I never agreed to that plan, Steff. I mean, I do appreciate the offer, but you work for me. I don't think it would be appropriate to exploit our relationship that way."

"But it's okay to exploit your *relationship* with a journalist who is doing a story on you in a major magazine?"

"Hi, Steff," I chime in. "That's not technically correct. I'm just here to gather data. Kent Larson is writing the story."

"How did the poster know your name?" Steff asks, suspiciously.

"I was just wondering the same thing," I say. I turn to Blaze. "You don't think it might have been that flight attendant, do you?"

"You mean ex-flight attendant?" Steff growls. "That's seriously not okay. I'm putting a call into the airline now. We'll get to the bottom of this."

"No! Steff, stop. It's not important who posted the photo," Blaze interjects. "The point is that whoever it was, they just did us a huge favor. I'm not wild about the subterfuge, but we're going ahead with operation decoy. Just not with you as my decoy. You're off the hook. I was going to tell you when I got to the hotel. We're going with Emily."

"You mean you want me to put *her* in the suite with you?" Steff asks, sounding shocked.

"Yes," Blaze answers. "She can have the bed. I'll stay on the sofa."

"Don't be ridiculous!" Steff and I say at the same time. Blaze shakes his head.

"It's your book tour," I say. "I'm just fine on the couch."

"But, where will I stay then?" Steff asks.

"In whatever room you booked for Emily," Blaze answers.

Steff is silent for a moment.

I look out the window. Still not much to see, but we're getting closer to the city. Traffic has picked up, and we're passing by blocks of apartments.

"I'll be honest, Blaze. I really don't like this." Steff sounds dubious.

"Well, those photos are already out, Steff. And we were spotted together at the airport. I don't know what to say. We're almost there."

Blaze checks his watch.

"Okay. I'll see you both in fifteen minutes. We'll talk more when you get here. I have to go sort out the damned rooms now. And you should probably delete the photos I sent you. Bye!" With no further warning, Steff abruptly hangs up.

blaze

. . .

"Imagine a world where people didn't pass on the right or treat lane changes like last-minute, covert operations. Here's a thought. What if everyone used their blinker when they were about to turn? None of us have the ability to read minds. Failing to indicate your intentions and communicate your needs runs the risk of putting your relationship on the skids."

— Blaze Smith, *Go Your Own Way*, on Communication and Mixed Messages

OF ALL THE times to meet someone I actually feel this kind of a connection with. And of all the people, it had to be a journalist who's gathering intel on me? There's nothing I want more right now than to call off the entire book tour, cancel the interview, and whisk Emily away somewhere.

I wish I'd never shaved my beard. I wish I could somehow still be Smitty.

But it doesn't matter what I want anymore. The moment our van pulls up onto the plaza above the Spanish Steps, we're no longer alone. We've arrived on an international stage. And we have an audience.

Steff is standing in the portico outside the hotel entrance, an overly bright, orange-lipped, open-mouthed smile pasted onto her face. She waves and nods eagerly at the car as we pull in, and then subtly tilts her head to the right, tipping me off to the presence of paparazzi.

"Looks like they're waiting for us," I tell Emily.

"Who?" She blinks at me, looking confused. She's had her face and phone pasted to the window ever since we entered the city, snapping photos. It's hard not to be impressed by the clash of thousand-year-old, marble-clad churches and Roman ruins, cozied up to modern shops, kiosks, and cafés.

"Paparazzi. Waiting to take photos of us when we get out of the car. Still sure you want to do this? Last chance to back out." I squeeze her hand. Suddenly, I'm not so sure I want to feed her to the sharks.

Emily scans the plaza outside the window. "Are you sure? I don't see anyone there."

"See that woman by the door? That's Steff, my tour manager. She just gave me a signal. They're probably over there by the trees," I say, pointing toward the top of the Spanish Steps. "Or maybe on the other side of the church."

"This is so weird." Emily's eyes are wide. "I'm not used to being on this side of the velvet rope."

"You'll get used to it this week," I assure her. "So, here's the plan. The bellhops will take care of our luggage. We'll just get out and give them a brief show. Nothing crazy, just confirmation we're together. Since we know they are somewhere over by the trees, we can position ourselves to give them a clear view."

I hate being so calculating, but it's a game, isn't it? Strategies and tactics.

"And after that?" Emily is still looking out the window suspiciously, trying to spot the paparazzi.

"Then we go inside. Steff already checked us in. They can't follow us into the hotel."

"Okay," Emily says, digging in her clown car purse. "Give me a minute?"

"No problem."

I place my hand on the door, opening it slowly for maximum dramatic effect. When I get out, I make a show of stretching, smiling, and looking around, taking it all in. *Here I am guys! So happy to be in Rome! Come and get me!*

The game feels a little like fishing. The line has been cast. I'm the worm. Wiggle, wiggle.

It doesn't take long before I hear it, somewhere off in the distance. The soft click of a camera shutter. Fish on.

I wait another moment or two, shading my eyes and glancing across the rooftops down to the streets below the plaza. They are all decked out for the holidays. It's going to look spectacular at night.

As if I'm in no particular rush, I lean back into the car and extend a hand to Emily, pulling her out in one smooth move. She's somehow managed to put on a large pair of sunglasses and apply lip gloss in the last thirty seconds. I think she's done something with her hair as well. It's no longer up. With the grace of a dancer, she uncoils herself and steps out, taking my cue and stretching languidly.

She fluffs and shakes out her hair, and her curls undulate around her shoulders, catching the sunlight. More clicks. The hook is set. Time to reel them in. Time for the money shot.

"Point something out to me," she says.

"Bernini's La Barcaccia Fountain is right down there." I point toward the world-famous staircase. "And the Pantheon is …"

But before I can finish my sentence, Emily is twining her arms around my waist, turning her back to the paparazzi and rotating me to face them. She steps closer to me, backing me up against the van.

"What are you doing?" I ask. "They can't even see you from this angle, they can only see me."

"Trust me," she whispers. I am close enough that I can see her eyes through the smoky lenses. "It's a better story if they don't see me yet. They only need to see you and that you're with someone."

With that, she places a hand on my chest and leans into me, pressing her entire soft, warm body against me and nuzzling her head under my chin. There's that honey smell again. I wrap my arms around her waist without thinking twice.

"Do me a favor? Spread your hand out over my butt?" she murmurs into my neck. I can feel the vibration of her lips against my Adam's apple.

"What?"

"These leggings do nothing for my butt." She sighs. "If that's all they're really getting of me, I just want to make sure there's a proper sense of scale."

"You have a fabulous ass, and you know it." I smirk, tipping her chin up to kiss her. It feels so natural. So unrushed and easy, like we've been at it for ages and we've already memorized each other's moves.

"Now would be a good time," she reminds me while gently biting my lower lip. She tastes like peppermints.

"If you insist," I say, obliging her. I hook my thumb in her waistband and spread my fingers wide to cup her ripe, juicy buttock. Too graphic? Too much too soon? Suddenly, I don't even care.

I pull her hips closer and delight in the feel of her breasts smashed up against my chest.

I should be hitting the brakes right about now, but I can't stop kissing her just yet. In the distance, the sound of clicking reaches a crescendo, like a swarm of cicadas descending.

Emily moans softly, and for a moment, the world falls away. I lose my sense of place and time. But then, just as abruptly, she pulls her mouth away from mine, leans back, and blinks at me.

We're both breathing fast—and hard. "Don't you think that's enough, Blaze Smith?" Her fingers trace my collarbone as she speaks.

I think it's the first time she's actually said my full name to me. It rolls off her tongue like a red hot, sweet and spicy. I want to hear her say it again.

"Say my name again." My hands are still on her hips. I'm not ready to let her go.

"Enough, Smitty."

Emily pushes away from me. She takes a few backward steps toward the door. At the last minute, she pivots. Head down, face hidden by the oversize glasses and a curtain of hair, she's left everyone wanting more. Myself included. I can hear the frenzied clicks echoing in her wake. Phones are buzzing. Voices are calling out to get her attention.

I'm pretty sure that none of the cameras are pointed at me anymore. Just as well. I'm still breathing heavily, and to be completely honest, drooling a little.

Steff gives Emily the once-over as she passes by, then turns back to wait for me. Her smile is slipping. She looks like she might vomit from the effort of maintaining it.

"What the fuck?" she mouths silently as I pass.

"Let's take it upstairs." I speak through an open-mouthed smile, like a ventriloquist, and put an arm around Steff's shoulder to guide her into the lobby. A bellhop follows close behind with our luggage. Steff hands him some cash and tells him the room number.

Emily lowers her sunglasses as we approach.

"Emily, this is Steff. Steff, this is Emily." I introduce the two women.

Emily holds out her hand to shake, but Steff ignores the gesture and spins on the heel of her pointy-toed, vintage-style shoe. She makes a beeline for the elevator.

"Nobody speaks till we get up to the room," she commands.

emily

. . .

THE HOTEL LOBBY HAS A PLUSH, hushed ambiance. Marble floors, gleaming brass-and-crystal fixtures, and soft, hand-woven carpets look both new and old, as if they've been beamed from another era. It smells of wood polish, fresh flowers, and old money. But I can't appreciate anything properly at the moment. On a scale of one to ten, I'm already at a twelve for sensory overload. My heart? Pounding. My brain cells? Frizzante.

I'm not even sure if there's actually Muzak playing in the background, or if it's my imagination supplying a jazzy soundtrack to calm me till my nervous system settles back down. It's just as well that Steff demanded we all remain silent until we get up to the room. It takes that long for my heart to stop racing.

Facing myself in the mirrors on the elevator, I see that my lip gloss is smeared. Steff looks disgusted when I wipe at it with the back of my hand. Maybe she's a germaphobe. Maybe that's why she refused to shake my hand?

Blaze squeezes my shoulder. "You were amazing out there, Emily," he praises. Steff glares at him.

"What did I say?" she warns.

Steff has reserved a penthouse suite on a private floor for Blaze to stay in during the tour. It's practically an apartment. There's a bedroom with an en suite bath, a sitting room, a dining room, and an additional bathroom with a shower off an entry foyer. A large balcony runs the length of the unit, providing sweeping views over the entire city.

I let myself out onto the balcony. The air outside is fresh and smells very faintly of woodsmoke.

"Amazing, right? This place is a splurge, but it's worth it." Blaze joins me at the railing.

"Oh my God, Blaze." I gesture at the view and shake my head. "I don't think I could ever get sick of this."

"It's pretty magical," he agrees.

"I don't know where to look first," I admit. "I wish I brought binoculars."

"You two need to come inside now," Steff calls out to the balcony.

"So, she's a little scary," I whisper to Blaze.

"She's really good at her job, though," he whispers back.

I follow him back into the sitting room.

Steff waits for the bellhop to leave, then opens the door and walks out into the hall to check if he's really gone before speaking.

"Kent didn't mention that you were so …" She holds out her hand and gestures in a spiral. Her face is disapproving.

"So what?" I stick my chin out and raise my eyebrows.

"I don't know, so … dramatic?" she suggests. She strikes me as the kind of woman who doesn't approve of drama, unless it's of her own making.

I feel the hairs standing up on the back of my neck. In fact, Kent used to love to accuse me of being overly dramatic. When I didn't want to be his plus-one at an event and insisted on getting my own press pass? I was being dramatic. When my grief over my father's death lasted longer than the "acceptable" six-week mourning period he'd penciled into his calendar? Dramatic. When I confronted him about sleeping with his coworker? Melodramatic.

But I'm pretty certain he wouldn't have wanted to jeopardize this assignment by bad-mouthing me to Steff.

"Drama is the *last* thing we need on this book tour." Steff looks down her nose.

"Who says Emily's dramatic now?" Blaze returns from putting his suitcase in the bedroom and stands by the table. "In my opinion, she's been nothing but accommodating."

He hands Steff a paper bag.

"Some things of yours were still in my room. You should probably take them to your own room."

Steff folds the bag over twice and tucks it under her arm. Her cheeks are red.

"Speaking of my room," Steff says, "this hotel is sold out. The only other place that was available was a single in a three-star hotel near the Trevi Fountain." She pauses for dramatic effect, raising her eyebrows at Blaze.

"Okay," Blaze affirms. "Thank goodness you found something."

"Well, when I booked it, I didn't think it was a big deal for *Emily* to be staying so far from you, but now, as your tour manager, I'm a little concerned. I don't think it's a good idea." Steff looks pointedly from Blaze to me.

"How far is it?" he asks.

"Ten-minute walk," Steff says.

"That's hardly the other side of town, Steff. I'm a big boy. I'm sure I'll be fine."

"I think we should stick to my plan," Steff asserts.

"I don't think there's any turning back now after the show we just put on." Blaze looks at me and raises one eyebrow. I feel my temperature go up three degrees.

"We can say she was a crazed fan." Steff folds her arms across her chest, still hugging the paper bag.

"Steff, you're good at spinning, but I'm betting at least one of them got it on video. There's no way I'd make out with a random person in a public place."

A tiny snort escapes from me, and Blaze looks over at me, realizing what he's just said.

"You were not a fan. You said I was full of shit," he backpedals.

Steff narrows her eyes at us.

"How much of a show was that out there? You two aren't an actual item, are you? Because if there's really something going on, I should know about it."

"Relax, Steff. That was a little inside joke. Emily and I met at a newsstand in SeaTac before I shaved and she didn't recognize me. She told me she thought my book was full of shit, only she didn't know she was talking to me."

"That's not very professional." Steff looks sidelong at me. "Are you sure you're up to doing the job Kent sent you to do?"

"I sure hope so. It's me or it's nobody," I say. Then I back off a bit because there's no point in antagonizing her. We're going to be stuck together for the next week or so. "Kent spoke highly of you, Steff, and so has Blaze. I'm a professional writer. I'd be happy to share my portfolio with you, but I'm really just here to get the background material for Kent's story, which he's writing. It'd be a shame for the tour to get canceled at this point and for you to miss out on this press. It has the potential to be a cover story."

Steff looks slightly appeased, and intrigued.

"You'll stick to the questions on the list?" she asks.

"I can do that," I agree.

"What's in it for you?" Steff asks.

"I have personal reasons for wanting to spend some time in Italy," I admit. "And I think with the additional access to Blaze, I'm much more likely to get the content we need to make this a cover story."

"Is that ethical?" she questions.

"Nobody knows I'm here to interview him, not even the editor." I shrug. "But anyway, Blaze and I have agreed to keep things strictly professional. That stuff out there was all for show. It was all for the paparazzi."

I fetch myself some sparkling water from the glass-fronted mini fridge and take it to the couch. I feel like I need it to wash down the lump that has suddenly shown up in my throat.

Blaze walks behind Steff and rubs her shoulders and neck, working her tense muscles like a physical therapist. He speaks to her in low, soothing, placating tones. "From now on, we'll loop you in. You can choose where we'll go for our meals out and make suggestions about where we should be seen together. We'll put ourselves in your capable hands."

I watch in dumbfounded fascination as Steff's whole face melts and threatens to pool on the floor. I suspect that if she were a dog, her leg would be kicking out and she might even pee a little.

Is he aware of the effect that he has on her?

Is that the effect he has on me? Are we both Blaze Smith's bitches? I shudder a little.

"Fine. I don't love it, but what's done is done. From now on, I plan everything." Steff rolls her neck and shoulders and settles herself into a seat at the table. She tucks her paper bag under her seat and produces a clipboard from her briefcase.

"Blaze, here's your schedule. We've got a book signing at an Italian bookstore this afternoon and a charity dinner with a local group of marriage therapists."

"Can you add Emily?"

"Sorry." Steff shakes her head. "There's no time for that."

Blaze frowns.

"I'll be fine. I have some work to catch up on," I say.

"Emily." Steff turns to me, removing a second sheath of papers. "The two of you didn't give me much time or warning, but I've drafted something for you to sign. It's a standard NDA stating you won't share any privileged information, and that you won't stay beyond the agreed-upon length of your arrangement."

I eye the contract warily. "Is this instead of or in addition to the agreement I already signed?"

Blaze jumps up, grabs the contract, and skims the terms, reading out loud.

"'Emily Romano will not touch Blaze Smith's torso in public or private. Ms. Romano will refrain from sharing food with

Mr. Smith. Ms. Romano will neither give nor receive *massages* from Mr. Smith?' What the hell is this, Steff?"

"I just felt we should cover all the bases. How well do you know this woman? It's all well and good that she's helping you out here, but the last thing you need is a paternity suit right when the next book comes out."

Blaze sighs and sinks back into his chair. "We've gone over this, Steff. This is the end of the line for the foreseeable future. Last book. After this, I'm taking a break. A much-needed hiatus."

"Sure." Steff snorts. "We'll see. That's what you said last time too."

"I mean it this time." Blaze tears the NDA in half. "And in the meantime, you're going to have to trust that I trust Emily."

"You can't blame me for doing my job!" Steff shrugs at me, then begrudgingly holds out a hand. I stand up and walk to the table in order to shake it.

"Welcome to the team, Romano."

"Thank you, Steff," I say. "Glad to be here."

Maybe it's the comedown from all the adrenaline, or maybe it's jet lag. Suddenly, I'm exhausted. I stifle a yawn.

"You're tired." Blaze looks concerned.

"I'll be fine," I say. "I just need some coffee. I didn't get much sleep the night before the flight."

"Why don't you take a shower and lie down in the bedroom?" Blaze suggests. "That way, if I come back between meetings, I won't disturb you."

"But we said you'd take the bed," I argue.

Steff taps her watch. "How about you two flip for the bed later. Right now, I need to get Blaze to a barber for a haircut before his book signing. And Blaze, you need to burn those clothes."

Blaze groans and runs a hand through his hair. "Do I really need to cut it? I kind of like it longer."

"I like it longer too," I say. "I just think you need to brush it."

Steff doesn't look amused. "Fine, leave it longer. I don't care. But we definitely need to get you trimmed and changed. I picked up an outfit for you. It's in the car. You can change at the barbershop. And I've got a stack of your books in Italian for you to sign before we get there. So, you know what they say. Prego!"

Blaze shrugs helplessly and looks back at me. "You sure you're okay alone here, Emily?"

"I'm sure." I smile. "I've got some reading to do." Then I reach into my bag and feel around for his book.

"You left it in the airport security lounge." Blaze smiles. "But I rescued it. And I even signed it for you. So, try and hang on to it this time?"

Blaze pulls the book out of his bag and places it on the table. Then he kisses me slowly on both cheeks, European style.

It would have felt more platonic if either of us were actually European.

blaze

. . .

"Crosswalks and four-way stops are inherently awkward. We lean on non-verbal communication. Vague waves that establish right of way. Half the time, we can't even figure out whose turn it is to go. Relationships have awkward intersections too. I went on a date once. The woman wasn't interested in taking it any further than dinner. She dropped me off and declined my offer to come in. Then she realized I'd left my doggie bag on her back seat. She came back to drop it off. I flung open the door passionately, wearing nothing but my boxers. She handed me my pasta."

— Blaze Smith, *Go Your Own Way*, on Awkward Intersections

IT'S midnight when I get back to the suite. I'm wrecked. Half blind with jet lag and still buzzed from the wine that kept flowing with our dinner. I can't wait to crawl into bed.

A tray in the hallway suggests that Emily ate her dinner alone, in the room. I feel a pang of guilt. She shouldn't have had to eat alone on her first night in Rome.

Hopefully, she didn't sleep all day. That only makes it harder to adjust. I'd been playing a game of chicken with my urge to lie down, all day. I use the keycard to let myself into the small foyer.

"Emily, are you up?" I call quietly.

She's asleep on the narrow sofa, hair fanned out around her. Moonlight is spilling through the windows, bathing her in silver light. Her lips are parted, and her long eyelashes are curled against her cheeks. I can see the shape of her cheekbones and notice, for the first time, that she's got a beauty mark there, just at the top corner of her cheekbone, near her right eye.

My first thought is that she looks like a fairy tale princess. A real-life princess. But not a prissy one because my second thought is that the couch looks pretty fucking uncomfortable. Hard, narrow, and barely long enough for an adult human to lay on. She doesn't even have proper bedding. There's just a top sheet and an undersize throw, both of which have slid mostly off her. The room is chilly. She's cold. That's obvious, going by the outline of her nipples under her slinky nightgown.

I force myself to look away and pull the throw over her. As I do, she stirs.

My book is on the floor beside her, lying open to the last chapter. I pick it up and flip through. She's circled several passages and written exclamation points and question marks.

Emily opens an eye.

"Blaze? Is that you?"

There's that witchcraft again. Heat rushes over me like a backdraft at the sound of my name coming out of her mouth. I've been hearing my name my whole life. It's never sounded that way before.

Emily pushes up on one arm, patting the sofa and feeling around for something. Her cell phone clatters to the floor. She sits straight up after retrieving it.

"Oh, shit. It's dead. I forgot to plug it in." She glances at her charger, plugged in next to the coffeemaker on the other side of the room.

I look around for an outlet and realize that there aren't any near the couch.

"How was the book signing?" She yawns. "And the dinner?"

"Molto bene." I smile wryly and sit on the sofa beside her. "Fine, but I kind of missed you when it was time for the photos. How was the rest of your day?"

"Good. I took a quick nap, then I went for a walk and checked out the Borghese Gallery. After that, I came back and finished your book. I ordered room service. I'll pay you back. Kent gave me a per diem."

"Don't be ridiculous." I shake my head. "I felt terrible that I didn't get your number. I wanted to text you to feel free to order whatever you need. The least I can do is feed my fake date."

She considers this for a moment, then agrees. "Okay, thank you. Dinner was delicious."

"What did you have?" I ask, shifting on the uncomfortable sofa. "You didn't order gelato without me, did you?"

"Of course not." She shivers and pulls the throw more tightly around herself. "I had the Cacio e Pepe."

"Why didn't you pull out the sofa? Isn't there any extra bedding in the suite?" I can't resist reaching out and tucking a stray curl behind her ear.

"Turns out this sofa doesn't fold out," Emily says. "And I didn't want to request a rollaway without discussing it with you first. It might—"

"Look bad?" I finish her sentence. I'm surprised that Steff booked this suite without making sure the sofa was a foldout.

Especially when she'd originally planned to be the decoy herself.

"Yeah. I thought the same thing." She sighs. "The hotel staff would definitely know we aren't sleeping together if we get a rollaway. It's not so bad. I'll manage."

"Emily Romano, you are a terrible liar. This sofa is hard as a rock and barely long enough to contain you."

I get up and hold out my hand. "You should just take the bed."

"I can't make you sleep on this thing," she objects. "You're the one who's here on tour. You need your rest."

"Yes, but I can't let you sleep here either. My fake girlfriend also needs her beauty sleep."

"What are we going to do?"

"Take my hand." I wiggle my fingers till she accepts it, and then I pull her up. "Here's what we are going to do. We're going to share the bed."

She looks at me suspiciously.

"I don't know if that's a good idea," she says.

"Do you have a better one? This hotel is completely sold out, and we can't get a rollaway. It's either the sofa or the floor, and I can't let you sleep on either. There's a logical solution. It's a king-size bed. Come."

I pull her gently after me, kicking the bedroom door open with my toe. The bed looks perfect, and I want to swan-dive into it, pulling her in beside me. I stop, though, suddenly remembering.

"Did you take a nap here earlier?"

"I did take a quick nap," she admits. "And that mattress is heaven. Housekeeping came in and re-made the bed and did turn-down service. That's why it doesn't look slept in."

"I see," I say, removing a foil-wrapped sweet from my pillow-case. "Chocolate?"

She shakes her head and continues to stand there. We're both staring at the bed like cartoon characters stare at an oasis in the midst of the desert. Thirsty, but suspicious. It could be a mirage. I lean into the awkward tension.

"Just get into the bed, Emily. Take the left side. Put pillows down the middle if you want. I don't know about you, but I fully expect to be unconscious the minute my head hits that pillow."

I kick off my shoes and throw my jacket onto a chair. "Go on, get in."

Finally, Emily pads to the other side of the bed and folds down the coverlet.

"Mmm," she moans as she lies back against the pillows. Then she sits up again, pulls a pillow out from behind her, and lays it across the center of the bed.

"There." She pats it pointedly. "This pillow is the DMZ."

"Better than an electrified fence," I say, and sit on the other side of the bed to take off my socks. The mattress is plump and inviting. Firm but padded. I moan a little, feeling the weight of my eyelids increase. "Oh, man. You weren't kidding. This bed is heaven."

Emily watches me as I unbutton my shirt and take it off. "Close your eyes," I admonish, as I stand to take off my pants.

"I didn't peg you for the shy type." Her lips twitch as she attempts to suppress a smile.

"Fair enough."

I toss my pants onto the chair with the rest of my clothes and slide into the bed, wearing only my boxers.

"You know, when I walked in the room earlier, for a second, I thought there was a princess sleeping on the couch."

"If I'm a princess, shouldn't you have turned back into a frog when I kissed you earlier?" Emily teases, sleepily. "I'd have settled for Smitty."

"Sorry." I roll on my side to face her, propping myself up on my elbow. "Too bad we have to wait till tomorrow to try again." I can smell her shampoo on my pillow. She must have lain down on this side earlier.

We stare at each other. Eyes locked across the DMZ. I lift an arm to touch her shoulder, then immediately snatch it back, as if the pillow divider really were electrified.

Abruptly, Emily swings her legs to the other side of the bed and stands up. "This was a stupid idea. I don't know what I was thinking. We can't possibly sleep in the same bed."

"Just come back," I say. "For the sake of your lower back. We can build up the DMZ with more pillows. Or sleep head to toe."

"No. I don't think it's a good idea for us to share the bed. I'm sorry, Blaze. I'm usually far more professional than this. I keep forgetting. We probably shouldn't even sleep in the same room."

She's standing at the foot of the bed now and I sit up slightly, observing the curve of her hips, the dip of her collarbones, the fullness of her breasts, backlit by moonlight. This image of her is going to be burned into my synapses now.

"You're right, we probably shouldn't, but what other choice do we have?"

I blink a few times and rub my eyes, trying to hit some kind of mental refresh button that will wipe the image away. It doesn't work. Emily is etched into my eyeballs, like they're connected to a compromised LCD screen. She's going to stay there like a ghost, haunting and taunting me.

"I'm not going to have sex with you, Blaze."

"I heard you the first time you said that, Emily," I say very quietly. It's a battle to keep my ego out of it.

"But I was talking to Smitty then. I had no idea who he … who *you* are."

"Got it. Now if you don't mind, I have an early morning tomorrow."

I hate myself for being short with her. But what am I going to say? Should I say that although I have a hard-on, I don't have to act on it? I'm not some kind of uncontrolled ape who can't take no for an answer. Plus, I have professional ethics.

But if she'd been into it?

I roll onto my side, facing away from her side of the bed, toward the windows. As tired as I was, I'm suddenly awake. I listen as Emily paces. She uses the restroom, heads into the living room. Pours herself a drink. I listen as she gets out her computer. The sounds of her typing do nothing to lull me to sleep.

I debate getting up and joining her out there. Twice, I sit up in bed, then lie back down after deciding against it. What would I even say?

Eventually, after another twenty minutes or so, she comes back.

"Blaze?" she whispers. "You still awake?"

I don't answer, feigning sleep.

"I just want to say I'm sorry for being so awkward," she murmurs. "I know you were trying to be a gentleman. And for the record, you deserve a real relationship, Blaze. You shouldn't have to pretend."

And then she climbs into the bed and curls up behind me, fully displacing the DMZ. The small of her back skims again mine. Moments later, I'm asleep.

———

Steff marches into the bedroom the following morning, waking us up.

"What the fuck, guys?" She looks spooked to find us in the bed together. "I thought the two of you weren't an item?" Steff looks suspiciously from me to Emily. I follow her gaze and notice that Emily's slinky nightwear has slipped sidewise. She's a millimeter away from a nip slip.

Emily sits up and pulls up the sheet.

Steff's shrewd gaze tracks back to mine.

"Ever hear of knocking?" I ask.

"I didn't think it was required," Steff says. "I expected you both to be up, decent, and ready by seven. I was going to offer to help clear the couch before anyone noticed anything. But I can see now that won't be necessary."

"Were you aware that the sofa has no bed?" I ask Steff.

"Really? That's odd." She sniffs. "Want me to pull an outfit for today?"

"No." I shoot her a warning look. "You're not my mother. I'm perfectly capable of choosing my own clothing, Steff."

"I'm sorry I overslept," Emily apologizes, and stands, swiftly pulling on a robe. "Just give me ten minutes. I'll use the other bathroom and I'll be ready."

"Take your time," Steff calls after her. "Don't forget to drag a brush through your hair. We need you to be camera ready."

Steff waits till Emily is gone before sitting down in the bed with me. She pulls out her phone and shows me a photo.

"This just hit."

The photo shows me and Emily kissing in front of the hotel, and the headline says something like, "Who is fanning the flames of the Love Doctor's heart?" At least I think that is what it says. My Italian is patchy.

"Clever of her not to show her face. Now everyone is trying to figure it out. Maybe she should stay behind today so we can string them along a little more."

"No," I say. "Emily isn't going to spend this entire tour locked up in this hotel suite. Nobody's going to buy that we're an item if she's not by my side."

"This would have been so much simpler if you'd just stuck with the original plan." Steff leans back and stretches out on the bed. "This bed is incredible. I have to find out who makes the mattress."

"Do you want to go down to the lobby and ask while I get dressed?" I suggest.

Steff laughs and smiles at me chummily. "No, I can ask later. I'm fine here, thanks. My back is actually killing me. I think the mattresses at my hotel are stuffed with old hay."

"Okay, but Steff, I need to get up to get dressed, and I'm only wearing my boxers."

"What's the big deal? Emily saw you in your boxers, right? I mean, what's the difference? We're all adults. Unless …"

"Unless what?"

"Unless there really is something going on between you two."

"Nope."

"So, I don't understand what the problem is." Steff takes a deep breath, looks skyward, and shakes her head a little. "We've been together for several years, Blaze. I've seen you in gym shorts and a swimsuit. I'm not going to faint if I see you in your boxers."

"Fine." I throw back the covers, stand up, and pull on my pants from yesterday.

"You're not planning on wearing those same pants again today, are you?" Steff asks.

"You know what, Steff? I could really use some coffee. How about you grab us some coffee and pastries while I take a quick shower? Emily and I will meet you in the lobby in twenty minutes. That should give us time to get to the Anglo-American Bookstore before the event, right?"

"I arranged for coffee and pastries for us at the bookstore." Steff dismisses the request and examines her manicure. Her nails are filed to a point and painted like little Christmas trees.

"Then how about an espresso?" I ask. "I'm really jet-lagged, and I would appreciate it."

She looks dubious about having to move, so I lay it on even thicker. "Honestly, Steff, I don't know what I'd do without you."

"Fine." She gets to her feet and pats the sheets smooth. "But I was hoping we'd have a few minutes for a private chat. I did a little research on Emily. Apparently, she and Kent used to be an item. He didn't mention that to me."

"Okay. But I don't see what that has to do with anything," I say.

"I just wanted you to know that I'm still here for you, looking out for you, and I always will be. I don't trust her, and I hate even leaving you alone in this suite with her. You should be careful around her."

I sigh. "I'm a grown man, Steff. I can take care of myself."

"I can see that." She wags her eyebrows appreciatively at me. "You're looking pretty buff after that month in the mountains. We should think about shooting some photos to go along with that article. I'm thinking a swimsuit—something with a lifeguard vibe. But instead of a cross, we do a heart."

"Absolutely not," I say, closing the bedroom door behind her. "But thank you."

emily

. . .

"HEY EMILY," Blaze calls through the bathroom door. "I'm jumping in the shower. I told Steff we'd meet her in the lobby in twenty minutes. I hope that's okay."

I'm sitting on the lid of the toilet in the suite's second bathroom, reading the texts that have come in overnight.

"No problem," I answer. "I'm pretty low maintenance."

"That's because you're a natural beauty," Blaze says. "I, on the other hand, am going to need to shave again."

I wait a moment till he's padded away before replying to Alexis's latest text, trying to be as vague as possible.

> Emily!!!! Tell me EVERYTHING!

Alexis is eager for details. She shoots over several stars, eggplant, and heart emoji, as well as camera ones. In addition to the photo from the plane, Alexis has texted over a shot from our arrival at the hotel.

> How did you even get all those pics?

I use two fingers to enlarge the photo, gratified to see my ass looks pretty good with Blaze's hand on it. But how good it looks is nothing compared to how good it felt.

> I set up text and Google alerts for Blaze
> Smith the minute you left.

> Nothing gets by you, does it?

> Anyway, I knew it! I just had a feeling
> something was going down on this trip.
> Speaking of which …

Alexis sends a string of every sexual emoji she can think of and a few that make no sense whatsoever. Easter Island Guy? What's he doing in there with the peaches and eggplants?

> Stop it, Alexis! Get your head out of the
> gutter.

> Please tell me you're wearing the lingerie?

I shoot a quick selfie in the mirror and send it to her.

> Girl, you are GLOWING. Glad you got some!

Applause hands, thumbs-up, glowing hearts, sunshine, more eggplants.

> Enough with the emoji. It's not like that.
> Nothing happened last night.

At least I can be truthful about that. Not telling my friends about the true nature of my relationship with Blaze is probably going to be the hardest part of our arrangement. Actually, no. That isn't true. It's the second hardest part.

Don't waste too much time. You're already in the taboo zone hooking up with an assignment. May as well enjoy it while you can. I'm so proud of you, Em!

I can't believe my oldest friend thinks I've totally abandoned my professional ethics, and her reaction is to tell me she's *proud* of me?

I have to go get dressed now. Blaze is doing a panel appearance with some romance writers at an English bookshop today.

Anyone good?

Actually, yes! Isla Fairfax. The one who has that Chance Encounters blog? She wrote the book about the mystical matchmaker. We talked about her a few months ago on Lit Lovers.

Wow! Jackson's going to flip when he hears that. Doing any sightseeing btw?

I'll probably wander this afternoon. The hotel is by the Spanish Steps.

Not by Trevi?

She includes a weeping emoji.

It's not far. Anyway, I think this place is even better.

Cool. Send pics, plz?

I will.

And promise you'll wear something nice?

Your good jeans and that sweater I pulled for
you then. With the sexy boots.

Ok. Gotta get ready.

Good luck! Keep me posted!

Alexis signs off with a trail of kisses, hearts, and eggplants.

Twenty minutes is not a lot of time to get ready for a day out, and I've already spent the last seven of them texting. Fortunately, my waves seem to like the humidity in Rome. After a quick spritz with my mister and some finger-raking, I'm satisfied with what I see. I slap on some tinted moisturizer, lipstick, and mascara and cautiously head back to the bedroom to retrieve my clothing from the closet where I've hung it.

Blaze is still in the shower. He's singing something. He doesn't have a good voice. In fact, it's so bad, I can't even make out the tune. So, he isn't so perfect after all.

I chuckle to myself as I smooth the bed and lay out my clothes. Blaze's book is still on the nightstand. I open it and flip to the title page, rereading his inscription:

To Emily, who looks like an angel and kisses like the devil. I'm pretty sure there's nothing in this book that you don't already know. You don't need my help stopping traffic.

Love, Smitty

What does it mean? Why did he sign it "Smitty" instead of using his real name?

I'm driving myself crazy, searching for hidden messages. To what end? He's probably used to flirting with every new woman he meets. Winding them up a bit, making them feel sexy. All part of his Love Doctor schtick. It doesn't have to mean anything.

After the tour ends, our paths are unlikely to cross again. I'll probably never see him in person again after this. And another more painful thought occurs to me. What if he feels sorry for me? I'd unloaded about Kent to him. He needed my help, but perhaps he also thinks I need his. Maybe all the flirting with me is just him trying to bolster my ego.

I mean, he said I looked like a princess. That was laying it on a bit thick.

I set the book back down and stand up to face the full-length mirror on the back of the bathroom door, taking a good, long, honest look at myself. I clean up well, but I'm no super model. I have a bump on my nose, thank you, Italian gene pool. I'm a bit pigeon-toed. And I'll never be thin. It's something I've really only come to terms with recently—post Kent. Breaking free from him and the relentlessness of his dieting has helped me embrace my curves.

I pivot to look at my butt. I *like* having a little more junk in my trunk. I'm strong, fit, and real, dammit! This sudden burst of self-acceptance couldn't have come at a more auspicious time. My future plans to become pregnant won't exactly make me slimmer. But I'm ready for it.

Whimsically, I arch my back, pushing my belly out as far as possible. Is this what I'd look like pregnant?

I rest one hand on my silk-covered, distended stomach and cross the other arm up my already large breasts, lifting them and squeezing them together in an exaggerated way. I test out a step sideways, watching myself waddle left then right, the green silk swaying and my breasts threatening to spill over the top.

"Ooh … what do you think, Em? Pretty sexy, huh?" I giggle at my reflection.

I don't get a chance to answer myself.

As the door bursts open, I catch a glimpse of my own shocked look flying by. Then, a very naked, soaking-wet Blaze skids to a halt. He stops a couple of inches shy of slamming into me.

"Oops," he says, wide-eyed.

"Oh, shit. I'm sorry!" I hold my hand up in front of my face, as if I can unsee what I've already seen. My eyes aren't fully closed. I'm peeking. I can't resist checking out his naked body between my outstretched fingers.

"You, uh … you're hanging out," Blaze says, staring openly at me.

"No, I just came in here for a minute to grab my stuff." I gesture to the clothes on the bed and bend to retrieve them, which is when I realize that he wasn't accusing me of hanging out, as in hanging out in the room. I shove my left breast back into the flimsy, silk gown.

"I didn't think you were done showering," I protest. "The water's still running."

"I forgot my razor," Blaze says, taking a single step back and reaching into the bathroom to pull a towel from the rack. He wraps it around himself, but it's too late. There's no pretending that I didn't see that hard-on. I bite both lips and force myself to look away from the line of hair that may as well be an arrow. It points down from his belly button to the edge of the towel.

Blaze captures my gaze and smiles wryly.

"This is completely my bad. I'm sorry, Emily. I'm not used to having a roommate." He turns to the desk and unzips a leather Dopp kit to retrieve his razor. "I didn't do the best job in the airport." He sighs, rubbing the shadow along his beautiful jaw. I wish I could rub it too. I can practically feel the sandy texture of his stubble on my fingertips, just thinking about it.

I ball my hands into fists.

"No, really, I'm sorry," I apologize. "I should have at least called out to warn you when I came back in here to grab a few things."

"So, um ... what, exactly, were you doing there?" Blaze asks, taking a step toward me and continuing to look directly into my eyes. I'm not used to this much eye contact.

"Nothing." I blush. "Just being stupid."

"Because it looked like you were pretending to be pregnant?" He raises one eyebrow and tilts his head to one side.

I can't take it anymore. I have to look away. I collapse into the side chair and cover my face.

"Can we just pretend this whole awkward moment never happened?" I beg.

"I think you'd look incredibly sexy pregnant, for what it's worth," Blaze says. I sneak a peek at him. He's not looking at me anymore. He's looking down at the tented towel. "But, uh, I guess that's already apparent."

"Ugh." I groan into my hands. "You've got to be kidding me, Blaze. We both know I looked ridiculous, and I'll probably look even crazier if I ever do actually get pregnant."

"I might be in the minority, but I happen to think that pregnant women are hot." Blaze shrugs. "I mean, it's not a fetish or anything, but it's so powerful. So magical. Creating a new life. Seriously, I can't think of anything that's sexier than wielding that kind of power."

"How are you still single?" I ask, shaking my head. "Honestly, you're so fucking evolved, it's painful."

"I don't know." Blaze shrugs and turns back toward the shower. "I could ask the same of you. Seems like there should be a long line of guys who'd kill for the chance to make babies with a beautiful, intelligent woman like you."

"The baby *making* part isn't the issue," I say. "It's everything that comes after."

"The right guy is out there. I refuse to believe that a woman like you can't have it all. That's my professional opinion," he says.

"Sucks to be us." I sigh. "Single, awesome, and so under-appreciated."

"I couldn't have said it better," Blaze agrees. "Sucks to be us." And then he closes the door behind him.

blaze

. . .

"ARE YOU READY FOR THIS?" I ask Emily in the car. The bookstore is only a few blocks away, but we're on a tight schedule, and Steff is worried we'll get waylaid by photographers on the street if we walk. She's probably right.

"Steff thinks there's going to be even more photographers today because everyone's dying to figure out who you are, Emily. Nice call on that yesterday."

"All part of the service," Emily says without looking up from her knitting. The tiny bootie she's working on is starting to take shape.

Steff reads from a brief about the two romance novelists who'll be on the panel with me. "Isla Fairfax is a Brit who writes romantic comedy with paranormal overtones, and Roxy Aubergine is American. She writes spicy romance. They're both expats who live here in Rome. I'm not thrilled about this particular arrangement, but hopefully there's some audience crossover."

"I'm a fan of Isla Fairfax's books," Emily enthuses. "Can't wait to meet her. Her blog is a lot of fun too. Lots of posts about modern romance. The comments are hysterical."

"Be that as it may, let's be clear. We're focusing on *Blaze* at this event." Steff addresses Emily as she hands me the folder with information about the authors' recent releases.

"I wish I'd had time to read their books." I sigh, skimming the summaries. These actually sound kind of fun.

"You enjoy reading romance novels?" Emily seems surprised.

"Sometimes," I admit. "I like reality TV too. There's a lot you can learn about relationships from pop culture. It's all a reflection. Kind of like parables and fairy tales. I mean, they're entirely unrealistic, but the archetypes do track."

"So, what archetype are you?" Emily asks.

Steff coughs and clears her throat. "Is this on the record? Because this was not on Kent's list of submitted questions."

I roll my eyes. Steff continues with her brief.

"So, this part is exciting. There's going to be a surprise guest today. I just got confirmation. Marco is going to make a quick appearance at the bookstore this morning!"

"Marco? What for?" I ask.

Emily stops knitting for a moment, looking from me to Steff.

"Who's Marco?"

"Only the 'sexiest man in Italy.'" Steff exhales. "He's a very, very popular cover model and also stars in a top Italian reality TV show—'*Pazzi per Amore.*'"

"Marco is the centerpiece of the show," I explain. "It's one of those matchmaking shows where there are too many people cooped up together. He's currently staying at the Villa dei Baci just outside Rome with a dozen of his fans all vying for the opportunity to date him."

"Every date is a reenactment of one of his famous romance novel covers," Steff enthuses. "It's pure genius."

"But what does this have to do with you, Blaze?" Emily asks me.

"Marco's down to his top three choices, and they're bringing me in to do some relationship counseling for the episode they're shooting later this week," I explain.

"They're going to film him stopping by the bookstore for the event. He'll surprise some of his romance reader fans and buy a copy of Blaze's book." Steff smiles smugly. "This is great news for us. It means we now get mentioned in two episodes of that show. Try to act surprised when he gets there."

Emily leans forward to look at the half-naked man featured on the cover of the Roxy Aubergine novel and raises an eyebrow. "He's got a reality show about dating his fans? Does anyone find lasting love on one of those shows?"

"Meow! Just because Kent Larson dumped you isn't a reason to be so cynical, Emily," Steff tuts. She pockets her phone and gives Emily a pitying look. "I'm surprised you're being so negative, actually. I would have thought you, of all people, would eat this event up."

Steff turns toward me. "Blaze, were you aware that Emily hosts a podcast about romantic fiction?"

She turns back to face Emily.

"For the record, before you even ask, we haven't agreed to doing anything with your little podcast, Emily. I hope you weren't getting your hopes up. I swear, if Kent had been more up front with me about your background and self-interests, I would never have agreed to all this." Steff purses her lips and frowns.

"I'm dying to hear more about Emily's podcast," I continue. "I've already added it to my queue."

"It's not *my* podcast," Emily clarifies. "Technically, it's my friend Jackson's show. I'm just a commentater. And by that I mean I'm the in-house prude."

"Not buying it." I shake my head.

"What even is that thing you're making?" Steff side-eyes the bootie Emily is knitting. "Some kind of mouse sweater?"

Emily shoves her project back in her bag. "Hey, you two don't mind if I run an errand after the panel, do you? I thought I might grab some more yarn while Blaze is signing books."

"Don't you think maybe it's a sign that you've run out of yarn for that project? I mean, I can't think of a more perfect metaphor. Why are you still stringing yourself along?" I ask.

Why do I give a damn who she's knitting stuff for?

"Excuse me?" Steff looks confusedly from me to Emily. "What are you two talking about?"

"Nothing." Emily shrugs. "Blaze just isn't a huge fan of my crafting."

"There's a yarn shop near the Trevi Fountain," Emily says. "It's not far. I can walk there."

"Maybe we can swing by there together after the signing," I suggest. "And get that gelato."

"Oh, look! We're here. We should make a plan." Steff interrupts us as the car slows to a stop outside the bookstore.

A sign above the door reads, *Anglo-American Books*. It's a quaint, little, independent bookstore tucked into a side street in the trendy area not far from the Trevi Fountain known for great shopping and cafés.

A sandwich board with a handwritten message has been placed outside the entrance. It explains that the store will be closed till noon for a private-ticketed author event and book signing.

Three large portraits are hanging in the window.

I'm front and center, smiling in my most recent headshot. Portraits of the two female novelists hang on either side. Beneath our photos is an artful stack of our collective books, arranged in a heart-shaped display.

"I should make sure the coast is clear before you head in," Steff says.

"That's okay, Steff. I got this." I throw open the car door and jump out. I'm aware that this event has been well advertised. Sure enough, the photographers are waiting. They flow out of the side alley and creep around the corner as soon as I emerge from the car.

"Mr. Smith, over here!" one of them yells. I wave before leaning back into the car. Emily pulls her bag strap up and onto her shoulder. We lock eyes before I grab both of her hands in mine.

"One, two, three," I count, pulling her to her feet on three.

"Mr. Smith, who's your girlfriend?" yells another pap.

Emily tips her head toward the photographer who's just asked the question and leans into me. I feel a strange, elemental urge to protect her from the cameras, which is utterly at odds with our mutual goal to get the good press this book tour needs.

One of the photographers approaches us boldly. He's snapping away with his camera held out in front of him. He's stepped a little too close for my comfort. I give him a warning look as we pivot away from his lens.

Emily follows my lead, turning effortlessly with me. It's as if we're on a dance floor together and have been practicing for ages. I pull her in front of me, and then to my other side, as easily as executing a dip.

"Come on, Blaze. Can't you tell us anything about your bella amore?" A younger woman holds out a mic, begging.

"Blaze, is your new girlfriend from Rome?"

"Well, her last name is Romano," I say, shrugging. Let them draw their own conclusions.

Emily slides a hand into my back pocket and pinches my ass —hard. I try not to react.

"What do you think about the city? Any holiday plans?"

"This book tour is already my favorite tour ever," I say. "I'm genuinely thrilled to be here at such a magical time of year." With this, I whisk her into the bookstore.

It's not what I expected. The shop's decor is so sparce and modern. Soaring, industrial-style bookshelves divide the loft-like space into a series of smaller spaces. The cement floors and stone walls don't compete with the stacks of paperbacks and hardcovers everywhere.

It's still early, and the other authors aren't here yet. The caterer is still setting out coffee and pastries, and the owner of the shop is rushing to set up folding chairs wherever she can fit them. Steff rushes in behind us, takes one look, and immediately demands that everything be rearranged.

"I'm going to need some shots of you in the front of the store before the panel begins." She holds up a finger as if she's about to say something else, but loses her train of thought when she notices that my books have been placed beneath the other authors' books in the window display. Her forehead creases. "Oh, hell no. That won't do. Stay there a minute," she says, rushing off again.

"I think I know exactly what to get you for Christmas," Emily buzzes in my ear.

The warmth of her breath in my ear is entirely distracting. Two can play at that game.

"What's that?" I ask, reaching to help her take off her woolly jacket. My thumbs caress her collarbones, and I watch with delight as her cheeks turn red. She looks down at my hands and then back up at my face.

"A shovel," she whispers. "To help with all the bullshit. Maybe a wheelbarrow too."

"You still think I'm full of it then?" I lean in to whisper back in her ear as I slide my arms inside her jacket, easing it off.

"I'm sure of it," she murmurs against my neck.

"I suspect your bullshit radar is broken." I drape her jacket over my arm, still speaking low, even though there's only staff and Steff here. "I wasn't lying, Emily. This is the most fun I've ever had on a book tour. Even if it *is* all make-believe."

Her eyes flash as she looks up at me. Then she glances out the window toward the street.

"Are we still being watched?"

"Who's to say?" I shrug. "You never know with the technology today. We should really act 'as if.'"

I place my hands on her upper arms and lean forward, claiming her lips. They are soft beneath mine. Yielding. And then they are not. She's kissing me back, giving as good as she gets. I let go of her shoulders and reach around to the back of her head, tangling my fingers in her thick, gorgeous hair.

The bell on the door erupts, announcing a new arrival.

"Oh, my stars!" The redhead with the upper-crusty British accent fans herself melodramatically. "*Do* believe the hype! These two are generating some serious page-one heat."

We pull apart, both of us flushed and dilated, blinking in an attempt to refocus.

"I'm Isla, and I know who this guy is here." She points at me. "But who are you?" The redhead slips off a pair of vintage-style, white gloves before holding out a hand to Emily.

"I'm Emily," Emily replies. "Emily Romano. Just thrilled to meet you, Isla. I'm a huge fan of your books. We featured your Mystic Matchmaker series on the podcast I cohost."

"Well, now I'm a huge fan of you, Emily Romano. Do you know where I might put my things?"

Emily shakes her head. "We just got here. I was just about to ask the same thing." She smiles at Isla and takes her coat back from me.

"Is that coffee I smell?" Isla asks.

"Yes, they were just setting up in the back of the store when we got here," Emily says.

"Thank God," Isla cheers. "I was afraid I was going to have to send someone to get some."

Just then, Steff returns with two giant stacks of my books in her arms. They are piled so high, I'm not sure how she is able to see where she is going. "It's too late to get the other authors' books out of the window," she laments, "but we can still add more of yours on top. Let's get these set up so we can get those photos done."

"Steff, this is Isla, one of the other authors on today's panel," I say.

"Oh!" Steff snaps to attention, setting the books on a nearby table. "Great to meet you, Isla. Such a pleasure. Don't mind me. I'm just Blaze's pushy PR person. I manage all his tours."

"Well, Steff," Isla says, "you might not want to put all his books in the window. How is anyone going to be able to buy them if they're all up there? Leave a stack or two where people can grab them. That's what I always do. That and swag. Everyone likes swag." She reaches into her bag and pulls out a roll of shiny, crystal-ball-themed stickers.

Steff taps her foot impatiently. Today's crazy shoes have a harlequin design.

"Why don't we leave these two to it and get ourselves some coffee?" Isla clutches Emily's arm.

"Can I grab something for you, Blaze?" Emily offers.

"Thanks, I'm good, though," I say. I lean over to plant a quick kiss on Emily's forehead. She closes her eyes. "Let's get that gelato and talk some more when I'm done here. I've got the whole afternoon free."

emily

. . .

THE BOOKSTORE IS SMALLER than I expected. It's divided into three areas, each with tables piled high with books. Along the walls, the shelves extend nearly to the high ceilings. The top shelves require ladders to access the books. Swags of silver tinsel garland and a few handmade ornaments indicate the holiday season, but it's nothing at all like an American bookshop. No Rudolph music playing on a constant loop or candy canes in the impulse aisle.

There's something about the smell of a bookshop. All that paper, and all the possibilities. Mix in the smell of coffee and pastries, and it's my own personal eau d' happy place.

Isla grabs my arm and pulls me back toward the coffee setup. As we pass, I see the table that's been set up for the three panelists. On the left-hand side, there's a stack of copies of her most recent book from the Mystic Matchmaker series, *Fate Dating*. The cover features colorful, cartoonish illustrations. There's a pair of starry-eyed lovers and a fortune teller with a crystal ball.

I check out Roxy Aubergine's stack. Her book has photography on the cover—a shirtless man, all airbrushed abs and piercing, blue eyes, stands on a windblown dock in the midst of a purple storm. His brown hair is tousled. The top half of his body is naked. He's wearing a pair of faded jeans on the bottom half. Unbuttoned.

The model, I take it, is the aforementioned "Marco," romance's current cover darling. No wonder his team is sending him over to shop. The store is already going to be full of his fans, and they are going to freak out.

In between the two romance authors, a few of Blaze Smith's books are stacked. A pile of his promotional bookmarks is spread out on the table. Miniature "One Way" signs, reformatted, say *Go Your Own Way.*

Isla drops her crystal ball-shaped stickers and a bag of fortune cookies on the table beside her books. She sees me looking at the Roxy Aubergine book and smiles.

"Do you know her?" I ask.

"No, can't say I do. And nothing against her, Emily"—she leans in to whisper conspiratorially— "but this event here today is why I don't do chest covers," she says. "It's so much easier to make cute swag out of an illustration."

"You mean, she's not handing out die-cut stickers of his abs?" I ask with mock horror.

Isla snorts. "I suspect that might be a hit if she tried it."

"Blaze too." I laugh. "He needs some sexy stickers!" I wonder again whose idea it was to pair Blaze Smith up with a couple of romance writers. Steff? "I can totally see him on a water bottle."

Isla agrees, "That'd be brilliant!" She takes off her woolly, green jacket, revealing a silk blouse that's covered with semi-psychedelic, colorful hearts. Not many people could pull this shirt off, but Isla can. With her flaming-red hair and pink lipstick, she has a positive Whoville vibe. Like a much prettier version of a Dr. Seuss character has popped off the page.

I like her immediately. Her accent, her quirky wardrobe. I have the distinct feeling that we're going to be friends.

"The romance section of the store is much bigger than I expected," I mention.

"Oh, this place is a staple. It's where all the English speakers shop. Most of the people who shop here are on holiday." Isla shrugs. "They stock a lot of travel stuff and books by Italian authors. But it's the TikTok famous stuff and the romance that probably sells the most. People like light, fluffy reads when they are traveling."

We make our way back to the coffee urn and serve ourselves.

"Now, come sit with me at my table until this thing starts and protect me from my fans," Isla says.

"I mean, I love them dearly, I swear I do, but I want to make it through this cup before the 'selfie with the author' requests start rolling in." Isla points at the side of the store where the other romance author has been waylaid on her way past the check-out stand. There's a group of four or five people who have just arrived, and they all seem eager to meet and snap selfies with her.

I glance around for Blaze and locate him with Steff. She is still snapping photos of him in front of the display up front. He catches my eye as I'm looking at him and tilts his head at me.

"Quick, before this event starts, you have to tell me about how you and Blaze met," Isla says, pulling me into Blaze's seat at the author's table. "Meet cutes are my crack."

"Really, there's not much to tell," I insist.

"Mm-hmm." Isla shakes her head at me. "Why do I get the feeling you're not telling me the truth? Did anyone set you two up?" She blows on her coffee and takes a cautious sip.

"No, nothing like that. We met at a newsstand," I offer.

"Interesting," Isla muses, studying me. "What kind of newsstand?"

"An airport one, actually." I smile.

Aside from the success of her popular rom-com books, Isla's claim to fame is her ability to custom-tailor meet cutes for people. To date, she's made over fifty matches, and they all have gone on to their happily ever afters. Some of them quite preposterously so. She's written about her delightfully mismatched matches on her blog, and we've discussed them on *Lit Lovers* more than once.

I'd love to ask her to be a guest on the podcast.

Isla's skeptical smile implies that she's entirely not satisfied with my story.

"An airport newsstand! Hmm. That's vague. Tell me more."

"Well, we got to talking, and we decided to grab a bite together." I improvise. "It turned out we were on the same flight, and I told him about how I've been dying to come to Italy." It's all technically true, if a bit out of order. I'm on thin ice here. Blaze and I should have agreed on an origin story. This is a serious fake relationship fail.

"Who doesn't want to come to Italy?" Isla empathizes. "I came here two years ago, and I still haven't left!"

I hate doing it, but I need a distraction. I offer up my grandparents as a red herring. I'm betting I can distract her.

"I wanted to come for personal reasons. My grandmother's past here in Italy has always been a mystery. After I inherited my grandparents' house, I found a bunch of old love letters in the attic. And some other letters, too, including one from my grandmother's childhood best friend. It turns out she's still alive, and she begged me to come and meet her."

Isla freezes in a mid-gulp of coffee. I can see the gears of her story brain whirring into motion. She sets down her coffee and peers at me with renewed interest before continuing.

"Oh my God, Emily. This is epic. Look at my arm. I just got gooseflesh. This is meaningful. You must tell me everything. Can I see these letters? Did you bring them?"

Her enthusiasm is infectious. I laugh. Across the bookstore, Blaze waves and points toward the back, gesturing that he's going to grab coffee now.

"I think your event is about to start, Isla," I protest gently. "But sure, I'd be happy to share the letters with you if you're interested. I'd love to hear what you think."

"Give me your phone." Isla holds out her hand. "I'm putting my contact info in there. I can take you to do some sightseeing later this week and then I'm taking you to lunch and you're going to tell me all about these letters, okay?"

I hand her my phone, and she quickly taps in her digits, sends herself a text message, and then picks up her own phone to reply.

"There, now we're friends for real." She squeezes my hand and looks to address Blaze, who has come to claim his seat. "I don't know exactly where you found this one, but she is a gem! Old love letters! That's my catnip. If you don't hang on to her this week, I might steal her away."

"You can try." Blaze offers his hand to help me up, then pulls me in for a quick kiss.

"Oof. I'm afraid I cannot compete with that kind of electricity." Isla fans herself with a book. "All I have is a hookup with a secret cannoli bakery."

"Carbs are my other love language." I smile.

The owner of the bookshop rings a bell to let everyone know the panel is about to begin, and the other author breaks free from her social media queue. She makes her way toward the table.

"Knock 'em dead," I say, and take my seat in the audience.

———

I never would have thought that pairing a relationship expert with romance novelists could yield such an entertaining conversation. Blaze is unpretentious and downright funny. This culminates when he proposes an impromptu therapy session with the mystical matchmaker main character from Isla's novel.

"So, you believe you're being guided by spirits when you set people up?" Blaze questions.

"I'm completely sure of it. It's magic," Isla responds, speaking for her character.

"But don't you think there's a little more to relationships than that?"

"I don't know. I sensed some real magic between you and your girlfriend earlier," Isla teases.

Blaze scans the audience and locks eyes with me. Then he winks.

"Well, I can't argue with that. Emily is pretty magical."

A dozen women and a few men "aw" and turn to gawk at me. Someone who is seated in the front row pulls out her phone to take a photo of me. Steff glares at her, and she puts the phone away.

"I think that we can take questions for the next fifteen minutes, and then all three of our authors will be available to sign books." The bookstore makes an announcement and wraps the panel up. It's my chance to break away.

"How long does the signing part usually take? I thought I'd duck out now to go to the yarn shop," I ask Steff.

"It'll be at least an hour, but you should be back here in forty-five minutes. I don't want to have to come looking for you. Oh, and make sure to use the back door. Marco will be here any minute, and I don't want the paparazzi getting distracted by you."

"Got it." I wave. "See you in forty-five."

———

After the warmth and closeness of the bookstore, the morning air feels refreshing. I pull up the Google Maps app on my phone and let it guide me toward the Trevi Fountain. It's just a few short blocks away, and as I round the bend, I catch my breath. Somehow, I hadn't expected it to be quite so large. Crammed into a plaza that seems entirely too small for it, the eighteenth-century Baroque fountain has the footprint of a decent size city swimming pool. Even in the winter, the plaza is crowded with tourists making the pilgrimage to Rome's most famous fountain.

I take a few photos and shoot some selfies to share with my friends. Then I indulge in superstition. I turn around and toss a coin, right hand over left shoulder, making the classic wish to return someday. I definitely want to come back. Now that I've had this taste, I want more. Days to wander through museums and sit at cafés.

Glancing across the plaza, I notice a café with tiny, round tables set up on the street. I didn't finish my coffee at the bookstore. I'm dying for a cappuccino. Checking my watch, I decide there's still time.

I pull out the bundle of letters from my bag while waiting for my drink. I unfold the one on the top.

Dearest Carmela,

How I long to see you again. I have been counting the days till you join me. Each night, I recall our long walks in Tuscany and all the plans we spoke of. And that is not all. When I close my eyes, I see the moonlight on your beautiful hair. The memory of your laugh, drifting on the wind, floats in and out of my dreams. Your sweet lips, Carmela. And speaking of sweet, I have planted a hazelnut tree in the back-yard so we will have filberts to make that delicious gelato…

The waiter brings my coffee, and I reluctantly fold the letter, placing it carefully back into its pouch inside my purse. I sip my cappuccino slowly, letting the fountain hypnotize me. The yarn store is only a block away. I still have plenty of time.

Did Carmela ever toss a coin in this fountain?

Of course, my grandmother never returned to Italy. Once she got to America, she never looked back. She never talked about her childhood in Tuscany or mentioned her parents, specifically. What she did share were delicious recipes and colorful superstitions. But without any context, these all felt like pages torn from a book. There was no way to make sense of it all. Her story—at least the one I was told—didn't go back any further than the day my grandparents met.

My grandparents had an excellent meet cute, something I'm sure Isla will be interested in.

According to the story I was told since I was a very little girl, my grandpa had knocked on my grandmother's family's door out of curiosity because they had the same last name. He was stationed nearby, and he was curious to see if there was any connection. The rest was fate.

Romano is a pretty common name. My father had a more skeptical take. He'd only shared this after both my grandparents were gone and unable to argue. If my grandfather had knocked on his mom's door, my dad thought it probably had more to do with the fact that Carmela was rumored to be the prettiest girl in the village.

Reading over the letters now, I wonder if my dad was right. But I still prefer the original story.

I'm hoping Maria can fill in the gaps.

Not all of the letters in the stack are correspondence between my grandparents. I'd been delighted to find a handful of letters in the bunch from a woman named Maria. She wrote repeatedly, begging to know how my grandmother was faring in America. She spoke of the village and her own life, including photos of herself and her family. When my great-grandparents passed, she sent their obituaries in a folded sheet of paper along with a few pressed flowers.

For decades, Maria sent these letters, the only link with my grandmother's past. I have no way of knowing if my grandmother ever wrote back. And I can only imagine Maria's surprise when I got in touch.

Because of the return address on Maria's letters, I was finally able to locate the village that my grandmother was from. But even more amazingly, my letter to Maria was answered.

She's still alive. We've been exchanging letters two or three times a month for the last six months. I've also been in touch with her grandson, Francesco, via text. He's helped arrange my visit to Tuscany.

I glance down at my phone to check the time and notice the new message notification. Almost immediately, I get a terrible feeling. The number is familiar. It's the number of my family doctor back in Washington State. My heart pounds ominously, making me regret all the caffeine. The call must have come in while my phone was silenced at the event.

It's just a little PTSD. They're probably calling to change my next appointment.

My doctor is a member of the same overall practice that treated my father. When he was sick, and I was taking care of him, I was constantly calling the main number and getting calls back. Those were never good calls.

Instinctively, I reach back into my bag and touch my grandmother's letters, feeling the smooth, silky fibers of the frayed ribbon holding the bundle together. Sometimes, it feels like the only thing holding me together is just as tenuous. I've never felt more alone.

My mother is out there, but we rarely speak.

My grandparents and my father were my real family. My whole family and my whole heart. Just them, and for the years we dated, I suppose it was Kent too. And now it's just me. Rattling around that big, old house I inherited, all alone. The house is hardly a comfort, with all the people who matter missing. A house is a place. People are home. My grandmother would be so disappointed in me, putting off trimming the tree for so long.

Rome wasn't built in a day.

I won't be alone forever. I have wonderful friends. I will rebuild. I can make my own family. That's the plan. Taking a deep breath, I hit play and listen to the message.

My doctor greets me in her cheery, slightly apologetic tone.

"Hi, Emily," she says. "I'm so sorry to leave this in a message, and I don't want you to panic. But I'm concerned that things might not be as straightforward as we'd hoped. Endometriosis can make conception more challenging. I'd like you to come in for some additional tests, and I recommend we also start working up a plan to do IVF, if you decide to go that route. Give me a call when you're back, and we can discuss the costs and the options."

Dammit.

I recall my doctor warning, years ago, that the condition could make conception and implantation a little trickier. But she had also said lots of people with endometriosis get pregnant naturally, so I'd happily stayed on birth control for years. The last thing I'd wanted when I was with Kent was a kid.

It doesn't matter what I want.

Savagely, I pull my knitting project out of my bag. I slide the circular needles out from the nearly completed cuff of the bootie. How many stitches had I completed already, each loop bringing me closer to completion?

I pick at the yarn and start unraveling.

The tears flow as I pull out my work. But there's also something so soothing about it. Like cleaning up a mess. I roll the soft alpaca yarn back into a ball as I go, trying to imagine what else it might be. Someday. When the time is right for it to be transformed.

"Emily? What the hell?" Blaze is standing next to my table, holding a paper bag. He drops the bag on the table and bends over to wipe my tears with his thumb.

"What are you doing here?" I ask, confused. "Shouldn't you still be signing books?"

"We wrapped it up early. I left some signed copies. Marco showed up after you left, and there was practically a stampede. I thought I'd catch up with you in the yarn shop, but you weren't there. So, I came looking for you at the fountain." He gestures at the bag. "I bought you some stuff, by the way."

"Thank you," I say. My voice catches between the two words, like an unbalanced spin cycle.

"Are you crying because of Kent, Emily? I'm sorry if I was too harsh about the booties."

"No, you were 100 percent right. But I wasn't totally up front with you."

Blaze pulls out a seat and joins me at the table. When the waiter starts to approach, he points at the cappuccino cup and holds up a finger to indicate he wants the same.

"So, what's this about then?" he asks, signaling at my destruction in progress.

"The booties weren't for Kent's babies," I say. "They were for mine."

"Wait! You're pregnant?" Blaze's eyebrows fly up and his eyes bug out, and I imagine him going back over the Bloody Mary, the wine on my dinner tray. Not to mention the Xanax.

"No! I'm not pregnant. But I was planning to pursue artificial insemination this spring." I quickly explain. "I decided that I don't want to wait till I have the perfect relationship or whatever. I don't know if that relationship—or any relationship—is ever going to happen. But I know I want a kid."

Blaze nods his understanding. "Okay, I can follow that. But then, why are you doing that?" he points at the ball of yarn that's still growing in my hands.

"Actually, can you help me? Just wind this as I pull on the loops?" I ask. "It keeps getting snagged."

I hand him the ball of yarn to wind and continue tugging at the mess I've made.

"You know what doing this is called?" I ask.

"Crazy?" he guesses.

"No, it's called frogging." I smile wistfully.

"Why frogging?"

"Because you 'rip it, rip it.'" I laugh dryly at my own joke, coming at last to the end of the stitches. The lump in my throat is receding. It's more like a bump now. It no longer feels lethal.

I hold out my hand, and Blaze passes the ball of yarn back to me.

"See? All better. This can be anything now. Pure possibility, zero expectations."

"That's actually kind of deep," Blaze says. "I might use that in a book."

"Feel free. My gift to you." I wave my hand, granting permission.

"So, clarify something for me? What expectations have we let go of here, exactly?" Blaze asks.

I take a deep breath and close my eyes, pretending for a moment that it's Smitty I'm speaking to and not this insanely charismatic, handsome creature who has to hide from photographers.

"I guess I'm releasing the expectation that I'm going to be able to get pregnant at all. I don't know why I just assumed it would be a slam dunk. My doctor just called, and she said that I might have to step it up."

"As in?"

"I don't know, IVF." For some reason, I can't force myself to meet his eye.

"Is there any reason to assume that's definitely going to be the case?"

"Well, no. But she said it might be difficult to conceive on my own via, you know, a donor."

Blaze reaches out and grabs the ball of yarn from my hand. He tosses it back and forth, keeping it away from me when I try to grab it back.

"Hey!" I yell.

"I don't care what your doctor said." Blaze winds a bit of yarn around his finger.

"Excuse me?"

"I think you're going to be a great mom one day, no matter what path you take to get there. And I'm sure when the time is right, you *will* get there. There's no reason to assume the worst, particularly when there's nothing you can do about it right now. But you know what? Right now, right here, this week in Rome? We can both choose to enjoy ourselves. Together."

My face burns with shame as I realize I've done it again. How many times am I going to go on and on and on like this with this man? Why do I keep talking about myself and moping like this? I wish there were a way to dive deep into the fountain and emerge on the other side as if I'd just arrived at the plaza. I'm imagining a sort of baptismal do-over.

"I'm so sorry, Blaze," I apologize. "That was a lot. It was wrong of me to unload on you like that. Maybe we can work on the background questions a bit?" I suggest.

"No, Emily. That's not what I was saying. What I want to work on with you today is something else entirely. I want to work on seeing this magical city with my new girlfriend. Let's let that be enough. We don't have to think about anything or anyone else."

Blaze leans across the table. He cocoons my hands in his, spreading warmth through my whole body. And then he leans in closer, pressing his forehead to mine. Our lips are close. So close. I can practically taste him. But he suddenly leans his head back and kisses a tear off the tip of my nose.

"You're so salty," he says, before bringing his lips back to crush mine.

Blaze tastes like coffee and the cinnamon that dusted our cappuccinos. His skin is still smooth from shaving. I like the feel of his clean-shaven face against mine—almost as much as I liked the beard.

I lay a fingertip against the cleft in his chin. "Sweet," I say.

"You think I'm sweet?" he asks, pulling my seat closer. He sweeps his tongue between my parted lips, teasing me. I am amped and exhausted at the same time. I feel like I've been on one of those carnival rides that lifts and drops you unpredictably, the heights all the more thrilling because you can't predict the next drop.

And then I remember. *We're pretending.*

"Um ... Blaze, I don't know that anyone's watching."

"Think of it like practice, Emily. Practice makes perfect. We never know when the paparazzi might be lurking."

"Mm-hmm," I mumble. I'm dying to slip a hand under his sweater, into his shirt. I'm imagining how his chest would feel against my palm. Instead, I sit on my hands. "What exactly do you want from me, Blaze?"

He leans back in his seat and sighs. "I don't know, Emily. It's going to sound stupid if I say it."

"Then you're in good company! All the more reason to say it. Please? For pity's sake, don't let me be the only one making a fool of themselves."

"Okay." He sits straight again and takes a deep breath before leaning forward. There's a mischievous gleam in his eye, but there's something else—a plea. "What I want …"

I fold my hands in front of me and raise my eyebrows, urging him to go on. "Go on, you can say anything."

"Okay, but before you tell me you're not going to sleep with me, for the third time, it's not that," he says.

I nod.

"It's not going to be something weird, is it?" I ask. "Like you're not going to ask me to wash your feet or let you eat sushi off my belly?"

"Is the sushi thing an option?"

"Blaze?" I try to look at him sternly, but he seems so genuinely nervous, I can't keep it up.

"Okay. So, we've agreed to this arrangement for the week. I know it's all pretending, but does make-believe have to be a chore?" He fiddles some more with the ball of yarn. "It doesn't feel like a chore to me. It actually feels pretty fun. I'm so damn tired of overthinking everything, Emily. I don't want to worry about tomorrow or who's watching us when and where. I just want to be able to spend this time in Rome with you, and I don't know … live in the moment? I guess what I want boils down to this. I want you to play with me. Would you play with me?"

Blaze rolls the ball of yarn across the table at me, and I block it before it rolls off the edge.

I send it flying back across the table, and he catches it and lobs it back. We continue the volley a few more times till he misses. The ball of yarn lands in his lap.

"Two points for me," I cheer.

"Is that a yes then?" he asks, tipping his head down and peering solemnly at me.

"Yes." I nod.

"Good." He grins. "Then let's get out of here and find somewhere to eat lunch."

He lays some bills on the table and then stands up. Still facing me, he takes a few steps back. He sticks his hand in his pocket, fishing around for a coin.

"Gotta do it, right? When in Rome …" Blaze tosses the coin over his shoulder, sending it sailing far. It lands with a splash.

"Did you make a wish to come back?" I ask.

"Something like that," he says.

"What does that mean?" I ask, standing and stretching.

"I'd tell you"—he takes my hand—"but then my wish might not come true."

blaze

. . .

"I'll never forget the first time I got on the freeway. I was sixteen years old and I'd been driving, mostly in parking lots, for all of two days. 'Be cool, Blaze,' I told myself. 'Just do what everyone else is doing. You just gotta make it to the next exit. And try not to die.' If you've got a driver's license, you've already been indoctrinated into the cult of 'fake it till you make it.' Welcome. We all gotta start somewhere."

— Blaze Smith, *Go Your Own Way,* on Faking It Till You Make It

IN BETWEEN CHEESE and olive tastings and bites of crusty bread drizzled with oil and vinegar, the sun peeks out from behind the clouds. It lights up the produce-laden market stalls in the Campo de' Fiori square. We warm ourselves with cups of hot, fruity, mulled wine—Vin Brulé—as we walk.

Like snow on the roof of a car, Emily's sadness melts away in the midday sun. Only a little shadow of salt around the edges remains. Otherwise, you wouldn't have believed it was there at all.

Next, we stroll through the Piazza Navona. We hold hands as we stop to admire each of the three spectacular fountains, just like millions of tourists who've wandered here before us. It's not my first time here, but I'm enjoying seeing it all through Emily's eyes. She brings a fresh perspective and enthusiasm that I hadn't known was missing from my travels. How have I never noticed the walrus and the dolphins in these fountains before?

"Ha! I found it. The octopus is right there," I exclaim. I have just completed her challenge—locating all the marine life in the plaza's fountains in under six minutes. "Victory is mine! What's my prize?"

"I'm afraid I'm out of stickers and lollipops," Emily laments, "but I can spring for a souvenir at one of those shops. Unless you have anywhere else you want to go?"

"I told you, I cleared the afternoon," I reassure her.

Emily lets go of my hand and reaches into her bag for her phone. She zooms in on the octopus in the fountain and shoots her thousandth photo of the day. She's a much better documenter than I am. Nothing is too trivial—the bottles of aged balsamic vinegar in the market, bags of penis-shaped pasta in a shop window, timeworn doors, and ceramic plaques and street signs. She even shoots a photo of the cobblestones beneath our feet.

"Give me your phone," I say.

She looks at me questioningly. "What for?"

"For a selfie with me," I say. She looks surprised.

"I think it's an ussie when there's more than one person."

"Whatever." I take the phone and pull her in closer. I hold the phone out and adjust it to frame Bernini's Fontana dei Quattro Fiumi behind us. Emily looks up at the screen and smiles goofily. No practiced posing or sly head tilt designed to only show her good side. She doesn't even demand that I adjust the camera angle or ask me to stand differently.

I tap the screen several times, as we spontaneously rearrange ourselves. In one shot, I point over-enthusiastically at the obelisk above the fountain. In another, we both make mock serious faces. There's no rhyme or reason to these poses, but when I check them, they look great. Silly, but great. How is it that we look so good together? Quickly, I text the photos to myself.

"Nope," I say when she holds out a hand for her phone. "I want to take one more." Impulsively, I hold up the phone again and pull her against me, kissing her. My eyes are closed, and I have no idea if I'm even getting the shot as I continue to tap the screen for another ten seconds. Finally, I lower my arm and slide the phone back in her pocket. We're still kissing. She doesn't push me away.

Emily's hands tangle in my hair, and the tips of our tongues test the current that's running between us. Every time our tongues make contact, there's a buzz. I savor the shivery shock of electricity.

Emily presses her hips against me. I have to swallow a groan. While our PDA might not look particularly dirty to passersby, my mind is taking me to indecent places. I add up all the places our clothed bodies are making contact, and then, in my imagination, I subtract the garments.

"You don't have to keep pretending." I pause to catch my breath and nuzzle her neck. "We don't have to keep up the act if you don't want to."

Miraculously, we've managed to wander, unnoticed, almost all afternoon. I haven't seen any paparazzi. The streets are crowded with disinterested tourists, too caught up in their last-minute holiday shopping to pay us any mind.

"Didn't you say practice makes perfect?" Emily asks. She dusts her lips across my jaw, down to my chin, and lingers there.

I lower my head and bring her lips to mine again. Deeper this time. Rougher. She tastes like the sweet, mulled wine from the market. My need for her is increasing. I can't imagine how I'll manage to sleep tonight, feeling the heat of her lying beside me.

"Blaze?" Emily pulls away. Her eyes are pools of honey, shot through with sage, cinnamon, and caution. She steps back and holds up one hand, as though resting it against an invisible wall to regain her equilibrium.

"I'm so sorry," I apologize. "I got carried away. You have that effect on me."

"And you on me," she admits. "This is exactly why we made the rules. This could get confusing otherwise."

"Are you confused?" I ask.

"I don't know what to say. What do you want me to say?" She reaches into her bag and pulls out an umbrella, popping it open the exact moment I start to feel sprinkles.

I want her to say yes. Yes! Yes, Blaze, I am very confused by this, and it's only getting worse with every passing moment.

I wish she would just say she feels the same way I do so I could know it's not just me. So I could believe that my imagination isn't playing tricks on me, blurring the lines between make-believe and reality.

"We both have jobs to do." Emily sighs, fiddling with the umbrella and looking away across the Piazza. "And we have very different lives. When this book tour is over, you'll be headed back to your regularly scheduled celebrity appearances. And I'll be headed home to my small town to get busy with a turkey baster"—she pauses here, frowning as she rethinks this—"or IVF. Whatever. You'll *Go Your Own Way*. I'll go mine."

Did she just use the title of my book to let me down easy? I feel the air being let out of my tires.

What was I thinking? That she'd be swept away by my celebrity? Hardly. She truly doesn't give a shit about it, which is refreshing. Did I think that she'd profess her love for me after knowing me for all of three days? It's way too soon.

But there's something here that feels stronger than a maybe. Something about Emily feels inevitable. The more I try to shake off the premonition, the more its tendrils pull at me, moving me imperceptibly closer to the edge of an unseen cliff.

You've already started to fall. You're gaining momentum.

"Anyway, I don't know when I'll have another chance to travel again, and certainly not in this grand a style," Emily is saying. "So, as awkward as it is to say this, I'm really grateful for this opportunity," she says, gesturing between us.

This *"opportunity."* The word hits me like a bucket of ice water. It's a word that people use after job interviews for positions they know won't ever happen. Thank you for this opportunity. Have a nice life.

"Of course," I say, pulling on a knit beanie and shoving my hands into my pockets. "I hope it all works out for you."

We walk in silence for the next ten minutes, both of us lost in our thoughts. When we come to the Spanish Steps, we pause. "So where to next?" Emily asks. "You want to go back to the hotel?"

"I still owe you a proper meal," I say. "You think you'll be up for it in an hour or two?"

"Ha! I'm Italian," Emily jokes. "I can always eat."

"Tell you what," I say, glancing up toward our hotel. "Let's go back to the room and freshen up. I'll get us a reservation."

Two hours later, we're strolling down the street in Trastevere, breathing like dragons, every exhalation producing streams of steam. Our fingers are intertwined again, Emily's hand tucked into the pocket of my overcoat. The skin-on-skin contact is what's keeping me warm.

I catalog Emily's features as we step inside the cozy restaurant, committing them to memory. Cascading waves of caramel-colored hair. Flashing hazel eyes. High cheekbones. The divot above her soft upper lip, and the swoop of eyelashes that sweep up toward her arched brows. She's a letter written in cursive. I want to steam the envelope open and unfold all her secrets.

"You're staring, Blaze." Emily blushes as I pull out her chair.

"You look amazing in that red dress, Emily." This is an understatement. She dazzles. The minute she took off her long coat, everyone in the restaurant was turning to look at her. The knit dress clings to her curves and dips at the neckline. It's not quite revealing, but it's also not quite demure.

Emily raises an eyebrow at me, then looks down at herself. "Are you sure that's it? There's nothing on my face. Or my dress?"

"You're perfect," I say. Then I attempt to change the subject. "It smells great in here. I'm starving."

"The smell reminds me of my grandma's kitchen." Emily sniffs. "She was such a great cook."

"You said she was from Tuscany?" I ask.

"Yes." Emily nods. "She was from the Maremma and grew up in Pitigliano. I'm looking forward to visiting next week."

The waiter appears with bottled water, and I hold up the menu to show Emily the wine I'm considering ordering.

"Perfect choice." She approves of my decision. The waiter makes a note and leaves.

"You mentioned a friend of your grandmother's who's still alive. Is there any other family?"

"My grandmother didn't have any siblings. Once her parents passed away, there wasn't anyone left."

"Cousins?"

"None that I know of. I'm a third generation only child."

"That's rough."

"You're telling me. I definitely want to have more than one." Emily pauses as the waiter pours her wine. She swirls it and takes a sip, nodding her approval. Then she finishes her thought. "I don't want my kids to be only children."

"Were you lonely as a kid?" I reach out for her hand again. I turn it over, looking at her palm, tracing the heart line.

"Blaze, do you read palms?" Emily looks surprised.

"A little." I'm tempted to concoct a story for her. She responds to the wicked gleam in my eyes and matches it with her own mischief.

"Oh, really now. Perhaps this is the best kept secret about you! No wonder you are so good at counseling couples and predicting love matches. As a fortune teller, you already see and know all." She shakes her head. "You really are a man of hidden talents."

I laugh. "And by hidden talents, do you mean 'charlatan?'"

"If the designer shoes fit …"

"It's nothing like that," I confess. "My older sister went through a phase when she was in high school. I was her guinea pig."

"All right then." Emily looks down at her hand in mine. "Enlighten me. Tell me what my hand says."

"Let's see," I say, looking a little closer and trying to remember what my sister used to say. I trace a finger down her lifeline. "Your lifeline is long and strong, so that's wonderful news."

Next, I turn her hand sideways, rotating it and examining the lines that form at her wrist. "It looks like you will have two— no, wait—*three* bambini."

She bites her lip, trying not to laugh as she looks skeptically at me.

"Three, you say? Oh my. What else does it say there?"

I turn her hand back over, probing the fleshy mounds at the base of her thumb and beneath her ring finger. I close my eyes, letting my imagination run wild for a moment. Then I open my eyes wide, sigh happily, smile smugly, place her hand facedown on the table, and shrug.

"Oh, come on. That is not fair," she protests.

"I can't tell you anything else until you cross my palm with silver," I insist. "I'm not just a pretty face, Emily. I have a special gift. It needs to be rewarded."

Emily laughs. "The hell you do."

"Well, then, if you're not a believer, there's no need to tell you."

"Out with it, Blaze!" she demands. She is so gorgeous in the candlelight of this restaurant. I'm sure she looks far more like a celebrity than I do.

"You sure you want to know?" I tease.

"It's my hand. Of course I want to know."

"Okay." I open my menu, using it as a shield to mask my smile. Then I say, in as dispassionate a voice as I can muster, "Your hand says you are a very selfish lover."

Emily's napkin flies over the menu, hitting me in the face.

"That's bullshit!" she exclaims. "I want my money back."

"Okay, okay." I laugh, lowering the menu. "I think what your hand actually says, from what I recall, is that you are a very passionate lover." I take her hand again, rubbing the Mount of Venus area. "See how soft and cushy your hand is here?"

Emily turns her hand over and grabs my wrist.

"Okay. Let me read you now." She smirks.

"You read palms too?" I raise my eyebrows.

"As a matter of fact," Emily says, "I do. My grandmother taught me. She always said, 'Emily, you must not trust those self-help guru types. They're full of shit.'"

"No, she did not." I chuckle.

"You're right." Emily acquiesces. "She didn't say that. She actually said, 'You want to see what's in a man's heart, you look in his hand.'"

She gazes into my palm, then dips a finger into her water to pull out an ice cube. Before I know what she's doing, she wipes the ice cube across my palm.

"What the hell?" I snatch my wet hand away.

"Don't be a baby, give it back." She holds out a napkin. "I find a little ice water works much better than silver to help me see the lines. Just be happy I didn't also spit on you."

"Is that actually a thing?" I ask at once, horrified and fascinated.

"Only if you're worried about someone being cursed with an evil eye," she murmurs, tilting my palm around near the flickering candle. She pauses for a moment. "You don't think anyone's cursed you lately, do you? You want me to spit?"

"Stop!" I bite my lip. "You can never tell my sister about the spitting. She'll want to make up for lost time."

Emily spends another minute concentrating on my palm, studying it by candlelight, before releasing me.

"It's just as I thought," she proclaims triumphantly.

"What?"

"You *are* full of shit." She leans back and folds her arms across her chest.

"That's it? That's all you got from all this?" I act unimpressed, laying my right hand out, face up on the table.

"Well, it also looks like three kids for you. But not with Viv. That relationship is definitely in the past now." She leans forward, looking authoritatively at a break in my love line. "Looks like a new relationship is in your future. And some big changes."

"Am I missing the poop emoji on my fate line? Where exactly does it say I'm full of shit?" I stare into my own hand.

Emily sighs and looks at me like I'm an ignorant child.

"Do you see all these little lines … here, here, and here?" Emily points. "And here? They're pretty much everywhere, and they say you are constantly questioning and second-guessing yourself. I suspect you overthink everything." She folds my fingers in and turns my hand over.

"In other words, Blaze Smith, you're full of shit."

"Couldn't all those lines mean I'm very sensitive?" I argue. "And doesn't being sensitive make me a better therapist? Empathy is an important attribute for a therapist," I contend.

"Mayyyyybe." She pries my fingers open again and taps her way around my palm. For a moment, she seems surprised. Then she smirks again.

"Out with it, Romano," I say.

"Well, Smitty, it appears you are very 'eager to please' in bed. Care to confirm or deny this fact?"

"So now I'm Smitty again?"

"I mean, this hand clearly is." She taps my right hand. "Want me to have a look at the other one?"

"Eager to please?" I repeat. "You couldn't put a more positive spin on that?"

"What's negative about being 'eager to please'?"

We're both leaning forward now, hands splayed out on the table.

"You know what I think my hand really says?" I ask.

"No, but I'm sure you're going to tell me your version."

"I think it says I'm a very *generous* lover."

Emily's eyes sparkle, and I can feel her pulse quicken as I take her hand. Without looking away from her, I rub my thumb in slow circles on her palm and wrist. I trace gently between her fingers, teasing and caressing the delicate webbing between each digit. She bites her lip, and her eyes close halfway as I slowly, deliberately, slide my index finger in and out of the sensitive spaces between her fingers.

Finally, she makes a fist and pulls her hand away.

"Fine," she says, a little breathlessly. "Generous? Have it your way."

"Yes, but at the end of the day, Emily, we're both up shit's creek."

"Why is that?" She gulps some water. I am pleased to see that she is so flushed.

"Because neither one of us has anyone to share all that unrequited passion and generosity with."

emily

. . .

BLAZE OPENS UP ABOUT VIV, as I carefully twirl my pasta.

"I just assumed that neither of us was pursuing anything till the tour was over. We agreed we'd announce our 'conscious uncoupling' afterward. No harm, no foul, no injured parties. And then we'd get on with our lives, Viv in LA and me in Seattle."

"How did the two of you get together?" I ask. Technically, it's one of the questions on Kent's background list, but I'm assuming anything we discuss at dinner is off the record.

"Funny story. If it wasn't for Viv, I wouldn't be famous. I'd probably have a private practice somewhere—an office with quirky art, a bowl of candy, and an overstuffed couch with an armrest you could balance a box of tissues on."

"Would you prefer that?" I ask.

"Honestly? I might," Blaze admits. "No matter how many books I've sold, I still feel most fulfilled by the work I've done with patients, one-on-one. I became a celebrity by accident."

"What do you mean?"

"Are we on the record here?" Blaze asks.

"I assumed we weren't." I shrug.

"Some of this is fine to share. I don't mind Viv taking the credit. I just don't want any of the intimate details of our relationship in the brief you're preparing for Kent, okay?"

"Got it." I nod. For once, it's not me doing all the talking. It's a relief to be in the 'listener' seat with Blaze. It's also a thrill knowing he feels comfortable enough to open up to me.

I take a small bite of my entrée and lay down my fork. I'm not even hungry anymore. I can still feel the slip of his fingers between mine, and I'm not entirely over it. On the heels of that, I'm not sure I want to picture the 'intimate details' between him and the blonde newscaster.

Still, I listen.

"I was dating Viv when she was new to the *Seattle Morning News*. We went out on a few dates. Then one morning, at about 4 a.m., she called me and begged me to come into the station. The therapist who was supposed to be on for the Valentine's Day segment had the flu."

"Let me guess," I say. "You rushed in to do the spot? Doctor Love to the rescue?"

Blaze nods and rubs his forehead.

"One thing led to another. I became a regular and even got my own weekly segment, discussing dating and relationship trends. I started doing appearances on national morning shows, afternoon talk shows, and then the book deal literally fell in my lap."

"And the rest is history?" I guess.

"Well, yes and no. There's more business to the business, but I won't bore you."

Blaze holds out a chunk of lasagna for me to taste, spinning the fork midair to spiral the long strings of cheese into a tight little package.

"So, what happened with Viv?" I lean forward, pausing before allowing him to feed it to me. "Off the record."

"Things were fine with Viv—at first. She loved it when she was able to tag along to New York, LA, Chicago, or whatever city I was headed to next. She schmoozed up the producers of every show. All the while, she was working her way up the food chain in Seattle."

I pause to take a bite of my chicken, and I have to close my eyes.

"That good?" Blaze asks.

"Life-changing," I admit. "It sounds like things were going well for you and Viv. So, when did you grow apart?"

"Right after I released my second book. Viv landed a host gig at a nationally syndicated entertainment show based in LA. Our schedules conflicted. We didn't have time to go out on dates anymore. Instead, we became each other's plus-ones at 'mutually beneficial' press events."

Blaze seems about to say something else, but then he appears to change his mind. He looks off to the side and sighs.

"That sounds rough." I lay a hand on his arm.

"That's showbiz." He shrugs.

"And showbiz isn't what you want long term?" I probe.

"You really won't repeat this?" Blaze asks, but there's a hint of warning to the tone. Whatever he's about to tell me, he really doesn't want me to write about it.

I nod. "As you've pointed out, it's not my byline, Blaze. I don't have any skin in the game, other than being tasked with gathering enough basic info for Kent to cobble his piece together. As far as I'm concerned? You can have Steff answer Kent's questions if you prefer."

Actually, I'm not sure why I didn't think of this sooner.

Blaze looks at me for a moment. "I'm sure Steff would love that."

"She would." I laugh.

"She means well," he says. "She's just doing her job. And I'm grateful. I'm grateful for her looking out for me, and for the fans, for all of this." He moves his hand in a sweeping gesture. "Trips to Rome, VIP treatment, whatever. But when you ask me if celebrity is what I want long term?" Blaze exhales, letting out a long, slow breath before continuing.

"The answer is no. Hell no, Emily. This life is not what I had in mind for myself long term!" Blaze runs a hand through his hair and looks over his shoulder. He lowers his voice. "Even right now, I'm wondering if someone is eavesdropping, or filming me, or taking a covert photo. It's always in the back of my mind, and it keeps me from really being present. I'm so sick of it. I want privacy. I want anonymity. And I want to have kids who grow up and challenge me like normal, screwed-up therapists' kids."

He smiles wryly when he references "normal" screwed-up kids. I don't say anything, but I nod to indicate that I get it. I can only imagine what it's like to live under a magnifying glass like he does.

"So no, I don't want to continue living in the spotlight and subject my future family to worrying about ending up in the tabloids," Blaze continues. "Jesus, what kind of normal woman would want that? How am I supposed to have a *real* relationship when I can't even check into a hotel without the press speculating?"

I take a sip of my wine before speaking, searching for the right words. There are none.

"I'm so sorry, Blaze. That really sucks," I say.

"Thank you, Emily. Most people would tell me I'm being ridiculous, that this is just the cost of celebrity and I should 'suck it up' and enjoy my good fortune and all the trappings that come with being famous. And maybe fame would suit them better. But I never asked for this."

"For what it's worth, I thought Smitty was pretty hot." I smile wryly. "So, if you ever consider the Witness Protection Program, I'd go with that persona."

Blaze's hand goes to his chin, which is already starting to show stubble.

"It was fun being Smitty. But I like this more. I'm loving being in Rome with you, Emily. We've had a good run at normal anonymity today."

Blaze maintains eye contact as he refills our glasses. He raises his cup.

"This might be a game of make-believe, but I can't think of anyone else I'd rather play with. To Rome for the Holidays," he toasts.

"Rome for the Holidays," I echo.

We clink glasses.

———

The next morning, I sleep in. I don't even hear Blaze when he gets up to go to the set of *Pazzi per Amore*. I'd camped on the couch last night, claiming a wine headache. But the truth was, I couldn't trust myself around him. And now, after tossing and turning half the night, watching moonlit shadows creep across the ceiling, I do have a headache.

Maybe it's the jet lag catching up. And maybe it's something else. Every time Blaze and I are alone, I get more confused. He makes my heart crash around in my chest like some kind of caged animal. I want to keep it safe, and I want to set it free. I'm afraid it will devour me. It's exhausting.

There's drool and mascara on my pillow. It's after ten on a weekday, a truly unprofessional hour to still be sleeping. I consider getting up to shower and do a little work, but I promptly fall back asleep, into a dream.

I'm talking to my father, asking him if he's ever read my grandparents' letters. And then my grandparents are there, too, and they are all laughing because why waste time reading the letters when we are all here and can talk to each other? A lion wanders through the room, and my grandmother pets it like a dog. My grandparents exchange a knowing look. My father asks if they're ever going to tell me.

Tell me what?

Someone is in the suite. My eyes flicker open. I'm still so caught up in the dream and my frustration at not hearing what my grandparents have to tell me that I fail to be alarmed at the fact that I am not alone. Instead, I am annoyed. Did whoever it was have to wake me up? Right at the part when I was about to hear whatever it was my grandparents were going to tell me?

Recognition dawns on me, followed by outrage.

"Steff? Why are you going through my bag?"

Steff is standing next to the table in the dining area. She has dumped the entire contents of my bag onto the table. My grandparents' letters are fanned out, and she is taking a photo of the prescription anti-anxiety meds that I brought along for the flights.

I leap to my feet. Steff glances suspiciously from the bottle to me.

"Overdo it last night?" She wrinkles her nose and sets the pill bottle down on the table. "You probably shouldn't mix drugs and alcohol."

"Don't be ridiculous. I have jet lag," I say.

"Uh-huh." Steff nods at me and adopts a condescending tone, as if she is speaking to a toddler. "Of course you do."

"Why are you here, and why the fuck do you think it's okay to invade my privacy and go through my bag?"

"Blaze is running some errands. He forgot his planner and asked me to check on you before we left. He was worried that you weren't answering texts." Steff taps her Christmas tree nails on the table.

"Bullshit."

I don't even think Blaze has my cell phone number. It occurs to me that we've never exchanged cell phone numbers.

"Check your texts, Sleeping Beauty," Steff sneers.

I pick up my phone.

Sure enough, there are three texts from Blaze. I scroll back through the messages and find the ussie we shot by the fountain yesterday. He'd used my phone and sent it to himself. That must be how he got my number.

And now I have his, too, I think. I'm not sure why that matters, but it gives me a little thrill. He's been texting since 7 a.m.

> Don't want to wake you. You look so peaceful. Grabbing breakfast with Steff, then headed to the Pazzi per Amore set. Text me when you get this?

Hey, Emily. Just checking if you got that last
text. Hope your head feels better.

Heads-up. Steff's on her way up to grab my
planner. You ok?

The last message was sent about ten minutes ago. Steff has her hands on her hips and a smug smirk on her face.

"I didn't sleep well last night," I say. "I'm sorry. I'm not the best at snapping into new time zones."

"You should try melatonin," Steff suggests. "And stay away from the hard stuff." She glances back significantly at my pill bottle that is still on the table.

"And you should try not going through other people's personal belongings."

I pad over to the coffeemaker on the counter and look around for some pods. What's the point of having a coffeemaker in the room if they don't supply it with coffee? I pick up the phone and dial housekeeping.

"Can we please get some more coffee pods when the room is refreshed?" I ask.

"I took all the pods back to my hotel. They charge a fortune for them there. I was just trying to be economical with Blaze's money. Sorry." She shrugs. Sorry *not* sorry.

"I don't really care about the coffee, but going through my things just isn't cool, Steff."

Steff pulls out a chair and sits down. She uses one finger to scoot my spilled possessions out of the way and sets down her phone on the table. Then she turns to me, her bulgy, blue eyes cold as steel.

"I'm just doing my job, Emily. Taking care of Blaze Smith is *my* job."

"Pardon?" I ask. "Are you insinuating that I'm trying to do your job?"

"You could never do my job," Steff sneers now. "You can't even wake yourself up before noon on a workday. You're a train wreck."

I flinch a little at her attack. In the mirror, I see myself. Mascara running, clad in the old, stained sleep tee I snuck back into my bag after Alexis left. My hair is a tangled mess, and there are creases from the pillow pressed into my face. But I am not on drugs.

With some effort, I manage to hold my head high. Steff continues her tirade.

"Blaze Smith is a *superstar*. I've worked hard to create and maintain his wholesome image, and I'm not going to let someone like you come along and threaten that. When Kent said he was sending a *colleague* to gather info for the article, I had no idea he was sending a gold digger like you. I never would have agreed to that."

A gold digger? Is she for real?

"I imagine it would have been up to Blaze, and not you, but that's beside the point."

"Sit down," Steff commands, pointing at the other chair by the table.

"No."

"Fine." She clicks her jaw and swings her leg impatiently. Her peculiar, purple Mary Janes remind me of witch shoes. On anyone else, they might be cool. But everything about Steff is starting to remind me of a cross between a witch and a troll.

"Here's the thing, Emily. I went through your stuff because I had to make sure that you weren't secretly recording Blaze or doing anything else to gather intel for nefarious purposes."

"Are you insane?" I laugh. "I am here to do a job. Kent is paying me to get the answers to those background questions. The ones that you and Blaze already approved. That is the whole reason I'm here. The only reason."

"The whole reason? Really?" Steff purses her lips and arches a brow. "Aren't you also getting paid to pretend you're his girlfriend?" Steff asserts. "Like some kind of amateur call girl. It's unseemly. It would be a disaster if that information got out."

"I'm not getting paid!" I spit out, horrified at her assumption.

"Well, that's a relief." Steff sighs. "I'd hate to see him throw away money like that. But it would still be a disaster for Blaze if this *charade* ever got out."

"Has it occurred to you that I've got a lot at stake here too?" I ask.

"Oh, I'll bet you do," she sneers.

"Listen, Steff." I make one last attempt to appeal to her sense of decency. "I care about Blaze. I don't want to see him getting torn up in the tabloids. That's why I agreed to do this. As a favor to him."

"Favor, trick …" She flicks my prescription bottle.

"Fuck you!" I snatch my meds and toss them back into my bag.

"Well, yes. Now that you mention it, if there's anyone Blaze Smith should be fucking, it's probably me, not you." Steff's eyes are narrowed. "Blaze and I go back almost seven years. I've been patient—super patient—waiting for his 'relationship' with Viv to end. Who do you think had her followed and got the Cabo pics to the press?"

Now I do sit down.

"You did that? Jesus Christ. Why would you do that?"

"Because it was only a matter of time before someone else leaked the story, and this way, I was able to stay ahead of it. I had a plan. A good plan. I was supposed to be his Rome romance. Which would have made perfect sense and would have worked out great for everyone. But then you had to come along and catfish him."

"I don't think that word means what you think it means," I say.

"I think you're a fraud, Emily. I know Kent dumped you, and maybe you think this is how you get him back, scoop him, whatever. But not on my watch. You need to end this arrangement with Blaze. I'll give you fifteen thousand dollars to pack up and leave today. Think about it. That money could be life-changing."

"No," I say flatly. "I think you need to go now."

She doesn't budge.

"Fine. Twenty thousand." She rolls her eyes.

"Still no."

"I think you need to reconsider my offer, Emily."

"Or what?"

"Or I'm going to make you very sorry you ever came to Rome."

I study her, trying to decide how much is real and how much is bluster. She's being sloppy. Emotional. I almost feel sorry for her. *Almost.*

"Does Blaze know how you feel about him?"

"I'm sure he does, on some level."

I doubt that. In fact, I feel pretty damn sure that he has absolutely no clue how she feels. I have no idea how he'd react if he did. Or if he'd even believe me if I shared this interchange.

"I'm not going to quit unless Blaze personally asks me to quit." I stand and walk away from the table, toward the door. "I've got things to do, and Blaze mentioned it was a long drive to the set. You should probably get going now, don't you think?"

Steff pushes back her chair noisily, banging into a side table.

"You're going to regret this," she threatens.

"Don't threaten me," I warn.

"Why not? What are *you* going to do to me?"

"Well, Steff, I'm your ticket to that magazine article, and as you've just pointed out yourself, I'm in a position to potentially harm your client. Furthermore, I now have dirt on *you* that I'm sure you'd prefer I don't share."

I don't know exactly where this burst of confidence is coming from, but my temper is definitely leading the charge. "So how about I do my job and you do yours, and you stay out of my business and my bags?"

I open the door and point the way out to the hallway.

"This isn't the end of—" Steff calls over her shoulder. I slam the door in her face before she gets out the rest of the sentence.

blaze

. . .

"Were you driving distracted? Take that turn too fast? Did you think you had more time, or space, or money in the meter? To err is human. To own up to your mistakes is divine. Skip this chapter if you've never fucked up. If you skipped this chapter, you're probably a narcissist."

— Blaze Smith, *Go Your Own Way*, on Admitting Fault

"WHAT'S UP WITH YOU?" I ask Steff on the way to the *Pazzi per Amore* reality show set.

The show is wrapping up their filming at Villa dei Baci, a luxurious, hilltop mansion outside of Rome. Not only have we had to sign multiple NDAs, we also had to agree to using their driver to take me there. Only Steff is allowed to accompany me.

The segment I will be taping involves me giving dating and premarital advice to the three remaining women and the handsome man-child who will be choosing between them —Marco.

"I hate this shit," I say flatly.

After meeting Marco at the book signing yesterday, I'm looking forward to this appearance even less. Things had rapidly devolved after he got there. The fans got stupid, the film crew got demanding, and Marco was predictably obnoxious. He hadn't been in the store for five minutes before jumping up on a chair and tearing off his shirt. Isla and I had slipped out the back entrance, leaving the film crew and selfie-seekers to their party. Steff stuck around to help clean up.

I check my texts. Finally, there's a message from Emily.

> Feeling better. Might meet up with Isla and
> do some sightseeing. Good luck today!

"Keep your head in the game, Blaze," Steff chastises me. She's been surly since I gave her the slip yesterday. This isn't stopping her from sitting too close. Her powdery, floral perfume in the enclosed space of the car is cloying. I crack my window and stare out at the rolling countryside, thinking about the village that Emily's grandmother was from. I haven't been to Tuscany. I'm jealous of Emily. I should stay a few extra days.

"Blaze?" Steff commands my attention with a sharp nudge of her knee. "Here's a brief about the three women who are left on the show. We should go over it. Giulia, the blonde, is the fan favorite for Marco. Just so you know who everyone is rooting for."

"And why is that?"

"I don't know." Steff flips through the folder. "I see here something about them 'making beautiful bambini' and her being a stay-at-home mom."

"Okay, but is that what Marco wants in a partner?"

Steff rolls her eyes. "You're totally missing the point here. It doesn't matter what Marco wants. Everyone who watches the show wants Giulia for him. If you want to sell books, you'll give the people what they want. Honestly, Blaze, you're paying me to do a job. The least you can do is pay attention to my advice. I don't do things half-assed. You know that about me, Blaze."

She stares meaningfully at me. At least, I think it's meaningful. But I also don't get it. Sometimes, I don't think we speak the same language. I take the brief from her, slide it into my bag, and give her hand a squeeze.

"We've worked together for a long time, Steff. I am assuming you'd tell me if something was bothering you. You're not usually one to hold back."

"Not something. Some*one*." It's her turn to stare out the window. "I'm concerned, Blaze. What do you really know about Emily? You know I found drugs in her bag?"

"Wait, you went through her bag?" I ask.

"Of course I did. It's my job to look after you and your reputation."

"That's a little much, though," I say. "Don't you think?"

"Is it?" Steff turns back to face me. "She sleeps when she should be working. She had drugs in her bag. She's constantly crawling all over you." She holds up a hand, ticking off imaginary offenses. "Has she even started working with you on the questions Kent sent over, or is she too busy trying to get into your pants?"

"Hey now!" I object, holding up my hands. "Do I have to remind you that you're the one who okayed her coming here to do the interview questions instead of Kent? And furthermore, my arrangement with her was all *my* idea, and part of the reason I thought of it was so that you'd be off the hook."

Steff snorts and resumes looking out the window. But not before I see the glassy sheen of tears in her eyes.

"Was the thought of faking a relationship with me really that horrible, Blaze?" she asks.

Understanding creeps up over me, cold and quiet as a tsunami. How had I missed all the warning signs? I'm such an idiot.

I try not to panic.

"It's not too late, Blaze," Steff says, placing a hand on my leg. "I've done what I can to suppress the story about you and Emily, but honestly, I'm not sure how much longer I can keep that up."

The tide is rising, threatening to wash away everything we've worked for, everything we've built over the last seven years.

I move her hand off my leg, gently. A sign by the side of the road gives me an idea. I cling to it, out of desperation.

"When was the last time you took a few days off, Steff?" I ask. "I'm taking the weekend off, and really, the only event left on Monday is *The Morning Show on Rai 1*. How about heading to a spa this weekend—on me?"

"Together?" She sits up straighter, looking hopeful.

Oh God. I didn't phrase that right.

"No." I shake my head. Steff wilts.

"I'm planning on laying low at the hotel, finishing the interview questions with Emily so she can enjoy the rest of her time in Italy," I say. "Without me," I add, making it clear that I haven't made any further plans.

Thinking about saying goodbye to Emily sends a sharp, stabbing pain through my gut. An actual physical sensation. But Steff seems somewhat appeased.

"The sooner you get rid of her, the better. We'll come up with a story for when people notice you're not together anymore."

But what if ...

The driver turns off onto a private lane and stops the car by a locked gate. A security guard in pressed pants and aviator glasses leans in to speak to our driver. He rolls down the back window so the guard can peek in. I wave hello. Steff looks out the other window. The guard waves us past.

"Don't worry," I reassure her. "It will all work out."

———

Marco is dripping wet when he greets me in the glassed-in pavilion behind the villa.

The young, female producer who led me here frowns and says something in Italian into the mic attached to her ear. It causes the wardrobe and makeup people clustered in the corner to abandon their card game and rush around, gathering their tools.

Marco shakes himself like a dog, proudly displaying the muscles that half the world is sighing over. The windows are steamed over from the heated pool, but it's still quite chilly in here, and he has goose bumps. The producer hurries over with a towel and a robe.

"Perdona me," Marco addresses me as he takes the towel. He wraps it around his hips. "I was just swimming. It calms me down. You have no idea how stressful it is to be the center of attention ..." Then he stops himself and slaps me on the back.

"What am I saying? You are the big, famous Love Doctor. Of course you know! Scusa! Mi da un momento per favore? (Can I have a moment with the doctor)?"

"Tienitila per la fotocamera, Marco," the producer protests. Quickly, she translates for me. "We prefer it if our cast doesn't engage in conversation outside of filming. Better to save it for the camera."

Marco gives her one of his signature, smoldering looks, and she checks her watch. "Dieci minuti, non di più (Fine, ten minutes). Then I need you back in the chair for hair and makeup."

"Grazie, bella!" Marco rejects the robe and blows her a kiss. Then he leads me to a seating area near the back door. He cracks the door and lights a cigarette, taking a deep drag.

"Okay, so first of all, Doctor Love, I already know which one I'm picking. But I wanted to make sure we put on a good show, so let's talk about what we're going to talk about."

"Cut to the chase!" I laugh.

"Cosa?"

"I mean, you are getting right to the point." I correct myself and remind myself, once again, to stay away from verbal idioms when I'm doing the session.

"Well yes, why not? Life is short. I already know, from the first episode, that I am choosing Giulia. She is the one for me. She's going to be a great mama for my bambini."

"Do you think that's what Giulia wants?"

"Of course. She's also going to start her own line of maternity skin care products. My cousin is already sourcing the—how do you say, package? The whole package." Marco smirks, indicating that this is a phrase he is familiar with.

"Well, it sounds like you're a man who knows what he wants," I offer. I'm not too worried about the session. There's always something to talk about. Even when people know what they want.

"Just don't mention the package, okay? This is a secret."

"I won't," I assure him.

"Do the other girls know?" I ask. Marco gives me a look like I'm some kind of idiot.

"Certamente! (For sure)," he says. "That is why they are still here. They are a couple. They will 'come out' after the show ends."

I shake my head. *Why am I even here?*

"You gotta love reality TV." I laugh. "It seems like you all have everything scripted. Is there anything I can actually help you with?"

"No. We do not script. We *sculpt*," Marco protests, admiring his own arm, flexing. The cigarette is dangling out of the corner of his mouth. "I look tough, no?" He grins, and the cigarette drops to the wet flagstones, sizzling as it fizzles out.

"You look great, Marco." The producer is back. "But I need you in the chair, now. We gotta get this show wrapped so the crew can get everything out by the weekend."

"Allora, I hear you have an Italian girlfriend." Marco stretches and then turns back to me.

"Where did you hear that?" I ask.

"It was on the news. Someone says she is an Italian American." Marco lights another cigarette before heading off somewhere to get his hair and makeup attended to.

The producer flops down on the couch.

"I cannot leave him alone for two minutes," she complains. "I didn't get a degree in Italian tourism and hospitality for this pazzi per cazzi bullshit. I've had it with these showbiz assholes."

"Pazzi per cazzi?" I ask.

"Pazzi means crazy and cazzi means dicks. It's kind of the unofficial name of the show." She rolls her eyes.

"So, you're an American too?" I ask.

"Yeah," she says. "My family is Italian, and I thought it would be fun to do an internship with a production company after college. One thing led to another, and here I am. They always stick me in the houses. It blows. I'd rather be leading wine tasting tours in Chianti."

"Interesting," I say. "I'd love to pick your brain about places to visit. I have a friend who's looking into her family's history in Tuscany. Maybe you have some suggestions about what to see in the area?"

"Would that be the girlfriend Marco mentioned?"

I smile, enigmatically.

"I'm Rory. Here's my card," she says, sitting up straighter. "Just don't call me after we wrap on Friday. My family rents a place in the tropics every year, and I plan on being drunk for the rest of the holidays."

"Hey Rory," I say, an idea occurring to me. "One more thing. Do you happen to know where I could get my hands on some costume items? I'd like to be able to do some sightseeing this weekend without being recognized."

I hear the echo of Steff's shoes on the flagstones as she makes her way across the pavilion. She shoots an incredulous look at me and an impatient look at the producer.

"What's going on here? Isn't anyone going to do my client's makeup? We need to do a light check in the kitchen before we film anything there. And would it be too much trouble to get us some club soda?"

The producer stands up and speaks rapidly into her mic in Italian.

"If you don't have any plans for Christmas, you're welcome to join me, Blaze." Rory winks at me. "Oh, and there are sodas in the fridge in the kitchen," she informs Steff. "Help yourself."

Her tennis shoes squeak as she takes off toward the kitchen.

"DO you know how many downloads and new subs we've had because of you this week?" Jackson asks on the video conference call.

It's just as well that Blaze and Steff are away for the rest of the day because today's the day we're recording *Lit Lovers* remotely. Later, after we wrap the episode, I've got plans to meet up with Isla for some sightseeing.

"Word is getting out about you and Blaze," Jackson says. "People are asking questions on the website."

"About that," I tell my three cohosts. "I can talk about anything today *except* Blaze Smith. He's 100 percent off limits for the podcast, okay?"

Jackson groans. His hands fly to his face, and he looks so comically bereft that, for a moment, he reminds me of the kid from *Home Alone*.

Meanwhile, Alexis looks at me like I'm the Grinch, and I've just cleared out all the gifts under her tree.

"Emily!" Alexis complains. "How can you do this to us? We *need* the vicarious details of your celebrity fling! It's cruel and unusual …" She sends me a text even as she is speaking.

You'll still spill to me after, right?

"Guys! Settle down. We need to honor Emily's wishes. It's not like there's nothing else to talk about. We can still chat about the trope of the week." Chelsea uses her high school teacher classroom voice to perfect effect.

Thank you, Chelsea.

"What's the trope?" I ask.

"Let's see." Chelsea flips through her notebook. "Looks like we penciled in 'Fake Relationships' for this week. Yay! Such a classic," Chelsea cheers.

Now it's my turn to silently scream into a pillow.

The fake relationship trope. Perfect. It couldn't be the brother's best friend? Grumpy guys and sunshine gals? Forced proximity? Professional rivals?

Chelsea gives me a thumbs-up.

"I don't think there's that much to go over if Emily's holding out on us." Jackson sighs disappointedly. "Should we get started?"

"I'm good," I say, plugging in my portable mic.

After a countdown, Jackson hits record and begins the intros. He says a word about our sponsors and includes a few notes about upcoming events in our area. Then we get down to business. He leads with the trope of the day.

"That's right, people. Today on *Lit Lovers*, we're talking about one of your all-time favorite tropes—fake it till you make it. The ol' 'fake relationship.'" Jackson purrs into the mic. "I should mention that our very own Emily Romano is joining us from Rome today," Jackson says. "And I'm interested in hearing all about what it's like to be in Rome for the holidays. But first, who can name some fake relationship classics?"

"The Proposal." I get mine in first.

"The Wedding Date," Chelsea says, "and I just read *The Love Hypothesis."*

Alexis offers up, *"10 Things I Hate About You."*

"Leap Year," I chime in with another one of my favorite fake relationship movies. And we're off.

Over the next half hour, we discuss the rules of fake dating and the inevitable outcomes. It's funny how different I feel about the trope, now that I'm in it. I want to scream at my cohosts.

It's all fun and games until someone's heart gets broken!

"Obviously, they're going to fall in love," Chelsea says, "so why do the main characters always act so surprised about it? They should know what they are signing up for."

It's called denial, Chelsea.

"Yeah, and why do they always have to have such dramatic changes of heart?" Jackson points out. "It's like a one-eighty every time. Never would they ever, and then, whoops! Whiplash!"

"Well, maybe it's because the pretending gets so confusing! It shakes everything up," I say.

Hopefully not too defensively, I backtrack a bit. "I mean, I *imagine* it doesn't start out that way, but maybe it's like method acting, when actors get overly invested in their roles and lose their sense of self."

"I don't buy it. Relationships are always confusing," Jackson says. "When it's a faked relationship, the boundaries are clearer. There should be less room for confusion."

"But that's just the thing with this trope," I argue. "The behavioral boundaries are crystal clear, but the emotional ones aren't. It creates a kind of cognitive dissonance."

"I'm trying to decide whether there is anything sexy about cognitive dissonance," Alexis says. "Give me a minute. Nope, not sexy."

"Cognitive dissonance also leads to awkwardness," I say. "So much opportunity for humor there. Like when the characters accidentally bump into each other when one of them is getting out of the shower."

I freeze, realizing what I've just said, mentally replaying the naked, post-shower collision with Blaze. It's a good thing that we've all turned away from our screens. Nobody can see my expression. Alexis continues the conversation.

"OMG, yes! Okay, you pulled it out with that one. I love a good naked mishap. And, of course, you have to have that moment where they kiss and it's so good. Like, shockingly good," Alexis adds.

Check and check. That's two for two.

"I like it when people are super mismatched in a fake relationship," Chelsea says. "That's always a lot of fun. Like in *Pretty Woman*."

"Yeah, but that makes it far less believable when they finally get together," Alexis argues. "They need to have something in common, like it was there all along, but they just took a minute to zero in and focus on it."

"I couldn't pull it off." Chelsea laughs. "I'm the worst actress."

"What if it was someone you already had a huge crush on?" I ask.

"Like Dean?" Jackson teases his sister.

"Shut up, Jackson." Chelsea shushes him. "You better edit that out. He might listen to the podcast."

"Who's Dean?" I ask.

"He was my BFF in high school. Football player but really into theater, and you guys all know what a theater nerd my sister is," Jackson explains. "She had such a crush on him! He's a prop guy now. Art directs the Titanium Man films, actually."

"Wow," Alexis says. "Can I get an intro to Rafe Barzilay?"

"I think Titanium Man is seeing someone new, Alexis," I mention, regretting the slip instantly.

"Oh, that's right, Emily! Whose girlfriend did Titanium Man steal? I know I saw something on TMZ." She takes the bait. Of course she does.

"Never mind. Tell me more about Dean, Chelsea?" I jump in, throwing Chelsea under the bus. Sorry, Chels.

"Ancient history. Dean is off the menu." Chelsea sighs. "He's got a beautiful girlfriend and a very successful career."

"You had it bad. Remember that time you asked him to take you to senior prom? When you were still a freshman?"

"Seriously Jackson? I was fourteen! Shall we discuss your high school obsession with Sarah Michelle Gellar and Alyssa Milano? The *poster* wall? At least I had a crush on a real person!"

"Sarah and Alyssa are real people," Jackson says defensively.

"I'm sure they were very real. In your dreams." Chelsea smirks.

"I had a fantasy about having a fake relationship with Mark Wahlberg," Alexis confesses.

"With Marky Mark? No way!" Jackson laughs. "Why him?"

"It was when I started working out a lot. He was so super fit, and he'd done this old workout video, and I was like, what if he asked me to be his pretend girlfriend just to prove he wasn't sizeist, and then he helped me get into really great shape, only to decide he was more into me when I was thicker. He fed me a lot of milkshakes in this fantasy."

"That is oddly specific," Jackson says.

We wrap up with a poll about the long-term viability of fake relationships, and then Jackson stops the recording.

"Well, guys," he says, "that was a little disappointing. I can't believe you're holding out on us, Emily Romano."

"It's complicated," I say. And then I remember what Blaze said about using 'it's complicated' as a cop-out. I sigh. "I signed an NDA."

"Yeah, but there's a best friend clause, right?" Alexis argues. "Off the record? Or do you need me to sign an NDA too?"

"How about I tell you everything when I get home next week?" I offer. It feels so far away—the other side of a rope bridge. Anything could happen. A million things could change between here and there. And I already have so many things I want to discuss with her, I'm dying.

"You're the worst," Alexis complains.

"I love you too," I answer, "but I have to go. I'm meeting up with Isla Fairfax to do some sightseeing."

"I can't believe you met Isla Fairfax." Jackson snaps back to attention. "We're talking about the same Isla Fairfax who writes the *Chance Encounters* blog and the Mystic Matchmaker series that we talked about a few months ago, right?"

"Yes! She lives here. I met her yesterday at a book signing!" I exclaim.

"Well, that's how you can make it up to us," Jackson suggests. "Get her on the show. I'm dying to expose her asinine theories about magical matchmaking."

"With an offer like that, how could she refuse?" I snort.

"I love her books and her blog," Chelsea interjects. "I'd love a signed copy of something if you can get me one."

"I already did." I hold up a copy of Isla's book and a few stickers. "Plus, swag!"

"That is going on my water bottle for sure!" Chelsea enthuses.

"So, you'll ask her?" Jackson asks. "What's she like anyway? Her picture isn't in her books. I'm picturing a little old lady who collects cats."

"She's our age," I say. "Can't say about the cats."

The minute we close the chat, Alexis texts me.

> You're really not going to tell me, your oldest friend, any more about what's going on with you and Blaze?

> Early days, nothing to tell!

> Bullshit. You are dating THE Love Doc himself. Something isn't quite right here. Now I'm worried about you.

> Everything is fine! I just don't want to talk about it yet.

Ugh! I do want to talk about it. Desperately. I want to talk about how confused I am every time Blaze kisses me. I want to explore how even though I know it's all for show, it doesn't make me want him less.

It makes me savor each and every performance and rack my brains for an excuse for an encore. And I'd like to talk about how dangerous my feelings feel. Just when I'd finally figured everything out. Just when I was finally feeling like I was out of my funk and back on my feet.

> This doesn't have anything to do with Kent,
> does it?

> Kent who?

I insert the laughing face and poop emoji.

> Seriously, don't worry. I'll leave you with this.
> Blaze is an amazing kisser.

> Tease!

My phone chirps to let me know I've got another message coming in, and I see it's a notification from Kent. As if we've conjured him by typing out his name. Maybe the twins came early. Maybe he's checking up on me. Either way, I don't want to read it. But it could have something to do with the assignment.

Warily, I switch over to the message from Kent.

> What the hell, Em. Anyone ever told you not
> to shit where you eat?

The irony.

> Hello, Pot. Checking in on the kettle?

Seriously, what are you doing? I am counting
on you. You better not screw this up. If I had
known you were going to sleep with Blaze
Smith, I would never have sent you. Steff
must be having a cow.

She's delightful. Thanks for the heads-up.

I wonder how far back he and Steff go. He did say that she owed him. Had she been another one of his "work trip" conquests? The thought of Kent hooking up with Steff makes me feel gaggy. I change the subject.

How are the buns?

Still in the oven. Are you trying to get back at
me? You don't want it getting out that you
bed your assignments, do you?

His thinly veiled threat makes me feel sick, but then I remember what a master manipulator Kent is and why I'm actually here.

You don't want it getting out that you sent
someone else to do your job, do you?

Get me the material ASAP. You look good,
Em. Even though you've put on a few
pounds.

I throw my phone at the couch.

———

Isla meets me on the plaza outside the Pantheon. It's pouring outside. We follow the shelter-seeking crowds inside, admiring the ancient edifice in silence, lest the docents shush us. It's obvious we're both dying to chat, and the rain seems unrelenting. We decide to ditch our plans to see the Colosseum in favor of grabbing a late lunch in one of the nearby cozy cafés.

"I'm a terrible tourist." I peel off my damp jacket and hang it on a hook beside our booth. "How can someone come to Rome and not visit the Colosseum? I'm worried my visa will be revoked."

"Don't be silly! There's no law you have to see anything in particular, or in any particular order. The Colosseum has been there for nearly two thousand years. I don't think it's going anywhere. Plus, ultimately, it's just a stadium, right? Are you really that into sports?"

"I'm probably more of a foodie than a sports fanatic," I confess.

"Well then, this is a much better venue on a day like today." Isla waves her hand as if presenting the café. Patterned tiles on the floor are punctuated with the occasional mismatch, due to repairs. The walls are covered with framed photos, many of them signed by celebrities. Still more signed by people I don't recognize. There's a pleasant buzz from the patrons sitting in mismatched, wooden chairs. It's warm inside, and everything smells like delicious bread and herbs. Isla insists on sharing the oversize slice of focaccia she's ordered. It arrives warm and smelling of earthy rosemary. We dip it into spicy olive oil, and quickly order a cheese plate to go with it.

"So, what is Blaze up to today?" Isla asks.

"He's taping something," I say.

"Oh, right! With that obnoxious Marco bloke, no?"

I nod and sip my cappuccino.

"What a wanker," Isla says. "You're lucky you left when you did. He showed up like he was God's gift to chick lit. Tried to mansplain to me how to sell books."

"Did he?" I ask, genuinely curious. "What was his advice?"

"Shockingly, his number one piece of advice for making your romance novel a bestseller was to have a 'hot, sexy cover.' He proceeded to rip off his shirt immediately after giving this advice, and I'm afraid I didn't stick around for the rest."

"I feel so sorry for the other author," I say. "Did she leave as well?"

"Oh, God no. Her books were selling like hotcakes."

"More like beefcakes." I giggle.

Isla covers her face. "Totally! It's embarrassing. But not as embarrassing as the fact that I actually bought one." She hides her face with her hands and laughs with me.

"Blaze seems lovely." Isla sips her tea. "I would have expected him to be a bit of a wanker as well, but I must say, I was pleasantly surprised. And he's clearly smitten with you."

"He's certainly full of surprises." I attempt an enigmatic smile.

"Big plans for the weekend?" Isla asks.

"Not really." I shrug. "I know Blaze is looking forward to a little downtime."

"Perfect! I have some cozy holiday suggestions for you and Blaze to consider right here," she says, waving a sheet of paper.

I look over her handwritten list.

Panettone at Roscoli
Christmas market in Piazza Navona
Christmas tree in Piazza Venezia
Christmas lights on Via Condotti and Via del Corso
Nativity scene in St Peter's Square
Lights on Via del Pellegrino
Roasted chestnuts, anywhere in the Centro Storico

"Aren't we meant to tour the Vatican and see all the art? What about all the churches and cathedrals?"

"They'll still be here next time. This list is more about living in the moment." Isla taps the sheet of paper. "Trust me, this is what you two need. It's just the right amount of 'worth getting out of bed for, but not too tragic if you stay in bed and miss it.'" She winks.

I fold the list and put it in my bag. "If you say so. But I still would like to do some of the tourist things before I head to Tuscany on Monday."

"Is that where your family is from?"

"It is," I say.

"And are you going to tell me any more about the old letters? I got chills when you were talking about them."

"Would you like to read them?" I ask, reaching into my bag to pull out the precious pouch.

Isla's eyes light up. "Do cats love sardines? Do kids love candy? Do Marco's fans love seeing him rip off his shirt? Of course I want to read them!"

"There's one condition, though." I tilt my head and pause before unzipping the pouch.

"Oh damn. You don't want my firstborn or anything, do you?"

"No." I laugh. "But I do want you to be a guest on the *Lit Lovers'* podcast sometime. Remember I mentioned that your books and blog came up in one of our episodes? I promised my cohost Jackson that I would invite you."

"Oh, that's easy then. Done!" Isla waves her hands like she's granting a wish.

"I should warn you, though." I hesitate before handing her the pouch. "Jackson, the founder of the podcast, isn't so fond of your theories about magical-meet cutes. He's very logical."

"Oh, is he?" Isla's eyes narrow, but she looks absolutely delighted. Her smile says *game on*. "Is he seeing anyone then?"

"No," I say. "I mean, he's perfectly eligible and all that, but he spends all his time working on his algorithm. He's determined to crack the compatibility code."

"His 'algorithm'? Ha! What hogwash!" Isla exclaims.

I smile. "Well, it seems the two of you have that porcine term in common, at least."

"You know what, Emily? I would *love* to be a guest on that podcast—and possibly do you one better. If this Jackson fellow isn't seeing anyone, I would love to have a crack at setting him up and write about it on my blog. Where did you say you live again?"

"You would come to Ephron, Washington?" I ask rather incredulously.

"Well, it's not the seventh level of hell or anything, is it? I do love a good challenge."

I hand over the packet of letters. "No. It's quite lovely, actually. We've got a lot of wineries nearby."

"Perfect." Isla smiles, unzipping the bag. "Can I get a little background before I read?"

I tell my new friend about my family. I tell her about my earliest memories of my grandparents. How my grandfather always stirred brown sugar into my grandmother's tea because he knew exactly how she liked it. I tell her how they always held hands when they sat on the sofa to watch television. And I tell her how it wasn't very long after my grandfather passed that my grandmother joined him.

She asks me about my father next.

It's harder to talk about him. Almost ten months out, but the loss still feels like a fresh wound. I limp through the story about how he once confronted a dance teacher who called me chubby, calling her "Fancy Pants" and making the entire class of ten-year-old girls giggle. Then I remember afresh that he won't be there when I fly home for Christmas. As long as I've been here—and particularly when I've been talking about him—it's been easy to pretend that the house I'll be flying back to isn't quite as empty as the one I'd left behind.

"I have no idea if he even knew about these letters, or about my grandmother's friend Maria," I admit.

"She's the one you're going to visit next week?" Isla asks, turning one of Maria's letters over to examine the postmark.

"Yes," I say. "Her grandson and I have set up a meeting in Pitigliano, where she and my grandmother were raised."

"Oh, you're going to love it there!" Isla claps her hands. "If ever there was a magical village…"

"It looks lovely online," I say.

"Just wait till you go. The photos don't do it justice." She picks up the letter again. "So, I gather your grandmother's friend was happy to hear from you?"

"Yes," I say. "She was so excited to hear from me. She said she was hoping, waiting, all these years to meet me!"

"What a story." Isla holds the letter against her chest and closes her eyes for a moment. "I hope I'm not overstepping any boundaries here, but I'd love to write a post on my blog about your grandparents' letters, Emily."

"Really?" I ask. I'm flattered, but also wary. "Why?"

"It's just such an old-fashioned, romantic story, and I love the way it's still unfolding. I'm sure my readers would also love to follow you on this journey."

"I should probably check with Blaze," I say, picturing Steff, not him. "He might not want me sharing anything that mentions him."

"Oh, I don't have to mention him at all," Isla says. "This isn't his story, it's yours. And I'm sure so many people will relate to it."

"Can I think about it?" I ask.

"Of course!" Isla hands the packet of letters back. "Have a look at my site and mull it over. I'm not the Colosseum, but I'm not going anywhere for the moment either."

———

Blaze texts when I get back to the hotel.

> The segment just wrapped. Grabbing dinner
> with the producers, Steff, and Marco. Don't
> wait up. We can finish the interview
> tomorrow. PS. Got some tips on touring
> Tuscany for you! PPS. Looking forward to
> taking Saturday off.

I change into my pajamas and order room service. I should probably be making the most of my time here, dining out and sightseeing. But it's raining relentlessly, and the thought of doing these things alone has lost its luster. I flip on the television and find a holiday film to watch.

While waiting for room service, I sort through the balls of yarn that Blaze picked out. There are two balls. The first is a rich, red, hand-dyed alpaca. The second one is an incredibly soft cashmere blend in a forest green. I don't have to think for very long. I can already sense what they want to become.

I take out my needles and cast on.

blaze

. . .

"They say you can't go back again, but we still try, don't we? We can't resist traveling over old, familiar routes. When they make us feel good, we call it 'nostalgic' or tradition. When they make us feel like shit, we call it a rut."

— Blaze Smith, *Go Your Own Way*, on Navigating Familiar Territory

IT'S RAINING AGAIN on Friday morning and colder as well. Soup weather. If I was back in the Pacific Northwest, I'd be putting up a pot of chili. But I won't be having chili tonight. We're wrapping up the week of appearances with a recorded "romantic" couples' cooking class with a local pizza chef.

Silly to be feeling homesick in a city as beautiful as Rome, but a part of me wishes I were back in my own bed, back to my own routine. I want to wake up, check the weather, and walk the dog. With all the travel I've been doing for the past few years, a dog has been out of the question. I can't even manage a dog with my schedule. How am I supposed to have a relationship?

The dog, at least, is something I can change. I make a mental note to call some breeders. Or perhaps I'll just go to a shelter when I get home and let fate have its way with me. One way or another, I'm getting a dog this Christmas.

Emily is awake, dressed, and working on her computer when I walk out to the living room. She's sitting at the table, sipping her coffee.

"Guess I'm the one who got smacked with the jet lag stick today," I say, placing a pod in the coffeemaker.

"You must have gotten in really late," Emily replies without looking up. "I fell asleep on the couch watching *Home Alone 3*."

"I noticed." I set my coffee down on the table. "I threw a blanket on you. You didn't look like you were going anywhere."

"I'm assuming it was you who plugged in my phone too. Thanks for that." She glances up at me, clad in an open robe and my boxers, and quickly looks back at her computer screen.

"What are you working on?" I ask, taking a seat.

"I was just filling in some of the background questions," she says. "I mean, we've chatted about a lot of this stuff already." She turns the computer to show me what she's written.

"You don't have to show me," I say. But I'm glad she did.

"This isn't exactly a normal interview situation. Anyway, I can't guarantee what Kent will use in his piece. I'm just collecting the raw material. I was hoping we could finish up today?" Emily closes the laptop and looks at me again, this time keeping her gaze trained on my face.

I'm struck yet again by how naturally beautiful she is. Not pretty in a calculated way. She hasn't got on any makeup at the moment, and her hair is piled on top of her head in a messy bun.

"I like having morning coffee with you. I'm going to miss this," I say.

She blushes. "Does that mean you don't want to finish the questions today?"

"I'm not going to hold you hostage." I sigh. "But I was hoping you'd still stick around through the weekend. My last stop on this blitz is *The Morning Show* on Monday."

"It'll probably take me a day or so to write everything up," Emily says. "But I have no plans until Monday night."

"Is that when you're meeting your grandmother's friend Maria?" I ask.

Emily nods. "It is. I just got off the phone with Francesco, Maria's grandson. He's got a rental property I can stay in Monday night. I'm a little nervous driving to Tuscany and finding the place, but he says it's pretty straightforward."

"I can send my driver," I offer. "Want me to call him?"

"No!" She shakes her head vehemently. "You don't have to do that. I'm an adult. I'm perfectly capable of driving myself."

"You sure?"

"Yes, I'm sure." She stands to make herself another cup of coffee. "Are you headed back home after Monday?"

"That's the plan," I say. "I'm looking forward to the downtime."

"No new book?" she asks tentatively.

"No plans at the moment."

"So, what will you do?"

"I don't know. Spend some time at my own place. Maybe work on my beard?" I rub my chin thoughtfully. "I haven't had time to even think about my New Year's resolutions. Taking it one day at a time."

"Okay. So, what's on tap for today then, other than chatting with me?" Emily asks. "Will you need me for any fake girl-friend public appearances?"

I might be imagining it, but she looks almost hopeful.

"Have you got other plans?" I ask, pretending to be wounded.

"No. You're the only guru I'm following and pretending to sleep with in Rome, at the moment," Emily teases.

"Well, that couples' cooking segment is taping this afternoon," I say. "I was just coming in here to let you know that I got the go-ahead for you to be in it with me. We're going to be a team."

"Steff okayed that?" Emily looks skeptical. "Wasn't she planning on being your partner?"

"Yeah, well, Steff's still doing the segment. Just not with me." I shrug.

"What?" Emily looks surprised, and a bit confused.

"She signed a new client last night—Marco."

"No!" Emily exclaims, then puts a hand over her mouth to hide her laughter. "I'm sorry. It isn't so nice of me to laugh. But Isla told me a little more about how he behaved at the book signing."

I don't know what to say, so I just sigh and shake my head. Her mirth is contagious. I have to bite my cheek to avoid cracking up.

"I suspect the chef is even more thrilled to have him there than me. He was fine with the last-minute addition. And Steff said she wouldn't mind buddying up with Marco for the class."

Considering how she was hanging all over him after a few drinks at dinner, I'm sure that's not all she wouldn't mind doing.

"I should figure out what to wear." Emily ponders.

"It doesn't matter. You look great in everything. You're so beautiful, Emily." I reach out to touch her hair. She freezes. We make eye contact, and I withdraw my hand.

"Sorry," I say.

"For what?" Emily waves away my apology. "It's fine."

"For making you uncomfortable. I'm not apologizing for saying you're beautiful. That's a fact."

"Stop." She shakes her head at me.

"You think I'd fake-date an uggo?" I question.

"Blaze! That's so rude!" She scolds me.

"I'm kidding," I say. "About the uggo part. Not about you being beautiful because you objectively are. But that goes beyond first impressions. There are plenty of beautiful people who are total uggos once you get to know them."

"Like Marco," she says.

"He's definitely an acquired taste," I say, thinking about how Steff has acquired him as her newest client and wondering if that is something I should be worried or grateful about. "He takes some getting used to."

"No thanks. I heard enough from Isla," Emily says. "I have a zero-tolerance policy for narcissists going forward."

"So, you don't think I'm a narcissist any more, then? Do you still think I'm full of shit?"

"Maybe not *entirely*." She reopens her laptop and types something in her notes. Without looking away she says, "There were a few good sections in your book, after all."

My cheeks burn with the effort it takes not to smile. I bite my lip and take a sip of coffee to try to mask my ridiculous delight at her admission. Some of the coffee dribbles onto the robe. It turns out, it is very difficult to drink coffee while suppressing a smile.

"You okay?" Emily asks.

"Never better," I assure her.

"For a second there, you seemed—"

"Don't say it," I warn.

"Eager to please."

"You are not as nice a person as you pretend to be, Emily Romano." I shake my head at her.

"And you are not as slick and polished as you pretend to be, Blaze Smith."

"What? You don't think I am slick? Is not, how you say, the whole package?" I imitate Marco, flapping open my robe and flashing my abs.

Emily throws a ball of green yarn at my face, and I catch it. I see there's a new project laying on the table beside her laptop. She's started making something with the yarn I bought for her. It doesn't look like booties.

"What's that?" I ask.

"You'll see." Her lips twitch as she bites back her own smile. "All in good time."

"Fine, fine. Be that way." I toss the soft yarn absentmindedly between my hands and change the subject. "Tell me how it went with Isla yesterday. You two seemed to hit it off."

"I really liked her!" Emily enthuses. "We didn't end up going to the Colosseum. It was so rainy, we just ducked into a café and got to talking. Which reminds me. She wants to do a blog post about my grandparents' love letters and my search for information about my grandmother on this trip. Would that be okay with you?"

"Of course. Why wouldn't it be?"

"I don't know … because we're here together this week? But she doesn't have to mention you in the post," Emily assures me.

"It's a sweet story," I say. "By all means, she should write it."

"Oh, good. It's a nice way for me to memorialize them. And Isla has agreed to be on the *Lit Lovers'* podcast too. I'll let her know it's a go."

"Why don't you message her while I go get showered and dressed," I suggest.

"I'll be sure to stay out here while you do that," Emily promises.

"That's a pity," I say.

"Them's the rules." She shrugs.

I strip off my coffee-stained robe, leaving it by the sink so I can get the stain out later. I can feel Emily's eyes on me as I stand there, nearly naked.

"Stupid rules," I say.

emily

. . .

"SOME COUPLES MAKE beautiful music together, but tonight, we're going to make a beautiful pizza!" The chef speaks English, but with a heavy Italian accent. This episode of his popular cooking show will be distributed internationally, just before Valentine's Day.

Blaze and I, along with three other "couples," are standing side by side in the brightly lit studio kitchen, awaiting our instructions from the chef. An assistant is circulating, bringing balls of dough to us at our granite-topped workstations.

We are arranged in a semicircle. There's a camera on a boom above us and another one on a dolly track. Steff and Marco are at the other end of the grouping, facing us.

"Very important. Before we start, the chef hat!" the host of the show says. "Every team will get their own colored hats."

An assistant hands two blue chef hats to us, then two red ones to Marco and Steff. The other two couples receive green and yellow. I pull on my blue hat, adjusting the fit with a little help from Blaze.

Across the way, Marco begins to wave his arms and snap his hands for the assistant to come back.

"Scusi! There has been a mistake. This hat is no good. I don't do red. It doesn't match my eyes." Marco points dramatically at his eyeballs and folds his arms across his chest.

"Shh, Marco. This is what I'm here for," Steff speaks up. She hands their hats back to the confused assistant. "I'm sorry, my client didn't approve of this color. He wanted"—she pauses—"what color did you want, Marco?"

"I wanted the blue, *ovviamente (obviously)*!" He petulantly points at our blue hats, and then gestures at his wide-open eyes, batting his lashes furiously to make his point. "Am I not famous for my blue eyes? What is this red?"

I kick Blaze under the table.

"It's not a problem, Marco. Blaze and Emily will trade with us, won't you?" Steff narrows her eyes at me, daring me to object.

"I kind of like the blue on Emily," Blaze says. He struggles to keep a straight face.

"It makes much more sense for your team to wear red, *Blaze*." Steff stomps her foot.

"Here, take them." I pull off my hat and thrust it at the assistant. Blaze shrugs and follows suit.

The chef steps into the spotlight at the center of our grouping and looks up at the overhead camera, speaking passionately.

"Now that we have our hats on, we will knead the dough. I want you to remember to work the dough with love. *Massage* the dough. Squeeze it. Feel it with your fingers. The more love you give the dough, the sweeter she will be."

I try to suppress a snort. "Is he for real? He wants us to make love to the dough?" I whisper to Blaze.

Blaze steps behind me and reaches around me on both sides to knead the dough while embracing me. "Just go with it, Emily. Release your passion," he whispers in my ear. My entire core liquefies, and I have to brace myself against the countertop. Tentatively, I poke the ball and then let my hands sink into the warm, sticky, pliable dough. Blaze places his hands over mine, caressing them momentarily, waiting for me, and then continuing to match my pace as I begin to knead. We fall into a pace together, him pressing into me, both of us pressing into the dough. Him. Dough. Him. Dough.

Oh!

"That's it, very good!" says the host, circulating to watch us. He pauses by our workstation, offering some coaching. "You want to push the dough, gently, gently, not too rough. Push, and push, and push. Yes!" he exclaims. "And then flip her over!"

"Thwack!"

The slapping sound of a big ball of dough being slammed against the counter echoes through the studio as Steff throws down. She is glaring at Blaze and me. Marco flinches and brushes some flour off his skintight, leather pants.

"Okay, Okay." The host heads toward them. "It's true. Some people like it rough. Just make sure you have a safe word."

Steff turns red.

"What is a safe word?" Marco asks. One of the other couples, an older pair, translates for him, and Marco nods slowly, smirking.

Steff punches the dough, still glaring at us. Marco looks from her, to us, to the camera that is pointed at us, and then back at the dough. He takes a deep breath, as if he's come to a decision. Then he whispers something in Steff's ear.

"Can I get some ice water, please?" Steff asks, summoning nobody in particular. She fans herself with a spatula and then commences fanning Marco as he unties the top half of his apron. The fourth couple stop their kneading to gape as Marco slowly strips off his shirt and casts it aside. Both cameras pivot and pan toward him as he reties his apron and positions himself behind Steff. She turns to admire him, licking her lips lasciviously. His eyes dart to the monitors. Upon seeing himself there, he smolders into the camera. Finally, he commences flexing one bicep, then the other, as he lifts up and squeezes the dough.

"Oh, my," vamps the host. "It's getting hot in here!"

"Technically, I'm not even sure that qualifies as kneading," Blaze says.

"Does it matter?" I laugh.

In the end, we don't even use the dough we've kneaded to make our couples' pizza. That dough is scrapped, and the chef's assistants bring us freshly rolled discs of dough, ready to be sauced and finished with our choice of topping.

"This is where it gets tricky, no? Even with a good foundation, things can still go tragically wrong for our pizzas. Any words of advice from Doctor Love?" The host sticks a mic in Blaze's face.

"Well, you're the chef, but I think it helps if a couple has a well-matched taste profile." Blaze winks at me. "And you have to be honest about what you're into. Some couples are into classic toppings, while others are all about the spice."

"Emily, can you tell us how Blaze likes to make his pizza?" The host sticks the mic at me.

I consider my answer before speaking.

"Blaze is very generous with his pizza," I say. "He likes to make sure everyone is well served."

Beneath the table, Blaze pinches me.

"Emily is passionate about her pizza," he says. "So very passionate."

There's a clattering noise as Marco clears a section of their countertop and lifts Steff up to sit on it. He uses his cast-off shirt as a makeshift blindfold and proceeds to feed her tiny spoonfuls of sauce and toppings, basing their choices on the ones that make her moan the most. It's practically pornographic, except there's no nudity.

"We can never unsee that." Blaze shudders as Steff licks truffle sauce off Marco's index finger.

"At least she looks happy," I offer. She may be blindfolded, but she's definitely smiling. I didn't know she had it in her.

"I almost forgot to ask you something really important," Blaze says, as we layer mozzarella, basil, capers, and salami onto our creation.

"What's that?" I ask.

"Where you stand on the whole pineapple on pizza debate."

"Abomination!" I declare.

"Thank God." Blaze breathes a sigh of relief.

———

After we're done taping and have washed up, Blaze checks in with Steff while I go outside to text with Isla.

I'm linking you to a drive with scans and photos of the letters that I don't mind you sharing in the post. Let me know if you need anything else.

This is fantastic! Hey, I just binge listened a
whole season of Lit Lovers. You guys are
hilarious! What are you and Blaze up to?

We just taped a couples' pizza-making
segment for a cooking show. With Marco.
Don't ask.

I pepper my text with pizza and shocked-guy emoji.

When are you leaving Italy?

My flight back is Wednesday. Headed to
Tuscany Monday.

I'm so jealous! Safe travels if I don't see you
before you leave. I'll get this post up
tomorrow and then back to my edits and
housecleaning. Call me if you need anything!
I'll be around. PS. I hate cleaning, so
seriously, call me. Xxoo

Blaze greets me on the street as I finish the text exchange.

"Ready to go?"

"Should we wait for Steff? Does she need a lift?"

"Oh, no. She's off to the spa for the weekend with Marco. They're celebrating his season, wrapping and hammering out the details of their working relationship."

I can't help but look a little dubious about this. "What about your working relationship?" I ask. "Isn't she supposed to be *your* tour manager?"

"I told her to take the weekend off." He rubs his hands together and blows on them. "It got so cold suddenly, didn't it?"

"It's not too bad," I say.

"Well, maybe I should stand closer to you so you can keep me warm," Blaze jokes. He pulls me in front of him and sticks his hands in my pocket.

"I liked making pizza with you," he says, nuzzling against my neck. It feels wonderful.

"There's nobody else here," I say.

"You never know if someone might be watching. Technically, we're in public." Blaze nips at my earlobe. I wish there was a way I could rationalize spending all the rest of our time together in public. Except, the things I really want him to do to me require privacy.

Steff and Marco come out of the studio, holding hands. Marco claps Blaze on the shoulder.

"Ciao, Dottore!"

Steff stares off into the distance. "The valet's here with your car, Marco."

"Have a nice weekend, Steff," Blaze says, attempting to catch her eye. She refuses to look in our direction.

"Oh, she will." Marco winks lustily at us and takes the keys to his Ferrari from the valet.

At the last minute, after she slams her door shut, Steff finally looks back at us. Blaze gives her an encouraging thumbs-up and she rolls her eyes, but it's clear she can hardly contain that smug smile. And then Marco floors it. With a loud roar, they are gone, into the night.

"Do you really think that's a good idea? Steff and Marco?" I ask.

Blaze shrugs. "Who am I to judge? They're both adults. I think she just needs to let off some steam."

"What about his match on that dating show? What if she sees this cooking show episode?"

"Giulia? I don't think she cares. But anyway, the show we just filmed isn't airing till Valentine's Day. I don't think it will be a problem by then." Blaze shrugs.

"Isn't Marco Steff's client now?" I ask, still trying to piece it together.

"Yeah, but it's none of my business," Blaze says. "Or yours." He raises his eyebrows at me in a way that suggests I should drop it, but I don't want to.

"So, it's fine with you because it means you're off the hook now?" I ask. "Steff has a new boy toy?"

He turns to glare at me.

"What exactly are you suggesting, Emily? I have never crossed the line with my manager."

"But she would have been happy to cross the line with you."

Blaze breathes in deeply and shudders.

"You know I'm right." I wrap my arms around myself. How could he *not* know?

"It was that obvious?" he asks.

"Yep." I raise my eyebrows and tilt my head back. "Painfully."

"To everyone but me," he says quietly, "until very recently."

I can't think of anything to say to this. I lean back against the stone wall of the building. Blaze paces back and forth in the alley, his breath leaving steam trails behind him.

"Maybe I really am full of shit," Blaze muses. He digs inside his coat for a beanie. "Our car will be here any minute.

Thanks for being such a great sport about everything today, Emily. I know it's been a lot," he says, pulling the knit hat on.

I open my mouth to object, to tell him that I haven't minded, that I've even enjoyed it. But before I can formulate a way to say the things I so desperately want to say, a car slides quietly to the curb in front of us.

Blaze opens the door for me and speaks first.

"I'm pretty tired, Emily," he says. "I'm just going to crash on the couch when we get back. Why don't you take the bed tonight?"

blaze

. . .

"Roll down the windows. Crank some tunes. Drive in circles. Get lost. Get laid in the back seat."

— Blaze Smith, *Go Your Own Way*, on Sunday Drives

I WAKE up on the couch feeling like I've been in a street fight, and I haven't fared well. But it wasn't a fight. It's just this damn, uncomfortable sofa. Everything hurts. My neck, my back, my shoulders, my groin.

Technically, I can't blame my groin pain on the couch.

Despite these physical discomforts, I'm in a great mood. For the first time in a long time, I have nowhere that I need to be, nothing that I need to do. No carefully rehearsed talking points to go over, no wardrobe checks, no lint rollers. Nothing. Even on my sister's farm, there was always work waiting. Goats to milk. Pens to rake. When was the last time I woke up to an absolute blank slate of a day?

I brew two cups of coffee, going over last night's conversations.

How had I been the last person to realize that Steff had feelings for me? Deep down, I must have known. But I didn't want to deal with it. So, I pushed the thoughts away. I'd liked being her number one priority. I just assumed she was super dedicated to her job. I never considered that she might have been motivated by anything else. Which kind of makes me an asshole. Sleeping on it hasn't helped.

I still don't want to think about it.

"Emily? You awake?" The bedroom door is cracked.

"Come in," she says, her voice still thick with sleep.

"I have coffee," I say.

She's belly down, sleeping star-fished on the bed with the covers kicked off. It's cold out today, but the hotel's ancient heating system must have come on in the night, making the room downright steamy. Her sapphire-blue nightgown skims her curves, covering her beautifully round ass without actually concealing anything. But it's her mask that gives me ideas.

"Mmm. Coffee?" She sniffs, sits up, and pulls off the sleep mask. "You said the magic word."

"Sleep well?" I ask.

"Like a baby. This mattress, and these sheets ..." She stretches and flosses her fingers in the rumpled bedding.

I roll my shoulder and massage it. "You deserved it after two nights on that couch. I haven't been in this much pain since I did goat yoga."

"Oh, my God. I'm so sorry, Blaze. You're taller than me. I shouldn't have let you—"

"Stop," I interrupt her. "I was fine on the couch. But scoot over, would you? I thought maybe we could have coffee and discuss our plans for the rest of the weekend?"

She looks at me warily.

"I'm not going to bite, Emily," I assure her.

Even though I would love to.

Emily sits up and fluffs the pillow beside her before leaning back against the headboard and holding out a hand for one of the mugs of coffee. I don't let her have it. Instead, I set both mugs on the nightstand and jump into the bed beside her, bouncing playfully.

"This IS a good mattress. Very springy." The bed creaks rhythmically, suggestively. I raise an eyebrow at her, and she rolls her eyes.

"You're awfully chipper this morning."

"I've been looking forward to today all week," I tell her. "I didn't even realize how much I needed a day off until I woke up on that bed of nails out there, and I was still overjoyed because there were no texts from Steff and no notes to review."

I bounce some more.

"Okay." She laughs. "What are you planning to do today?"

"It kind of depends on you," I say, looking at her hopefully. "Were you planning on working?"

"I emailed the brief to Kent last night," she says. "But we could go back over my notes today, if you want. I don't think he'll even look at them till Monday."

"No. Absolutely not. What's done is done."

"Okay. So, what do you usually like to do with your downtime? Do you want to stay in and read a book? Watch a movie?" Emily tosses out suggestions.

"Emily, we are in ROME. Up and at 'em!" I energetically bounce on the bed some more, like I've unleashed my inner Tigger. The headboard thumps against the wall.

"Blaze! Cut it out!" she chastises me, but she also can't help but crack a grin at my juvenile antics. "Besides, it's still early. What's your rush?"

I stop, and then resume my bouncing much, much slower. "Oh, we can take it slow. Slow as you want."

Squeak. Pause. Squeak. Pause. Squeak.

Emily groans, and our neighbors pound on the wall, causing us both to giggle like naughty children.

"Scusi!" Emily calls out, banging back on the wall.

"Oops!" I say, wiping a tear from my eye. I hand over her coffee, and we both take sips as we regain our composure.

"So, as far as going out somewhere today, it's definitely not a problem for me. But for you?" She imitates a paparazzi, snapping photos.

"Let me ask, was there anything specific you wanted to do?"

"Isla gave me a list of holiday-related things to do," Emily says. "But I guess I assumed I'd be doing them alone. I'm pretty much out of camera-ready clothing at this point."

"Not a problem." I smile.

"If we head out together, you know we're going to have to be ready to put on a show." Her eyes meet mine, and I feel the lights flicker.

"You don't have to pretend to be the 'Love Doctor's' girlfriend today," I suggest. "I have an alternative plan for you to consider."

"Hold that thought a moment?" Emily gets up to use the restroom.

While she's gone, I lean over and breathe her scent on the pillow. Damn. I'll have no right to miss that scent on my sheets, but I know I'm going to. I sit up quickly, before she gets back.

"Okay, tell me more." Emily hops back into the bed and sits facing me, legs crossed, hands wrapped around her mug.

I reach out and adjust the strap of her nightgown, sliding my finger beneath it and lifting it back up onto her shoulder. I linger there a moment, my finger tracing her collarbone. Her warm skin seems to buzz and vibrate beneath my touch.

"You're done with your work, and you owe me nothing at this point. But I hope you'll consider spending some time with me today anyway."

"I am grateful you didn't call the tour off. I really needed this trip for a lot of reasons," Emily says. "Kent's wife is being induced today, by the way. Good thing he sent me to cover."

Emily seems lost in thought. She's staring out the window. Her shoulders are tense, practically at ear level. I reach out a hand and squeeze her shoulder, and she sighs, turning back toward me. She smiles with her mouth, but it doesn't quite reach her eyes.

"Are you thinking about Kent?" I ask.

"No, I'm thinking about all the doctor appointments I need to make when I get home," she says.

"That sounds like future Emily's problem," I say. "Can present Emily come out to play today?"

"You sound like my friend Alexis," she says.

"Would she be the same friend who suggested a one-night stand?"

Emily smiles and shakes her head. "Yeah, but as you may have figured out by now, I'm not a one-night-stand kind of woman—not in the past, present, or the future."

"But you are a 'kiss a stranger in the airport lounge' kind of woman," I tease.

My pulse quickens as I notice that Emily has a fistful of sheets in her hand. Her breathing is shallow and her lips are parted. She is so close that I could just lean forward and brush my mouth against hers, tracing a trail of kisses down her sternum. The smell of her hair is all over the pillows, distracting me from the plan I came in here to propose.

Screw my big idea. I'd rather take the cup of coffee out of her other hand and lay her back against the pillows.

"There's a reason for the rules, right?" Emily reads my thoughts and whispers.

"Now that you're done with the article, I'm not sure the rules still apply," I say, realizing that we are both leaning in. The gap between us is slowly growing smaller.

"I need to get dressed." Emily turns abruptly and swings her legs over the edge of the bed. She stands and walks to the dresser.

"Wait. Hang on a second," I say. I run my hands through my hair, giving it a tug in an attempt to rid myself of this distracting carnal fog. Perhaps chatting in bed had not been the wisest move.

"I'll be right back. Just hear me out on this."

I head back to the living room closet to fetch the bag of items. They were delivered to the hotel last night. Rory, the producer, had come through.

I peek inside the bag. It's all perfect—plenty of fodder for us.

"What's in there?" Emily asks when I place the bag on the bed.

"Remember how we were both pretending to be someone else at the airport? It was kind of fun, right?"

"I guess." She looks cautious, but curious.

"What if we could both be somebody else for a day? Anyone we want. Nobody in particular. A true day off. Not just from our work, but from ourselves."

I dump the contents on the bed. There's an assortment of wigs, several pairs of sunglasses, and some very unfashionable clothing to choose from. There's also fake facial hair and a stage makeup kit.

Emily busts out laughing.

"I would NOT have pegged you for someone who's into cosplay!"

It's my turn to blush now.

"I'm not!" I exclaim. "I mean, not that there's anything wrong with it. Some of us just need a little more help getting out the door unrecognized."

"Just giving you a hard time. Where the heck did you find all this?" Emily laughs, picking through the pile.

"I asked the producer from the *Pazzi per Amore* show. She called around for me and had some stuff sent over from another production that just wrapped."

Emily bites her lip. "It's too bad we can't step out in period garb. I kind of AM into cosplay. I just dressed up in a regency-era gown for a masquerade last month."

I close my eyes, willing myself not to try and imagine this, or worse, ask for pics.

"I don't know if I got your size right. I guessed. We could probably get more options sent over if you don't see anything."

Emily pulls on a platinum-blonde wig and oversize sunglasses. "I think I can work with this. How do I look? Too *Real Housewife*?"

I pull on a shaggy, brown wig and hold up a stache. "I'm calling this look *The Bavarian Tourist*."

"The track suit jacket would really sell it." Emily nods approvingly. Then she takes off the wig and glasses. "You're serious. You want to go sightseeing in Rome with me, in costume?"

"So much"—I find myself grinning—"I can't think of anything I'd rather do today."

"And you're not afraid of our cover being blown?"

"The paparazzi are not out there looking for a Real House-wife and a German tourist," I say.

"So, you've done this sort of thing before?" She still looks a little dubious.

"No," I admit. "But it always works out for Scooby and the gang, so I figured it's worth a shot."

"Are you sure you want to do this, Blaze? I mean, what if you do get recognized?"

"No press is bad press?" I shrug. "You don't have to do this if you don't want to, Emily."

"Everyone needs a day off from being themselves some-times." She toys with the hair on the wig, then thinks of something. "Can I call you Smitty again today?" Her eyes sparkle.

"That's Herr Schmitty to you."

"Okay, then. Fine. Whatever. I'm in. This is going to be fun!" Emily drops back into the bed and bounces excitedly enough for the headboard to thump against the wall again.

A loud thunk from something hitting the wall next door echoes through the room.

"What do you think that was?" Emily asks.

"I don't know? Maybe they threw a shoe?"

Emily responds by bouncing up and down on the bed some more, pretending to moan and calling out, "Herr Schmitty, OH, Herr Schmitty!"

"What are you doing?" I ask her, wide-eyed.

"Just seeing if we can get them to throw the other shoe." She winks.

emily

. . .

"QUICK! The coast is clear. Nobody's in the hallway right now." Blaze peeks out the door and waves for me to follow.

I'm wearing a platinum-colored, bob-style wig, oversize sunglasses, and a short, furry coat, paired with my own jeans and boots. The costume "kit" included blingy, fake jewels, which I have layered on generously. I'm also sporting a fair amount of contouring and highlighting over an orange-toned foundation and a fatter upper lip, thanks to the magic of makeup.

I look ridiculous. But it's also kind of awesome.

Blaze is wearing a fake beer belly under an oversize, nylon track suit jacket. He's chosen a shaggy wig, fake sideburns, and a pair of aviator-style sunglasses that read somewhere between rap star and math teacher.

"Ready to do this?" Blaze offers me his arm as we step into the elevator.

We snap ridiculous selfies all the way down to the lobby, making duck lips and peace signs in the mirrored elevator interior. We did such a good job. There's no way anyone would recognize us. Not in a million years.

The hotel staff looks suspiciously at us as we hustle through the lobby. "Scusi, Signor? Signora? Are you lost? Can I help you with something?" The concierge follows us.

Blaze looks at him solemnly and wags a finger.

"No thanks, hon. We were just leavin'," I say, adopting a fake Texan accent. Cheekily, I blow a kiss.

"I think he thinks we just pulled a heist," I whisper, aware of the eyes still on us as we head toward the door. We picked the wrong disguises if we were hoping to blend in at this hotel.

Blaze quirks a smile. "Looks like we're getting away with it."

The doorman holds the door for us, and then we are out of the building on the cobbled street and crossing the plaza.

We stroll right past a group of paparazzi clustered under a tree near the Spanish Steps. Blaze waves enthusiastically at one of them, a man who is sitting on a low wall, smoking a cigarette. He looks at Blaze with a mix of pity and disgust, then pointedly checks me out.

"I think we fooled them!" I say, once we're past the group. "Nobody recognized you."

"That one dude seemed much more interested in you than me, Blondie." Blaze gestures toward the paparazzo who's already back on the job, monitoring the hotel door for celebrity sightings.

"His loss!" I hook arms with Blaze as we head down the Spanish Steps.

"Where to first?" he asks.

"I have a list from Isla," I say, reaching into my pocket for the slip of paper. "She recommended some things to do and see."

"Give it here," Blaze says, holding out a hand. He reads through her suggestions.

"So, we've got the Christmas markets, some bakeries where she has suggested we go to try the panettone and pane d'ouro, assorted nativity scenes, ice skating and, of course, the holiday lights. We don't have to go far for that." Blaze sweeps his hand across the plaza, where every cross street is festooned with swags.

"We don't have to do everything on the list," I say. "I think I'm okay with shopping and wandering for a bit, actually."

"Well, then, I think we're in the right place. Via Condotti, Via del Babuino, or Via del Corso? Pick your poison."

The pedestrian shopping streets splayed out below us are already crowded with holiday shoppers eager to score deals on designer goods. The crinkling sound of tissue paper and multiple bags being shifted on shoppers' arms is like a collective sigh. There's an expectant atmosphere, ripe with newness and the emotion of gifts about to be given. I smell delicious things on the breeze as well. Coffee, roast chestnuts, cinnamon, and mulled wine.

"I don't even have a tree," Blaze is saying. "I don't think I'll have time to get one. How about you?"

"Oh, I have one," I say. "I just haven't trimmed it yet. My friends are going to help me when I get home. Trimming the tree was always a dad and me thing."

"Tell me about it." Blaze squeezes my hand, pulling me to sit on the steps for a moment.

"We chose new ornaments every year and hung them in chronological order. We'd start with the ones my grandparents gave him for his first tree. When they were alive, we all did it together, taking turns to select an ornament and find the perfect spot."

"That sounds amazing," Blaze says. "My mom had a few special ornaments, but mostly, we bought new ones every year."

"Ours were always a combination of store-bought and hand-made. We'd hang the newest ones last and say why we chose them. They always represented places we'd traveled to that year, current trends, and obsessions. We never had a tree like you see in the movies, with single-color themes and matching bows. Our tree was perfect, though. Always."

"It sounds beautiful." Blaze wraps his arm around me. "I'm so glad your friends are helping you trim it this year. They sound like great friends."

I take a quick, sharp breath of the cold, clear air to ward off the tears that are gathering, willing the grief squall to pass without damaging my makeup efforts. Thanks to my over-size, black sunglasses, Blaze doesn't seem to notice. I jump up to my feet.

"Daylight's burning. Let's keep moving." I know if I sit for another minute, my grief will catch up with me, and I don't want to ruin this day or my carefully applied makeup. I hold out a hand to help Blaze up. He takes it and holds on, lacing his fingers with mine. We swing our arms together as we continue to walk.

"How did the podcast taping go on Wednesday? I forgot to ask. Were you able to record the episode?" Blaze asks.

"Yes, too bad you missed it."

"Oh, really? Why?" he asks. We've stopped to watch tourists filling their water bottles by the boat fountain at the foot of the Spanish Steps. Holiday music snippets thread through the low hum of multilingual chatter on the plaza. I turn back toward Blaze.

"You would have appreciated that the trope of the week was fake relationships." I bite my lip.

"You're kidding!" Blaze turns to me, eyes wide. "Your friends don't know, do they? Do you think they suspect anything?"

I shake my head. "No."

"What have you told them about us?" I can see the mischief sparking in his eyes as he asks.

"I've told them as much as nothing." I shrug. "I mean, I did sign an NDA, and I'm pretty sure Steff would have no problem calling in a few favors to get my body tossed in the Tiber if I didn't honor it."

"So how do your friends even know we're together, then?" he asks.

Now I take off the sunglasses to give him the full WTF look.

"Are you honestly that out of touch? One: They know I'm here with you. Two: My friend Alexis set up a Google alert and has been following your social feeds. Three: She saw the selfie that *you* posted of us, but even if she hadn't seen that photo in your feed, we've been all over the tabloids."

Blaze stops in his tracks and frowns. "Oh, God. I'm a dumbass. Why didn't I think about all of that? This must be awkward for you, not being able to tell the truth."

"I'm okay." I shrug. "We made it through the week. We're almost in the clear now. Just have to hang on till Monday."

And then what?

We still haven't discussed our plan for the breakup. Ending the deception should be a relief. But thinking about it makes me feel nauseous.

"I'm sorry I didn't plan better." Blaze squeezes my hand. "At least you don't have to lie to them for much longer." His hand is warm, and I don't want him to let mine go. He reads my mind, blowing on my fingers and pulling me closer.

"Let's get you some gloves today before you freeze." He warms my hand with his breath, blowing on it. His lips are so close, they are almost brushing against my fingers.

"What about you?" I ask. "What have you told your friends and family about me?" I pretend to be fascinated by a jewelry display in a shop window. Like I couldn't care less what he's told his family about me. *If* he's told them anything.

Blaze looks up at the clouds, watching the sky for a bit before he answers.

"I haven't told my family anything, actually."

I'm surprised at how hurt I feel. I shouldn't feel gutted about this. It's not like I really matter to him. I'm just passing through his life. Like the clouds. A small part of the ever-changing scenery.

"What about the photos?" I ask. "The tabloids?"

"My mom and my sister don't read them," Blaze says. "My sister lives pretty much off the grid, raising goats in the mountains. And my mom is in a memory care facility. Even if she did see the photos, she wouldn't remember them the next day. She'd like you, though. She knits too."

"I'm so sorry, Blaze." I'm not hurt anymore. Instead, my heart hurts for him. "How about your dad?" I ask. "Is he in the picture?"

"Out of the picture since I was ten," Blaze answers. "The one blessing about my mom's disease is that she only seems to remember the good parts of their relationship."

"Not as nice for you, though?" I guess.

"Actually, in a weird way, it *is* nice." Blaze smiles wistfully. "I always had such a hard time understanding what she saw in him and why she put up with him as long as she did. But when she talks about him now, there's no bitterness or resentment, and I can picture where they started, not just where their relationship went."

I consider this for a bit.

"I wish I could see my mom that way. I have no idea why she ended up with my dad. They had nothing in common and wanted totally different things in life, and ultimately they made each other miserable. Yet, here I am."

"Maybe they found each other irresistible because that was what had to happen to make you."

"Gross," I say. "Don't make me think about my parents like that."

"Don't tell me you're not a romantic. You've been walking around Italy with your grandparents' letters?"

It's so nice just being out with him, lost in a crowd. I'm in no rush to do any actual shopping.

"There's just one part of the story I don't understand." Blaze wrinkles his brow. "How did your grandfather know the people living in a particular house in that village had the same last name as him? And isn't Romano a really common name, kind of like Smith? How many doors was he knocking on?" Blaze asks.

"I don't know," I say. I'm almost embarrassed to admit that I hadn't considered any of that. "Maybe these are questions I should ask my grandmother's friend Maria."

We reach a store with a crowd outside. The sign in the window simply reads "The Christmas Store."

From the look of the place, it appears to operate year-round, offering a selection of Italian-made ornaments and holiday decor. Everything from handblown glass balls to campy, folkloric holiday characters. Like a belle being presented at the ball, the store is having a moment. A long line of shoppers is waiting for their chance to go inside and select holiday-related souvenirs. We pause to stare into the lavishly decorated windows. But I'm no longer looking at the unique items in the display. Instead, I'm gawping at our ridiculous reflection. Somewhere between the Spanish Steps and here, I forgot about our disguises.

In the light of day and crush of the crowds, we are both drooping. A tuft of my brown hair has sprung free from beneath my wig. It's poking out like a rat tail, hanging down just behind my left ear. Blaze's faux paunch, meanwhile, has taken a right turn without him. It's hanging over his hip.

"Herr Schmitty, you're a little off center." I step closer and wrap my arms around him, giving the faux gut a nudge.

Blaze pulls me closer, wriggling against me to straighten himself out. The faux belly is a ridiculous lump between us.

"You smell so delicious, you are making me quite hungry, Liebchen," Blaze says, nuzzling my neck with his nose, and then his lips. And his tongue. Oh, God. His tongue.

"You know you don't have to do that." I moan. "Nobody is watching. And even if they were, nobody knows who we really are."

"That makes me want to do it even more." Blaze places a hand behind my neck and stares into my eyes. His thumb strokes tiny circles beneath my ear that send my desire spiraling out of control.

"We had a deal," I say.

"No, *we* didn't. Blaze and Emily had a deal." His eyes lock on to mine. There's no mistaking the hunger there. And the question. "We aren't those people today."

"So, who are we, then?" I ask breathlessly.

"You can be whoever you want to be," Blaze says. "And I'll be whoever you want me to be."

"Herr Schmitty. You *are* eager to please."

"And you are quite passionate, Frau Schmitty."

The word 'Frau' hits me like the klieg lights coming on in the auditorium at the end of a junior high school dance. Like a bucket of ice water. I can't help it. I crack up. And once I start laughing, I can't stop.

"You know what, Blaze? There is nothing sexy about the word Frau. I'm sorry. I can't." I bite my lip gasping, wiping a tear and trying not to laugh.

"What about 'Herr'? Herr is not exactly a sexy word either. It's like a cross between hair and herring." Blaze starts to shake with laughter. "Also, this belly has got to go." He bends forward, reaches under his shirt, pulls the faux stomach out, and slings it over his shoulder.

An older woman stops to gaze at us, horrified, and makes the sign of the devil before continuing on.

"Can I tell you a secret?" I ask.

"What?"

"I already did all my holiday shopping. The gifts are sitting in my house, in the hall closet."

"I don't need to do any shopping either," Blaze says.

Blaze takes my hand, leading me into the doorway of a closed shop. Once there, he tips my chin up and kisses me properly, with tongue. He tastes like cinnamon and vanilla. When he bites my lower lip, I feel my pulse throb and quicken in my core. His stubble feels scratchy against my face. I hold a finger to the cleft in his chin, and then I kiss him there, poking my tongue out to taste him. I know I shouldn't be doing this. But I don't have the willpower to stop anymore.

"It's really not fair how beautiful you are," I complain.

"I suspect that's just me basking in your light," he says. "I'm dying to see you Emily—all of you."

"What exactly are we doing here?" I ask. Desire and confusion are making everything murky for me. "Are we still playacting?"

"No, Emily, I don't think we are."

blaze

. . .

"Are we there yet?" Some people have to ask this question before you even pull out of the driveway. Some will refer to a map, counting down the miles till you get there. Sometimes you get there fast, and sometimes you miss the boat."

— Blaze Smith, *Go Your Own Way*, on Getting Physical

WE HUSTLE on our walk back to the hotel room. The Spanish Steps seem to have multiplied. Were there really that many steps before? We don't speak as we climb. Now that we've set our course, there is nothing but breathless anticipation.

The paparazzi don't even look up as we slip past them again. I want to laugh. I take Emily's hand and revel in the electric buzz that's traveling between us. It's like a drug. We take turns stealing furtive glances at each other as we make a beeline for the hotel's glassy entrance.

Does the doorman hold the doors, or did they open automatically? It doesn't register. Only the obstacles do. We have to step around a line of people at the desk waiting to be helped. Someone from the housekeeping team is mopping the floor near the breakfast room and we have to detour, taking a wide path around the fountain to avoid the still-wet marble floors. Every extra step that slows us down feels like a cosmic cockblock.

We duck into the elevator and wait a millennium for the doors to close. By the time they do, we have both ossified in place, staring straight ahead and hoping for a miracle lightning strike to crank up the juice on this snail cab. I sincerely regret booking the penthouse.

"I'm dying to kiss you again." I'm looking at her in the mirror because I know if I turn to face her, I won't be able to resist. The mirror is safer. The weirdest thing is, I don't see the wig in the mirror, or the makeup, or the crazy outfit. I just see the mosaic of colors in her eyes. The single curl spiraling out from beneath her costume, like the irrepressible tendril of a tenacious vine. I hold my breath.

"I want you too." Emily holds my gaze. "But maybe without all of this." Still watching in the mirror, she pulls off the wig, shaking her hair free.

I peel off my sideburns and unzip the track jacket.

"The next time I kiss you, Emily Romano, it's going to be us. Just us. No costumes. No tabloids. No secrets and no lies."

Her goose bumps travel like a wave across her body and onto mine, as contagious as a yawn, but far more thrilling.

Finally, the elevator jerks to a halt on our floor. I've already got the keycard in my hand.

Emily touches the iron plaque with our room number that's mounted on the door, and so do I, though I'm not even sure why. It feels like that moment when you slide into home base. You can quit running. You're safe.

"I'm going to take a shower," Emily says, "and get all this makeup off."

"Take your time," I say. "I'm going to wash up and change, and then I need to check in with the front desk about something. I'll probably be back before you're out, but just in case, please don't go anywhere?"

"Okay," she says, slowly stepping backward toward the bedroom, turning at the last possible moment.

I head to the second bathroom and shower quickly, scraping off the rest of the faux facial hair. Then I throw on a hoodie with my favorite jeans that I flew here in. It feels so good to be myself again, until I hear other people in the hallway. I yank the hood up and keep my head down, trying to avoid recognition until I'm standing in front of the concierge's desk.

It's the same man we slipped by unrecognized earlier. But he sees me now.

"Mr. Smith! How may I help you? Do you need an umbrella? The weather is not supposed to improve for the next day or so."

"Well, then, it's a good thing I'm not planning on going anywhere," I say. "I do have a special request, though."

I unfold several bills and hand them to him. "It involves a lot of gelato. I'm assuming you'll know the best place to get some."

———

The shower is still running when I get back to the suite. I'm so tempted to strip and slip into it with her. Instead, I take a seat in one of the bedroom chairs and wait till I hear the water stop.

"I'm back," I call out.

"I didn't even know you were gone," Emily calls back.

"Has the Polyjuice worn off? Are you back to yourself again?" I stand up and lean against the bathroom door.

"Can you hand me my robe?" Emily asks. "It's on the chair." I pick up the silky robe and pass it through a crack in the door.

"Emily," I say.

"Yes, Blaze?"

"What was your favorite book as a kid?"

"Anything by Roald Dahl," she says, opening the door and stepping out in her robe, hair wrapped in a towel. "And Eloise, of course. Come to think of it, that might be part of why this whole arrangement seemed so appealing. You're catering to my hotel brat fantasies."

She flops into a chair, looking relaxed and fresh-faced and ten times more beautiful without the makeup.

"You don't seem like the spoiled brat type to me," I say, sizing her up. "I haven't heard you complain once about the thread count on the sheets."

"Those sheets have a higher thread count than the cumulative thread count of all the sheets in my linen cupboard."

"And you haven't complained about the room temperature."

"It is a bit steamy in here. Perhaps we should crack a window?" She gestures to the windows, which are fogged. "Oh, wow! It's really coming down now, isn't it? I'm glad we didn't get stuck in that."

"We made the right choice coming back," I agree, watching Emily struggle a bit with the window. It won't budge.

"I think it opens from the top," I say. "But we don't have to open it. We could just take off our clothes instead."

She sucks in a breath.

"Blaze," she drawls.

"Emily," I growl. "I love how you say my name, Emily. Like a slow burn. But I want to make you shout it."

"Are we really doing this?" she asks, glancing toward the perfectly made bed. Too neat. Too orderly.

I want to yank off the coverlet and send the pillows flying. "I sure hope so," I say, stepping closer. "But only if you want to."

"And our deal?"

"I promised I wouldn't try to seduce you while you were still working on the background for that article."

"I haven't slept with anyone in a long time," Emily admits.

"Okay." I nod. "Neither have I."

"Really?" She looks at me suspiciously. "I find that hard to believe."

"Why does everyone assume I'm a man whore?"

"Because you're famous, and you're great at telling women what they want to hear, and Christ, just look at you." Emily pauses in front of me, running a fingertip down my jawline, over my stubble to my chin. "You could have any woman you want."

"The only woman I want right now is *you*."

"But why?" she asks. "Because I told you that you were full of shit? Or is this just some kind of ego play because I said I wouldn't sleep with you at the airport?"

I can hear the frustration in her voice. She needs to hear the answer. She isn't just fishing for a compliment.

"Is that really what you think of me? You think I'm that brand of narcissist?"

"No." She plops into a chair. "I actually don't. I don't think you're like that at all. But I'm having a hard time understanding what you see in *me*. I'm just a normal girl. I don't have huge career goals, other than being able to pay the bills, and hopefully, not hate what I do. And other than that, I just want to be a mom. I'm not a starfucker, Blaze."

"No, you're not. But I think it's fair to say I'm a bit of a fucked-up star."

"You're totally out of my league."

"No, I'm not. You're perfect, Emily. I love that you had no idea who I was when I kissed you in the lounge. And you still kissed me back. I've never been happier to see anyone else seated next to me on a long-haul flight."

"Smitty was an excellent kisser." Emily sighs. "I kinda miss that beard."

"I can offer you this stubble." I move to kneel in front of her and present my chin.

"I like this face, too, though. I'm not sure I could give it up now that I've seen what was under all that facial hair." Emily touches my cheek. She leans back to look at me.

"You really don't know how good-looking you are, do you?" she says.

"Oh, please. I'm no Titanium Man." I smile wryly. "People think I'm attractive because I'm a celebrity. It's not the other way around."

"No, Blaze, you are objectively hot," Emily insists. "You already know I'm not a starfucker, so how else would you explain the effect you're having on me?"

She places my hand on her chest, and I can feel how hard, how fast her heart is beating. I can also see the outline of her erect nipples through the silk robe.

I pull her hand to my chest, where my heart is also beating like a wild drum, counting down the hours, the minutes, the seconds till it can be set free. Emily glances down. But it's not my heart she's looking at. My arousal is obvious, and my need is suddenly more overwhelming than even I am comfortable with. I need a moment.

"Can I get you a drink?" I ask.

"Okay," Emily says. Her eyes are all pupil. "That would be nice, actually. I'm a little nervous. I've never done anything like this before—slept with a stranger."

"We aren't exactly strangers anymore, are we?" I pop the cork on some champagne and pour it into two flutes. "To exploring together."

"And being real," Emily adds. "Or should that have been 'being authentic?' I'm not up on the self-help lingo."

"You don't have to pretend to be anything you're not with me, Emily. There's nobody else here. It's only us."

We clink glasses, and I take a sip. Emily drains her glass.

"Emily? I want to kiss you now. But before I do, you have to promise you'll tell me what *you* want. Tell me what you like. There's no need to worry about what I think because the thing I want the most right now is to please you. Right here, right now, there's only you and me."

"You know, I could be into some really weird shit?" Emily raises a brow.

"Are you into anything unusual?" I ask, trying to remain calm.

"Aside from addressing each other as Frau and Herr Schmitty?" she jokes.

I notice her hands are shaking a little. And the humor is surely a ploy to deal with her nerves. I get it. I haven't felt this vulnerable in a long time. Possibly ever.

I lay my hands on hers, a little surprised to see mine are shaking as well.

"I'm making an effort not to hide anything from you, Emily. So, I'm going to be completely honest. You've been making me crazy since SeaTac. I keep imagining all the things I want to do to you. And that mouth of yours. The only times I wasn't pretending was when we weren't alone, and all I've really wanted was this."

"We're alone now," Emily says.

"No more pretending."

We lock eyes, and something shifts as it becomes crystal clear how much we both want this.

She leans forward, speaking quietly but with confidence and determination. She seems sure of what she's about to say.

"I want you to tease me, Blaze," she says. "I want you to tease me until I can't take it anymore. But first, I want you to take off your shirt."

My hoodie is halfway over my head when I ask her, "How will I know when you can't take it anymore, Emily?"

"Because it will be the only time you'll ever hear me beg," she says, untying her robe and allowing it to fall off one shoulder. "Now, kiss me, please."

The robe continues to slide down her arm, revealing one juicy, round breast. Her nipple is rosy and pebbled and I am mesmerized, unable to resist. I can feel the texture of her skin on my lips even before I touch and taste her.

She runs her fingers through my hair, dragging my head back to look up at her. "This wasn't exactly what I meant." She moans.

"I know," I say, biting her gently and flicking my tongue. "But you were teasing me with this, and I intend to do the same."

She closes her eyes as I slide her robe entirely off her shoulders.

"I'm going to kiss the other one now. And then I'm going to kiss you everywhere else, Emily. But not necessarily where you ask. And I'm going to keep kissing you all over until you beg me to do something else, okay?"

"Okay." She nods.

And then all I can think about is how I'd like to make driving Emily Romano crazy my new, full-time profession.

emily

. . .

THERE'S a knock on the door. Somewhere off in the distance, there is knocking. I'm aware of it like I'm aware of things that happen off camera in my dreams. The exquisite sensations that I am currently experiencing seem far more compelling. If we just ignore the knocking, surely it will go away.

But Blaze doesn't ignore the knocking. He kisses my inner thigh before pushing himself up to a standing position and pulling on a robe. He reaches down to grab my robe from the floor and tosses it at me.

"Here," he says. His eyes drink me in, lingering in all the places he has recently kissed, or licked. "You might want to put this on before I let them in."

"If we ignore them, won't they go away?" I ask hopefully.

"It'll just be a minute." Blaze kisses me on the mouth and heads to the living room of the suite. Curious to see what could be so important, I pull on my robe and stand to follow him.

Room Service? He stopped doing that to answer the door for room service?

It's the same slight, elderly waiter who has brought my dinner every night that I've stayed in to work this week. But he's not serving us dinner, I don't think. Crisply starched linens are draped on the now familiar rolling cart, but I don't see any plates or silver domes. I'm also not smelling the delicious, savory smells that I've tried very hard not to get used to. The waiter nods at me, and I see the slightest twinkle in his crinkly eyes.

As I look closer, I can see that both tiers of the cart are filled with ice buckets. Four on each level. And inside each ice bucket are multiple servings of gelato, perfectly and artfully scooped into small cups. The server shows Blaze that the ice buckets are each tagged with a number, and that the number corresponds with a handwritten list, describing the flavors contained within each bucket.

He glances at me and smiles as he hands the list to Blaze for him to inspect and approve.

"I forgot to ask. You're not allergic to anything, are you?" Blaze hesitates for a moment before signing for the delivery. He reaches for his wallet on the counter and hands the server a bill before the man excuses himself, exiting as silently as a shadow.

"No. No food allergies," I say, trying to peek at the list. Blaze folds it and sticks it in the pocket of his robe.

"Blaze, what have you done?" I ask.

"I promised you gelato." He smiles. "And I was thinking I'd like to do an experiment with it."

"That's a lot of gelato to tease a girl with." I smile. I'm suddenly realizing I'm famished. "Please don't say I have to choose between sex and gelato because that would be cruel."

"What kind of a monster do you take me for?" Blaze looks horrified. "No, I was thinking about gelato and flavor

profiles. Some combos work, and some things don't, but ultimately, it's all so personal, right? What tastes great to you
might not taste so wonderful to me."

"It's gelato. It's all wonderful." I laugh.

"Yes, but you might not put"—he takes the list from his
pocket and examines it—"lemon sorbetto together with
chestnut gelato. Then again, what the hell do I know? I'm a
relationship guru, not a gelato expert. It might be amazing.
We might be surprised. Shall we try it?"

He looks genuinely excited, almost like a little kid, as he peers
into the containers, removing a couple to sniff them.

"Sure, I'm game." I laugh.

"But not in here." He winks, pushing the cart back toward
the bedroom. "And not in these robes." He unties the belt on
my robe as he walks past me, and tosses his own onto the
couch.

"I'm not done teasing you either," he says. "Where's that
sleep mask you had on earlier? We're going to need that."

———

"I think it's safe to say that we have created a rather sticky
situation here." I gesture lazily to my torso, still slick with
sugar and cream. Blaze rolls on his side and rains light kisses
encircling my breast.

"Nougat," he says. "But on you, it tastes like milk and honey.
You will always be milk and honey to me."

"Does that make me the Promised Land?" I raise my
eyebrows.

"Quite possibly." He licks his lips.

"You're dark chocolate, cinnamon, and bourbon, maybe a little coffee?" I sigh. I lap a streak of dark chocolate from his cheek.

The sleep mask is on the floor, along with most of the bedding. We're lying in a nest of towels, which have certainly saved the sheets, but I am starting to feel a little bit guilty about the mess.

"We should probably shower," I say.

"Not yet." Blaze rolls on top of me, placing a knee between my legs. Instantly, my pulse quickens.

"Again?" I smile because I can hardly believe he has the stamina for a third time.

"Again," he says, staring into my eyes. "Must be all the delicious carbs we've loaded up on. Or maybe it's just you." Blaze unrolls what appears to be his last condom and pauses above me, looking for permission. I lick my lips and nod. There's no question. Of course I want him again. I want to feel him inside me. I want to feel us stuck together.

If it's all the time we'll ever have together, I want to make the most of it. I want to lick the bowl clean.

Without taking his eyes off me, Blaze thrusts. We both laugh when the headboard hits the wall and the springs creak. Our skin sticks together, peeling apart with a slightly stinging sensation that only intensifies everything, everywhere.

"No more teasing." Blaze places a finger under my chin as he looks down at me. "And no more begging. Tell me what you want."

"I want to be on top," I say, suddenly sure of this. Why hadn't this position ever occurred to me before? If it had, I must have dismissed it, too caught up in my desire to please my partner. Perhaps I'd worried that the demand would sound selfish.

But Blaze doesn't make me feel selfish. My needs only seem to further inflame his desire for me. His gray eyes deepen and flash in response to my request. If he were a genie, his eyes would be saying, "Your wish is my command." And it wouldn't be a trick.

"Wrap your legs around me," Blaze says, rolling smoothly with me. Without breaking stride or missing a single beat, he is suddenly on his back and I am straddling him. Our eyes are still locked together, as if held by a magnetic force.

I circle my hips slowly, changing the rhythm. First in one direction, then the other, squeezing him tightly inside myself and savoring every sensation. He groans, and his eyes start to slide shut. His body rises up to meet mine, and he grips my hip bones like handles. He's pulling me closer, pushing himself deeper, touching me in even more sensitive places. I have to struggle not to lose myself to this too quickly.

"Be still now," I instruct him.

I pause for a moment, stilling myself as well, and I feel his thighs tense up under me. He closes his eyes tightly as he strains against the urge to thrust.

When the dimple on his chin quivers, it nearly does me in. I have to look away as I squeeze my muscles around him, fighting my own urge to rock. We stay like this until we can't take it anymore, and I hear my own greedy moans as I begin to rock. Blaze sits up to rock with me, keeping me perched in his lap. We are swaying together, skin on sticky skin, sweat glistening in the overheated room.

My thoughts cease to make sense at this point. All the rationalizing, all the justifications, all the considerations and the fears. There's just this man and this bed—and my overwhelming desire. I want him like I've never wanted anyone or anything before. I want to feel him exploding within me. I want to possess that climax. I know, without a doubt, it's going to tip me over the edge as well.

"Let me feel it," I whisper in his ear, and bite the lobe, moving faster, squeezing harder.

Blaze rumbles again and grabs my ass, doing the impossible, pulling me closer and plunging himself deeper.

"Come with me?" he asks. I whimper as he groans. "Are you ready?"

I answer with a gyration, and we are both spiraling, waves breaking over us in a vortex. It's the most complete orgasm I've ever experienced, going on for what seems like an impossibly long time. Or maybe time stops.

Yet moments later, I hit a wall that takes my breath away. I feel alone. Worse than alone. I feel something akin to grief. A profound and inexplicable sense of loss washes over me after Blaze pulls out and goes to the bathroom to discard the condom.

When he returns, Blaze touches a finger to the tears pouring out of my eyes. "What's this?" he asks. "Are you okay? Jesus, Emily, did I hurt you?"

"No. It's nothing like that," I say, slightly embarrassed that I cannot seem to get ahold of myself. I can't even coherently explain to myself why I'm crying. "I just … I don't think I've ever come like that before," I admit. "It was a bit metaphysical, actually. What the hell was in that ice cream anyway?"

"Our flavors combine well." Blaze pulls me to him, spooning me under a sheet.

"Mmm," I say, willing away the slightly empty feeling. "They do."

"Can I tell you something crazy and a little shocking, Emily?"

"Sure," I say, tears still stinging. Whatever it is, it can't be worse than my embarrassing waterworks.

"I wished I wasn't wearing that condom just now."

I freeze and feel the burn as the tears come back with company in the form of a massive lump in my throat.

"I know, that's a little weird. I've never felt that way before, and I guess that's a really selfish way to feel. But there it is. At that moment, I just wanted to make love to you so badly without the condom, damn the consequences."

"Me too." I sigh, feeling slightly better and less alone.

"Just putting it out there," he says. "I'm not sure we need to unpack that right now."

"Or ever," I murmur, my lids suddenly feeling heavy despite my determination to make the most of every moment left together.

Blaze brushes my hair aside to kiss the back of my neck. "I love how curly you are," he says. "I could get entirely tangled up in your curls."

And then we both slip into a deep sleep, our bodies spent and wrapped around each other's.

blaze

. . .

"Airport runs are tricky. You want to swing it so you're dropping off the people you hate and picking up the ones you love. It's so much easier saying goodbye to assholes. Maybe this is why we need to villainize our exes. It makes it so much easier to kick them out on the curb."

— Blaze Smith, *Go Your Own Way*, on Departures

"WE SHOULD TALK ABOUT THIS," I say, handing Emily her hairbrush.

She shoves it into the side pocket of her suitcase.

"All good things come to an end, Blaze." She picks up the signed copy of my book and places it on top of the folded clothing in her bag. "I'm not going to leave this behind again. I promise."

It's still raining outside, and we haven't left the hotel all day. Although, I'm not sure we would have left even if the skies were clear. We barely got out of bed. No art gallery or ancient wonder could compete with a tour of Emily's freckles. All the sights I needed to see were right here. We didn't even bother getting dressed. We're both still in our robes.

"Stay an extra night," I suggest. "We didn't even get to go see the lights."

"We didn't get to see a lot of things," she says. Her smile says she doesn't mind.

"Screw the bucket list." I hold out my hand. "I don't regret a thing."

"Me either." Emily sits on the edge of the bed now. "Though I might have to change my return ticket. How can I go home without touring the Colosseum? I feel terrible I've only seen it in passing."

"So, stay another day. We can go see all those things together after *The Morning Show* taping tomorrow. I'll book a driver," I offer. "It's my fault you didn't get to see those things."

"It's hardly your fault." Emily stands to zip her bag. "I was here for work, not as a tourist. And when it came down to making decisions about my free time …" Her voice trails off. "I'll have other chances to see this city." She turns to touch my face, tenderly. "But this? Being here with you, Blaze? The last twenty-four hours have been like a lightning strike."

I place my hand over hers, willing her to stop packing and listen to me.

"We need to talk about what happened here, Emily," I say again.

Her phone rings, and she excuses herself to take the call in the sitting room where she can take notes. I assume she is speaking with Maria's grandson, as she switches between rudimentary Italian and simple English, getting directions and making plans to meet up.

I follow her into the room and clear our dinner dishes, wheeling the cart out to the hallway as she chats. Then I pour myself a cup of tea and review the schedule for tomorrow. I need to be at the TV studio by 7 a.m. for my appearance on

The Morning Show. It's the last stop on the tour, and then I'm free. Only now, I don't want to be.

Emily hangs up her call and comes to sit at the table with me.

"So, when are you headed home?" she asks.

"I'm flying back on Wednesday," I reply. Too soon. I'm not ready. "I don't want you to go tomorrow." I take her hands in mine. "I don't want this—whatever this is—to end."

"This has been amazing," Emily agrees. "But we both know it's not reality."

"Who says what's real? We're the only people who get to make that distinction."

"But we just met, Blaze. This has been magical, but it's a travel fling. It's not our lives. I don't know if you live in an apartment or a house. I don't know if you like to read or binge-watch TV shows, or if you know how to ice skate, or if you have a favorite color."

"I have a house. I like historical novels, but I'm not above reading rom-coms and binging on television series. Loved *Outlander*. I do skate. I played ice hockey a lot as a kid, though not well. What else? Oh yeah, my favorite color used to be green, but now I think it's the color of your eyes," I monologue. "And you already know my favorite flavor of gelato. Your turn."

"Blaze." She looks a little sad and hesitates before speaking. "I don't think we should do this now. It's only going to make it harder. If anything, we need to discuss the story for our official breakup tonight. I'd like to get an early start tomorrow and get to the airport to grab my car before it gets too busy."

"You're not planning on coming to *The Morning Show* with me?" I ask, trying not to sound petulant. I don't know why I'd assumed.

"Do you really need me there?" she asks.

"Yes," I say, attempting not to pout. "It might look weird if you don't come."

My phone rings, and I see that it's Steff, FaceTiming. "Do you mind if I pick up?" I ask.

Emily shrugs.

I tap the screen to accept the call. Steff is not alone. She is in a hot tub with Marco. It looks to be the same hot tub from Villa dei Baci. Neither one of them appears to be wearing clothing, and mercifully, the phone is pitched at an exclusively "shoulders up" angle.

But still.

"Where are you?" I ask. "I thought you were going to a spa?"

"Marco and a few friends decided to stick around. He's rented the Villa dei Baci for the holidays. He's asked me to stay and help him spitball his media for the New Year. And I mean, how could I refuse an offer like that?"

In the background, Marco flexes and makes a peace sign.

"Where's Emily? She hasn't left yet, has she?" Steff asks, worriedly looking at me as if she's trying to see over my shoulder.

"No, she's right here," I say, rotating the phone.

Emily waves. "Hey, Steff."

"Thank goodness," Steff huffs. "*The Morning Show* folks just called me to ask that we make sure Emily's there tomorrow. Apparently, that blogger, Isla, from the bookstore event wrote a post about Emily's grandparents?"

"Cool. She got that done fast," I say.

"Why didn't you clear it with me?" Steff's tone is icy.

"There's nothing about Blaze in that post at all," Emily chimes in. "Isla promised."

"That's beside the point," Steff snarls. "Nobody would give a damn about you or your grandparents if you weren't dating Blaze. There wouldn't be a story if you weren't dating him. So even without mentioning him, you're still cashing in on his celebrity."

I frown. "That's totally out of line, Steff. I think you owe Emily an apology."

"I think the story about Emily's grandparents is very beautiful," Marco pipes up, "even if that author Isla makes such sad cartoon book covers. She could sell so many more books with me on them. Emily, do you think she will write a book about you and Blaze? I could portray the dottore on that one, no? Steff, you will call her for me?"

Steff splashes Marco exasperatedly. "No, Marco, there won't be any book about Blaze and Emily. Try and keep up. Their whole relationship was a PR stunt for this tour. It's fake."

Marco looks taken aback and squints as he peers at us through the phone screen.

"No!" he exclaims. "Say it isn't true!"

"Which reminds me," Steff continues. "Have you two agreed on a story for your breakup? You definitely need to show up together at the taping, but we can leak the news about your split any time after. Maybe when Emily flies home alone? I talked to Viv, and she's game to resume the old deal for a few more months. Things didn't pan out with Rafe."

Steff raises her eyebrows and nods encouragingly at me as she dangles this news. It's like she's trying to placate a child with a bribe. As if I were the least bit interested in resuming anything with Viv. I look over at Emily, and she shakes her head, looking at me expectantly.

"We've got everything under control here," I assure Steff. "Really, you don't need to worry about anything else for this tour. Enjoy your spa time. I'll make sure your last payment gets wired as soon as I'm home, and then I think we're done."

"Okay. We can chat about your next book after the New Year," Steff says, leaning into Marco, who is now aping at the phone, using it like a mirror to check himself out. "You're still on with Viv for New Year's Eve, right?"

"No, Steff. I meant it when I said I was done for the foreseeable future. With Viv, the books, all of it. I'm taking a hiatus."

Steff laughs. "Very funny!"

"I'm not joking," I say. Emily nods at me and squeezes my hand. "Look, Steff, we had a good run, but your services are no longer needed."

Marco's eyes widen as he looks from the screen to Steff and back. "I am confused," Marco says. "Perdona me, but did you just say 'you're fired!' to my manager?"

Steff narrows her eyes at Emily.

"Emily! You conniving little—"

"Emily has nothing to do with this," I assert.

"Bullshit," Steff snarls. "What did she say?"

emily

. . .

BLAZE IS PACING in circles around the sitting room, fuming.

"So, you've known this whole time that my own manager set me up," he reiterates. "And you chose to keep that information to yourself?"

"It wasn't the whole time," I say. "Just since Thursday morning."

"Long enough. Why didn't you say anything when we talked about her? You knew she was plotting. Why didn't you tell me the whole story, or mention what had happened? Don't you think I would have wanted to know that someone who works for me was threatening you?"

I can't tell who he is maddest at—me, Steff, or himself.

"Maybe I should have told you." I stare down at the patterned carpet. "But it was none of my business, and put yourself in my shoes for a minute. I didn't think you'd believe me."

"Dammit." Blaze strides to the balcony and throws open the doors, cooling his temper in the icy night air. His fists are clenched and his jaw is tight, but as he stands in the doorway, I can see some of the tension begin to dissipate. He lets out a deep breath.

"I'm sorry, Blaze, you deserve better," I say.

"You shouldn't be apologizing to me," he says, turning toward me. "It's my fault you got dragged into this whole charade. I've made some bad choices in both my personal and professional life."

"Just because you're a relationship expert doesn't mean that you have to have the answers to everything," I say. "You're also a human being. Nobody expects you to be perfect." I lay a hand tentatively on his shoulder.

"Don't they?" Blaze says. His lip curls and he blinks, taking a step out into the night. Closing his eyes, he turns his face to the evening sky.

"Nobody who matters expects you to be perfect, Blaze, except maybe you."

"My mom's care facility called me on Thursday. They told me she probably can't handle traveling anymore, and don't think the trip I planned for us this Christmas is a good idea. Even with a full-time aide. She's having too many bad days."

"I'm so sorry," I say, stepping out into the rain with him. It's a soft rain, more mist than downpour, and I turn my face up to the sky as well. "What will you do?"

I think of my own plans, or lack thereof, for Christmas.

"I haven't decided." Blaze shakes his head. "It's up to my sister. My mom's caregivers suggested we still head to the resort without her. She won't know the difference."

"I'm sure she'd want you to be happy, whatever you do," I say.

Blaze sighs and turns to me, pushing a curl behind my ear.

"I'm sorry Steff sucked you into this whole drama," he says. "But if I can be selfish for a moment, I'm also not sorry. I feel more like myself with you than I've felt in years."

Below us, millions of Christmas lights lining the streets and rooftops sparkle and twinkle, forming a reverse galaxy. Blaze sweeps his hand across the panoramic view. "This is really something, isn't it?"

"It is," I agree, though I'm not sure if he's referring to the lights or to us.

"Come to the show with me tomorrow? One last appearance?"

"I promised Maria I would be in Pitigliano by dinnertime." I sigh. I was hoping to slip out tomorrow morning while Blaze was still asleep. The thought of having to say goodbye in daylight, in public, makes my stomach form knots. I've never been great at goodbyes.

"You heard Steff. She wouldn't have suggested you stick around unless the station really wanted you there."

"I don't think the station actually cares about me," I scoff.

"I care about you." Blaze folds me into his arms. "Screw the station. Stay for me. Just this one last appearance."

"You're only making this harder," I argue.

"It doesn't have to be so hard," he says, tipping my chin up and meeting my eyes. "This doesn't have to be fake anymore."

"You don't mean that." I break away. "Our worlds are entirely different. I have a boring life to go home to, and you would get sick of me. I knew what I signed up for when I agreed to go through with the whole fake relationship plan. Let me leave with my dignity intact. You don't owe me anything.

Besides, you heard Steff. Shouldn't you resolve things with Viv?"

Blaze snorts. "I don't think so. That ship sailed a long time ago." He considers me. "And you? Are you sure you're really done with Kent? You're not planning on knitting blankets for his babies now, are you?"

We eye each other warily. His nearness makes me want to cling to him. It makes me want to run away. It makes me want to cry. Why hadn't I anticipated what this new loss would feel like? Fresh on the heels of so many others. I'd signed up to pour salt on my own wounds.

Eventually, I turn away from the lights and lean back on the balcony. "You know what I'm doing on Christmas Eve? I signed up to volunteer at a pet shelter. I didn't want to crash anyone else's parties, but I also didn't want to be alone."

"This is what you really want?" Blaze asks, seeking my eyes. "You want me to let you go tomorrow, Emily? Because you're wrong about me. I'm pretty sure I know what I want, and I'm also pretty sure that nothing's ever been more real than this fake relationship. From the moment we met. But I will honor your wishes, if that's what you really want—to walk away."

It's not what I want. Of course it isn't. But what other choice do I really have? Better tomorrow than in another week, month, or year. Better when I can still walk away with a piece of my heart intact.

I nod at Blaze, willing the lump in my throat to disappear. I try to memorize and crystallize every detail of this week, this night, his face, so I can take the memory out and turn it over in my palm like a cherished ornament.

"We'll always have this, right, Smitty?" I gesture in a sweeping motion, back toward the lights below and the cozy warmth beckoning from the room within. Our "Rome for the Holidays."

"The night isn't over yet," Blaze says. "And if I only have you till morning, I don't want to waste any of that time. You're mine till tomorrow."

———

Blaze pulls me back through the double doors leading to the bedroom, stopping only when he reaches the bed. He sits down and grabs hold of my hips, pulling my sex toward his mouth and kissing the mound, breathing hotly between my legs.

"Is this what you want?" Blaze asks.

I moan at the feel of his tongue through my robe, inching me apart, willing me to open myself to him. When his hands snake up my legs, tracing loops against my inner thighs, I have to place my hands on his shoulders for balance.

"Take this off," Blaze demands, pulling the sash on my robe with his teeth. The robe falls open, exposing my nakedness underneath. He stares up at me with shining eyes.

"I hardly know where to start with you, Emily. I want to touch you everywhere. Taste every part of you. Take my fill and fill you up."

He demonstrates this with a flick of his tongue that captures and pinpoints my desire. And then he applies his whole mouth, licking, lapping, and kissing me at my center, like I am gelato, needing to be enjoyed before it melts.

His hands continue their swooping journey, seeking out my slippery center. When he places two fingers inside of me, I have to beg him to stop. It's going too fast. I don't want this to be over.

"Stop," I beg. "Allow me to be generous, too, tonight."

I let my robe fall to the floor and reach forward to untie his before dropping to my knees between his legs. I place my hands on his knees and kiss a trail up one leg, then the other. All the while, I am watching and reveling in his response. His shaft shifts and strains with every touch, as if it has a will of its own, a destination it's desperate to reach.

I graze my fingernails against his inner thighs, scratching lightly as I lean forward to taste him, like he tasted me.

Blaze tangles his hands in my hair as my tongue flickers against his base.

"Oh God, Emily. You have no idea what you're doing to me, do you?"

But I do have some idea because I know what his touch does to me. And what I'm doing to him now isn't only about him. I'm still buzzing with excitement, growing wetter with each lick.

As I make my way slowly up the thick, smooth length of him, he makes a gutteral sound somewhere between a growl and a rumble. The sound sends aftershocks through me as well.

By the time I reach his tip, he is vibrating.

I twirl my tongue around his tip, lavishing all of my attention on this one spot. His hand is on the back of my head as I kiss the salty drop off the tip. I part my lips and take him in, flattening my tongue and drawing on him.

His grip in my hair tightens, and he tugs me back.

"No, you need to stop. This isn't how I want to be with you."

"Am I doing it wrong?" I ask, suddenly worried.

"Oh God, no. It isn't that. If anything, you're doing it too well."

Blaze is shaking now. He shrugs the robe off his shoulders and stands. Then he pulls me to my feet and embraces me in a full-body, naked hug.

"I'm shaking," he says.

"I think I am too," I admit.

"You are." He nods into my neck, kissing the hollow along my collarbone.

He shifts himself, aligning our bodies more closely, pressing harder as he runs his hands down the length of my spine and over my buttocks. I imagine my nerves like a roadmap, running off the page and into his, electricity jumping across the bridges between our pages. It's a miracle we aren't shocking each other.

"I need to be inside of you." Blaze grips and lifts me, raising my welcoming entrance closer to his throbbing need. I wrap my legs around him, pressing myself closer, loving the feel of his length against me and the way that we align, tip to target, still buzzing with anticipation.

Blaze spins with me and lays me back against the bed.

"Just you and me," he says. "No barriers?"

I nod my acquiescence. "I want to feel you," I say. "I need to feel you."

There should be alarms going off in my head. One of us should be reaching for a condom. But we don't.

We both gasp when he finally enters me. It's more than nerves. It's an unexpected homecoming. An undeniable rightness to the moment.

"Do you feel that too?" Blaze asks, moving against me.

"I do," I say.

"Can you think of anything more real?"

I can't.

"This is beyond real," I say, contracting my muscles to hold him tighter as he moves within me. I'm starting to see stars.

"Oh God, Emily, I don't want to pull out." Blaze moans.

"I don't want you to either," I say, placing my hands possessively on his buttocks. The feel of his thrusting muscles under my fingertips only drives me closer to my own climax.

"Tell me now," Blaze insists. "Tell me what you want me to do."

I don't even need to think about it. My body answers for me.

"I want you to come inside of me," I say. "I want to feel you do that, Blaze. Do you think you can do that for me?"

His answer is a groan that catapults me over the edge, all of my senses exploding and overflowing as he pleases me.

blaze

. . .

"I'm not going to tell you that punching the gas and doing donuts isn't thrilling. There's a reason that nobody makes movies about parallel parking. I'm just going to tell you that calculated risks are still risky. And nobody but you can do that math."

— Blaze Smith, *Go Your Own Way*, on Risk Taking

THE AIR IS thick with fog, and the city is still waking. The alarm went off too soon. Leaving our warm bed feels like a punishment. It's early, so early, and we were up so late.

We didn't use a condom.

I should be worried about what we did, but I'm not. Not even a little bit. Which is weird. I know Emily was afraid she might have problems getting pregnant, but even if she wasn't concerned, I don't think I would have stopped just then. I didn't feel like I had a choice in the matter. And I was, and still am, willing to accept whatever the outcome might be.

Was a part of me wishing for it? Wishing for an excuse to stay in each other's lives?

We shower and dress silently, then sit on the couch holding hands, waiting for the front desk to let us know that our van is here. When the call comes, Emily takes one last look around the suite to make sure she hasn't forgotten anything. She shifts her overloaded shoulder bag onto her suitcase before we head downstairs.

"That's okay, I've got it." She refuses when I offer to help.

I hate the clattering sound of Emily's bag rolling across the cobblestones. There's a stark finality to that sound. No turning back now. She's really leaving. I can't take it. I pick up her bag, if only to stop the noise, and carry it the rest of the way to the van.

Not long after departing, the van comes to a stop.

"It's not here, is it?" Emily asks.

"You can't leave Rome without trying Sant Eustachio Coffee," the driver says. He returns quickly with our to-go order.

Emily breathes in deeply, closing her eyes at the smell of her coffee, then takes a sip. "This really is amazing."

"Thanks for coming today," I say. "It means a lot to me."

"You don't need me, or anyone, on your arm to be taken seriously, Blaze. You do know that, right?"

"I may not need you there, but I definitely want you there," I say. "I'm not ready to field questions about being dumped again. Especially not on a morning show. Way too early."

I sip my coffee.

"Who says I'm going to be the one dumping you?" She seems surprised at this.

"Well, who's going to buy me breaking up with you, Emily?" I shake my head sadly.

"It's probably best if we say the breakup is mutual. Call it a fling." Emily stares out the window. "I'm looking forward to being able to do anonymous grocery runs in pajama pants and a sweatshirt again."

"Good luck with that. I think you may have your own following after this."

Her phone dings with a text. She reads it, gasps, then types furiously in response.

"What is it?" I ask. "Everything okay?"

"It's Kent. Honestly, I don't know what his problem is now. But whatever it is, I'll deal with it later." Emily is curt and dismissive. But I can see whatever was in that text really bothered her.

"Let me see?" I ask.

"No. It's my problem, not yours." She pockets the phone and changes the subject. "So, what do you think they're going to want to talk to you about today?"

I'm dying to know what Kent sent her, but I know better than to push it. I try to hide my feelings and answer the question.

"You know, the usual holiday relationship stuff. Romantic gift suggestions, how to keep your wife from finding out about your mistress when she sees the credit card bill ..."

"Seriously?" Emily's jaw drops.

"It's Italy." I shrug. "I'm prepared for almost anything."

Almost anything. I'm not sure how I'll answer the one big question I'm pretty sure is coming.

So, what's the deal with you and your new girlfriend?

"Why do you think they wanted me there?" Emily asks.

"Probably because they plan to grill me about you." I sigh. "And it's better TV if the cameras can pan to you in the audience."

"Oh, shit." Emily pats her face.

"Don't worry, you're gorgeous. And that top is perfect for TV." I compliment her close-fitting, hunter-green sweater. "It really brings out the gold and green in your eyes."

She blushes. "I have to admit, I feel very awkward in your world," she says.

"The secret is that everyone does. We're all faking it," I say. The van pulls into the parking garage and stops at an unmarked, gray door. There's a woman waiting there, holding a clipboard and wearing an earpiece.

"We're here," I say.

"Great!" The assistant claps when she sees us. She is speaking perfect English with a vaguely British accent. "Let's get you into chairs now for hair and makeup. We are so happy you agreed to be on the show today, Emily! Such a great story!"

Emily looks quizzically at the assistant and back at me. I shrug.

"What do you mean by 'on the show?'" Emily asks.

But the assistant doesn't answer. She is too busy speaking into her earpiece, answering someone else. When she turns back to us, she is in a hurry. Her eyes dart back and forth as she looks around for someone to escort us.

"Loredana will take the lead for Blaze's segment," she explains. "She will be chatting with him in English, which will be translated with subtitles for local viewers. He's at the beginning of the show, and there's a break after, so you can leave if you don't want to stay for the whole taping. This way," she says, leading us to the hallway and pointing toward a set of open doors. "I'm sorry, I have to run now. Good luck!"

———

Emily's phone dings again while we are being fussed over by the hair and makeup crew. Worriedly, she grabs for it.

"Is it Kent again?" I ask.

"No," she says, setting the phone back down on the ledge in front of her. "It's late back home, and he's a brand-new dad. He's probably sleeping."

"Okay, good." I nod, still wondering who the text was from but determined not to ask. I stare down at my hands, twiddling my thumbs. "None of my business."

"The text was from Maria's grandson." Emily sighs, rolling her eyes at me. "Just telling me where to park when I get there tonight."

A hairdresser comes at Emily with a curling iron, touching up her curls, while another fusses over which shade of lipstick.

"Is this really necessary? I'm just going to be in the audience, right?" Emily lets the makeup artist choose a deep-red shade.

"It's time to wire you two up." A very young-looking sound guy comes in with lav mic kits. He can't be more than twenty. He's got a patchy beard and is wearing skinny jeans and an Adventure Time tee.

"Do I need to wear a mic even if I'm sitting in the audience?" Emily looks a bit worried.

"The producer says ..." The sound guy shrugs as he clips the lav to the collar of Emily's sweater and hands her a small box that's attached by a wire. "Can you please put this down your shirt and wrap it around to the back?" He clips the box to her waistband.

"But I'm still going to be in the audience?" She looks warily from him to me again.

"Si! You are in the audience. This is just if they speak to you, ask you a question."

"Okay." She nods, looking relieved.

"It'll be fine," I say, clipping on my own mic. "Just follow my lead. It's a short segment. They can't possibly be asking us much more than what we have planned for the holidays."

Emily's phone rings, and the sound guy looks over at it, alarmed. "You must turn that off now!"

emily

. . .

I SEND the call to voice mail before shutting my phone off. It's a UK number, not one I recognize.

"Okay, team, let's go!" The sound guy hustles us back down the hall, directing Blaze to the green room. "You wait here. I will bring Emily to her chair."

Blaze hesitates at the door. "See you on the other side," he says. For a second, I think he's going to kiss me, but our recently styled hair and makeup has rendered us untouchable. He reaches out and squeezes my hand instead.

The sound guy looks impatient. My stomach spasms. Unlike all the other times I've appeared with Blaze, I am nervous. It's ridiculous. It's not like anyone I know will ever see this segment. And it's not like it's actually about *me*. For all intents and purposes, I'm still acting, appearing in the role of Blaze Smith's girlfriend.

But I'm not acting anymore.

I don't have to pretend I have feelings for that man. Whatever seeds were planted back in Seattle have burst into bloom. I keep trying to stuff their wild tendrils back in my bag, but they won't behave. They're like weeds, reaching out to take root anywhere, even when there's no ground for them to grow on.

I allow the sound guy to lead me to the seating area opposite *The Morning Show's* set. There's a small audience in the stadium-style seats opposite the compact set. A couple dozen spectators are already seated, waiting expectantly for the show to start. He points at a metal folding chair directly behind one of the cameras. It feels awfully close to the action. The butterflies in my stomach flap harder.

While the crew does their final checks, I surreptitiously check my phone inside my bag, rereading the rude, cryptic text from Kent.

Are you kidding me, Em? I can't fucking believe

what a starfucking bitch you are! And I can't

believe he fell for it.

Had I missed something? Was Kent on something? Perhaps new-dad sleep deprivation had induced the equivalent of drunk texting?

I swipe over to my visual voice mail to see if the caller from earlier has left a message, fully expecting to see that it's spam. But it isn't. It's from an editor at the magazine Kent was writing the article for. Part of the transcription doesn't come through, but the part that does goes a long way toward explaining his angry text.

"We're holding the February cover for you and Blaze if you're willing to offer us an exclusive. We're thinking something like, 'In Love with Love'—a tell-all about your relationship with Doctor Love himself. Call me ASAP?"

My heart jumps around frantically in my chest. Does this mean they're canceling Kent's article? How did they even think to get in touch with me? I switch the phone off and stash my bag under my seat before the sound guy can come back and chastise me. The show is about to start.

A bunch of things seem to happen all at once. The lights in the audience area go dark. Two bright spots come up on the stage, revealing the two female *Morning Show* hosts seated on a curved, tan sofa surrounding a round table. There's a white-painted, wooden set wall behind them and a large-screened monitor, displaying *The Morning Show's* logo.

The hosts' smiles seem frozen as they sit there, hands in their laps, staring blankly in my direction. It's disconcerting until I realize that they aren't looking at me. They're waiting for some sort of signal from the cameraman. There's a teleprompter screen mounted to the camera in front of me.

The show's theme music comes on, and everyone in the audience is urged to clap. When the fanfare dies down, one of the hosts, Loredana, an attractive woman in her forties, greets the public with a joke about the weather and a few words about today's guests. My Italian is spotty, but I am able to follow along when she mentions Blaze. She refers to him as the Love Doctor and promises that he's going to be talking about holiday romances. Other segments include winter travel with pets and clever ways to wrap presents.

I settle back in my seat, finally feeling less nervous about the actual show now, but just as nervous about saying goodbye to Blaze and dealing with the Kent situation afterward. Nothing seems real anymore. I can't believe I'm here right now. And I also can't fully process that after today, I'll probably never see Blaze again.

I can't stop thinking about what we did last night. How reckless we were. Even though we knew nothing was likely to come of it, there was still some risk involved. We'd both taken a chance. Willingly. What had we been thinking?

We weren't thinking. At least not with our heads.

The show's hosts laugh as they trade makeup tips and complain about the weather. It's so surreal, but I also can't imagine being anywhere else. Ephron seems like it's a million miles away. It's hard to picture myself existing there now. Without Blaze.

I swore this wouldn't happen. I was so sure I could play this week-long game with Blaze and walk away unscathed. I hadn't just been fooling the paparazzi—I was fooling myself. I got troped.

I realize the studio audience is clapping again. Reflexively, I slap my hands together, as the lights switch and the show cuts to a break.

Makeup artists rush in to do touch-ups, and camera men reposition themselves in a flurry of activity. The sound guy shows up again and kneels beside me, asking me to say a few words while he checks my levels.

"Say … Blaze Smith is my dream," he teases.

"You are seriously pushing it," I say instead.

He shrugs, eyes twinkling in an "Oh well, I tried" way. Then he holds up a hand, giving the "okay" sign to someone in another part of the studio.

"Be ready," he says. "You are next."

"You mean Blaze is up next," I say.

"Si, si." He nods slowly, checking my mic one last time and hurries away. The lights readjust, and the countdown to live starts again: 3-2-1 …

This time, the hosts start their chat with a few words about Blaze Smith and his latest book. I see the cover of *Go Your Own Way* come up on the monitors, and they take turns passing around a hard copy of his book. The monitors fade to white, and then a series of press photos of Blaze appear. The slideshow ends on the same handsome photo of him from the cover of the book—clean-shaven, dressed expensively, overly tanned, groomed and styled for the camera.

A different slideshow plays in my mind. A fan favorite series, for one. Smitty, in his colorful airport attire. Herr Schmitty with his ridiculous costume belly. Blaze sliding out of the shower, nearly careening into me. Hot, sticky Blaze, licking gelato off my belly.

Stark-naked Blaze asking my permission to finish, no barriers between us. The memory makes my still-tender center spasm.

And then, there he is, walking out onto the soundstage, looking so much more handsome than the press photo. Not because he's perfect. Because he's not just a fantasy. He's real. His eyes find mine in the audience, even before he takes his seat at the table with the hosts.

"Are you looking for someone else, Blaze?" Loredana says, feigning jealousy. "Here I thought you were coming to see me today, but you seem distracted."

Blaze shakes his head, smiling. "You know I'm genuinely thrilled to be here today. How may I be of service?"

Placated, the host pulls out a stack of notecards.

"Since the Love Doctor is in, we have some burning questions from our viewers that we were hoping you could answer today." Loredana mugs at the camera and looks at the audience for a reaction. There's mild whistling, clapping, and a few cheers.

"Hit me," Blaze says.

"Is that your way of saying you like it rough, Doctor?" Loredana quips, holding a hand over her mouth in mock theatrical shock.

"What *I* like isn't the point." Blaze smoothly redirects her. "Haven't you read Chapter 19 of *Go Your Own Way*: Rough Ride Ahead?"

The host licks her finger and smolders into the camera before opening the book, supposedly to that chapter, making a shocked-looking face. The audience wrangler waves his arms, prompting forced laughter from the crowd.

Blaze smiles blandly, but I see the tic in his jaw, indicating he is not amused. I don't know how he can stand it.

"Okay, all kidding aside, we're anxious to get your feedback on these classic holiday dating dilemmas." Loredana leafs through her stack of printed questions and chooses one.

"Dear Doctor Love, I've been exchanging text messages with my boyfriend's older brother. Now I'm not sure which one I want to kiss on New Year's Eve."

"That depends. Which one is a better kisser?" Blaze says. The audience laughs. "All joking aside, you're playing with fire if you're dating one brother and messaging the other at the same time. It's not fair to either of them and likely will cause a family rift. It's okay to date more than one person, but if you don't want to burn bridges, you should probably avoid dating siblings."

Blaze gazes past the camera, looking directly at me as he speaks, and I find myself nodding, proud of his ability to cut through bullshit.

"You know, I always like to ask myself, 'Where am I going with this relationship?'" Blaze says. "It's a lot easier to imagine your route when you've decided on a destination."

"Speaking of destinations," the host says, now looking at the camera in my direction as well. "We're all wondering if you're planning to make Italy a more prominent destination in your future travels. We have it from a good source that your new bella girlfriend is Italian, and she's spending some time doing research on her family heritage while you two are here. You must have read the love letters between her grandparents. Is this not the most romantic thing ever?"

Quotes from my grandparents' letters come up on the monitor. It's a montage of the lines I'd copied for Isla's blog post.

Beloved Wife, I am counting the days until you arrive. The house is almost ready. There is a small garden that I have planted for you, a large kitchen, and a room that is perfect for a nursery. I miss you every moment. I can't wait till we make this house a home.

Man of my dreams, for that is surely what you must be, the answer to my prayers. I will be with you soon. I can already feel your arms around me and know I will be safe with you.

Loredana translates some of the quotes into Italian, and the audience oohs and aahs and makes swooning sounds, egged on by the audience wrangler. Suddenly, the cameras are swiveling toward me, and I see myself on the monitors.

"Emily! We are so thrilled to have you here today. Come on up here."

For a moment, I remain frozen, staring at my digital reflection. Even if I could run, I have no idea where the exit is. I stand up, feeling more like a marionette than a creature with free will.

Seeking out Blaze's face, I can tell that he's been blindsided, too, his mouth set in a hard line, brows drawn together. He looks pissed. I see all of this in the fraction of a second before we make eye contact. He takes a breath and recovers quickly, standing and holding out a hand to me.

"We can't wait to hear more about your family and your grandparents' great love affair," Loredana suggests, patting the sofa and beckoning me to her side like a dog.

I ignore her. Blaze's hand is my lifeline. It can't be more than a few yards, but it seems like I'm traversing miles as I dodge the cameras, stepping over taped lines. I hold my breath until he pulls me into the space beside him.

"Oh, look how cute you two are together," Loredana fawns. "I can see why you chose someone like Emily. You two even make an old cynic like me believe in true love again."

blaze

. . .

"How many dates till we have sex? How long should we be dating before we get engaged? How long should we be married before we have kids? There's no schedule, people! Your ETA and your mileage will vary. Just ask anyone who's driven anywhere in LA. Timing is everything. The same trip might take you twenty minutes one day and three hours the next. It's all about the current conditions."

— Blaze Smith, *Go Your Own Way*, on Schedules

"THERE'S no way I'm letting you drive to Tuscany alone now," I say. "It isn't safe."

Emily's hands are still shaking when the sound guy comes back to the green room to collect the mics. He hands her purse back to her. She gives him a disappointed look.

"You could have at least warned me," she chastises.

He shrugs. "Not my job. You two were great, though."

Emily turns to me. "So, this is how Steff gets her revenge on me?"

"I don't think the segment itself was her doing," I disagree, "although I do suspect she left out some of the details on purpose."

"What's done is done." Emily reaches into her bag to retrieve her phone, checking quickly to see if she has any new notifications. "I need to get on the road. I just want to get out of here. Can we go to the airport and get my car now?"

"Emily." I put my hands on her shoulders. "Hang on a minute. Let's go somewhere and talk. You can't just jump in a car and go to Tuscany now. Think about it. The press isn't going to leave you alone."

"Sure they will. We can just speed up the announcement that we've broken up. Let's stage a fight in the hallway. Make a scene, and I'll be on my way back to blessed obscurity."

"It doesn't work like that." I sigh. "Half the country is swooning over your grandparents' love story. They don't even care about me anymore. You're the celebrity now. They're invested. They're not going to just leave you alone. Even if you make a scene. *Especially* if you make a scene."

The sudden and loud ringing of the phone in her hand shocks us both like a jump scare. Emily jabs at the screen, answering the FaceTime call from Isla.

"Oh my God! You guys!" Isla is flushed and excited. Clearly, she was watching this morning.

"Oh my God is right. Did you know anything about this? Did they check in with you?" Emily asks.

"Uh-oh," Isla says. "That doesn't sound positive. I had no idea they were going to mention my post. But I thought it was super cute. You weren't happy with it?"

"Hey, Isla." I lean in, letting Isla know that she isn't only speaking to Emily.

"Oh, hi Blaze," Isla says. "I hope you aren't upset with me as well?"

"I'm not upset with you!" Emily assures her. "It's not your fault we were blindsided."

"You didn't know this would happen," I say. "The issue is that Emily was planning to head to Tuscany this afternoon —alone."

"Well, that can't happen now!" Isla says. "She's likely to be followed and harassed. You can't let her go alone, Blaze!"

"That's what we were just discussing," I say. "I'm glad you're on the same page as me. Maybe you can help me talk some sense into Emily. At the very least, I think we need to send her with my driver."

"I don't need a babysitter," Emily insists. "I'm a perfectly capable adult!"

"Okay, this is between the two of you," Isla says. "Emily, I'd offer to drive up with you, but I have to meet with my editor later today. If you can wait till tomorrow, I'm free."

"No, it has to be tonight," Emily says. "I made plans. I'll figure something out."

"I'm sorry, Emily," Isla says. "I didn't expect the story to blow up like it has. The traffic on that post has been insane. I don't know what to say. People are really into you. Call me later and let me know what you decide to do?"

"Thanks, Isla. We'll be sure to check in later," I say.

Emily hangs up the phone and tosses it back into her purse.

"I never should have let you talk me into coming here this morning." She paces between me and the door. "I could have been there already."

"I swear I didn't know," I say. She hitches her bag up on her shoulder and hugs herself.

"I believe you." She nods.

"But I'm also not entirely sorry now," I admit. I run my hands through my crunchy, oversprayed hair, making a mess of it.

"Want to know why I'm not sorry?" I take a tentative step toward her, and when she doesn't retreat, I pull her into my arms. Her hands form fists against my chest, and her forehead presses into me.

"No," she says, shaking her head against me.

"I really didn't want you to leave me yet," I say. "I'm not going to apologize for feeling that way. So even though I hate that this happened, I'm grateful. Let me come on your trip with you, Emily. Please?"

Her body judders as she sucks in a rough breath and breaks. Tipping her chin up, I see the tears falling, leaving black mascara trails in their wake.

"I didn't want to leave you either, stupid." She bangs her fist against me, punctuating each word with a soft punch. "And. This. Isn't. Making. It. Any. Easier."

"Yes, it is." I kiss her. "This is the universe's way of telling us that we shouldn't be apart. We just have to stop fighting it. Please don't cry." I kiss her more, covering her cheeks, her forehead, and pulling her against me as I kiss the top of her head.

"This isn't real," she says into my chest.

"Who's full of shit now?" I ask.

"It's barely been a week," she insists.

"So what?" I shrug.

"It's too crazy."

"Maybe. But I don't care. I've seen some shit, Emily. I've talked to people who have been married for decades, and I swear they didn't feel one tenth of the feelings I'm feeling for you right now."

"Stop! Don't say it!" She braces as if it's bad news.

"How do you know what I'm going to say?"

"I know what I want you to say," she whispers. "But it would only make it harder for me to walk away from you."

"I don't want you to walk away from me, Emily. I'm falling in love with you, and I'm not afraid to say it. I don't want to regret not saying it later on down the line. I can't let you go your own way. Take me with you."

emily

. . .

I PULL off the highway and into the service area, at Blaze's request, so we can use the restrooms and stock up on snacks. After a quick stop back at the hotel for him to pack a bag, we'd finally made it to the airport, picked up my car, and hit the road just after 1 p.m.

Plenty of time to make it to Pitigliano for dinner. But no time for lunch.

"I'm telling you, you have to see this," he says. "It's nothing like rest areas in the United States. Five-star service. It's like Whole Foods. No better place to buy your free-range wild boar salami."

"I'm starving," I confess. "I'd be happy with almost anything, although I might take a pass on the boar."

"You don't have to settle. Are you craving sweet or salty? I'm sure they have Toblerone." Blaze is bouncing in his seat, clearly excited. He's channeling that wild Smitty sparkle that I haven't seen since the Seattle airport.

"You're really into road trips." I laugh.

"You've discovered my secret. I *love* road trips, Emily. Especially spontaneous ones. Are you okay with the playlist I've put together?"

"Your playlist is perfect." I smile, pulling into a parking spot. "Magical. Although you can't really take all the credit."

After a bit of initial discussion about our road trip responsibilities, we'd decided that I'd do the driving and Blaze would do the navigating and playlist management. He took the cheesy, yacht rock playlist off my phone and tripled it, filling the new list with five hours of selections that made me laugh and familiar-sounding songs that I'd totally forgotten about.

And then he'd programmed our route into the Google Maps app on his phone. Without stops, we were two and a half hours away.

"What made you go with yacht rock?" Blaze asks as we sit in the car, letting the Fleetwood Mac song "Go Your Own Way" finish.

"Do not hate on the yacht rock," I warn him.

He holds up his hands, eyes wide and innocent. "Nope. No hate here! There are no better road-tripping tunes, in my opinion. I just can't believe how in sync we are on this."

"Are you making fun of me?" I challenge, squinting my eyes at him.

"Hardly. I took a lot of road trips with my mom and my sister when I was little," Blaze says. "My mom loved the classics from the '70s. She and my sister would sit up front, arguing over the radio stations. Remember life before satellite radio and cell phones? I got the whole back seat to myself. Me, my dog, my action figures, and a big, old paper map. We went all over the west. Yosemite, Joshua Tree, the Pacific Coast Highway …"

He sings along to the familiar tune and winks at me. Something clicks.

"Your book!" I exclaim. "Was this the inspiration?"

"Maybe subconsciously. Those were great times." He smiles, remembering. "Simpler. And so full of possibilities."

"My dad loved this music too," I say. "On the weekends, when we went to my grandparents' house for dinner, he'd insist we put on 'his' music. It was always playing in the background, kind of like a soundtrack for my childhood. When I hear certain songs, it's like I'm right back there with him."

"Music can be a portal like that. Tell me a memory."

"For this song? I remember my dad giving me unsolicited advice about dating," I say. "We were rocking on the porch swing."

"Did he have good advice?"

"Probably. But I was determined not to take it." I laugh. "He was never a fan of Kent."

"Good man." Blaze nods his approval.

Now that we're out of the city, everything feels less hectic. Maybe it's the absence of the paparazzi. It no longer feels like we're running away. It feels like we're heading toward something. The dread I was feeling all morning is gone. In its place is a sort of delicious anticipation.

I roll down the windows, look around, and consciously try to make a new memory. I sniff the air, which smells like a mix of grass, petrol, and really good coffee coming from the service station. Azure winter skies and winter-brown fields. Blaze in the passenger seat. The landscape rolls in waves toward a distant horizon, inviting us to follow, come closer, and crest the next hill. I file it all away, hoping the song will act as a solidifying agent, preserving it all for later retrieval.

When the song ends, we get out of the car and stretch our limbs. The gravel crunches underfoot.

"My dad would have loved to be on this road trip." I sigh. "He never made it to Italy. We always talked about coming, but it wasn't meant to be. I guess I just wanted to listen to that music because it makes me feel like he's here with me."

"I'm sure he is."

Blaze wraps his arms around me, and we stand like this for a moment. I add the secure feeling of his strong arms caressing me to the memory. He literally has my back. I can't remember the last time I had that feeling. And I'm not crying, I realize. I was able to talk about my dad without crying.

"Thanks for making my playlist more awesome," I say.

———

After we stock up on snacks and some flowers for Maria, I fire off texts to Isla and Alexis, alerting them of our change of plans. Even though it's nearly morning back home, Alexis texts me back immediately, demanding a selfie as we're merging back onto the highway.

Blaze snaps a photo of me at the wheel, and another of us in the car together, and sends them back.

Whatever anxiety I had about driving to Tuscany slowly dissolves away as we get closer. Even when the well-appointed highway gives way to curving country lanes, I feel a sense of homecoming.

"People drive much more sensibly than I expected," I say, making my way around a tractor that's slowed for me to pass.

"Tell me about it. I'd rather be on these roads at 4 p.m. than driving through LA on the 405."

"Do you like LA?" I ask, all too aware that this is where Viv lives, and that she's the main reason he would have to spend time there.

"Not really," Blaze says. "I'm more of a country guy. I mean, the California Coast is spectacular, but I'm not a fan of the entertainment industry. I won't miss it." He looks at me significantly, then leans across to turn up the James Taylor song that's playing and starts singing along.

I can't help but join in, and before I know it, we're both belting out songs, cruising through forests and around hillsides that move past us like we're flying on our own personal magic carpet. Up and up into the hills we roll.

As we get closer, the sky starts to turn pink around the edges, and the light shooting through the tree branches takes on hues of honey and gold.

"It's the magic hour," I say. "Good thing we're almost there. I'm not so sure these roads would be as fun in the dark."

"Pull over if you see a turnout? I want to take a photo of you."

"Seriously?" I ask.

"Emily, you have no idea how gorgeous you look in this light. I just want to remember today. Please? Just for a moment. We're only a few miles away. According to the map, there's an overlook coming up in about three-quarters of a mile. It says there's a panoramic view of the city."

"Fine," I agree, slowing down. My heart is beating in anticipation of my first view of the town where my grandmother lived. "It's got to be right up here."

And then we round the bend, and I am not at all prepared for the sight before me. I am so gobsmacked by the sight of her village that I almost miss the pullout.

"Holy shit!" Blaze exclaims as I slam on the brakes and throw the car into reverse to back up into the carved-out parking lot set into the side of the hill. There's a trailhead there and a sign with the image of the Virgin Mary. But that isn't what nearly caused me to drive off the cliff.

Across the ravine, towering over the valley, is the stone-cut, hilltop village of Pitigliano. The buildings rise up out of the cliffs almost seamlessly, as if the entire town is a fairy tale castle formed by some organic process. The city shimmers in eyeshadow palette shades of pink, bronze, and rose gold, lit by the setting sun. It's like a CGI fantasy, except it isn't. It's an actual village that's been there for hundreds if not thousands of years.

We get out of the car and stand cliffside, in front of the guardrail, to gape at the view. I hold up my phone to take a photo, then turn it sideways, try zooming out, and finally give up. There's no way to capture it all without shooting in panoramic mode, stitching the pieces together.

"I've seen photos, but none of them do this view justice," I say.

"Let me take your picture?" Blaze asks. "For posterity."

Standing alone by the guardrail, I feel vaguely dizzy. I grip the railing and try not to look down.

"Would you mind taking one with me?" I hold out my hand shyly, beckoning him to come over. It still feels slightly strange to ask him for a photo. Like I'm a celebrity selfie-seeker. But Blaze is more than willing. He cheerfully complies, coming to stand behind me, pulling me back against his chest. He feels solid as I lean into him, a wall of safety that instantly vanquishes my fears of the void on the other side of the guardrail.

He takes my phone and holds it out to shoot the selfie.

"I can't believe we're really here. It doesn't look real," I say.

"Who's to say what's real?" Blaze kisses behind my ear, prompting me to turn to face him and kiss him properly. "Does this feel real?"

"No," I confess. "You feel like a dream."

"Then I don't want to wake up yet."

blaze

. . .

"My ex hated highways, so we always took surface streets. But the weird thing is that long after we split, I still found myself mindlessly driving her preferred routes, even while out on a date with someone new. Force of habit. It made me think about who's really riding shotgun. We've all got some ghosts hitching a ride and making stupid decisions for us. Every once in a while, it's a good idea to burn some sage."

— Blaze Smith, *Go Your Own Way*, on Getting Rid of Ghosts

I **FETCH** our bags from the back of the car while Emily applies red lipstick. It's the kind of lipstick that says, "Sorry, you can't kiss me right now," which only makes me want to kiss it right off her.

"You sure it's okay if I tag along?" I ask. "I could find dinner myself and meet up with you later if you prefer," I say, checking in again and making doubly sure she is fine with my presence at this meeting.

Now that we've come this far, I am also anxious to meet Maria. I'm dying to hear the story about how Carmela met Joe. I want to know why she never came back to this magical place.

The sound of suitcase wheels on cobblestones is different in stereo. When it's two bags, it sounds like adventure. New beginnings.

"I want you to come along," Emily reassures me.

"Good." I heave a sigh of relief. "Because I was going to have to resort to spying on you. I'm so curious to see how this all turns out."

Emily smiles distractedly. Her eyes are wide, taking in what they can in the dying light of the day. We cross a plaza and pass a series of fountains as we enter the historic district of the city. The entire old city is a pedestrian-only zone.

"It's a bit of a hike to the restaurant where Maria's grandson wants to meet," I say, reassessing the map. "Do you want me to take both bags?"

"Don't be silly, I've got it. I'm wearing my comfy shoes." Emily sticks out a sheepskin-clad foot, showing off the boots I haven't seen since the airport. "Very on trend, no?"

"Now I feel underdressed." I wink, pulling out my orange puffer vest and layering it over my blue fleece.

"Oh dear, what would Steff say?" Emily giggles. "If the paparazzi could only see us now."

"Steff can stuff it," I say.

"I like the sound of that." Emily nods. She stops to check her phone when a message comes in. "Francesco says he'll bring the keys to the guest apartment with him to dinner. It's near the restaurant and close to Maria's place."

"It's nice of him to put us up."

"He insisted. Maria owns the apartment. He manages it for her."

I'm not sure where to look first. The entire city looks like a movie set, with narrow alleys and steep staircases cobbled together, converging at impossible angles like an Escher print. We pass by pottery shops and leather goods stores. There's vintage and upcycled clothing and shops selling specialty kitchen items. I imagine the scene is very different on summer nights, when days are longer, more filled with tourists.

"How long has Maria's family been here?"

"Several generations," Emily says. "I'm not clear about my family's presence. My grandmother didn't have any siblings, so when she left and they died, that was it." Emily shrugs.

"Didn't she miss her parents?" I ask, finding it hard to picture leaving a place like this and never looking back.

Emily shakes her head. "I don't know. She didn't talk about them—ever. And before you say it, I know that's strange. But it's just how it was. She was still very young when she came to America, and it was after the war. Lots of people didn't talk about the past."

"Did you tell Francesco and Maria I was coming?"

"They said you are more than welcome. They saw the segment this morning. I'm not sure who they are more excited to meet now, you or me." Emily shrugs. "Maria said she feels like a celebrity."

We pause outside a tiny shop with a taxidermied boar's head perched in the window. The boar is smoking a cigarette and surrounded by hanging salamis.

"I have to get a picture of this for Alexis and Jackson!" Emily snaps, while I check my map.

"It's not too much farther. The restaurant should be in the next square," I say.

"Emily?"

Before we have a chance to walk any farther, we are greeted by a well-dressed Italian man wearing leather loafers, perfectly pressed trousers, and a thick, vintage wool blazer topped with a finely woven scarf.

"Francesco?" Emily looks up from the boar to wave at Maria's grandson.

"Si! Welcome!"

Francesco hastens his step to her side and proceeds to swiftly kiss her on both cheeks. "Bella!" he enthuses. "I have heard how beautiful your grandmother was, but now I can see for myself and believe it!"

There's something familiar about this man, and for a moment, I wonder if I might have met him at an event somewhere. Or seen him in a film. His old-fashioned clothing gives the impression that he might have popped out of another decade and into this square on his way to send a telegram or to pick up some pipe tobacco.

He eyes me suspiciously, taking in my orange puffer vest with obvious surprise—and distaste.

"Dottore Amore?" He holds out his hand to shake. The handshake is firm, even if his gaze is disapproving. He looks from me to the bag by Emily's side.

"Prego! I will take this bag," he insists, whisking Emily's roller bag away before she can protest. He gestures for us to follow. "My nonna, she is already waiting in the restaurant. She is going to be so happy to see you, Emily. Come!"

———

The restaurant is cozy inside. Red-and-white checked tablecloths cover tables topped with flickering tea lights. The bar has been decorated with swags of holly and tiny, twinkling lights. Like Francesco's clothing, there is a timelessness to the place. The rough-hewn, stone walls have probably remained unchanged for centuries, though different generations of customers have come and gone. Francesco stashes our bags near the entry, then stops at the bar to retrieve a tray of drinks.

"Prosecco. We must make a toast." He distributes the drinks and leads us to a private room in the back, where an ancient yet oddly robust woman sits with perfect posture. Her cheekbones are high and her skin is weathered, but it's her unusual hazel eyes glimmering in the candlelight that stop me in my tracks. She has the eyes of a much younger woman. Hazel eyes. Not unlike Emily's, I realize.

"Please don't get up, Maria!" Emily insists as she bends to hug the woman.

Maria places her hands on Emily's cheeks.

"Bella, bella," she says. She turns Emily's head from side to side, looking at her. I don't need to understand Italian to know what she is saying next. It's clear how significant it is for her to be meeting Emily. The two women seem as if they would be content simply staring into each other's eyes all night, but Francesco breaks the spell, tapping a glass with his spoon.

"To old friends and family!" he says.

We all hold up our glasses and toast, making eye contact. Maria's grandson, I notice, also has the same hazel eyes as Emily. It further explains why he looks familiar. I wonder if it is a quirk of the region.

By the time our coats are off and we are all seated, the waitstaff is piling food on the table. Thick, crusty slabs of freshly baked bread. Spicy olive oil and bowls of olives. Plates of cheese and salami. Soft jazz music filters in from the main dining room as we all make short work of a bottle of Sangiovese.

"I have so many questions for you, Maria," Emily says. "I don't know where to start."

Maria nods. "I'm just grateful that I'm alive to answer those questions and that I'm still here today." She turns to me to explain. "I am heading to Amalfi tomorrow. Francesco will take me. We're spending the holidays with my daughter-in-law." Maria makes a face, indicating that she is not entirely thrilled about this prospect.

Emily and I exchange a glance. Seeing this, Maria answers the question we're too polite to ask. "I prefer my holidays at home. My daughter-in-law is very annoying."

"Nonna!" Francesco warns.

"What? You know it's the truth. Your mama's food is terrible, and she never stops talking," Maria says. Then she pats Francesco's cheek. "But she did give me a beautiful grandson."

"Your English is excellent," I compliment her.

"My nonna taught English. She learned it after the war. Her family had a British boarder," Francesco supplies. "He never left. He became my grandfather."

"Shh. I can speak for myself." Maria shakes a finger at her grandson. "And I don't need you to mess up the story. I did not learn English from my late husband, although he gave me the chance to practice it. Carmela and I actually began to learn English long before that. We thought maybe we would meet a handsome soldier and go to America with him. We wanted to be prepared."

"It worked out for Carmela!" Francesco claps.

Maria dips her bread in the olive oil and turns to address Emily before taking a bite. "How much did your nonna tell you about her life here?"

"Very little," Emily confesses. Maria chews slowly and swallows. She takes a sip of her wine before continuing.

"She didn't mention me or my family to you then?"

"No." Emily shakes her head. "That's why I was so glad to find the letters. I can't imagine why she didn't talk about this place. I mean, it's so beautiful. But my grandmother never talked about her life before she came to America. Except maybe when she was talking about the recipes she learned as a girl."

At this, Maria snorts and has to set down her wineglass.

"The recipes she learned as a girl? Oh, that is good. Very funny."

"What? What's funny about that?" Emily asks.

"Your grandmother's cooking was worse than my daughter-in-law's. I loved her dearly, but she could barely boil water."

"I assure you, Maria, my nonna was an excellent cook." Emily speaks defensively with her chin raised. "She taught me how to make all of her family classics."

"Really?" Maria looks dubious. "Well, this is interesting. Tell me about them? What did she make?"

"Chicken Parmesan, Fettucini Alfredo with Chicken, Spaghetti and Meatballs ..." Emily ticks off entrées on her fingers.

Maria shakes her head and wipes a tear from her cheek. "Oh Emily, cara mia, I am so sorry to tell you this, but your grandmother did not learn any of those dishes from her parents. We don't eat these things in Italy. But I am glad she finally learned how to cook. And I am sure she loved you very much if she learned to cook for you."

Francesco meets my eye, brows raised, in the awkward silence that follows. Then he turns to Emily.

"You are a journalist?" he asks.

"I am." She nods.

"You should write about my grandmother. She fought with the resistance in the war."

"That's not true, Francesco. You can hardly count translating a few letters, badly, as fighting in the resistance."

"Well, your brother fought with them, no?" Francesco argues. "And you helped him with the letters."

"I didn't help him enough." Maria sighs, looking back at us. "He died."

Emily and I both lean forward. "I'm so sorry, Maria." Emily lays a hand on the old woman's hand.

"This village seems so beautiful to you now, Emily, but things were very different in the war and the years following. Life was difficult. For me and for your grandmother. But possibly worse for your grandmother."

"Why is that?" Emily's brows are furrowed now, and I can see the cogs turning as she tries to imagine it—life in a different time, her grandmother as a young woman.

"Her parents were very strict. I would even say cruel. She spent a lot of time with my family because she couldn't stand being home alone with them. War has different effects on different people. Her parents were older, and very nervous. They didn't want her talking to anyone. They wanted her to stay home, not make any trouble."

"Oof. That wasn't her nature." Emily shakes her head.

"No." Maria laughs. "It was not."

Francesco chimes in, "So your grandmother was not only beautiful, but it sounds like she was spicy?"

Francesco leans across the table to refill Emily's glass, and I clock the shift in his interest. He is gazing attentively at her, lips parted, eyes flickering hungrily in the reflected candle-light. "Are you cold, bella? Take my jacket. It's very warm." He pats the jacket reverently and offers it to her.

Despite the fact that Emily is too lost in thought to notice his ministrations, I am struck by the overwhelming desire to punch him in the throat. Maria looks at her grandson, and then back at me, and rolls her eyes. Then she glances from me to Emily and back, and if I'm not mistaken, she winks. It all happens so quickly that I can't be sure I didn't imagine it.

I take a sip of my wine.

"Emily told me that her grandmother taught her to read palms," I mention in an attempt to lighten the conversation.

"Did she?" Maria grins. "Well then, give yours here."

"Do you read palms as well?" I raise a brow, but offer up my right hand.

"Who do you think taught Carmela?" Maria pulls on a pair of glasses that are dangling from a beaded chain around her neck. She dons them before gazing at my hand. She then purses her lips and begins to make expectorating noises.

Would it be rude to pull my hand away? Is she actually going to spit on me? I freeze.

Maria bursts out laughing. "Poor boy. You should see your face. I am only teasing. I will not spit on you."

"Try some ice!" Emily uses a spoon to fish an ice cube out of her own glass and places it in my palm.

"You, too, Emily." Maria indicates I should pass the ice cube to Emily. She pulls our palms together, side by side, to examine them.

"This is very interesting. I see something very big is happening here. But maybe it doesn't feel so real at the moment. There's some confusion. Things are not what they look like, no?" She holds our hands and looks into my eyes. "Maybe it's because you are such a big, famous person, Blaze. Nothing is what it seems. But I can tell you are a good man."

"I cannot believe that you have never read my palm, Nonna!" Francesco pouts. "I've only been your grandson for thirty-three years, and this is the first I hear about this talent?"

He places his palm next to Emily's and uses his thumb to stroke the back of her hand. When she turns to look at him questioningly, the overattentive smoldering is back.

"Put your hand away, Francesco." Maria scowls. "Leave Emily alone."

"What! Don't you want to see if maybe there could be something between me and your oldest friend's granddaughter? I don't see a ring on her finger."

Francesco shoots me a winning grin and nods at me, as if this is a game that I have agreed to play with him. May the best man win. He clearly thinks he is the best man. The balls on this guy!

I withdraw, biting my tongue and folding my arms across my chest, fists tucked under my elbows where they can do no harm.

Emily quickly pulls her hand away as well, drying her palm with her napkin.

"I think I'm good. Maybe you should read Francesco's palm, Maria."

"I don't need to read that fool's palm to know he has no future with you, Emily." Maria raises an eyebrow. She removes her glasses, letting them fall like a mic drop. "In our family, we do not marry our cousins."

emily

. . .

"THIS IS NOT A STORY FOR A RESTAURANT," Maria says. We have reconvened in her kitchen with freshly brewed coffee and fruity slabs of panettone.

I'm impressed that Maria is still able to live alone at her age, but Francesco assures me that she has a lot of help and is rarely alone.

"We all look after her," he says, pouring the coffee. "I live next door, and during the day, she has a helper to prepare food and drive her places. She still sits outside on the stoop on warm nights to spy and gossip."

"I don't have anyone left to shock with the most juicy gossip. And I miss the view from my old bedroom," Maria laments. "I don't go up the stairs much anymore. Everything I need is down here. I even have a washing machine. But it doesn't get things as clean. I still prefer to handwash my own undergarments."

"She is impossible," Francesco complains.

"Blaze, caro mio, can you reach the cabinet above the stove?"

Maria directs Blaze to a high cabinet. He has to stand on a stepstool to reach the box that's been stashed there. A cloud of dust swirls around him as he gingerly takes it down, making him sneeze. The box itself is also coated with a thick layer of powdery dust. Blaze uses a rag by the sink to wipe the dust off before he brings the box to the table. Then he fetches a fresh rag to clean off the counter.

"Grazie, Blaze." Maria smiles gratefully and lifts the lid off the box with shaky hands. The corners of the box are cracked, and the lid is dotted with water stains that look suspiciously like tears.

"Tell me exactly what your grandmother told you," Maria says as she rifles through the contents.

I repeat the story that I could recite in my sleep at this point. The coincidental same last names, the knock on the door, the instant connection, the love letters that they traded in the months that they were apart. Then I place the stack of letters from my bag onto the table for everyone to see.

"They both insisted it was love at first sight," I end. "And I can vouch that they loved each other till the very end. My nonna didn't want to live without Grandpa Joe. So, I'm really confused about what you are suggesting here. How can we be cousins?" I ask, pointing at Francesco, who is helping himself to one of the letters. He sets aside the thin, pink ribbon.

"Careful with that," I warn. "It's fragile."

"Non preoccuparti (Don't worry)." He dismisses my concern. I am not convinced.

"Here is what I was looking for." Maria pulls out a black-and-white photo of a young man, along with a ribbon that matches the one that's bound the letters together for all these years.

I reach out to touch the fragile, pink, silk scrap. I need my fingers to confirm the sameness that my eyes see.

"How is this same ribbon here?"

I lift the ribbon off the photo, only to drop it immediately. And I gasp.

"Does he look familiar to you?" Maria asks, almost hopefully.

Blaze steps down from the stool and drops his rag in the sink.

"What is it?" he asks, brushing off his hands and coming to stand beside me. He places a hand on my shoulder and bends to study the face of the young man in the photo.

"Oh, wow," Blaze says. "I can definitely see a little resemblance to Francesco."

Francesco sets down the letter he was reading and considers that. He shrugs. "Maybe a little, when I was younger. But I am named after this man, so no big surprise."

I'm still processing what I'm looking at. Words feel like loose marbles in my mouth. I cannot organize them. Instead, I reach for my phone, scrolling back through the album I put together almost a year ago. When I've loaded the one that I'm looking for, I lay my phone on the table beside the photograph.

"This is my father from his high school yearbook," I say. "His name was Frank."

Blaze's other hand comes to my other shoulder and squeezes, rooting me there. Holding me together.

"I don't understand?" Francesco says.

"Who is the man in this photo?" I ask, tapping the paper print.

"He was my brother—my twin brother, also Francesco—but we called him Ciccio." Maria picks up the photo to look at it. "We were all eighteen years old when he was killed."

She plucks another photo from the box. This one is more faded, giving the entire image a ghostly look. In the photo, a half dozen children sit around a table. I recognize my grandmother at the center, staring at a slice of cake with a candle and grinning. She has teeth missing. She can't be more than seven or eight.

"This is me here, and Ciccio." Maria points at herself and her twin brother, sitting on either side of my grandmother, gazing at her with complete adoration. She hands the photo to me, and on closer inspection, I notice that Ciccio is holding a small, wrapped package. I point at this.

"Ribbons for her hair," Maria says. She picks up the frayed remnants of the ribbon from the box. "I bought her chocolate, but she always liked his gifts better. The only thing my brother and I ever fought over was who loved Carmela more."

"So, Grandpa Joe wasn't …?" I can't complete the sentence. It doesn't seem possible that the words should exist in a sentence together.

"I am sure that Joe Romano was an excellent father to Frank and a wonderful grandfather to you. But no, he was not the biological father of your father."

"I have to sit down," I say, ignoring the fact that I am, in fact, already sitting down. Maria pats my hand.

Blaze pulls up a chair beside me and rubs my shoulders gently. "This explains why the three of you have such similar and unusual eyes," he says.

"There's a little bit more," Maria warns. "But maybe this is too much. It doesn't matter. Obviously, your grandmother loved your grandfather very much, and they had a good life together."

"The best." I nod tearfully, remembering the tender way my nonna held Grandpa Joe's hand as he took his last breaths, telling him he could go but he'd better wait for her.

"Maybe it can wait until tomorrow," Blaze suggests. "It's getting late."

"We are leaving for Amalfi in the morning," Francesco says. "I am sorry. I wish we had known sooner that Emily was coming." He checks his watch and stands. "I can take you to the apartment any time. There is only one bedroom. Maybe the Love Doctor wants to sleep on the couch. You are not a married couple."

"Sit down," Maria says to her grandson. "You are being rude."

"Tell me the rest," I urge. "Please?"

"I don't want you to think your grandmother was a loose woman. She and Francesco were very much in love. And they had agreed to get married. In their minds, they were already married. We knew what he was doing was very dangerous. But we were too young to believe the worst might actually happen."

Blaze pauses rubbing my shoulders to take Maria's hand. "But it did," he says. "I'm so sorry. You both must have been destroyed."

Maria nods and blinks back her own tears.

"Carmela blamed me because I had encouraged him to fight. When her parents found out she was pregnant, they forbade her to see my family again and made arrangements to send her to a convent."

"My God, poor Carmela," Blaze says. "And poor you, Maria."

"Yes, I lost my twin brother and was losing my best friend too."

"So how did Carmela meet Joe?" Blaze asks. He continues to rub slow, comforting circles on the back of my neck and shoulders. I am suddenly so grateful he is here, asking the questions I need the answers to while I struggle to process everything.

"Thank you for having my back," I turn to him and whisper.

"Always." He nods back at me.

"It was simply a chance encounter. Her mother sent her to the store to fetch something, and she stopped by the fountain to make a wish."

"I wonder what she wished for?" I ask.

"Who knows?" Maria shrugs sympathetically. "But she was sitting there, crying, when Joe saw her. He was passing through town with his unit. They were stationed nearby. He wouldn't leave her side until he knew she was okay. Your grandmother sent for me to translate."

"I thought you both studied English?" I ask.

"Carmela was more interested in studying my brother than learning English. Her English wasn't very good at that point." Maria shakes her head sadly. "Anyway, I was the one who came up with the plan and who wrote most of the letters you have here."

"What?" I splutter. "What plan?"

"The fake relationship plan." Maria sighs. "Joe felt very sorry for Carmela. He wanted to help her. He told us he had a big house back in the USA that he was headed home to. If they got married, Carmela could come with him. She wouldn't have to go to the convent, and nobody would take her baby away from her."

"Grandpa Joe grew up in an orphanage!" I gasp. That tracks that he wouldn't want to see another kid go through something like that.

"So many soldiers were marrying Italian women then," Maria continues. "Joe was the exact type of man I'd hoped to meet when I studied English all those years. I have to confess, I was a little jealous. But he couldn't take both of us back with him."

"He didn't mind that she was pregnant?" I ask.

"No. He had injuries from the war, and he wasn't sure if he would be able to have his own." Maria glances down at her hands.

Francesco shifts uncomfortably in his seat.

"Joseph was very kind. He told her she was free to stay with him, or not. He just wanted her and her baby to have the opportunity. We wrote the letters to make the sudden 'love affair' more convincing, should anyone question them."

"What did Carmela's parents think?" Blaze asks, once again beating me to the punch.

"They threw her out of the house as soon as they found out she was involved with this soldier." Maria frowns. "She came to stay with me until it was time to go to America. We were afraid she wouldn't get there before the baby came. I wished that this would be true. I wanted to see this piece of my brother."

"So, this whole time, when she was writing these letters"—I tap the pile—"she was living with you, where? Right here? And you were the one writing them?"

"Not all of them." Maria smiles. "While we waited, Carmela studied English for real. And after a while, she decided to start writing her own answers to Joe's letters."

"But they were *faking* it," I say. "That whole time. My whole life. They didn't tell my dad or me the truth."

"Did you really need to know?" Maria shrugs. "Was it really any of your business?"

"Yes, I think we deserved to know that none of it was real," I argue. "I've carried these letters halfway around the world, like a talisman, trying to convince myself to believe in love again, and it turns out they're forgeries?"

"Who's to say what's real?" Maria smiles enigmatically at me. It's maddening how infuriated I am with her. I have no place to put these emotions, and the uncomfortable itch of them makes it impossible to sit still any longer. I push back from the table and stand to pace.

"Why did you even tell me all of this, Maria? Why now?"

"Because you found my letters to Carmela, and you contacted me. You asked. And because when I'm gone, there will be nobody else to set the record straight. And I know you thought you were alone now. But the truth is, you aren't. You still have family here."

I shake my head. It's all too much. I'm so tired. I need to walk. I need to sleep.

"Take this box," Maria says. "There are some photos of you in there too. Carmela didn't write often, but she always sent news of you and your father when she did."

"I can't take them," I argue. "They're yours."

"No. They're yours. I was only saving them for you. But you can bring them back when you visit again. Maybe for Easter? It's lovely in the spring, and if you stay with me, I won't have to listen to my daughter-in-law."

"Nonna!" Francesco reprimands.

"Or this one," Maria adds, using her cane and her grandson's shoulder as levers to stand. "He needs to find a wife already. Hopefully, one who is not a relative."

blaze

· · ·

"Get yourself a safe word or two before you need them. They're not just for sexual situations. Safe words are the relationship equivalent of a roadside emergency kit. Those silver shock blankets and road-side flares are real life savers."

— Blaze Smith, *Go Your Own Way*, on Bumpy Territory

DESPITE THE FACT that the mattress is lumpy and the sheets are scratchy, we sleep like the dead. The following morning finds us tangled in the dip at the center of a suspiciously small, so-called "double" bed.

"It's a good thing I like you." Emily pulls her knees to her chest and tips her head back onto my shoulder as I spoon her.

"Same," I say, stroking her hair. "How are you doing after last night?"

She groans. "Ugh. Don't remind me. I was hoping this headache meant I drank too much wine and it was all a bad dream."

Maria's box is sitting on the dresser.

"When do you think you'll want to look through that?" I ask.

"I don't know. Later? I'm just not ready yet," Emily says. She rolls away from me, hoisting herself up and out of the mattress valley. "I need to find something for my head. Don't go anywhere."

Barefoot, hungover, and wearing an old tee, her curls are drooping, but she's still achingly beautiful in these simple surroundings. The apartment where we've spent the night is humble, but comfortable. Stone, tile, wrought iron, and wood are the primary elements making up the three rooms. On the ground floor, there's a small living room and kitchen. A short staircase separates the cozy sleeping area and bathroom from the living space.

"I'm sorry if this wasn't the fun, romantic road trip you were expecting," Emily says.

"I didn't have any expectations." I sit up in bed and reach for my tee. "You don't have to apologize. We could be in a ditch, and I'd probably still be happy to be on an adventure with you."

She seems like she wants to say something, but stops. Instead, she pulls on some thick, handmade socks and grabs her phone from the nightstand. "I'm just going to poke around the kitchen for caffeine. I'll be right back."

After she exits the small room, I roll up a pillow to place between myself and the wrought iron headboard. Then I reach for my phone. It's early—only 7 a.m. I hear the sound of diesel engines rumbling and shutters slamming in the distance as the village wakes up. There's nowhere that we need to be today, and I'm happy to follow Emily's lead. This gives me another day to decide what to do about the holidays and seeing my mom. Lazily, I scroll through my feed, browsing the news and not looking for anything in particular.

I would have missed the post on the celebrity gossip site entirely if Steff hadn't texted me a screenshot.

"One hundred percent Smokeshow, 0 percent Fire—Relationship "Expert" Blaze Smith Fakes Relationship with American Writer While on Holiday Book Tour in Italy."

The photo shows Emily and me outside the Anglo-American Bookstore. Chest thumping, I click the link.

"Sources close to these two have revealed that the entire relationship is a lie, fabricated to mask the fallout from Blaze's recent breakup with his anchorwoman girlfriend. Blaze is allegedly heartbroken over having been dumped for Rafe Barzilay, a.k.a. Titanium Man. It is unclear how the relationship guru and Ms. Romano met, but according to local news and a post on popular romance novelist Isla Fairfax's blog, Ms. Romano is researching her family history in Italy. The not-really-a-couple were last seen headed to the small town of Pitigliano in Tuscany."

Steff texts again, asking if I've read it yet.

> Give me a minute. I'm just reading it now.

> How did this happen? Who leaked it? Who did you tell?

> Seriously? I have no clue. You tell me!

My mind is lit up like a switchboard, looking for connections. Someone from the hotel? Isla? One of Emily's friends from home? As far as I know, none of her friends know about our agreement. We were so careful.

> I hate to say I told you so. But I warned you about her. She was in it for herself all along.

> You are not seriously suggesting that Emily is the one who leaked this?

If the shoe fits.

Emily's scruffy, sheepskin boots are sitting innocently by the bedroom door.

What about Kent?

No way. Kent's not that kind of idiot. Where are you now? The paps are going to be all over you. What's your evacuation plan?

I pull on my jeans and start packing. She's right. It's only a matter of time before the vultures show up.

Emily returns to the room holding two mugs of tea, her phone precariously tucked between her shoulder and her ear.

"I don't care how much you're offering," she shouts in the general direction of her collarbone. "I'm never writing that article, and I don't have any kind of a statement for you. Jesus, I thought you were a reputable publication!"

As she turns to glance at me, the phone flies out and clatters across the floor, coming to a halt somewhere under the bed. I can hear the tinny, abrasive voice of the editor still trying to persuade her.

"We're talking about a cover story, Emily. We're prepared to double the offer we made when we just thought you were dating him. Don't dismiss it out of hand. Six figures. International exposure. I realize that this might be a little sensitive for you due to the sex worker overtones, but people want to hear your story—from you. And they deserve to know what kind of shyster that man really is. I mean, what kind of relationship expert fakes a relationship, right? He's totally full of shit."

Shyster. Full of shit. I flinch.

Emily sets down the mugs of tea on the dresser and dives under the bed for the phone.

"Fuck. Off," she says as she presses the button to disconnect the call. She stares at me, wide-eyed and horrified.

"Blaze I … I don't know how to tell you this, but I think somebody leaked our story."

"Was it you?" I ask.

"What the fuck! I can't believe you would even ask me that! You heard me telling her to go to hell."

"I also heard her repeating all the same things that you told me in the airport. That you think I'm full of shit."

Emily is livid. She narrows her eyes and shakes her head at me.

"You know what? You *are* full of shit if you think it's okay for you to say that to me right now."

Hastily, she pulls on clothing and commences stuffing items back into her bag.

"Why was Kent texting you yesterday?" I ask, recalling how secretive she was about the exchange.

"Kent's piece got canceled. They offered it to me if I was willing to write a tell-all about what it's like to be Doctor Love's primary patient. He was pissed. I probably should have told you when they called me yesterday at the studio, but I was hoping if I just ignored them, they'd lose interest and leave me alone."

"So, you weren't just upset about being blindsided on the show," I say. I knew there was more to it. "And you thought Kent was just going to let it go?" I ask.

"Yes. I didn't think he'd risk his entire career over it. I still don't. Especially now that he's a new dad. Ouch! Dammit!"

she curses when the zipper pinches her finger. She kicks the unbalanced bag, and it wobbles on stuck wheels for a few inches before falling over.

I sit back on the bed and take a deep breath, trying to calm myself, assess the damage, and keep this situation from spinning out of control. Emily sucks on her finger.

"This is ridiculous," I say. "I'm sorry. I'm totally overreacting."

She looks at me warily.

"It's not the end of the world," I insist. "I just wasn't expecting it."

"I haven't read it yet," Emily admits.

I hand her my phone with the article pulled up. She scans the photos before reading.

"On the plus side, they don't have any photos of us in the costumes," she says.

"That is looking on the bright side," I agree. I give her time to finish reading, staring at the over-steeped tea cooling on the dresser.

"This really sucks," she says when she finishes. "Much more for you than for me. Do you have any idea what you're going to do?" Her eyes are sympathetic, but I don't want her pity.

"You didn't tell any friends about our deal?"

"No! I wish I could have talked to them. It's been killing me to lie to Alexis. And Isla. I just met her. What's she going to think?" Emily stops talking and looks at me defiantly. "But why does it have to be someone on my side of the equation? Maybe it was someone from your team."

Our conversation is interrupted by a loud banging downstairs.

"Emily! Blaze!" Francesco's voice is urgent as he continues to pound the door to the apartment. "Wake up!"

"Go," I say. "See what he wants. I'll dump these." I pick up the mugs and head into the modest, tiled bathroom.

As I rinse the mugs, I hear the pounding stop. Francesco's footsteps echo in the living room below. The door slams, and I catch the sound of the deadbolt.

"I am sorry to wake you like this, but it's an emergency. I have come to warn you!" Francesco's dramatic announcement echoes across the apartment.

"Is Maria okay?" Emily asks worriedly.

"Yes, my nonna is fine. That is not the problem."

"Okay, then. I would offer you some coffee, but all I could find was tea and two mugs," Emily says. "Would you like to sit down? I'll just fetch the mugs."

"Here they are," I say, coming down the short flight of stairs to join them. I place the mugs on the counter.

In the light of day, Francesco is a little less put together. His coat looks rather worn, and he has bags under his eyes. But oh, how similar those eyes are to Emily's.

"What's the trouble?" I ask.

He glares at me.

"I should ask you the same, Dottore Amore!" He sneers. "How dare you bring this army to my town. To my nonna's house!"

"Oh no. What happened?" I ask.

"They came at six in the morning. In the dark! When I came to fetch her to leave for Napoli, they had her place surrounded! They might have scared her to death. She is a very old woman."

"Okay. By *they*, do you mean paparazzi?" Emily clarifies.

"Si, yes! The paparazzi! Who do you think I meant?" Francesco looks at us as if we are deliberately missing the point. "Five men and two women. Right away, they start with the shooting and the … how do you say, booms!"

Emily and I exchange a look as Francesco continues, clearly relishing his self-important role in our drama. He lifts his chin, staring off into the distance, as if recalling war-torn memories.

"It is not safe for you two here anymore. You need to leave. Subito (immediately)."

"We're already packed. I'll get the bags," I volunteer. I'm back with them in a matter of moments. Francesco presses a hand-drawn map into Emily's hands.

"Stick to these alleys. This is the safest route out of the city," he says.

He looks at me gravely upon my return with the suitcases. "If anything happens to my cousin …"

"I will do my best to keep her safe," I promise. "But you have to realize that it's hardly a matter of life and death, Francesco. Worst case scenario, someone takes a bad photo. Where are the paparazzi now?"

"Nonna invited them all into her house for breakfast." Francisco shrugs. "She is making eggs. She sent me out for pastries and to warn you so you could escape. She says she will keep them busy for a while."

"Oh my God, Maria." Emily shakes her head and chuckles.

"I'm starting to see where you get it from," I say.

emily

. . .

WHEN WE GET in the car, my only plan is to get out of town. I retrace our route back through the city's ancient stone gate, heading down toward the valley below. I don't stop until we cross the valley and crest the next hill. When we reach the overlook, I pull over. This time, we don't get out. We remain in the front seat, staring at the view. The colors are different in the light of day. Some of the magic is gone. But it's still an almost otherworldly sight.

Aside from the sound of the wind in the trees, bird calls, and the occasional passing car, everything is silent. I wish I had coffee. I didn't even have time to drink the tea.

"Where to now?" I ask.

"We should probably go back to Rome to regroup." Blaze sighs. "But we could stop somewhere on the way if you want. I'm sorry, Emily. I'm sure you wanted to spend more time there."

"I'll be back," I say, feeling certain. "The timing isn't right now."

Now that we know we're being pursued, every car that passes us releases fresh waves of anxiety. Every glance in our direction feels suspect.

"I guess I'll drive toward Rome, then," I say. "We can stop for coffee at the service station."

"Okay," Blaze says. "Do you want me to put any music on?"

"No, it's okay. I think I prefer it quiet right now."

I pull back onto the two-lane highway and put all my attention into the winding road. I'm grateful for the mesmerizing curves. They keep me from obsessing about last night's earth-shattering info dump. It's going to take some time for the pieces of my life to reassemble. I have a great-aunt. Cousins. A whole family history that I knew nothing about.

I glance in the rearview mirror at the paper box. It's in the center of the back seat, buckled in like a child.

On the next straightaway, I steal another glance at Blaze, surprised to see he's looking at me as well.

"So, Steff texted me earlier. Obviously," he says.

"Why obviously?" I ask. "I thought you fired her?"

"Yes, but she's not just my tour manager. She's been handling my PR for a really long time. And I don't know who else I'd call to deal with a crisis like this."

"Well, as long as we're sharing, I texted Kent back while I was making the tea," I admit.

"What the hell for?" Blaze scowls.

"To make it clear to him that I had no interest in stealing his byline."

"Is that really it?" Blaze asks. "I mean, was that even necessary?"

"I felt like it was. It's one thing to ghostwrite for him. It's another to steal his byline."

"I wish you would have," Blaze grumbles. "He certainly doesn't deserve any favors from you."

"I wouldn't be here now without him." I shrug. "I don't regret coming. What if I never found out the truth?" I glance back again.

"Tell me the truth, Emily. Did you inform Kent that our relationship was fake?"

I don't answer right away.

"Well, that explains everything." Blaze lifts his phone to start texting.

"Explains what?" I glance sideways at him and then have to overcorrect on the next turn.

"Hey! Keep your eyes on the road, please?" Blaze says.

"He called me a starfucker, Blaze. I came here to do a job for him, and he had the wrong impression. Besides, I know this man. He would never leak anything that he's attached to in any way. He's far too afraid of making himself look bad."

"Sure," Blaze says tersely.

"Who are you texting?" I ask, struggling to keep my focus on the road. We've descended out of the forest now and into open, rolling hills full of fields with scattered cypress trees and olive groves.

"Who do you think?" He sounds exasperated.

"It wasn't Kent," I say. "He didn't leak this."

"Then who was it, Emily? Six figures is a big paycheck. Much bigger than Kent was sharing with you, I imagine. Six figures to write a tell-all about someone you'd already decided was full of shit? For all I know, this was the plan all along!"

Is he for real?

"Are you texting with Steff right now?" I ask.

"Did you or did you not say I was full of shit in the airport last week? Christ, I can't believe that was only a week ago."

Focus on the road, I tell myself, easing up on the clutch and downshifting into the downhill curve. Deep breath in.

"You're a celebrity relationship expert, Blaze. It's fair to say that there are a lot of people who think you are full of shit. Especially idiots like me who hadn't ever read your books. But I've done a total one-eighty. Obviously." I reach out to touch his arm.

He leans away.

"Is it that obvious, Emily? You are the one who keeps insisting that this isn't real. You're the one who was trying her best to leave yesterday! Why am I even here?"

I don't even have time to shift gears before the boar charges across the road in front of us. It happens so quickly, but also in slow motion. A flash of tusks, hooves, and leathery skin with wiry hair, he trots jauntily across the road and toward us. He's moving fast but doesn't seem to be in a hurry. Like he isn't the least bit concerned about becoming sausage. All that's missing is the cigarette dangling from his hairy jowls.

I scream as I slam on the brakes and swerve to avoid the massive beast.

As we spin, I am aware that I've lost all control. There's nothing to do but wait to see where it stops. How can so many thoughts pass through my head in a split second? I see Blaze, braced for impact, and in the rearview mirror, I spot the box of photos, still secure. My imagination—surely it's that—places my father beside it, resting one hand protectively on the lid.

Then, with a sickening thud, we land in the ditch. Mercifully, the airbags do not deploy.

"Jesus! Emily! Are you okay?"

The car is facing the wrong direction. We are pitched forward and to the side at an awkward angle. For a second, I sit there, stunned, thinking I should get out of the car, but I can't possibly open my door. Blaze unbuckles my seat belt.

"You're not bleeding. I don't think anything's broken," he says, looking me over and touching me tentatively.

"I'm fine," I say. "How about you? Are you okay?" He looks all right, but we could both be in shock. I've never been in a car accident before.

"I'm fine too," he insists. "All things considered, I think we're pretty lucky we just landed in the ditch."

"We didn't hit it, did we?" I ask, suddenly worried that the sound I heard wasn't just the sound of us hitting the ditch.

"No, but it was close. That was some amazing evasive action there. That thing was huge. It could have killed us."

"Fucking wild boar." I shake my head. "Unreal."

"We should get out," Blaze says. He opens his door and jumps out. He's clearly all right. He reaches back in for me. "Are you okay to climb out on my side?"

"Yes, I just want to grab the box," I say. I reach into the back seat and release the seat belt, handing the pictures out first. Then Blaze helps me out.

"I'm calling for help right now," he says, turning away from me and walking up the road.

Maybe it's the way he's speaking in low tones. Or maybe it's the fact that he walked away from me to make the call.

I go back to the car and retrieve my own phone from between the seats. Then I manage to get out my suitcase, which I use for a makeshift seat in the field.

I scroll till I find the contact I'm looking for.

Hey, Isla, what are you up to?

Nothing much. How's Tuscany?

Not so great.

Oh no. What's up?

I text her the link to the celebrity gossip site.

She responds with a horrified face emoji.

It's not true, is it? I don't believe it. I saw you two together.

As awful as that article is, I have another problem.

I shoot a photo of the car.

Holy shit, what happened?

I answer with a boar emoji, thinking this is the first and hopefully last time I'll ever use it.

He was a hairy boar. A very scary boar.

Are you okay? Do you need anything?

Blaze's suitcase squeaks as he rolls it over to join me in the field.

"Help is on the way, and my driver will meet us by the rest area off the highway."

"Everything is so simple when you have money and a staff." I sigh. I should be more grateful.

"You'll have to file a police report for the rental company, but I'll make sure the car is paid for and fixed," he offers.

"Thanks for that," I say, flatly.

"Of course." Blaze positions his suitcase and settles himself down on it. He glances at the sky. "Good thing it's not raining."

"Who did you just call?" I ask.

"Why does it matter?"

"It matters." I steel myself for the answer.

"Look, I was already texting with Steff when we got in the accident. She would have sent out a search party if I hadn't responded."

"Has it ever occurred to you that Steff might have been the one to have leaked that story?" I ask.

"Don't be ridiculous." Blaze shakes his head. "She may have a problematic personality, but she is very good at her job."

"Problematic?" I question. "She set you up before. Why wouldn't she do it again?"

"Because this could destroy her whole career."

"You think she cares more about her career than she cares about you?" I ask, incredulous.

"Absolutely." Blaze nods.

"But you think that Kent doesn't care as much about his career?" I ask.

"It's hard to say what Kent cares about. His priorities seem pretty fucked up from where I sit." Blaze crosses his long legs in front of him.

"Is your career the most important thing to you?" I ask.

"I think you know the answer to that." Blaze picks at the grass. "I'm grateful for it all, but it's gotten away from me. It's not what I want going forward."

"And you think that my career is all *I* care about?" I kick at the dirt, wishing help would come sooner.

"I didn't mean it like that," he protests.

"I know." I sigh. "You were texting with Steff. That was her messing with both our heads. But the point is that you let her. You keep suggesting I'm not over Kent, but I'm not the one who's put another person in the driver's seat on their journey —you are. You've even dragged her along on this trip with me. I feel like she's the one riding shotgun."

I can see flashing lights and a tow truck in the distance.

We both stand, and he waves at the approaching vehicles. Blaze sucks in a deep breath before he looks at me.

"Clearly, we still have a lot to talk about," he says.

"No, we don't," I argue. "After we do the paperwork, Isla is coming to get me. No more make-believe. This is where it ends."

blaze

. . .

"The sticker on the mirror says 'Objects may be closer than they appear.' So, are you going to believe the mirror or the sticker?"

— Blaze Smith, *Go Your Own Way*, on Going with Your Gut vs. Taking Advice

"**DO** you want to make any stops?" My driver glances back from the front seat of the Mercedes sedan. It seemed pointless to ask for a van when it's just me.

"No. Let's just head to Villa dei Baci."

The silence in the car is anything but comforting. It covers me like a wet blanket. Clouds are gathering, and the landscape has lost its lushness. Everything appears grayer and duller than yesterday.

I fiddle with my phone. I could call Steff to let her know I'm on my way, but I would prefer to have the element of surprise. If there's any chance that Emily could be right, I can't give Steff the time to spin.

The argument continues to replay in my head. Sample headlines too. They pop up between my thoughts, like unwanted ads playing too loud.

Once again, I sift through my complicated emotions about coming on this tour. The timing was awful, with my mom's condition worsening and the holidays looming. I hadn't really wanted to come. The scandal with Viv could have been the perfect excuse to bow out. It would have blown over. People don't actually care that much about my breakups, and their attention span is short. There's always another story. If I'd called it, it wouldn't have been so bad.

Instead, I'd behaved like some kind of crazy, fucking storm chaser who gets in the car to evacuate and then decides it'd be much more fun to drive toward the tornado instead.

It would be easy to blame everything on Steff's scheming and manipulation, but Steff didn't force me into a passionless and complacent PR-driven relationship with Viv. For years! I'd just gone along with it. It hadn't been fair to either one of us. No wonder she stepped out with a superhero. Steff also didn't force me to keep writing books when what I really wanted to do was get back to private practice. It was just easier to put it off. And Steff didn't force me to get on that plane.

The only person who's forced me to do anything is Emily. She's forced me to face the truth. And the truth is that it's been so much easier to be a passenger lying in the back seat, studying my maps and pontificating, than to buckle up, pick a direction, and drive.

The irony of having this epiphany in the back seat of this chauffeur-driven Mercedes is not lost on me.

So, I'm not going to confront Steff now because I want—or even need—her to fix things for me.

I'm going because I need to know the truth. If it was Steff who leaked the story, then I'm not even sure how I'm going to apologize.

I don't think it was Steff. Emily insists it couldn't have been Kent. I know in my heart that it wasn't Emily. How could I have thought, even considered for a moment, that she leaked this story? Now I'm not going to rest till I figure it out.

It's too late to call my mom, but there's a chance my sister is still awake, and I need to talk. I dial her number.

emily

. . .

"PLEASE KEEP an eye out for wild boars," I beg Isla.

Isla is playing classical music in her beat-up, ancient, orange Volvo wagon. I take comfort in the fact that it's built like a battle tank. The rain has really started to come down, and the wipers beat a steady spludge, spludge, spludge as we make our way south.

I can't thank her enough for rescuing me.

"Oh please! I had nothing on for today besides cleaning," she assures me. "My mum isn't coming in till tomorrow. You've saved me from the misery of housework. Plus, I'm dying to hear the story about the letters. You must tell me everything, or I won't let you leave!" Isla pushes a strand of red hair behind her ear. She is wearing hot-pink glasses and a bright-blue raincoat.

"Where to start," I say, conjuring up a vision of Francesco. I describe my second cousin in detail, down to his shiny shoes, pocket square, and eyes so similar to mine.

"He's single," I mention casually.

Isla laughs. "Nope. I don't date Italian men. They come with Italian mothers."

"You say that like it's a bad thing," I joke. And then I dig into my bag, fish out my knitting project, and launch into the tale. I'm determined to finish the story and my knitting before we get to the Rome Airport. It seems right to be done with both before I get on the plane home.

"So, Maria is your great-aunt, and all this time, you had family in Italy that you didn't know about?" Isla is incredulous.

"I didn't suspect a thing. And neither did my father, I'm sure of it. We knew nothing about the fake relationship, the letters, all of it. I still can't wrap my head around the fact that Maria wrote the letters!"

Isla glances at the box sitting between us on the bench seat.

"But she didn't write *all* of them," Isla corrects. "She said your grandmother took over at some point, right?"

"Yes, I suppose."

"Maybe she did that because she was starting to have feelings for Grandpa Joe."

"Maybe." I pause to pick up a dropped stitch.

"Your grandparents were very much in love. You told me as much at the café. It's part of what made you want to investigate the origins of their love story, right?"

"That's what I thought," I say. "I'm not even sure what to think anymore. My grandparents always set the relationship bar for me, and they set it high."

"What if you'd never found the letters?" Isla asks.

"Part of me wishes I hadn't," I admit. "I don't want to give up their love story. It gave me hope."

"I think you're looking at it the wrong way," Isla admonishes. "This information may change the story details, but it doesn't change the fact that they loved each other. Truly. If anything, I think it makes it more romantic. Think about it. Think about the chance that they both took, barely knowing each other? And think about how it all worked out."

"They were each other's perfect match," I say, recalling the little ways they always cared for each other.

"Right. And while the death of Maria's brother was tragic, who's to say how that would have panned out? Your grandmother got a second chance and she took it, without looking back. And look where that got her. It got her *you*."

I feel the sting of tears starting to well in my eyes and look down at the yarn in my lap. I've completed the last row.

Isla takes the exit for the airport. Now there's nothing left to do but cast off.

blaze

. . .

"Why don't I like 'Park at Your Own Risk' signs? To me, these are red flags. That's the last thing you want to see when you're in uncharted territory. You need to know nothing crazy is going to happen when you walk away from your shit for two minutes. Imagine if people wore these signs? We'd never let our partners out of our sight."

— Blaze Smith, *Go Your Own Way*, on Trust Issues

THERE'S no security when we pull up to the gate to Villa dei Baci this time. The iron doors are propped open wide. We park next to two other cars in the circular drive, one of which I recognize as Marco's custom, purple Ferrari. This is encouraging. It means that it's likely that Steff and Marco are at home.

I'm not exactly sure what I'm going to say to Steff when I march up to the door. I just know that this is a conversation we need to have face-to-face.

The iron, lion's head door-knocker at the center of the massive oak entry is the size of a baby's head. I lift it and release it. It hits the wooden door with a satisfying clonk that shakes the large holly wreath mounted above.

For a moment, I don't think anyone will answer the door. I try the latch, only to find it's locked. But then I see movement through the glass window beside the door, and I hear footsteps echoing on the travertine inside.

A tall, blonde woman, who I recognize as the final contestant, Giulia, from the TV show, answers the door. She is wearing a short bathrobe and a facemask.

"Oh!" I say, surprised to see her. "I'm sorry. I was looking for Marco and Steff?"

"Si, si. I think they are shooting some holiday photos in the pavilion." She points in the direction of the pool. "You know the way, no? If you don't mind going yourself, I am working on some TikTok videos for my skincare line."

"Thanks," I say, stepping into the foyer. "I hope things are going well for you and Marco?"

"So well," she enthuses in broken English. "I am almost a million followers!"

"Good for you," I say, quite aware that she hadn't answered the actual question I'd asked. Yet in a way, she had.

The house feels different without the crew and all the activity. Empty. It's not just missing people. The set dressing is gone as well. There's not a lot of furniture left and no art on the walls. The floors are bare stone, which makes every sound echo.

I make my way through the granite kitchen and out to the glassed-in pool area.

"Hello?" I call. "Steff? Marco?"

Contrary to Giulia's tip, there doesn't appear to be anyone here. The pool is still full, though, and the familiar Jacuzzi is turned on and bubbling away. Steam is rising from it, fogging up the glass.

But it isn't the Jacuzzi that's occupying pride of place anymore. It has been upstaged by a larger-than-life-size red sleigh parked beside the Jacuzzi. Gone is the small seating area we sat in last week. This is the Ferrari of sleds.

Up front, the seats are upholstered in sparkling, glittery, white vinyl. In back, there's plenty of room for presents or to stretch out on the full-size, fur-covered mattress that cushions the interior. The sled's exterior is decorated with giant, shining jingle bells and tinsel streamers. The license plate on the back reads "I SLAY." I can only hope no reindeer were harmed in the execution of this monstrosity.

But no Steff and no Marco.

Before going to search for them, I duck into the restroom for a quick pitstop. As I relieve my over-full bladder, it occurs to me I should have asked my driver if he needed to go as well.

I'm just about to flush when I hear them coming into the pavilion. The clack of Steff's shoes is unmistakable. And her brittle laugh.

"I'll just place the tripod over here," she says. "You look so naughty, Santa."

"No, no. Santa is never on the naughty list. Be a good little elf and show Santa how you do your magic."

My hand freezes on the lever. I hear some giggling, and then someone turns on the song "Santa Baby." Good Lord, what have I walked in on?

Cautiously, I peek through the wooden slats on the door. My view is partially impeded by a potted palm, but in between the fronds, I can make out a foot in a high-heeled version of an elf shoe.

The foot steps forward, revealing a leg wearing red-and-green-striped stockings. My eyes follow the lines to mid-thigh. There are red, sequined garters holding the socks up. And above that?

Oh God. My eyes.

As she moves into full view, I can see that Steff has on elf ears. And not a whole lot more. Her spiky, frosted hair has fake snow in it, which is frankly a terrible look. It looks like reindeer dandruff. She's holding up a phone and merrily shooting photos, all the while shaking her assets to the tune.

"That's it, Santa, show me your package." She giggles.

Unfortunately, I see Marco too. He is wearing a shiny, red thong, furry, white boots that match his faux-fur beard, a Santa hat, and … is that a cape he is tossing over his shoulder?

Marco jumps into the sled and shakes his hips. I hear the sound of jingle bells coming from his behind.

"Want to take a ride with Santa?" he purrs. "I can take you places that the dottore never could."

"Let's not talk about my other clients. Let's stay present, Marco. I mean, Santa. Now show me that North Pole!"

Oh, my fucking Lord. I should just flush the toilet, and come out now. I don't want to hear this. Or see it. I'm not sure which is the worse fate.

"This is the real deal, Steffelfie. True north! You never have to make a fake anything with this."

This promise is followed by loud, slurpy noises. A quick, cautious peek out the slats confirms that they are seated in the sleigh and have their tongues down each other's throats.

"You are a very, very naughty little helper." Marco growls.

"Tell me how I can work harder for you, Santa," Steff rasps breathily as the song changes to 'All I Want for Christmas.'

"Well, you know, all Santa wants for Christmas is for Marco to get some good American press. Maybe some live appearances in Hollywood. And a film. A film would be a nice touch. You like the touches, no?"

Steff moans. "That's a long list, Santa. It's going to take me a little time in my workshop to put it all together. I might not be able to deliver by Christmas."

"That's okay. I know you will have lots of time now that you are not working with the dottore. Dottore Amore is finito, no?"

"Uh … what do you mean?" Steff's tone changes.

"I mean the truth has come out. I know you had to protect him when he was your client, but I don't have this problem. I give the press a big, fat present this year. I tell them the truth about Dottore and Emily!"

That's it. I slam the lever down on the toilet, hit the hand sanitizer and kick open the door.

"You absolute piece of shit!" I roar.

Marco freezes, eyes wide, a half-naked Steffelfie still straddling him in the sleigh.

"I'm so sorry, Blaze!" Steff starts to climb off him, looks down at her pasties, then thinks better of it. She stays where she is and leans into Marco, reaching around the back of him, trying to steal his cape.

Marco, mistaking her ministrations for a hug, smiles smugly at me.

"Dottore! Have you come back to give me more directions? As you can see, I've got everything under control here. Santa is driving the sleigh!" He slaps Steff on the ass for emphasis and she squeals, finally freeing the cape.

"Please don't get up on my account, Steff," I say. "I've done everything I need to do here. I've heard enough."

"Blaze! Wait! Let's talk. I can fix this!" Steff stalls, still trying to cover herself.

"No need. Really. This was illuminating. I'll just be on my way now," I say. And then a naughty thought occurs to me. "But first"—I pull out my phone and hold it up to capture the scene, myself included—"let me take an elfie."

emily

. . .

THE GATE AGENT tells me I was lucky to change my flight and get this seat—the last one on the plane. But I don't feel half as lucky as I felt on the way to Italy.

I set myself up in my modest economy accommodations for the duration of the flight. Nowhere near as luxurious as business class, but at least I got a window. Before the cabin doors are closed, I manage one last text exchange with Alexis.

> Thanks for agreeing to meet me at the airport.

No problem. I had a meeting in the city anyway. I thought you weren't getting home for another day, though?

> Change of plans. I got done early.

What about Blaze? It's not true is it, Em?

> Long story.

What does that mean?

> It means I have to shut my phone off in a
> minute. I can't type that much that fast.

I knew something was up when you didn't
call or text me.

> I wanted to. I promise I'll tell you everything
> when I get home. There's so much to tell you.

Great way to leave me hanging and make
sure I don't leave you stranded at the airport.
We still on for tree trimming?

> You bet. I missed you so much. Gotta
> go. Xxoo

I turn off the phone. My eyes ache from tears both shed and unshed. My lids are heavy, but I am pretty sure I won't be able to sleep.

The movie preview flashes in front of me and I consider the Titanium Man flick, but it only reminds me of Blaze. In the wake of the "fake relationship" news about me and Blaze, speculation is spinning out of control. Jackson has sent me a link to a reddit thread, suggesting that Rafe Barzilay and I are the real deal. Allegedly, we met while I was in Israel researching a falafel piece.

I have never been to Israel, but I do love falafel.

I flip off the screen and leaf through an *Inflight* magazine. Nothing terribly notable. It's full of the types of stories I normally write and cannot wait to get back to. "Ten European cities you have to see in the fall," and "How this European beach town's fishermen are making 'Fish to Table' a thing."

I make a solemn vow to myself to stick exclusively to writing about places and things. No more people. No celebrities.

Especially ones with ash-gray eyes who are eager to please me, in bed.

As the plane lifts away from the earth, I feel like a sweater, unraveling. Like a piece of me got stuck on a fence and is still tethered to the ground. There's the tug and pull of something releasing, until there's nothing left to cling to. Not even a ball of yarn that can be made into something new.

I check my watch.

Right about now, Isla is probably doing the last favor I'd requested of her. She is stopping by the hotel to deliver the red-and-green mittens I made for Blaze with the yarn he bought for me. I cast off the last stitch in the parking garage.

"You really do love him, don't you?" Isla had said, holding the package we put together with tissue paper and a bag from an airport shop.

"I think maybe I do." I'd nodded. "But it doesn't matter. It wasn't meant to be."

"We'll see." Isla had swung the bag on one finger. "I'll pop by the hotel on my way back to my place and deliver your gift."

I lie back in my seat on the flight, suddenly aware that I hadn't had a single attack of flying nerves, even without Blaze holding my hand.

And then I picture him unwrapping the mittens and slipping them onto his beautiful, strong hands, and I start to cry.

blaze

. . .

"Thanks for coming on this trip with me. Remember, your mileage may vary. Hopefully, you won't hit too many speedbumps or get stuck in traffic circles. If you do get in an accident, I hope it's not serious. Patch up your tires and keep on trucking. While it's important to go your own way, you don't always have to go it alone. Don't give up on love. Get in the driver's seat."

— Blaze Smith, *Go Your Own Way*, Conclusions

ISLA FAIRFAX IS VERY hard to miss with her bright-red hair, electric-blue coat, and neon-pink eyeglasses. She is waiting for me on a sofa in the hotel lobby when I get back.

"Oh good, you're here." She stands, holding out a bag. "This is for you. Merry Christmas. It isn't from me, though."

"Where's Emily?" I ask, taking the bag from her.

"I've just left her at the airport," Isla says. She looks hopeful. "I'm not sure her flight has left yet. Do you need a lift? I've always wanted to do one of those crazy, last-minute airport runs!"

"Wait, she's flying home today?" I ask, confused.

"She got her flight changed." Isla nods.

I pull up the airline's website. It looks like the last plane to Seattle has just departed.

"Too late," I say. "Dammit."

"Oh dear. You've fucked it up, haven't you," Isla says.

Coming from almost anyone else, this would sound like an admonishment. But coming from her, it's oddly encouraging. Like a kindergarten teacher about to comfort a clumsy pupil.

"You think?" I raise an eyebrow.

"Well, I'm just a romance novelist/blogger. I don't have your expertise." Isla smiles. "All I can offer you is a cup of tea and a shoulder to cry on."

"That's actually very kind of you," I say, "but I might need something stronger." I gesture toward the lobby bar.

We settle into chenille club chairs in the back corner and place our drink orders.

"So, Emily told me you thought I might have leaked the fake relationship story." Isla purses her lips and raises her brows, forcing me to come clean.

"I was grasping at straws and completely wrong about that," I apologize. "I'm sorry."

"I'm probably not the one you need to apologize to," she says.

I nod contritely. "I was really hoping I'd have the chance to do that tonight."

"Do you know who it really was then?"

"I do." I nod.

The waiter deposits our drinks on the side table and I sign for them, waving away Isla's offer.

"Thanks for getting Emily. Was she okay? She get to the airport all right?"

"She did get to the airport all right. But I don't know that she was okay." Isla tastes her tea and adds honey.

"Did she tell you everything that happened in Tuscany?" I ask.

"She did." Isla stirs the honey into her tea. "Shocker about her grandparents. I can't imagine getting that kind of news *and* being in a car crash *and* breaking up with someone all within twenty-four hours!"

"You can't break up with someone if the whole relationship was fake." I down a third of my whiskey, enjoying the burn.

"Was it fake for you, then?" Isla asks.

"No." I swirl the drink around in my cup.

"Then why don't you tell her?" Isla feels around for her bag. "I'm sure there's another flight. I haven't had anything to drink. Come on! Grab your things! Chop-chop! Let's go to the airport!"

I have to laugh.

"Hold your horses, Isla. This isn't one of your novels." I finish off my drink. "I've already rebooked my flight, but it's not leaving until the morning. And I can't go to see her directly. I have a stop to make."

"But you'll get to Emily's in time for Christmas?" she asks.

"That's the plan," I say. "And while I don't need a ride to the airport, there is something you can do for me."

"Will you let me have that gorgeous, orange puffer vest if I do?" she asks.

"It's yours." I take it off. "You just have to post the rest of the story about the fake relationship on your blog."

"I can't write the rest of the story about the letters without permission from Emily and her family." Isla frowns.

"Not that story." I hand her the vest. "*My* story. Classic fake relationship trope. And I want to write it."

emily

. . .

I TELL Alexis the whole story on the way home from the airport. She listens, without judgment, and then asks what she can do to help. Like Isla, she doesn't see any reason to question what my grandparents had. And she wants to hear more about what went on with Blaze, but I just can't.

There's no room for me in his chauffeur-driven world.

"It's just going to take time to get used to all these shifts in my reality," I say, trying to convince myself that this is true. Right now, all I want to do is sleep for days.

It seems unlikely that any paparazzi would follow me back to Ephron, but just in case, Alexis insists on staying with me for the three nights leading up to Christmas. She won't take no for an answer.

"Your house is so much nicer than my apartment. You'd be doing me a favor. I don't even have space to wrap presents at my place!" she insists.

She gives me twenty-four hours to rest. Then, as soon as I wake up from my jet lag-induced coma, the whole *Lit Lovers'* crew descends on me with boxes of tinsel and garland to complete my tree.

"Christmas is tomorrow. We can't let Nonna Carmela down!" Alexis says. She helps me get the box of ornaments down from the attic and go through them.

We stream classic holiday films and drink cocoa with cinnamon schnapps while we hang them. Jackson sets up timers for the tree and the lights by the front door. Chelsea bakes one of her famous casseroles. My friends Kenna and Georgia even stop by, bringing muffins from the diner and some homemade bath bombs for me to enjoy later. It's not the same as being with family—I miss my father and my grandparents desperately—but it's nice having my friends there. It takes my mind off Blaze as well. I can't help but wonder what he's doing now, and if he's back from Italy.

I have to block this thought from my mind, like I have him from my messages and my feed.

"Are you really sure you'll be okay spending tonight volunteering at the Kismet Pet Shelter?" Alexis asks one last time before leaving for her mom's house on Christmas Eve. "I'll just be down the street if you need anything."

"I'll be fine," I insist. "Who knows, maybe I'll get a dog. Georgia's been working on me for a couple of months to adopt." I show Alexis the dog sweater I knitted from the leftover yarn from Blaze's mittens.

"I'll just keep trying this on different dogs, like Cinderella's slipper, till I meet my soul mate," I joke.

"So, you're still on the fence about the baby plans, then?" Alexis asks gently, turning over the sweater. "Not knitting any more booties?"

"Not right now," I say. "I know it's something I want to do, but there's still time. I'm going to give it one more year and then look into fertility treatments or adoption, if need be. There are plenty of ways to build a family."

I glance up at the tiny, pink bow on the star at the top of my tree. I'd taken the scrap of ribbon from my grandmother's letters and tied it on there.

"Okay. Well, before I go, you should open this." She hands me a small, white box tied with a thick, gold, satin ribbon.

"What, no more sexy lingerie?" I joke.

"It's not from me, actually." Alexis shrugs.

"Who is it from, then?"

"Open it," she insists. "Carefully, it's delicate."

I open the box slowly to reveal a set of three ornaments. There's a blown-glass version of The Colosseum and one of the Trevi Fountain. The third ornament is a snow globe, with an image of the Spanish Steps inside.

"Where did you get these?" I gasp.

"Someone left it on the porch while you were out running errands. There's a card inside," she says, pointing at the package.

I open the box again and a small, white card drops out.

"Some sweet Italian memories for your tree this year. Miss you for real. XO, Smitty."

I wipe away a tear.

"He remembered," I say. Carefully, I place all three ornaments on the tree.

"I don't know, Emily. He seems pretty solid for a fake boyfriend."

I pull up to Kismet Pet Shelter's new location, a renovated barn on a rural road just outside Ephron. A small porch has been added recently, leading visitors to the shelter's office. There are stars and constellations painted all over the side of the barn and the front door, similar to the mural at Celestial Pets. Georgia, the owner of the local pet boutique and benefactor of the shelter, has done a great job with it. Star-shaped wind chimes are lilting in the breeze. It's brisk outside, but cozy inside.

There's a small reception area when you first walk in. A wall-mounted television is usually tuned to the Animal Network, and a massive bulletin board is plastered with photos, holidays cards, and letters from pet owners who have adopted in the past. A small fish tank in the corner is the permanent home of "Fins," the shelter's resident betta.

Behind the counter is an area set up like a makeshift living room, complete with a sofa that's covered with throw blankets. It's perfect for doing prospective pet intros.

"Thank you so much for coming, Emily!" Angie stands to greet me. She's a short, athletic, kindly woman in her seventies who has been the chief admin of the Kismet Pet Rescue for decades. Tonight, she's wearing an "ugly" Christmas sweater, featuring a corgi with reindeer antlers. It looks a lot like one of her own cherished pets. "I appreciate you being here after all your travels. You must be jet-lagged!"

"I've been sleeping a ton since I got back," I assure her.

"Okay. Hopefully, it will be quiet this year, but you'd be surprised at the number of people who get it in their heads to give pets as gifts without checking to see if the recipient is allergic or even allowed to have pets in their apartment." Angie shakes her head and tuts at this. "We've got one pup in the kennel right now, a real cutie. Just came in today."

She goes over the list of who to call in an emergency, making sure I have the number for Mac at the vet clinic, as well as her cell phone number and Georgia's. "If you want to take the puppy out of its cage for a cuddle, that's just fine. She could use some socialization."

"So, you're saying all I have to do is sit here, watch Netflix, drink cocoa, and play with an adorable puppy?" I ask.

"That's it." Angie smiles.

"Best Christmas Eve ever!" I joke. "Where do I sign?"

"Just give me a call before you lock up around midnight," Angie says. "You can drop the keys in the lockbox. We have some volunteers coming bright and early tomorrow morning."

After Angie leaves, I go back to the kennel to check out the puppy. She's even more adorable than advertised and clearly happy to see me. Her tail wags and thumps as she whimpers excitedly at the sight of me, her big, brown eyes imploring me to set her free from her cage.

"Well, hello you," I say, opening the metal door to let the curly, cream-colored fluffball out. She launches into my lap, licking my face all over.

"Easy there," I say. "There's not even any mistletoe in here." I laugh. I've never owned a dog before, but I can understand the appeal of this much unbridled affection.

"How about we go hang out up front and watch a movie?" I suggest, patting my leg to encourage the pup to follow me. Much to my surprise she does, happily running beside me and jumping in circles around me.

I set up a water bowl and fluff the pillows on the low love seat where I'm planning to sit and snuggle with her.

"There we go. I've got my cocoa and you've got your water. Would you prefer *The Holiday* or *Love Always*?" I use the remote to turn on the wall-mounted television. The puppy barks. "Okay, *The Holiday* it is!"

Then I remember the dog sweater in my bag. I dig it out to try it on her, pulling it over her head. I didn't think it was possible, but she looks even more adorable. I have to laugh. I get out my phone and crouch on the floor to take a photo with her, which I immediately text to Alexis.

Perfect fit!

I hear the bell on the door chime, but before I can stand up to see who it is, the puppy hurls herself at me again and knocks me flat onto my back.

"Oof!" The wind is knocked out of me as I land. The pup, thinking this is great fun, promptly jumps onto my stomach so she can enthusiastically lick my face. I wrap my arms around her and attempt to free myself as I call out, "Hi! Merry Christmas! Be right with you!"

"Lucky dog," says a familiar voice. My heart stops for a split second, and then starts beating again, the whoosh like the sound of an open gas line meeting a lit match.

All I can see from my position on the floor are the mittens—red and green stripes, dangling over the edge of the counter directly above me.

"You got the mittens," I say, rolling onto my side and attempting to catch my breath.

My eyes are probably still puffy from the tears I shed in the car, and I'm wearing plaid pajama bottoms and a sweatshirt with my sheepskin boots. I don't want him to see me like this.

"You once said I'd be lucky if I got you to knit me a pair of mittens. So, I won't be so greedy as to demand an afghan, but what do I have to do to get you to knit me a sweater like the one that dog is wearing?"

Blaze leans over the edge of the counter, taking in the scene below. There's nowhere for me to hide.

"Need a hand up?" he asks.

"I can't believe you're here," I say, heart pounding as I study the baseboards beneath the counter.

"I am here," he confirms.

"For real? I didn't just hit my head, did I?" I ask, still afraid to look up. The puppy is standing on my hair, which I'm sure I didn't even brush before coming here tonight. Not that I need to dress up for Blaze. I just would have preferred to look less like a character in a Zombie apocalypse drama.

I push the puppy off my hair, freeing myself to sit up.

"I mean, I haven't been here very long, but you don't appear to have a head injury. You look great to me. My God, it's good to see you, Emily."

Blaze extends a hand down to me and I take it, accepting his help to pull me up.

Now that I'm upright, I steal a look, noting the dark circles under his eyes and the beginnings of another beard. I can also see he's not alone. I'm surprised to see a petite, dark-haired woman in a navy puffer jacket and hiking boots standing behind him.

"What are you doing here?" I ask him warily. Meeting his gaze feels too dangerous. Instead, my eyes perform a visual sweep of the entire room with him in it, like passing your finger quickly through a candle flame.

"I wanted to get a dog this Christmas." He shrugs. "This seemed like as good a place as any to do that."

"You can't have this one. She's mine!" I say, putting a protective hand on the puppy, who is now standing on her hind legs, trying to sniff him.

Blaze laughs. "Oh really? Do you have papers for her?"

"No, but I was planning on adopting her," I say, feeling strangely protective.

"That's going to be tough." Blaze uses his arms to raise himself to a seated position on the counter, then swings his legs over and jumps off to stand in front of me. I recognize his jeans and that jacket. But I still can't look at him.

The smell of him is harder to avoid. That bourbon, coffee, and cinnamon smell. I close my eyes and inhale him before responding.

"What, you don't think I'm fit to take care of a puppy?" I ask, folding my arms across my chest.

The puppy promptly loses all interest in me and transfers her attention to Blaze. She jumps at his legs, and he picks her up in his arms, holding her like a baby and letting her lick his face.

"No." He laughs. "You just can't have this one. She's mine."

"What? Angie didn't mention anything about that!" I protest, feeling my pulse quicken and anger build. The nerve of him!

The woman in the doorway clears her throat. "Hi? Sorry to interrupt, but does anyone want to introduce me?"

Blaze sighs. "I'm sorry, Carina. Emily, this is my sister, Carina. We've just come straight here from seeing our mom and getting her settled at a new facility that is closer to both of us. Carina, this is Emily. See Carina? I told you Emily was real."

"Yes, I can definitely see that now." Carina walks over to the counter, holding a pink leash. Her blue eyes crinkle at the corners as she smiles warmly at me. "Why don't I take Maisy for a little walk and let you two talk? Give her here."

Blaze hands the dog across to his sister.

"What's going on?" I ask, looking between them. Carina raises her eyebrows at her brother, prompting him to explain as she clips the leash to the puppy's collar.

"We were in here earlier," Blaze explains. "And I filled out the paperwork for Maisy then. But Maisy wasn't the real reason I came here," he says, taking a deep breath and speaking more quickly. "Do you want to hear the real reason?"

I nod slowly. Carina looks back and smiles reassuringly at me, waving as she heads out the door.

But I still force myself to look directly into Blaze's eyes. It still hurts too much. I wrap my arms protectively across myself.

"You said you were working here on Christmas Eve," Blaze says tenderly.

"So, you thought you'd come steal my puppy in addition to breaking my heart?" I address my elbows.

"I owe you an apology, Emily. I'm so sorry for even suggesting that it might have been you who tipped off the press. I didn't mean it. I was upset, but you were the last person I should have lashed out at."

"So, it was Steff all along?" I keep my arms folded, preparing to be vindicated, and feeling no sense of victory.

Blaze reaches out to touch one of my curls.

"Not exactly," he says, "but close. It was Marco."

"Marco?" I ask, looking up in surprise before I have the chance to stop myself. That's all it takes. Blaze bends his head down to meet my gaze, and just like that, we are both swimming in each other's eyes, seeking answers in a separate side conversation from the one using words.

Now I'm dying to touch him too.

"Apparently, he wanted Steff all to himself," Blaze continues.

"How did you find out?" I ask. As hard as it was to look at him before, now that I have, I can't look away, and it's making me breathless.

"After I left you at the service station, I went straight to Marco's to confront Steff. I wanted to get to the bottom of things, but I got more than I bargained for. I'm done. So done."

Blaze reaches into his pocket for his phone and pulls up a photo. "I have to warn you, you can't unsee this."

"What is it?" I ask, glancing downward.

"I like to think of it as a parting shot. This is how I found them, discussing the details of the leak."

I am unprepared for the image of Steff and Marco on his screen. My eyes bug out as I grimace. "Oh! I'm not sure I even want to know what's going on here."

"I probably should have warned you more," he says. "I'm sorry. I've been driving for two days, just thinking about all the things I wanted to say to you and show you."

"No driver?" I ask, somewhat surprised. I realize that while Blaze writes about driving quite often, I've never actually seen him behind the wheel.

"No driver." Blaze smiles wryly. "And the only person riding shotgun was my sister."

"Who you've told about me." I say this more as a statement than a question.

"I've talked about you so much, she's probably ready to put a muzzle on me." Blaze looks sheepish, but unashamed. I can feel the tension between us loosening.

"There's something else I want to show you. It just went live." He takes back his phone to pull up Isla's blog. "It's a guest post," he says. "About a chance encounter in the airport and an instant connection."

I scan the header. The post is attributed to him, and there's a photo of me—one of the ones he took outside of Pitigliano.

"Did you really write this? Or is this just another one of Steff's ways of doing damage control?" I ask, almost afraid to hear the answer.

"Steff had nothing to do with this. I haven't exchanged a word with her since I left the villa. Ask Isla if you don't believe me, but I wrote every word of this post. The only person I'm interested in doing damage control for is you. You were so right. I was letting other people run my life and dragging you into it. Can you ever forgive me?"

My eyes scan his words as I scroll with a single, shaky finger.

"Falling in love with Emily wasn't a choice. It was a foregone conclusion. From the moment I met her, I knew it was inevitable. Like gravity. You can try to resist it, but gravity always wins."

I shake my head in disbelief, my tears making it difficult to read the beautiful, heartfelt post he's written.

"I love you, Emily. Please believe me? Let me show you? I don't give a damn about what anyone else in the world thinks. I know I'm not perfect, and I don't have all the answers, but if you can find a place in your heart for me despite all this?"

Blaze folds me into his arms, and we stay that way for a while. Just holding each other like we did in the booth in the airport lounge.

Finally, I speak.

"So, you're asking me to love you even though you think that I think you're full of shit?" I ask. I need to place my hands on his face so I can feel his rough stubble. I pull his chin close to mine and kiss his rough cheeks. "I *don't* think that, by the way. I think you make a lot of sense. But if I'm being honest, I'm kind of over the road trip analogies. I love you despite them."

"How do you feel about culinary analogies then?" Blaze asks. "Can we work with gelato?"

"You'd do anything for one of my hand-knit afghans, wouldn't you?" I laugh.

"Yes. Yes, I would." Blaze nods solemnly.

"Good. Because I want to keep Maisy." I gaze up at him. "I felt an instant connection. It made me believe in true love again."

"That's going to be tough," Blaze speaks between kisses. "Because I, too, felt an immediate connection." He kisses my eyelids, my nose, my cheeks, and my chin. "I've only heard about this sort of thing in the past, but I believe it genuinely was love at first sight."

"I'm not sure how we're ever going to work this out." I grin.

"There's only one solution," he says. "Package deal. Two-for-one holiday special. You'll just have to take us both."

acknowledgments

I had far too much fun writing this book, acting out scenes in my desk chair, making weird faces and waving my arms around to test out hand gestures. I cracked myself up a lot. As adults, we don't get enough chances to playact and pretend, something that the characters in this book were all too aware of. They wanted the chance to be someone else, somewhere else. I feel that way, too, sometimes. When I write, I get to be all my characters, if only in my mind.

I'm so grateful to my family for giving me the time and space to play this way. Marly, Ani, Fox, and Leo, you are *all* my favorites. I am so grateful for your support, Brian, but also for your excitement about reading back the "dailies" and for your Cookie Monster voice.

Libby Chapman, Nicole Carcerano, and Courtland Jeffries, your kind words have meant so much. My own kids have to be nice to me, but you three don't.

Rachel Zitin, I'm not sure what's more impressive—your encyclopedic knowledge of the city and its history, or your ability to drive around Rome like it's NBD.

And thanks, once again, to my "team," including developmental editor, Anya Kagan, of Touchstone Editing, my copy editor, Joyce Mochrie, owner of One Last Look, and Jillian Liota of Indie Graphic. You all make me—and more importantly, my stories—look good.

about the author

Ciara Blume met her husband in a comedy improv troupe. This sealed her fate as a rom-com writer. She lives in Southern California with her husband, four amazing kids, and an odd-eyed cat. Ciara enjoys reading, crafting, and traveling, especially in Italy.

This stand-alone holiday romance is the second title in the Lit Lovers series.

For more information and news about Ciara's upcoming releases, visit her website at: www.ciarablume.com

Scan the QR code below to join Ciara's mailing list and receive free bonus chapters and original stories, recipes, crafts, giveaways and more.

Dearest Reader,

I had a blast researching and writing this book, and I hope you've enjoyed reading it too. If you did, I'd appreciate you leaving a review to let other readers know about it and/or a shared link on

social media. Don't forget to tag me if you share. You can also email me to let me know what you think at: Author@CiaraBlume.com.

Your feedback is so important to me.

Ciao & Grazie!

Xo, Ciara Blume